MW00639591

BRIGHT SHARDS

Ink Sigil Press
www.megpechenick.com

Publisher's Note: This is a work of fiction. Names, characters, places, and incidents are a product of the author's imagination. Locales and public names are sometimes used for atmospheric purposes. Any resemblance to actual people, living or dead, or to businesses, companies, events, institutions, or locales is completely coincidental.

Book Layout © 2016 BookDesignTemplates.com

Bright Shards/ Meg Pechenick. -- 1st ed.
ISBN 978-1-7323123-1-9

For Sarah C., who knew the ending before I did

CONTENTS

PART ONE: ARKHATI

PART TWO: AZDRETH

PART THREE: IVRI KHEDAI

PART ONE: ARKHATI

It was with a mixture of awe and relief and a little sadness that I watched the tiny pearl-white bauble that was Arkhati Starhaven expanding to fill the entire field of the viewscreen before me. Part of me dreaded the idea of leaving the *Pinion* behind. The little ship with its crew of eleven had been my world for the last three months. It felt safe and familiar. But I now knew those feelings to be illusory. The explosion that had ripped through the cargo holds two weeks ago had compromised whole sections of the hull. The delicate membrane of air and warmth that sustained my life, and the lives of my crewmates, had revealed its astonishing soap-bubble fragility. All of us owed our continued survival to a combination of blind chance and brilliant Vardeshi engineering. In the ten days it had taken us to reach Arkhati, one system after another had threatened to fail. Whatever my misgivings about leaving the *Pinion*, the ship that had carried me away from Earth, and my first home among the stars, there could be no denying that it was time to move on.

I leaned forward, ambivalence giving way to eagerness as the starhaven swelled on the viewscreen. From a distance its starlit curves had seemed as ephemeral as blown glass. At close range, it was massive and reassuringly solid, acres of cold white metal and textured shadow. It looked like an elongated teardrop upended in space, its narrow end ringed with irregular extrusions like petals or feathers. Until now, my experience of Vardeshi structures had been limited to two shuttles and the *Pinion* itself; Arkhati was the first large-scale habitation I had seen. To my eyes it was both fantastical and a little frightening, a far cry from the crude blocky space stations currently circling Earth in low orbit. As Rhevi Ziral, the ship's pilot, guided the *Pinion* with her customary deft touch toward one of the upper projections, I belatedly identified them as docking platforms.

"Ready to go?" said a voice beside me. I turned to find Zey Takheri, my closest friend among the Vardeshi, grinning up at me. With his enormous dark eyes and feathery silver-white hair, Zey was a perfect illustration of one of the first nicknames my people had given his: namely, "Pixies." He and I shared the title of novi, the lowest rank in the hierarchy of the Vardeshi Stellar Fleet, but Zey was technically my superior due to seniority, a fact he never tired of pointing out. It didn't seem to trouble him that he had actually earned his title through the mandatory three years of training at the Fleet Institute, while mine was strictly honorary. He was just glad to have someone to share the novi work. Our duties were largely menial, which was the only reason any Vardeshi had thought a human might be able to perform them.

I flattered myself, though, that while the title might be only a courtesy, I had more right to it now than I had when I'd left Earth. When the *Pinion*'s communications network was sabotaged a month ago, I had been framed for the damage. After a humiliating sham trial, I had found myself demoted and confined to my quarters, a prisoner on the ship that had so recently begun to feel like home. With no way to contact Earth or my crewmates' homeworld of Vardesh Prime for mediation, I had been desperate for a way to exonerate myself and locate the real saboteur. The explosion in the cargo holds had forced my hand. I had proven my innocence the only way I could: through telepathic contact with Zey's older brother, Saresh, a senior officer on the *Pinion*. I was lucky that it had worked, and luckier that it had left my mind intact, given the potential incompatibility of Vardeshi and human minds and bodies. Saresh and I had discovered that the real traitor was the *Pinion*'s commander, Vekesh. We had shared the truth with his second-in-command, Hathan, the third member of the Takheri family serving on the *Pinion*'s tiny crew. With Zey's help, he had subdued Vekesh and gained control of the ship, but not before Vekesh put Saresh and me in the ship's medical bay, him with a bullet in his leg, me with a deep graze on my arm from a second shot meant for my heart.

Vekesh had done his best to take down the nascent alliance between humans and Vardeshi. He had failed, but it was a close thing, and all of us—the crew of the *Pinion* and the respective governments of Earth and Vardesh Prime, the United Earth Council and the Echelon—were still picking up the pieces. Over the past two weeks, with Vekesh himself locked safely away in his quarters awaiting trial on Arkhati, I had made my peace with my crewmates. They had been quick to offer the necessary apologies and explanations. I had been equally quick to forgive them. It helped that I liked them. I always had. They had been misled by Vekesh. They had misjudged me. That didn't make me like them any less.

However, they had fallen out of favor with the Echelon.

The Vardeshi were a proud people. Possessed of technology infinitely superior to that of Earth, they were inclined to see themselves as superior in other ways as well. They had labored to eradicate poverty, disease, and inequality in their territories. Humanity, on the other hand, was still mired in war and bigotry, "the darkness within," as the Vardeshi called it. There had been a presumption on both sides that if the alliance failed, it would be our fault. Vekesh's treachery, and the subsequent revelation that it had been orchestrated by an anti-alliance faction, had been a mortifying reversal for his people. While I spent my days on Arkhati resting, healing, and discovering the anthropological delights of a deep-space settlement no human had ever visited before, my crewmates would be defending their actions to the Echelon in a sequence of formal hearings. The stakes were high; if the Echelon ruled against the *Pinion*'s crew, I would be continuing my journey toward Vardesh Prime on a ship crewed by strangers. For many reasons—friendship, and loyalty, and something even more compelling—I hoped they ruled in our favor. At present, though, it was anyone's guess what the outcome would be.

But that was a question for another day. For now, I had my friends back and a starhaven to explore. I shouldered my paisley duffel bag and grinned back at Zey. "I'm ready. Let's go."

Most of the crew would remain on the *Pinion*, initiating shutdown procedures and assisting the equipment-transport teams from Arkhati, but Zey had been cleared to escort me onto the starhaven. So had Sohra, the *Pinion*'s Systems specialist. Pensive and mild-mannered, with long dark hair and blue eyes that made her look at times startlingly human, Sohra was another whose friendship I had come to prize. The three of us walked down together through the ship to helix one, the lowest level, which housed the largest cargo bays—including the two that had decompressed in the explosion—and the shuttle hangar. Beyond the hangar doors was another door whose function I had never known. Now Zey punched in a code and the panel slid back to reveal a chamber lined with the same globe-shaped lights familiar to me from the *Pinion*. "Are we on the starhaven?" I asked eagerly.

Zey laughed. "We're in the airlock." I followed him to the end of the chamber, where another panel slid open at his touch. The room beyond it was dark and vaulted, lit from below by a scattering of blue and green lights. Zey made an expansive gesture with the hand that wasn't holding an overnight bag. "Now we're on the starhaven."

I tilted my head back, trying to take in the scope of the chamber. I had the impression of a series of levels above our own, but I couldn't make them out in the dimness. Zey and Sohra went confidently up a ramp that climbed along one side of the enormous room toward the second level. I hurried after them, quickening my pace to avoid being left behind, but I had gone only a few steps when an impossibly familiar voice behind me said, "Hey, Stranger."

I swung around and said incredulously, "Kylie?"

It was unquestionably her: Kylie Braswell, my closest companion from my two weeks of accelerated prelaunch training in Switzerland. She stood grinning at me, her blond highlights gleaming in the eerie underwater lighting. She wore faded jeans and a yellow and white track jacket I recognized from the Villiger Center. How she had come to be here before me I didn't know. It didn't matter. I dropped my bag and threw myself at her, overcome with relief and gratitude. Her arms closed tightly around me. How often in the last three months had I longed for the touch of a fellow human, for a real hug, rather than the cautious embrace of someone inconceivably stronger than myself? I leaned into her warmth and solidity, breathing in the ghost of her shampoo and the faint familiar musk that underlay it, the unmistakable scent of human skin. It was a long time before I let go.

Finally I stepped back. "I can't believe this. What are you doing here? How did you get here before me?"

"I launched in the second wave, remember? I was only two weeks behind you to begin with. We were due to arrive tomorrow, but the Council wanted me here to meet you when you docked. Dr. Okoye thought it would be good for you to see a familiar face. So we pushed our speed a little and got in last night." She picked up my duffel bag. "Come on. I'll take you to my rooms. They're fantastic. It's like being royalty or something."

"Shouldn't I be staying with my crew?"

"They'll be close by. All the visitor quarters are grouped together. And this way we can share a kitchen. It'll be easier all around. Trust me, there's plenty of space."

I looked at Zey and Sohra, who were watching with indulgent smiles. "You knew," I said accusingly. "You knew she was already here."

"We knew," Sohra agreed. "Go get settled in. We know where to find you."

"But isn't there something I'm supposed to be doing right now?"

"Yes," Zey said. "Unpacking. Go."

I looked back at Kylie and laughed, giddy with excitement and surprise. "Well . . . okay. Lead on!"

It wasn't actually Kylie who led us to her quarters, but a young silver-haired woman in an unfamiliar red and black uniform who introduced herself to me as Officer Seshan Nerev, a member of Arkhati's security force and the head of Kylie's personal protection detail. "We'll have escorts everywhere we go," Kylie explained as we walked. "No one here has ever seen a human before. We're going to attract some attention. And after what happened to you, the Echelon isn't taking any chances with our security. Arkhati is a big place. People are constantly coming and going, and not all of them are going to be in favor of the alliance."

"How many people live on the starhaven?" I asked Officer Nerev in Vardeshi.

I saw the flicker of surprise, swiftly controlled, on her face before she answered. "There's a permanent crew of about two thousand, and another thousand or so passing through at any given time."

"It's like a city," I said wonderingly.

I quickly discovered that, in terms of its size, Arkhati Starhaven was indeed like a city. It seemed to have been designed on the same spiraling, vaguely organic principles as the *Pinion,* but on a vastly larger scale. Enormous vaulted chambers like the one where Kylie had met me led into long, curving, segmented corridors that sloped unpredictably upward or downward. Twice we stood in small rooms that I took for elevators of some kind, although I couldn't see or feel any evidence of movement, and the corridors we stepped out into looked identical to those through which we had entered. I didn't see any of the thriving and colorful interstellar marketplaces my years of Vardrama consumption had led me to expect, and I wondered if we were being deliberately shunted into less-trafficked areas of the starhaven.

Kylie had been right: Arkhati was immense. I was glad I wasn't trying to navigate it alone. On my own, I would have been lost almost at once, but more than that, something about the place made me uneasy. I knew the starhaven was centuries old, and I thought I would have known it even if my crewmates hadn't told me as much. There was a sense of accumulated age, of floors traversed by countless feet and door panels that had been touched by many fingers before my own. Time weighed heavily here. It was a feeling I associated with cathedrals and old forests on Earth. It was unsettling to feel it here, on a manufactured island in the depths of space.

There were other things too. The lights were a little too dim for my comfort; I found myself peering into shadows whose depths I couldn't quite make out. Now and then I caught wafts of stale odors on the recycled air, traces of alien food and sweat that the atmospheric scrubbers couldn't entirely eliminate. All those impressions together spoke to what Dr. Okoye, the psychiatrist at the Villiger Center, would have called my animal self, whispering that I was a trespasser here. I felt an impulse to flee and fought it down, knowing retreat was impossible. The *Pinion* wasn't home anymore. There was nowhere for me to go.

We encountered a few dozen Vardeshi on our route, many in Fleet uniforms. I looked eagerly at each new face in turn. They generally resembled my crewmates: wide-set eyes, high foreheads, hair in every length from spikily short to a waist-length curtain, and every shade from brilliant snow-white to inky black. However, I saw an intriguing range of skin tones, ashy gray and powdery blue in addition to the typical alabaster white. Were those people from different planets? Or was skin tone a cosmetic choice? I saw one or two excitingly novel hair colors as well, deep glossy red and vibrant gold. I guessed those were artificial. I didn't know if they were meant to imitate human coloring. Most of those we passed ignored me and stared frankly at Kylie, whose messy bun and bright jacket marked her immediately as foreign. A few looked closer, and I saw two or three distinct double takes as they registered my uniform, then my bare right hand, lacking both the ink sigil denoting birth house and the gold one denoting marriage house, and finally my—to them—exotic features. My hair was a duller shade of blond than Kylie's, but my coloring—not to mention my height, which placed me at eye level with all but the tallest Vardeshi men—marked me indelibly as human.

As we walked, I began to notice small illuminated panels bearing helix markings at each corridor junction. I stopped to look more closely at one of the panels. "Helix seventy? How many levels are there?"

"The main structure has seventy-two," said Officer Nerev.

"So the guest quarters are at the top?"

She nodded.

"Just like on the *Pinion*," I observed. "What's at the bottom?"

"Crew quarters and docks. Your official tour is scheduled for this evening, after the formal reception." She sounded a little amused.

"Reception?" I repeated. I looked over at Kylie, whose blank expression indicated that she hadn't followed our exchange. "There's a reception for us?" I said in English.

"Oh, yeah. The official welcome ceremony. It's dinner and then a tour or something. Here we are." She stopped in front of a door, brushed her fingers across the panel to activate it, and keyed in her door code without hesitation. It was jarring to see another human operating Vardeshi tech with such facility. *You were never the only one*, I reminded myself. *It just felt that way.*

"I'll be outside if you need anything," Officer Nerev said as Kylie stepped inside.

I paused. "I do have a couple of questions. What are the water restrictions here? Are they the same as on the *Pinion*? And where do we sign up for showers?"

She was definitely amused now. "These are diplomatic

suites, not novi quarters. You have a private shower in your room. And there are no water restrictions."

I grinned. "Perfect."

As I followed Kylie inside, I saw that she hadn't been exaggerating. Her rooms were palatial. I stifled a laugh, thinking of my snug little berth on the *Pinion,* which was approximately the size of a storage crate by comparison. There was an expansive central room whose gauzy hangings and cushioned platforms resembled those in the *Pinion*'s lounge. Half-hidden doorways set into the walls promised other rooms, and I followed Kylie in turn to three different bedrooms, a sanitation room, the longed-for private shower, and a galley on whose gleaming surfaces a set of cooking gear identical to my own had been halfway unpacked. Each room was a little different from the last, but there was a richness of color and texture throughout that I hadn't expected. These were rooms for royalty, I thought, or at least for esteemed foreign dignitaries. I paused here and there as objects caught my eye: a green enamel table inlaid with amber spirals, a wall design of stone and pale wood tiles arrayed with geometric precision. I stopped to stroke a hanging the color of smoke shot through with glinting copper threads. It was unexpectedly soft beneath my fingers, silky even, though it looked more like linen. The contrasting shades called to mind the embroidered detail on Hathan's surcoat at officers' dinner a few nights earlier. I had had ample time to study the detail on his sleeve that evening while I was trying not to betray myself by looking into his face.

It had come as a considerable shock to me to discover during my brief telepathic contact with the eldest Takheri brother that I had fallen in love with the middle one. At a glance, there was nothing terribly captivating about Hathan. Saresh was the striking one in the family, at least to human sensibilities. Tall and slim, with long platinum hair and brilliant blue eyes, he was almost comically good-looking. Next to him, Hathan, smaller and slighter, with the monochrome coloring more typical of his people, nearly disappeared. I had seen at once that he was intelligent. It had taken me weeks to understand that his reserve concealed an acerbic wit, and longer to see the distinction in the narrow cast of his features. The light in his gray eyes was watchful and meditative and laughing by turns. Almost from the start I had longed for his approbation. Not until I found myself a fugitive on a wounded ship, so desperate to clear my name that I would put my mental integrity at risk, had I understood why. And by that point he had already decided to hate me.

Of everyone on the *Pinion,* Hathan had been the most susceptible to Vekesh's poison. He had known Vekesh and respected him for years. I, on the other hand, was a stranger, a literal alien, invited for largely political reasons into a menial position—Ambassador Seidel, describing the title of novi to me, had called it "effectively a service role"—for which it was generally assumed I would prove inadequate. I had no relevant training and no facility with Vardeshi technology. From the start, Hathan had been distant and wary of me. A sequence of badly timed encounters had caused me to slide even further in his esteem. His astonishment at learning me to be innocent of the charges leveled at me by Vekesh must have been nearly equal to mine at discovering my true feelings for him.

To his credit, he had been quick to acknowledge his error in judgment. But he could hardly have done otherwise. I had learned early on in my journey that the vast majority of Vardeshi possessed latent telepathic powers. A scant few were Blanks, completely impervious to telepathic contact, or Voxes, in full and conscious command of their abilities. Zey was the former, Saresh the latter. It was for that reason, we assumed, that he had been able to access my memories in the Listening. For the Vardeshi, there could be no exoneration more complete than the word of a Vox. In the eyes of my crewmates, not to mention the Fleet and the Echelon, Saresh's declaration of my innocence was the final word on the subject.

Saresh had gone into my mind looking for the truth. He had found more there than either of us expected. He now knew my secret. I wished, at times desperately, that he didn't. Left to myself to choose a confidant, I would hardly have chosen Hathan's brother. I had to admit, though, that in the two weeks since Saresh had learned of my feelings, he had been perfectly discreet. He had to be; he was bound by the Vox code of ethics, which required him to keep in confidence any and all truths revealed during the Listening. I was grateful for the code, and for my knowledge, founded upon my friendship with Saresh and strengthened during my brief glimpse of his mind, of his fundamental kindness and integrity. Without those things, I would have had no choice but to abandon my crewmates and continue my mission toward Vardesh Prime on a different ship. The risk would simply have been too great. I could think of no torment worse than finding myself confined on a tiny ship with Hathan, months out in the darkness between starhavens, after he realized that I was in love with him.

Kylie's voice broke into my thoughts. "Picked a room yet?"

"This one," I said without hesitation, and she deposited my duffel bag on the floor of the smallest bedroom. It was still twice as large as my novi quarters, and had a shelf bed tucked against a wall. I wasn't sure I could sleep any more without my shoulder pressed into a bulkhead thrumming with the pulse of distant engines.

As we wandered from one chamber to the next, I felt my tension beginning to ease. The lighting in Kylie's rooms was warmer and brighter than anything I'd seen elsewhere on the starhaven. I wondered if someone had thoughtfully adjusted the frequencies in advance of her arrival. The temperature seemed a little warmer too. Those facts, and the fineness of the furnishings, confirmed what Officer Nerev had said in the corridor: We were diplomats here.

The reminder was a salient one for me. Under Vekesh's command, I had been an envoy of humanity in name only. In reality, I had been the lowest-ranking and worst-regarded member of a tiny staff, immersed in the petty concerns of shipboard life. With our arrival on Arkhati, my status had markedly altered. That meant elegant rooms and private showers, but it also meant different expectations. I would be representing my people on a wider stage now. All eyes would be on me and Kylie at tonight's reception, and my hard-won knowledge of the different Vardeshi factions told me not all of them would be friendly. I was intimidated by the thought, but not as much so as I might have been months or even weeks ago. In an odd way, Vekesh had unintentionally given me a gift. What would it signify if I dropped my fork or forgot a few names at dinner? Short of actually pulling out a gun and shooting someone, it would be hard for me to embarrass my people more thoroughly than he had already embarrassed his.

"This is the best part," said Kylie, leading me back into the main room. At its far end a short flight of wide, shallow steps led up to a terrace with a series of arched viewports serving as its exterior wall. The terrace was furnished with a scattering of the familiar padded stools and low tables, but I picked my way through them with hardly a glance, drawn toward what looked at first like an enormous piece of abstract art rendered in black and white. As I approached the viewports, the image resolved itself, and I realized what I was seeing: the bulk of the starhaven itself in stark white silhouette against the blackness of space. As I stood looking out, stunned by the scale of the place, a flash of movement drew my eye. A craft of a type I'd never seen, spindly and slender-winged as a dragonfly, was lifting off from one of the landing platforms far below. It drifted upward, seemingly aimless at first, gaining speed as it rose. When it flashed past the viewport, I realized it was much larger than I'd thought. Its iridescent skin, reflecting the stars and the lights of the starhaven, shone blindingly bright. It rose a little higher, then changed course abruptly and arrowed away into the night.

"Holy shit," I said to Kylie, and we both started to laugh.

2

We lingered on the terrace for a few more minutes, scanning the platforms below for other docking or departing ships. When none appeared, we made our way back down to the galley and started rifling through Kylie's food supplies. "There's more in storage," she said, "but this is most of my food for the month. I haven't even started to sort through it yet. I thought we could do something simple for lunch. Pizzas, maybe? I have the dough already thawed. Here." She sloshed white wine from a half-empty bottle into two glasses and handed one to me.

"To the Strangers," I said, referencing the nickname the hundred human representatives sent to live among the Vardeshi had adopted for ourselves.

"To Avery Alcott," Kylie countered, "the heroine of the exchange."

I made a face. "Please tell me no one's actually calling me that."

"They are." She grinned. "In both languages."

"I don't feel very heroic."

"You took a bullet for the alliance," she pointed out. "What would you call it?"

"I don't know, bad reflexes?" I looked down, swirling the wine in my glass. When I looked up again, I found her watching me, her brows drawn slightly together. She didn't say anything. After an uncomfortable pause I added, "Vekesh shot me in the arm and I fell down. Not exactly the stuff of legends."

"They imprisoned you," Kylie said quietly, "and you risked your mind to save them."

"I had help," I said. "I wasn't alone. Not ... at the end."

She clinked her glass against mine. "To not being alone, then."

I had forgotten what it felt like to share a meal with someone else, both the work of preparation and the pleasure of consumption. On the *Pinion,* food had been an irritation more than anything else, a visceral reminder that I was different from my companions. As yet little was known about the compatibility of Earth foods with Vardeshi physiology and vice versa. My prelaunch training had included strict instructions to keep my cooking and dishwashing procedures entirely separate from those of my crewmates. I was permitted to eat in the same room as them, but that was all. I couldn't sample their dishes; they couldn't sample mine. Even breathing in the aromas of their foods had been discouraged due to the risk of inhaling airborne allergens. Cooking, formerly a pleasure, had become a chore, solitary and ideally sterile.

Now I rediscovered food as a source of community. With Kylie, there was nothing to guard against, no danger of cross-contamination or olfactory offense. We were just two women sharing a kitchen. She scattered flour onto the counter and began rolling out the dough with the empty wine bottle. I lit the camp stoves and assembled the toppings, leaving the containers open so that we could sample them as we worked. It was sheer decadence to handle food without compulsively washing my hands afterward. Even something as minor as handing Kylie a slice of pepperoni was revelatory. While the pizzas cooked, we leaned against the counter, drinking our wine, talking about the best and worst of the prepackaged meals we'd brought from Earth.

"Worst: vegetable curry," Kylie said. "No question."

I smiled. "I don't know. I kind of liked that one."

"All right, what was your favorite, then?"

"Maybe the carbonara?"

She nodded. "Good choice. Let's make that tomorrow."

When the pizzas were sufficiently cool, we carried them to the terrace and ate them with knives and forks directly from the pans. "I'm changing my answer," I said after the first savory bite. "This is definitely the best meal of the trip." Kylie laughed and poured more wine into my glass. Not since the Listening had I felt so profoundly close to another person.

Afterward, drowsy with wine and food, I stood up and began stacking the dishes for easier carrying into the galley. "Leave the washing-up for later," Kylie commanded. "Go get comfortable in the main room. I've got a surprise for you." I went obediently to settle myself on one of the cushioned platforms. A few moments later, Kylie batted the curtain aside and stepped in, her laptop open in one hand. "They told me about your tech," she said. "I won't have the same shows as you, but it's got to be better than nothing. We can watch anything you like." She placed the laptop in front of me with a flourish.

I drew it reverently toward me. "Oh, thank God. This is exactly what I need right now." I scrolled through the list—mostly British sitcoms—and chose one I'd watched a couple of years earlier. Five minutes into the first episode, I was fast asleep.

The next thing I knew, it was several hours later, and Kylie was shaking me gently awake. "I thought you'd want time to get ready. We have a bit more than an hour before we have to leave for dinner. Shower's all yours." Her hair was damp, I saw, and she was wrapped in a terrycloth bathrobe.

I sat up and stretched elaborately. "I had no idea I was that tired."

"Dr. Okoye said you'd say that. She messaged me and said not to worry if you essentially collapsed once you felt yourself to be safe."

"She's been spot on with all of her predictions since the shooting," I said. "I'm starting to think it was her and not Saresh poking around in my head."

"She's seen trauma before. She says trauma with aliens is still trauma."

"She's right about that too," I muttered. My head felt cloudy with wine and sleep, and it took longer than it should have to track down my water bottle and retrieve my toiletries from my duffel bag, but after standing under a scalding hot shower for fifteen minutes, I felt fully refreshed. I toweled my hair dry and went to see what Kylie was wearing to the reception.

I found her in her room, putting the finishing touches on her makeup. She looked trim and confident in a navy sheath with white piping, her hair in a sleek knot. "Wow," I said. "You look like an ambassador."

She winked at me in the mirror. "That's the idea."

"I wonder what I'm supposed to wear?"

"Why don't you ask?"

I took her advice and sent a quick text to Zey before

beginning to style my own hair. I was finishing my own minimal makeup routine when the response came back: *Uniforms.* How concise, I thought, half-amused, half-exasperated. The brevity of the response was oddly disappointing. I missed Zey. I missed all of them. It was odd to think that I'd gone almost an entire day without seeing any of my crewmates. Even during the worst days of isolation on the *Pinion*, I hadn't been apart from them for more than a few consecutive daytime hours. I wondered what they'd been doing.

"I see you've decided to go as Novi Alkhat," Kylie said when I rejoined her.

I brushed self-consciously at one immaculate sleeve. "My crewmates will be in uniform. I thought I should too. Why? Do you think it's a mistake?"

"No." She held up two different earrings, and I pointed to one. "But," she went on thoughtfully, "it is a choice, and the Vardeshi are going to see it that way too."

"What do you mean?"

I watched our adjacent reflections in the mirror as Kylie spoke. "You're human. You're here to represent humanity. Tonight's reception isn't just a dinner, it's an official diplomatic welcome. Earth formal wear would be the predictable choice. Wearing the uniform sends a signal—it shows solidarity with your crew. You must know they're not exactly in favor with the Echelon right now."

I sighed. "I think you're better at this stuff than I am. I'm not . . . political."

Kylie checked the contents of her purse and slung it over one shoulder. "You learned Vardeshi. You can learn this too."

I went back to my room to look at the two formal dresses I'd packed, but before I'd had time to do more than slide back the wardrobe panel, the door chime sounded below. Officer Nerev identified herself and inquired whether we were ready to go to dinner. Kylie looked at me. I nodded. "We're ready," she confirmed. "Lead the way."

As we moved through the starhaven, I tracked our progress against my mental diagram of the place. The nap had restored some of my alertness, and I found I could identify the different stages of the journey without difficulty: the elevator descent through the visitors' section, the partial circuit of the starhaven's main structure, the second, longer drop into the administrative area. The room to which Officer Nerev showed us was almost as appealing as Kylie's suite, though much larger. It had a high arched ceiling hung with elaborately carved lanterns which cast a soft glow over the furnishings and the people below. There were a lot of them, I noted apprehensively. I scanned the group and saw civilians in their dark formal wear mixed in with Fleet officers in the familiar gray and gold uniforms. A handful of others wore a different uniform, one I hadn't seen before. I was immediately struck by its severity. "What's the black and white uniform?" I asked Kylie under my breath.

"Echelon," she murmured.

As if summoned by the word, a man and a woman garbed in black and white broke off from the main group and approached us. I looked them over curiously. Both appeared to be of middle age. The man wore his hair long, like Saresh, although it was gray rather than silver; his companion's was white and cropped shorter than my own. Her eyes were as piercingly blue as Sohra's, but I read little warmth in them. The pair stopped in front of us and the woman extended her hand in what was so clearly an Earth handshake that I took it without even attempting a Vardeshi greeting.

"Hello," she said. "Welcome to Arkhati Starhaven. I'm Irza Tavri, First Rank officer of the Echelon here on Arkhati. You might say . . . governor?" The hesitation was artificial; her English was flawless. I knew enough of Vardeshi kinesics to suspect that her smile of welcome was artificial too. It was a bit off-putting after the neutral expressions my crewmates on the *Pinion* customarily wore, but she might simply be trying to set us at ease. I smiled back and thanked her in English for the warm greeting.

"You must be Avery," she said. "We're honored to have you with us. You've made quite a name for yourself in the Fleet. Your crewmates have been singing your praises all day."

"Well," I said awkwardly, "I'm doing my best, but Khavi Takheri will tell you I'm still learning to make a decent cup of senek."

"I think you mean Suvi Takheri," she corrected smoothly.

"I'm sorry?"

"The promotion was temporary. Hathan Takheri has resumed his previous rank, pending the outcome of the hearings."

"Oh. Right. I forgot."

Studying my uniform, she said, "It strikes me that I may have been remiss in not issuing the dinner invitation sooner. Given more warning, you could have brought some of your Earth clothes from the *Pinion.*"

"Oh," I said again. "I did. But my crewmates are in uniform." I looked around a little helplessly. "Or they will be. When they get here."

"You feel allegiance to them," she observed.

"Of course I do."

"I find that remarkable, given what you've been forced to endure at their hands."

I said tightly, "We've all had a lot to endure."

Kylie chose that moment to interject a light comment about the tribulations of novi quarters. I listened with relief and some envy while she and Governor Tavri embarked on effortless small talk about Kylie's tenure on the *Black Moon* and the delights of the diplomatic suite. They were a matched pair, I thought: two winning smiles, two pairs of hard blue eyes. At an appropriate pause, the governor introduced her companion, Councilor Zirian, who offered his own greetings in English nearly as polished as the governor's. After a few more pleasantries, they passed us off to a cluster of civilians whose names I instantly forgot. I knew a cocktail hour when I saw one, and the ritual here on the starhaven appeared more or less the same as the Earthbound variety. I fielded my share of questions about life on the *Pinion,* but as much as possible I shifted the spotlight onto Kylie, who seemed to have an endless supply of amusing yet inoffensive cultural anecdotes queued up for delivery. At some point each of us was handed a glass of sparkling wine. I held mine without drinking it, looking wistfully around for a familiar face.

Zey appeared at my elbow. "Hey."

"Hey! I was starting to think you weren't here."

"I wasn't. They only released me from the hearings twenty minutes ago. I haven't even seen my quarters yet."

"You've been in hearings all day?" I looked him over. He did look a little tired, but not enough that I would have noticed it on my own. His hair was always tousled, and Zey could make even a fresh uniform look rumpled.

"We all have. Hathan and Ziral are still there."

I frowned. "I don't understand. You were barely involved in what happened. Except for the part where you knocked Vekesh down and saved the day. What could they possibly have to say to you that would take that long?"

"Oh, they're not done with me yet. They barely scratched the surface. The Echelon wants to know everything about the mission, from the very beginning. They spent an hour just grilling me about the language policy." He sighed. "It's going to be a long week."

At that point we were joined by Councilor Zirian, who invited us to take our seats for dinner. I was discouraged to see that Zey and Sohra had both been placed out of comfortable speaking range. I found myself at what was clearly the highest-ranking table, with Zirian himself, Kylie, Governor Tavri, and a couple of Fleet officers and civilians who looked vaguely familiar from the cocktail hour. One of the Fleet officers, bearing a khavi's insignia on his sleeve, I tentatively placed as the commander of the *Black Moon*. There were two empty seats at the table, and as people were finding their places, Saresh arrived to claim one of them. He smiled at me. The marks of fatigue were plainer on his face than they had been on Zey's. I felt an unbidden flare of resentment toward the Echelon. Saresh's injury had been more serious than mine; he was still walking with the aid of a cane. Surely providing medical attention to a wounded man ought to take priority over subjecting him to hours of debriefing.

When everyone had been seated, Governor Tavri rose to offer some boilerplate remarks on the historic moment in which we found ourselves, the promise of interspecies cooperation embodied by Kylie and me, and the honor our presence represented for Arkhati Starhaven. "We're particularly glad to have Avery safely among us," she said. *Avery,* I thought; the affectation of familiarity was a convenient way to sidestep the choice between an English and a Vardeshi title. Tavri continued, "Her path here hasn't been an easy one, and I know I speak for all the citizens of Arkhati when I pledge to show her a different face of the Vardeshi people than she has seen thus far." It was a little unfair, I thought, to dismiss the entire crew of the *Pinion* so cavalierly, as if Vekesh had tarnished them all with his betrayal. Keeping my expression carefully neutral, I glanced across the table at Saresh, who raised an eyebrow very slightly in response to my look.

When Tavri finished speaking, there was a moment of respectful silence, the Vardeshi version of applause, and then conversations resumed at the various tables. I turned to ask Kylie a question about the *Black Moon* and saw Hathan making his way through the tables in our direction. I wondered how much of Tavri's speech he had overheard. He slipped into the empty seat on the far side of the table, which happened to be beside Saresh, and they exchanged a few words too soft for me—or presumably anyone else—to overhear. Governor Tavri made the obligatory introductions. Her manner was cool and formal, reinforcing my impression that the warm greeting she had offered Kylie and me had been exaggerated for diplomatic reasons.

I hadn't been privy to the dinner arrangements, but Kylie clearly had, as our first course arrived in tandem with that of our hosts. "Who cooked this?" I asked as a bowl of steaming onion soup was placed in front of me.

"One of the chefs on the starhaven," Kylie said.

"Is that safe?"

Councilor Zirian said, "The research teams on Earth have made a great deal of progress over the past few months. You may not be fully up to date on their findings. It appears that it's safe for us to handle each other's food, with a few exceptions."

"Lemons and macadamia nuts," Kylie specified. "And coriander."

"Fortunately, the risk seems to be limited to contact and ingestion, not airborne exposure," the Councilor went on.

"Does that mean I can go to hydroponics?" I said

hopefully.

"Not only that, but you can sample a few of the crops," said Governor Tavri. "A number of Vardeshi foods have been approved for human consumption. You'll have to have an allergen test first, of course."

"Senek's been cleared," said Kylie. "And that gray beer. Not the whiskey, though—something in the distillation process doesn't agree with us."

"Senek?" I exclaimed. "Really?"

Kylie laughed. "Been letting your inbox pile up? Senek was the first thing to clear. That was almost a month ago now."

"Our communications network had already been disabled at that point," Saresh said quietly. "And the last two weeks have been . . . eventful."

"God, that's right. Sorry, I should have thought." Kylie's chagrin was obvious.

To smooth things over, I asked brightly, "So what else have I missed?"

Kylie took a sip of wine while she considered. "Let's see. There are the dull ones—lots of soaps and detergents. We can wash each other's dishes and scrub floors and all that. You'll be glad of that one. No more gloves when you're doing your novi chores."

"Oh, good," I said, a little guiltily. I hadn't worn gloves after the first week. It had just seemed like too much trouble. From the trace of a smile on Saresh's face, I could tell that he knew what I was thinking.

"And we can all shower with our own toiletries again," Kylie went on.

I nodded. "I thought I smelled real shampoo."

"You did. But you should try the Vardeshi soaps. They have some incredible fragrances. We can't wear perfume though. Supposedly they're a nasal irritant, but I think the

Vardeshi just don't like them."

"Can you blame them?" I said.

As the first course was cleared away, Kylie listed a few more scientific breakthroughs. The most exciting one was that each of our species appeared naturally immune to the other's most commonplace ailments. "At this point we've more or less abolished quarantine procedures. There doesn't seem to be any point to them. The Strangers are all in terrific health after three months of exposure to Vardeshi pathogens, and it looks like the worst thing the Vardeshi on Earth have to worry about is a bad sunburn. They're not catching the common cold, and we're not catching the . . . what is it? The summer flux? Whatever it's called."

The others at the table had been listening in evident amusement to our conversation, but they hadn't interjected. When Kylie reached the end of her list, however, Hathan said, "That was a comprehensive summary, Ms. Braswell, but you've forgotten one thing. The last item on the approved list."

Kylie glanced at him. "What's that?"

"Interspecies sexual contact."

I had just taken a sip of wine. I choked so violently that the Vardeshi nearest me recoiled in alarm, reaching for their flexscreens. Kylie, convulsed with laughter at my reaction, hastened to assure them that I didn't need medical attention. When I could speak again, I gasped, "What? How? I mean, not how. Who?"

Kylie pushed her glass of water toward me. "Officially, no names have been released. And they won't be. But I think it was one of the Vardeshi delegates with someone on Earth. Not one of the Strangers."

"Why not?" Saresh asked.

She grinned at him. "Because if it was one of us, I'd know

about it."

A thousand questions sprang instantly to mind: What were the genders of the participants? Had the encounter been satisfying for either party? Had it been a one-time experiment, purely in the interests of science, or was there now a human-Vardeshi couple in existence? It might have been permissible to ask—certainly the others around the table had greeted Hathan's introduction of the subject with almost clinical calm—but I wasn't at all confident that I could match their composure. I'd never been good at disguising my feelings, and this topic was closer to my heart than any of them (except Saresh) had reason to suspect. Deciding to save my questions for a more private venue, I ventured a harmless query about the Vardeshi foods that had been approved for ingestion by humans.

Thus steered back into safer channels, the conversation continued through the remainder of the meal, guided in about equal proportions by Kylie, Governor Tavri, and Councilor Zirian. In deference to Kylie's still-developing language skills, everyone spoke English. I understood the reason for the choice, but it still made me vaguely uncomfortable. It seemed too easy, almost like cheating, a feeling I suspected was a hold-over of Vekesh's Vardeshi-only decree. There was a brief exchange between the councilor and Saresh that drew my interest, suggesting as it did an old acquaintance between the former and Senator Takheri, but I wasn't able to overhear much of it. I was fully aware that the others at the table were making light, disarming conversation in order to keep me from having to talk about the last few weeks on the *Pinion*. I let them do it. Hathan said almost nothing. It would be difficult, I thought dryly, to equal the impact of his first contribution.

When the savory plates and postprandial drinks were passed around, I watched longingly as Kylie poured herself a cup of senek. "It's safe," she said. "I've already had my scratch test."

"What does it taste like?"

"It's no fun if I tell you." She raised her cup to me in a mocking toast.

A bottle of Earth whiskey had been thoughtfully provided for Kylie and me, and she had a glass of it to accompany her senek. I opted for coffee instead. It arrived at the table strong and hot, obviously freshly prepared. I cradled the cup in my hands as I looked down the table. As the end of the evening approached, the mood had relaxed perceptibly, and most people had fallen into low-voiced discourse with their seatmates. Councilor Zirian had poured whiskey for both Takheri brothers with a generous hand when the decanter was first passed around. Now I watched Saresh top off his own glass and lean over to refill Hathan's without asking. They were both too controlled to betray the strain I knew they must be feeling, but I had never seen them sitting together in silence for so long without work of some kind to hand. That fact alone was revealing to anyone who knew them. I looked over at Governor Tavri and saw that she was gazing in their direction too. I wondered how well she knew them.

All at once I noticed that the lanterns strung high overhead were growing fainter, their radiance softening to the dim glitter of candlelight. A young woman in flowing crimson garments reminiscent of the uniform worn for ranshai, the principal Vardeshi martial art, stepped forward to claim the attention of the seated guests. "Good evening," she said. "If you would join us in the anteroom, the performance is about to begin."

"Performance?" I whispered to Kylie as everyone began getting to their feet.

She bent down to retrieve her bag from under the table.

"This must be the cultural exchange portion of the evening. I think they're doing some kind of ritual dance for us."

We walked together through the doorway and into the smaller room, where people had begun to gather along the outer walls, leaving the central space empty for the performance. Those in front of Kylie and myself stepped politely aside to allow us a clearer view. The young woman who had previously spoken was waiting in the middle of the floor. When the flow of traffic out of the dining room had ceased, she said, "We give you the traditional harvest dance from the western mountains of Khafal Province."

Kylie was on my left side; I looked over to see that Hathan had arrived soundlessly on my right. "Where's Khafal Province?" I whispered.

"On Arideth. The first planet we colonized after we acquired long-range spaceflight capabilities."

"A harvest dance from a world that was settled by spacecraft?"

"It must sound incongruous."

"It does to me," I agreed. "But then science and mysticism have never meshed very well on Earth. I guess your people found a way to reconcile them."

"Or we just realized that we needed them both." I glanced at him again, a little surprised by the sentiment. He went on, "Those early explorers, in their rickety shuttles, with faulty navigation systems and no comm network to speak of . . . I don't envy them. It would have taken a belief in something, call it what you will, to get me onto one of those first colony ships. And I would have done every ritual dance I could think of if I managed to set it down in one piece."

I had known for a long time now that a vein of humor and lightness was present in him, hidden deep beneath his taciturnity. Only in the days since the revelation of Vekesh's guilt, and consequently my innocence, had I been permitted to share in it. I was still smiling when the dance began.

Three male and three female dancers, all dressed in crimson, all with closely shorn hair, advanced with balletic lightness of step into the center of the room. The woman who had announced the dance had retreated to a corner, where she now took up the spiral instrument threaded with silver bells that I had seen played on the *Pinion*. To the accompaniment of the bells and a low, resonant drumbeat from another corner of the room, where a second musician was shrouded in shadow, the dancers began to move.

The six of them wove around and past each other in figures that were simple yet precise. After a few passes, they separated, the women to one side of the room, the men to another. When they reunited, each performer was carrying a length of cord with a clear globe attached to one end. The globes had what appeared to be tiny flames flickering inside them, and although I was sure the fire was an illusion of some kind, I had no idea how it worked.

The second phase of the dance was swifter and somehow more martial, as the performers whirled their flames in complex and flawlessly synchronized patterns. Yet there was something about it all that held me at a remove. Unlike the music I'd heard my crewmates play, the time signature here was unfamiliar. I couldn't quite catch the rhythm of the drums, and the pattern seemed to start over at random. The dance, too, was as forbidding as it was beautiful. I thought it would have reminded me of ranshai even if the costumes had been different. The movements were a little too quick, too smooth, as if to emphasize the fact that the dancers possessed strength beyond the merely human. I wished Dr. Sawyer, the linguist who had secretly trained me in Vardeshi throughout the final year of silence before the Vardeshi themselves returned, were here to watch it. I wondered what he would have made of it as a display ostensibly selected to make two humans, far from home and weary with travel, feel welcome in a strange place.

When the dance concluded, I nearly applauded out of habit, recalling just in time that the Vardeshi showed their appreciation through silence. After the dancers had cleared the floor, I felt Kylie's hand brush my sleeve. "Wish me luck," she whispered as she stepped forward.

"Where are you going?" I hissed.

She turned back just long enough to reply, "It's our turn," before crossing to the center of the room, the click of her heels clearly audible in the hush. She seemed completely untroubled by the fact that everyone present was staring at her. I didn't know what to expect—that she would start singing, maybe— but she reached into her handbag and pulled out her phone and a portable speaker, which she proceeded to set up on a low pedestal that one of the dancers carried back onto the floor for her. She explained in a voice pitched to carry that the Council had asked her to choose a piece of classical music to play on the occasion. "It would be impossible to condense the richness and diversity of our world's music into a few minutes," she said. "Our culture, like yours, resists simplification. So let this piece be, like Avery and me, a symbol rather than a summary."

I was desperately grateful that the most public aspect of the evening had fallen to Kylie. Utterly poised, she rejoined me at the side of the room before pressing the key to begin playback. The strains of Bach's Cello Suite No. 1 filled the air. Unexpectedly moved, I shifted nearer to Kylie and rested my head on her shoulder. She put her arm around me and pulled me closer. I didn't look to see how the Vardeshi responded to the music. It was perfect, and I knew it, and for once I didn't care in the slightest what they thought. I closed my eyes and drew in a breath that seemed to go on forever. I didn't know which I had been craving more, a beloved piece of beautiful music or the warmth of a friend's arm around me. But I had the sense that a well deep inside me had been tapped dry over the past three months, and at last the cool, sweet water had begun trickling in again.

3

After the cello music, and the brief appreciative silence that followed it, Kylie went back to retrieve her speaker. I stood watching with Governor Tavri and Councilor Zirian as the guests departed. A few came over to say personal farewells. Most of the *Pinion*'s crew exited en masse with no formal leave-taking—I watched them go a little enviously—but Zey and Saresh swung by to say good-night. "See?" I said to Saresh. "Not all of our music is overproduced garbage."

"Each offers its own insights to an observant mind," he said, then added with a smile, "but I can't deny that I preferred the classical."

I nodded to his cane. "When do you go in for surgery?"

"Tomorrow afternoon. The Echelon wants a thorough debrief of the Listening before I undergo anesthesia."

"At least you get a break," Zey muttered. "I'd let them carve up my leg if it meant I could skip out on the hearings. Both legs, even."

"I'll just have to do them afterward," his brother reminded

him.

"Good point. Well, we'd better go." Zey raised one in a casual farewell. "Have fun on your tour, Eyvri."

"You're not coming?" I said without much hope.

"No way. I'm wrecked after all those hours of questioning. And also I wasn't invited."

It didn't appear that anyone other than Kylie and I had been invited on the tour. We set off down the corridor with Zirian and Tavri, trailing Officer Nerev and a handful of her red-and-black-garbed fellows. I spent the first few minutes of the tour waiting for the Echelon representatives to hand us off to a subordinate, but it seemed they had chosen to do the honors themselves. I was glad I had picked coffee over an after-dinner drink. It wasn't only the exalted company in which we found ourselves that demanded alertness. The corridors around us had begun to fill up with people. Most of them were out of uniform, and that fact, added to the lateness of the hour, told me they were pursuing errands of pleasure rather than business. This time, disconcertingly, I seemed to be the focus of their interest. Something about the governor's presence made the connection between Kylie and me plainer than before. Whereas earlier their glances had slid off me and onto her, now they studied me—my uniform, my face, my hair—with avid curiosity. The bars were open, I thought, and people were starting to relax a little. I heard my name murmured over and over again, *Alkhat,* the Vardeshi rendering of my surname. Sometimes it was preceded by *novi,* sometimes it wasn't. One or two passersby even went so far as to touch their arms, fingers brushing across their sleeves, miming the path of a bullet.

Kylie and Governor Tavri had taken the lead. Councilor Zirian dropped back to walk beside me. "How does it feel to be a celebrity?" he asked. The question itself was a disquieting echo of Kylie's earlier reference to heroism. Still, I was flattered, and somehow relieved, that he asked it in Vardeshi.

"Undeserved," I said.

"Really? You're a human in a Fleet uniform. That alone would be worthy of note, even if you hadn't also survived a Listening. And an assassination attempt."

"All right, maybe not undeserved then. But uncomfortable."

Zirian said, "You were comfortable on the *Pinion?*"

"Not most of the time, no. But I had time to get used to things. And the crew got used to me. If I was uncomfortable, it was because I was making mistakes. Or getting in trouble with Vekesh. It wasn't because I was human."

He nodded. "When the *Pinion* was chosen to host a human representative, and then to be in effect the flagship of the exchange program, there were objections. Some people said the ship was too small, that it would be isolating, or stifling, for the human."

"Those people haven't met me," I said.

"Indeed. Ambassador Seidel clearly has, though."

"Why, what did he tell you?"

"I believe his exact words were, 'She'll try to disappear. Don't let her.'"

I was immediately intrigued, but before I could question him further, we stepped through a high arched doorway into a room that was like nothing I had ever seen before. It looked as though a section of the cylindrical core of the station, a few hundred meters across and several stories tall, had been transformed into an open-air market. We stood on a narrow catwalk set just under the ceiling. The catwalk ran along the perimeter of the room, but two perpendicular bridges spanning the void permitted a more direct crossing. Both the bridges and the shoulder-high barriers enclosing them were made of a clear glassy material. I looked out at the narrow arched walkways, supported by nothing I could see, and my stomach churned.

A couple of stories beneath our catwalk was a wider balcony, thronged with pedestrians weaving their way between what I tentatively labeled food and drink stalls. Each stall had a standing bar built into it or a cluster of stools and tables nearby, and most of the seats were occupied. Below that balcony was a second, broader one, similarly full of customers and food stalls. I stepped closer to the transparent barrier and looked farther down. The floor of the space was obviously a marketplace, teeming with carts and stalls and tables on which vendors displayed their wares. The market looked hectic but at the same time highly organized, with a network of curving paths laid out for shoppers to wander at their leisure.

Here, then, was the alien bazaar I had been hoping for. It wasn't exactly what I had pictured. Even in a crowded marketplace, the Vardeshi kept their voices decorously low, and there were no competing shouts of hawkers or skirls of wild music. Visually, too, the scene was muted. The shops and food stalls were mostly built of what looked like bamboo. I assumed, given our distance from the nearest forested planet, that it was a synthetic material. The colors of the scene were subdued, ochre and tan and dull green. I might have found the entire spectacle a little anticlimactic were it not for its most striking feature. The air above the market was filled with banners, scores or hundreds of them in every imaginable color and shape. Some were covered in Vardeshi lettering, some bore abstract swirls or patterns, some were of one solid color emblazoned with a sigil or mark in a contrasting hue. They didn't appear to be suspended by strings, but rather by some application of the hover technology I knew the Vardeshi possessed. Many of the banners were stationary; a few drifted aimlessly on currents of air. The highest banners floated just below our feet.

"Welcome to the Atrium," said Governor Tavri, "Arkhati's central marketplace. All our most successful vendors can be found here. The competition for a place is intense—many of these stalls have been handed down through generations. The market has been running continuously for over six hundred years. Everyone who visits the starhaven passes through here at some point."

"What are the banners for?" I asked.

"They're advertisements for shops or restaurants, both here and elsewhere in the starhaven. If you scan a banner's insignia with your flexscreen, you'll be given directions to the stall and information about the goods for sale." Kylie and I both pulled out our flexscreens. I activated my camera and panned it slowly across the profusion of banners, selecting one in deep blue with a starburst design in white. "Zenesh Fine Tailoring," the governor read over my shoulder, translating into English for Kylie's benefit. "Handmade apparel of the highest quality, guaranteed ready before your launch date. Two hundred years of exquisite custom designs. Find us at Stall 171."

"They don't say anything about their prices," I noted.

"With a stall in the Atrium, you can assume they're exorbitant."

Kylie turned her flexscreen questioningly toward me. "House of Three Moons Senek Shop," I translated. "Tier Two, Stall 38."

Councilor Zirian smiled. "I get my senek there every morning."

"Would you like to see the marketplace?" the governor asked.

"Yes," Kylie and I said in unison.

We descended to the floor via a narrow spiraling ramp built of the same transparent substance as the bridges. I knew rationally that the material must be sturdier than glass, but it was perfectly clear and unnervingly thin, and after one quick glance downward, I opted to keep one hand on the rail and look out at the banners instead. Once in the maze of shops, I was instantly captivated by the variety and workmanship of the goods on offer. I saw vendors selling clothing, shoes, jewelry, musical instruments, tapestries. A few sold only memory crystals, the blue gemstones the Vardeshi encoded with their most precious images and audiorecordings. One aisle was entirely devoted to whiskey, senek, and rana, the drug that unlocked latent telepathic powers. I stopped to examine a pair of whiskey glasses each carved from a single glittering gray crystal. The shop owner watched me narrowly when I picked one up for a closer look, but he smiled with genuine warmth when I thanked him. Kylie and I were both drawn to a display of intricately embroidered sashes. The vendor, a young woman, explained that they were traditionally worn by expectant mothers. I translated, and the vendor laughed with me when Kylie dropped the sash she was holding in horror. I lingered so long at another stall, where jeweled pendants hung like stars against a velvety dark cloth, that Kylie had to drag me away by the elbow. "We'll come back," she promised. "You have plenty of time."

When we'd walked from one edge of the market to the other, we climbed another ramp to the first tier of food and drink shops, where a vendor served the other three with senek and me with water. He refused payment for the drinks, insisting it was an honor to serve his first human customers. The exchange prompted a thought, and I said in an undertone to Kylie, "How do we pay for things here?"

I'd underestimated the keenness of Vardeshi hearing. Councilor Zirian said in English, "As an employee of the Fleet, you draw a weekly salary, and Kylie, you've been provided a stipend as well. You both have currency accounts linked to your flexscreens. It's difficult to estimate the conversion rate, but . . ." He swirled his cup thoughtfully. "A cup of senek costs roughly six units, and a full meal is around sixty or eighty. A good piece of bespoke clothing should cost about four hundred. That whiskey glass you were looking at, Avery, would be about six hundred. As a novi in the Fleet, you earn about a thousand units a week. Kylie, your account has twenty-five thousand units in it. Any vendor will be able to check your balance on your flexscreen."

Kylie elbowed me. "Looks like there's no money in drudge work."

I laughed. "And it pays so well back home."

"If you're ready to move on, we're not far from the Arboretum," the governor said.

The Arboretum was located at the very top of the starhaven's main column. I found it as breathtaking as the Atrium in its own way. It was like a little woodland enclosed under a transparent dome, its floor sculpted with natural-looking rises and depressions to disguise the artificial flatness of the horizon. Soft globe lights hanging from the boughs of the trees provided a gentle illumination without obscuring the stars that glimmered beyond the dome. Leaves rustled in a manufactured breeze, and a tiny stream whispered over stones in its bed. Another sound, faint yet distinct, stopped my heart for an instant: the night-call of a bird or an animal, unseen in the dimness somewhere overhead. I stood in the entryway, transfixed, breathing in the scents of a night forest. The fragrances of the individual trees were unfamiliar, but there was an underlying resinous tang that evoked the woods of home.

"During the day, the ceiling panels turn opaque and emit simulated daylight," Zirian explained. "The starhaven has several hydroponics bays as well, of course, but the Arboretum is something special. We come here when we want to remember the feeling of being soilside. And it isn't only ornamental. The trees play an important role in our carbon dioxide processing and oxygen production, and the aquatic plants are part of our filtration system for reclaimed water."

We followed a winding path through the trees. It was startling to feel soft soil underfoot again. Passing under a low-hanging branch, I reached up to brush my fingers across the cool undersides of its leaves. The little stream crisscrossed our path a handful of times, and at one point we came upon a place where the water ran into a pool encircled by a grove of trees. Several hexagonal stone seats were placed beside the water. The clearing was more brightly lit than the paths on either side, and as I gazed down at the pool, I caught an unexpected gleam of sapphire in its dark depths. I knelt to look closer. Even as I recognized what I was seeing, Governor Tavri said, "They're memory crystals. People started leaving them here a hundred years ago or so, and it's become something of a good-luck ritual. This pool is filled with the memories of all the Vardeshi who have passed through Arkhati. Every few years we collect them all and expel them into space. We have to: otherwise they'd carpet the whole Arboretum by now."

"What kinds of memories?" I asked.

"I'm told they're mostly images of loved ones. There's a superstition that leaving someone's image in the pool invokes a kind of protection. But some people leave memories of those they've lost. It's a symbolic way of forgetting, I suppose."

"You're told?" Kylie repeated. "You don't look at the crystals?"

"Certainly not," Tavri said in surprise. "Our people would consider it an intrusion."

Kylie shrugged. "Ours would say that if you leave your memories lying around in plain sight, you can pretty much assume someone's going to look at them."

"Maybe the Vardeshi have better self-control," I said. "Or maybe they're just not interested. Pictures aren't that exciting when you're used to getting memories straight from the source."

"You'd know better than I would."

The words were Kylie's, but for an instant all three of them fixed me with speculative looks. I shivered. I didn't like feeling like a specimen, particularly when one of the people examining me was human.

After exploring a bit further, we emerged from the trees near a doorway, possibly the one by which we'd entered, though I wasn't sure. I checked my flexscreen, took note of the late hour, and tried unsuccessfully to stifle a yawn.

"I think you've seen enough for one night," the governor said, alert as ever. "You'll be seeing the medical and bureaucratic levels tomorrow, in any case. Avery, your hearing is tentatively set for one o'clock, with a medical examination to follow. Will that be acceptable?"

"It sounds fine," I said.

"We recommend that you bring at least one companion to your hearing. You're not on trial, and we'd like you to feel as comfortable as possible. I assumed . . ." She hesitated delicately.

"Kylie," I said. "Of course. If you don't mind," I added to Kylie herself. "And . . ." I paused to think. "I'd like Rhevi Daskar to be there." Daskar was the *Pinion*'s physician. Her calm maternal presence had been a source of comfort to me more than once in the tumultuous events of the last few weeks.

"Certainly," the governor said. "We'll see that she's informed."

The appropriate thanks and farewells were exchanged, and Tavri and Zirian took their leave of us. They weren't accompanied by any security personnel, at least not that I noticed; apparently Nerev and the three others who had been keeping pace with us all evening were solely for the benefit of the humans. Kylie and I didn't speak much on the short walk back to her suite. I started stripping off my uniform as soon as we were safely within her rooms.

"I'd offer you a cup of tea," she said, "but I know you're ready to crash."

"I'd love one tomorrow, if the offer doesn't expire."

"Sure. We'll talk then. Sleep well."

"You too." I went into my little gray and copper room, finished pulling off my uniform, and dropped it in a heap on the floor before stretching out on the bunk. It was considerably wider than my bed on the *Pinion,* but the tilt was identical, and while the hum emanating from the bulkhead wasn't a perfect match for the one I'd left behind, it was close enough. I reached for the blanket folded at the foot of the bunk and found it to be far softer than any of my Earth-issue bedding, the exact twin of the one in Zey's quarters that I'd been coveting. Maybe he'd gotten it on Arkhati. Maybe I could find one for sale in the Atrium. Hell, I was a diplomat now; maybe I could just take it with me. I burrowed under its cloudlike softness and fell immediately asleep.

* * *

I woke to the smell of bacon frying. I fumbled for pajamas and made my way into the galley, where I found Kylie busily putting together a feast. In addition to the bacon, there were eggs, toast, butter, marmalade, and tea in a real English teapot. I sat down and pulled the teapot toward me. "You're a miracle worker. How long have you been up?"

"An hour or so. I've been going through the publicity photos from last night." She waved at her flexscreen, which was sitting on the counter in what I judged dangerous proximity to the pan of bacon.

"Publicity photos? That's a Vardeshi thing?"

"No, but it's a human thing, so the Council asked the Echelon to assign a photographer for major events. I'm supposed to review the photos and send the best ones home. I'm basically my own press secretary." She wiped her fingers on a towel, logged into her flexscreen, and passed it to me. I skimmed through the pictures while she finished crisping the bacon. There were a couple of me and Hathan talking together at the beginning of the dance performance. I flicked past those quickly. I would have liked to examine them more carefully, on the off chance that not all of them were catastrophically unflattering, but I couldn't, not with Kylie only a few feet away and casting intermittent curious glances over my shoulder. There was one candid close-up shot I liked of myself and Zey laughing about something. I sent it to my own account and pushed the flexscreen to one side as Kylie set the plate of bacon between us.

We ate in ravenous silence for a few minutes. Then I poured myself a second cup of tea and went to light the camp stove to boil another pot of water. As I sat down again, I said cheerfully, "So, sex with aliens? Tell me about that."

Kylie let out a bark of laughter. "You don't waste any time, do you? Let me guess. It's Saresh, right? You're in love with Saresh."

I eyed her narrowly over my teacup. "I don't remember

saying anything about love."

"Oh, well done," she said approvingly.

"And no. All joking aside, I'm not in love with Saresh. I couldn't have done the Listening if I were."

She gave a grudging nod. "All right. It's hard to argue with that."

"I'm asking out of general interest. But I am interested. Who wouldn't be? I felt awkward talking about it in front of them, but they're not here now, so fill me in, because you obviously know more than I do."

Kylie reached for another piece of toast. "I don't know that much. Your commander, whatever his name is—"

"Hathan," I said.

"Right. He oversimplified a little. All we've been told is that there's been one confirmed report of consensual sexual intercourse between humans and Vardeshi. Vardeshi male, human female. Apparently the mechanics worked just fine, although I don't know how much either of them enjoyed it. The report was quite vague on the details. And it seems to have been a one-off, since there haven't been any updates since the message went out a couple of weeks ago. In any case, we've been given the green light to proceed with extreme caution. Naturally there are about a thousand regulations in place. Both parties have to sign a waiver documenting their consent and the activities planned, right down to the positions. You should look at the form—it's good for a laugh. A physician has to sign off, and obviously you're expected to use protection."

"Why?" I said. "It's not like anyone's getting pregnant."

"No, but with only one case on the books, all bodily fluids are potential biohazards." Both of us grimaced at the word. She went on, "And if you do take the plunge, so to speak, you're supposed to check every inch of your skin for signs of a negative reaction afterward. If you ask me, it's all pretty much guaranteed to squelch any romance that might be in the air. Or the vacuum."

I shook my head. "I can't see how it would even happen. All the Vardeshi I know are engaged. Or married. Playing the field doesn't really seem to be their style."

"Well," Kylie said, "it's happened once. So we know it's possible. The bigger question, to my mind, is whether it was any good."

"You'll have to let me know when you find out," I said.

"What makes you think it's going to be me?"

"What, you think it'll be me? My ship has ten people on it! And only five of them are guys. And, like I said, they're all taken." I held up my right hand with its imagined gold sigil turned toward her.

"All's fair," she murmured.

I ignored that. "It would be like hooking up in a minivan. Whereas Arkhati is basically a giant airport. Odds are that in the next six months you'll meet someone passing through who wants to satisfy his, you know, curiosity. It's a numbers game. I bet you could pick up someone in the Atrium tonight if you really wanted to."

"What about you? You'll be here a week. And you're the Vaku."

"I'm not a Vaku." I could feel myself blushing.

"You are," Kylie insisted. "You're a total fangirl. You're a little bit in love with all of them. The women too. You just are. You can't hide it, not from me. Honestly, given the chance, I'm not even sure I'd want to fuck one of them. I think they're a bit creepy sometimes. Those long fingers. And they're so controlled. Sometimes it's like talking to a bunch of really polite robots. I like my men a little rougher around the edges. But you don't see any of that. Tell me I'm wrong."

"You're not wrong," I admitted. In truth, she was more right than she knew, and I was lucky she hadn't looked any further than Saresh for the object of my hypothetical infatuation. With any luck, Hathan would escape her notice entirely.

We cleaned up our breakfast dishes, and I took another shower, an indulgence so hedonistic after months of water rationing that I felt a pang of guilt. I reminded myself that, as Councilor Zirian had explained during our tour, there were elaborate systems devoted to reclaiming and processing the starhaven's wastewater.

Shortly before one o'clock, Officer Nerev rang the chime and entered to escort us to my hearing in the administrative wing. It was amazing, I thought, how even on an ancient space station built by the hands of another race, bureaucratic hallways were instantly recognizable. There was a uniformity and drabness about the long, silent corridors with their identical gray doors. Save for the eldritch green lights and the nameplates etched in Vardeshi script, I could have been going to renew my driver's license.

The young man who conducted my hearing had Sohra's coloring, and, with his uncharacteristically round face, he looked so human that I wondered if he'd been chosen for that very reason. He wore the now-familiar Echelon uniform. When we entered his featureless little office, he was talking to Daskar, who had arrived before us. I caught a few words of their conversation before he interrupted himself and rose to greet us. They seemed to be talking about someone's language proficiency—mine, I guessed. The Echelon representative offered the standard Vardeshi greeting, first to me, then to Kylie.

"Novi Alkhat," he said in Vardeshi, "I'm Deputy Zekhan. My understanding is that you're capable of conducting this interview in Vardeshi, but for the sake of your companion, we'll continue in English, unless you have any objections."

"None," I said.

He switched languages at once. "Good. Please have a seat."

I sat down next to Daskar, thanked her for coming, and introduced her to Kylie, who claimed the stool on my other side. Deputy Zekhan seated himself and accessed a menu on his flexscreen. "I'm going to record our conversation. That way, we shouldn't need to call you in for additional sessions. Could you describe for me your interactions with Reyjai Vekesh, beginning with the day you arrived on the *Pinion?*"

"All of them?" I said.

"Please. Be as thorough as you can."

I talked for over an hour. It was easier than I'd expected to speak dispassionately about the events of the last three months. Talking to the deputy, whose affect remained neutral throughout my retelling, wasn't like talking to Kylie. It helped, too, that the past couple of weeks had been so dramatic. A few days removed from the action, it all started to feel a bit farfetched. I felt like I was explaining the plot of a Vardrama to someone who'd missed a few episodes. When I was done, the deputy asked several questions that were clearly directed at establishing who among the crew had attempted to help me and who had remained indifferent to my struggles. Daskar and Saresh, I knew, were already on record as my partisans, having appealed directly to the Echelon on my behalf. I spoke warmly in defense of Zey and Sohra. It was with a sick feeling in the pit of my stomach that I described my disastrous attempt to seek help from Hathan. I knew total honesty was required; my account would inevitably be cross-checked with those of my crewmates, and they would be telling the truth. I remembered what Hathan had said to me when I showed him the draft of my report on the shooting. *We can speak for ourselves.* I hoped they could.

The hearing ran a little under two hours from start to finish. When it was over, the deputy thanked me politely for my compliance and said I was free to go. "Your security attendant will show you to your next appointment on helix twelve. Enjoy your time on Arkhati."

"Thanks," I said. "Do you know how long we'll have to wait for a decision about my mission? Whether it will go forward with the original crew?"

He exchanged a look with Daskar. "Progress has been slow. I wouldn't expect a ruling for several days at least."

Officer Nerev was waiting for us out in the hallway with a male guard I hadn't seen before. As they led us away from the office I said, "What was that about? That look he gave you?"

Daskar said somberly, "It's more or less what we expected. The Echelon isn't disposed to let anyone on the *Pinion* off lightly. At the moment, rumor has it they're leaning toward dispersing the crew to other assignments."

"But I asked for everyone to be kept together."

"I know," she said.

"I thought . . . The Echelon told me I had a say in what happened next. They said it was up to me."

"They said the destination was up to you. Did they say anything in their message about the crew?"

With a sinking heart I said, "I don't remember. I thought it was the same thing."

"Regardless of the exact wording, I don't think you're wrong about the intent of the message. Your voice carries weight with the Echelon. But it's only one of many voices they're hearing right now. Some of the other ones are very powerful. You may need to fight to make yourself heard."

"How do I do that?"

"For now, there isn't much you can do except wait for the

results from the crew hearings. But if I were you . . ." She paused. "I'd want to know who my allies were."

We had arrived at a corridor junction. With that cryptic proclamation, Daskar left us, bound for another questioning session. Kylie and I followed our pair of security officers into an area marked "Medical." I commented as we walked, "You're awfully quiet. I don't think you said a word the whole time we were in the hearing."

Kylie said slowly, "I didn't know about any of that."

"You knew about the Listening, didn't you? And the attack?"

"Of course, but I didn't know you'd been put on trial. Or stripped of your rank. Or kept in bloody isolation for two weeks. I didn't know you weren't allowed to speak English, for God's sake. And I thought there'd been some kind of accident with your tech."

"Oh," I said. "Yeah. Not an accident. Pretty deliberate, actually." In an early attempt to distance me from my crewmates, Khavi Vekesh had forbidden me to communicate with them in English. Upon discovering that I was secretly watching recordings of old Vardramas with Zey, who as a Blank was captivated by Earth entertainment, he had confiscated my technology. Several days later, after I was imprisoned as a suspected spy, Hathan had ordered it disassembled, thoroughly checked for spyware, and the pieces ejected through an airlock.

"I've spent these three months, I don't know . . ." Kylie gestured vaguely with her hands.

"Drinking senek?" I suggested. "Engaging in profound philosophical debates about culture? Hosting Earth poetry readings in the ship's lounge?"

"Well . . . more or less."

"I know," I said. "That's what I thought I'd be doing too. Plus, you know, mopping floors and cleaning toilets. Things have gone a little differently than I expected."

She frowned. "Avery . . ."

Officer Nerev said, "Forgive the interruption, but we've arrived. The doctor's office is through that door."

"Could you tell her we need another minute? Would that be all right?" I asked.

She nodded and went in. Our second attendant moved down the hall to stand a discreet distance away. Not too far, I noticed; he could probably hear every word we said from there.

Kylie began again. "Avery, are you really sure you want to stay with your crew? Are you sure that's the right thing to do?"

"You sound like the Echelon," I said half-jokingly. "I thought you were on my side."

"Have you considered that the Echelon might be right? You've been through hell. Why spend another minute with the people who put you there? If I were you, I'd want to get far away from them. From all Vardeshi, maybe, but certainly the ones on the *Pinion*. They had their chance, and they blew it. And you almost died. I know I've been teasing you about being a Vaku, but are you at all worried that you might not be thinking clearly right now?"

"What are you saying, that you think I have Stockholm syndrome?" I'd tried to say the words lightly. They didn't sound light. This was a challenge from an unexpected corner. And rehashing my struggles in exquisite detail for the last two hours had apparently affected me a little more than I'd realized, because I found myself suddenly on the verge of tears. In the strained silence that followed my words, Officer Nerev emerged through the door and nodded to me.

Kylie said quietly, "If you did, you'd be the last one to know it."

I folded my arms. "So you're a psychiatrist now, is that it? You're taking over from Dr. Okoye? One day with me and you're an expert on my problems. That's got to be some kind of record."

She raised a placating hand. "I didn't mean—"

"You know what? You're right. You figured me out. I am in love with them. All of them. Every single one. Especially Khavi Vekesh. So what if he trashed my laptop, or locked me in a room, or shot me? He's not a bad guy. He's just fucking misunderstood!" My voice rose perilously high and cracked on the last word. I wasn't sure when I'd started shouting. I hadn't even known I was doing it until I heard the startling quiet that rushed in to follow my words.

"I think maybe we should talk about this later," Kylie said.

"Think whatever you want." I slammed my hand onto the control panel, and the door leapt open as if startled by the violence. I went in. Kylie followed a few seconds later. The tension between us was palpable, but the doctor, whose name I missed in the struggle to compose myself, gave no sign that she was aware of it. She performed a thorough but tactful examination. Ordinarily I would have undressed in front of Kylie without a trace of self-consciousness. Now I avoided her eyes. I could feel them lingering on my ribs, which were noticeably more prominent than they had been when I'd launched, and on the dark ribbon of scar tissue that banded my right arm. My body offered its own mute testimony to the trials I had endured.

The doctor's last act was to perform a series of scratch tests with fine-gauge needles on my left arm. "This looks promising," she said. "You aren't showing evidence of any immediate allergic response to the most common Vardeshi foods. I'd like to see you again in twenty-four hours for a recheck, but barring a change between now and then, you should be cleared to start sampling our food and drink tomorrow night. I'll have the most current list of approved foods sent to your flexscreen."

"Thanks," I said stiffly.

As we left the office, Kylie started to say something. I cut her off. "I think I need some space. I'm going for a walk in the Arboretum. I'll see you back at the room in a bit, okay?"

She said, "Okay," although she didn't look pleased.

Kylie followed Officer Nerev back the way we'd come, and I went with the male security officer down the hall to one of the silent elevator rooms. Sunk in my thoughts, I scarcely registered the journey to the Arboretum.

As we stepped through the doorway, however, I relaxed at once. There was something about the Arboretum, with its cool fragrant air and rustle of leaves overhead, that spoke directly to my animal self, urging calm. There were a few other people strolling the paths, but I avoided their eyes, and they left me alone. My security escort followed at a discreet distance, permitting me the illusion of solitude. Without meaning to, I found myself retracing our steps of the night before to the little clearing with the memory pool. I sat down on one of the hexagonal stones and rested my elbows on my knees, staring down at the surface of the water. In the daytime it glittered with simulated sunlight. I had to look harder for the elusive glints of blue.

Kylie's words had shaken me. More than that, they had stirred up a cloud of disquieting echoes from half-forgotten college anthropology classes. Stockholm syndrome. Inferiority complex. Gone native. Was she right? Had my infatuation with the Vardeshi caused me to lose all perspective? There was nothing I wanted less at this moment than to turn around and go back to Earth. But was that fact in itself a sign that I'd let things go too far? Had my judgment been compromised?

And if it had, then whose could I trust? The Vardeshi knew nothing about human psychology. They had only my word that I was competent to continue. Dr. Okoye had given me provisional approval to go on if I felt up to it, but she had only a few minutes of video and a handful of written reports on which to base her diagnosis. The Council wanted me to stay in the field. But Ambassador Seidel had been candid about his willingness to use me as a pawn to advance the alliance. Wherever my mental health ranked among his priorities, it wasn't at the top. What about Kylie, then? We didn't know each other well. We'd only been at the Villiger Center together for two weeks, albeit two intense weeks. Still, she was a friend, and more importantly, she was human. Alone of the thousands of other souls on Arkhati, she could size up my mental state at a glance. Her instincts were unerring. And they were telling her that I was acting irrationally. I had accused her of armchair psychology, but the simple truth was that, amateur or not, her diagnosis might be the most accurate one available.

The part of my mind that was cynical—or paranoid—pointed out that even Kylie's opinion wasn't entirely innocent of bias. For all that she was a friend, she was a rival as well. She had already beaten me to Arkhati. The first human steps on Vardesh Prime had yet to be taken, the history books yet to be written. If I quit now, Kylie moved up a place on the list. Daskar's words came back to me. Did I know who my allies were? Did I have any?

4

When I got back to Kylie's suite I found her sitting on the terrace with a bottle of wine and two glasses on the table in front of her. One of the glasses was half full, the other empty. She must have heard me approaching, but she didn't turn her head. I sat down on the stool next to hers. In silence we watched a landing craft like the one that had shuttled me from Zurich to the *Pinion* travel in a slow arc across the viewport. When it had disappeared from sight I said, "Sorry I was an asshole before."

Kylie said, "It's nothing."

"Don't tell me, Dr. Okoye told you that might happen too."

"She said you might lash out and that, as your friend, I'd be a safe target."

I sighed. "What you said last night about the Vardeshi being so controlled all the time . . . I think I've been trying to do that. For way too long. I guess I finally cracked."

"You're probably better off for it. We're not meant to keep

everything in. That may be their way, but it's not ours." Kylie poured wine into the second glass and slid it toward me. "The way I see it, you've done your hearing and your medical exam. There's nothing left to do now but wait for the Echelon's decision. I'd say you're officially on vacation. We have a whole starhaven to explore—what do you want to do first?"

"Dress up," I said. "Go out. Get drunk."

Kylie clinked her glass against mine. "Good answer."

If she still resented my earlier outburst, she gave no sign of it. I was grateful for her forbearance. She would have been within her rights to make things awkward for me for a while. I had expected that. Instead, she topped off her glass and told me to choose the dinner music while she lit the camp stove. We made risotto and drank more wine. After dinner, we got dressed for our first night out on the starhaven. Paradoxically, since I had fewer options to choose from, I was slower getting ready than Kylie.

"Finally," she said when I came downstairs at last. "I thought you were never going to take off that uniform."

I grinned. "That's a good line. You planning on using it tonight?"

"It wouldn't be the first time." She studied my outfit appraisingly. "I think you need another necklace."

"I think you need my leather jacket." I ran back up the stairs to get it. As I was on my way down again, my flexscreen lit up with a message from Zey. *Hearings are over for Sohra and me. We're going to the Atrium to celebrate. Meet us?*

The relief that crashed over me was dizzying. Seeing my crewmates last night had reinforced my longing for them; crossing paths briefly and publicly was almost worse than having no contact at all. I'd been toying with the thought of messaging Zey, but I'd been wary of straying into clingy girlfriend territory. What was the protocol in a situation like ours?

We weren't on the *Pinion* anymore. Arkhati was an enormous floating city with ample entertainment and social options. Maybe he would want to be left alone. Now, with clear evidence to the contrary glimmering in my hand, I didn't stop to question the rush of exhilaration I felt. I texted back immediately, *On our way!*

Downstairs, I passed the jacket to Kylie, who slipped it on at once. "You have your drinks?" she asked.

I patted my bag and heard the clink of bottles within. "Right here." As we went out the door I said, "Okay if we meet up with some of my friends from the *Pinion*?"

"Yeah, great. They can show us around."

We stepped out into the hallway. Officer Nerev had been replaced by another member of Kylie's security detail, a young dark-haired man who studied the directions Zey had sent and then led us toward the Atrium. "You sure have a lot of security," I said to Kylie as we walked.

She said matter-of-factly, "So do you."

"I do?" I looked around. "Where?" There was no one near us in the corridor save for Kylie's guard and a couple of men in Fleet uniforms who had paused to look at something on one of their flexscreens. Neither glanced up as we passed them.

Kylie shrugged. "Seshan says they're keeping a low profile for now, gauging the level of anti-human sentiment on the starhaven. You won't see them until you need them. But you can be sure they're there."

We found Zey and Sohra at a stall on the upper tier of food and drink stands, one that served senek and beer and offered a commanding view of both the lower tier and the marketplace below. I introduced Kylie, who offered greetings in rapid if ungrammatical Vardeshi. My crewmates already had drinks in their hands. After making their acquaintance, Kylie turned to the stall owner and ordered herself another of the same, which seemed to take all three Vardeshi equally by surprise. The owner glanced pointedly at me. "Just one?"

"Just one," I confirmed. At Zey's puzzled look I explained, "I just had my allergy test. By this time tomorrow, I'll be able to drink with you guys. I hope."

"What else did they test?" Sohra asked.

I pulled my flexscreen and a beer out of my bag. "I'll show you. You can tell me what to try first."

I hadn't known whether Kylie would mix well with my Vardeshi friends—combining groups was a risky enough proposition even when everyone involved was the same species—but conversation flowed easily among the four of us. As I would have expected in someone immersed in a difficult language without adequate time to study the essentials, Kylie's speech was laced with technical flaws, but they didn't impede her ability to communicate. She lost no time in finding points of connection with both of the others. She remembered seeing Zey at the Villiger Center on my last day of training, and upon hearing his surname, she linked it to his father's with admirable speed. Senator Novak Takheri had been a member of the original group of five representatives sent to Earth to make first contact twenty-five years ago. When Sohra mentioned a member of her graduating class at the Institute who was serving on the *Black Moon*, Kylie knew that name too and had a story to share. I felt a faint trace of envy as I watched her easy rapport with my crewmates. I told myself firmly that this was Kylie's particular gift. She excelled at making quick connections with strangers. She had done it with me at the Villiger Center, and she had undoubtedly done it with the crew of the *Black Moon*. In her six months on Arkhati, she would be asked to do it countless more times. It was her job, and if she was good at it, so much the better for the alliance. All the same, I felt a slightly guilty satisfaction at each error in tone or verb tense. Language was my area of specialization, and while I knew Kylie might have been equally proficient given my year-long head start, I saw no reason to let that fact cloud my triumph. I knew my own speech and writing were still far from perfect—it would have been hard to think otherwise when my crewmates, mainly Hathan, continued to point out mistakes with maddening regularity—but I also knew how far I'd come. Three months of complete immersion had done their work. And my idioms, thanks to Saresh, were perfectly on point. An unexpected side effect of the Listening had left me with a complete stock of Vardeshi idioms and him with an extensive collection of American pop-song lyrics.

For the most part we talked about the exchange. The other three seemed fairly current on exchange-related gossip, and listening to them made me realize how thoroughly insulated I'd been from everything beyond the walls of the *Pinion*. It was quickly clear that no one else among either the Strangers or the Vardeshi on Earth had a story to match mine for drama. "You're still the celebrity," Kylie assured me. Nevertheless, there had been some intriguing developments, and I'd missed all of them. Inevitably, there had been a few dropouts. Seven humans and three Vardeshi had quit the program, all within the last month. Replacements for all ten were currently en route. I didn't recognize any of the departing participants' names. Most of them had simply failed to conquer their environment shock, but one of the humans had suffered a total nervous breakdown and had to be evacuated for health reasons.

"He was already a month out," Sohra said. "That has to be the longest medical evacuation in history."

"And the most humiliating," Zey agreed.

Additionally, a Vardeshi delegate had changed her stance on the alliance after seeing the living conditions on Earth and asked to be discharged on ethical grounds. "Where was she stationed?" I asked.

"Hyderabad," said Kylie.

I bit my lip. "Damn."

"What's wrong with Hyderabad?" Sohra asked.

"Nothing. It's just . . ." I looked at Kylie.

"Have you been to India?" she asked.

"No," I admitted.

"I have. And, honestly, I think it's one of the best places they could have sent a delegate. It's all of humanity crammed in together and jostling for your attention. It's thrilling and colorful and sometimes terribly sad." Seeing my frown, she said firmly, "You can't cherry-pick the good parts of Earth and leave the bad ones behind. That's the nature of the exchange. It's all or nothing."

"Which representative was it?" Zey asked Sohra. She said a name. He waved dismissively. "Don't worry about it. She's South Continent. They're all soft."

"Aren't you from the South Continent?" I asked.

He grinned. "Yeah. But Fleet makes you tough."

"Remember who you're talking to," said Sohra.

Kylie punched my shoulder lightly. "Avery was tough to begin with."

Still disheartened, I said, "It's not like we lied. We never said we were perfect."

"It'll be fine," Zey insisted. "What's one person out of a hundred?"

"But does she still get a vote at the end of the year?"

"Probably." Kylie grinned. "But so do we."

We lounged against the railing with our drinks, watching as the artificial dusk deepened and the lights came on. Each shop or stall had its own form of illumination, some as muted and natural as starlight or candlelight, some garish as any neon sign in an Earth metropolis. The scene was lit from above, too, by the soft glow of the banners. I watched in fascination the endlessly exotic parade that passed beneath our vantage point. The number of uniforms, both Echelon and Fleet, dwindled as the proportions shifted: fewer workers headed home, more evening revelers. Vardeshi going-out clothes still tended toward the dark and formal, at least to my eyes, but I saw shades of purple, indigo, and orange mixed in with the gray and black, and some more daring looks interspersed with the typical jumpsuits. The women favored tops that were high-necked and conservative in front but strappy and barely there in back. I saw plenty of exposed shoulders and arms and the occasional gauzy blouse over little or no underclothing. People seemed to clothe their lower bodies more modestly, and I looked dubiously at the length of leg visible between my boots and skirt before deciding not to let it bother me. Kylie's skirt was even shorter than mine, so there was solidarity, of a kind. Both genders of Vardeshi wore vests, some long and flowing, some cropped just below the arms. A number of these featured strikingly high collars or complicated fins on the back that made me think perhaps the Vardrama costumers of past decades hadn't been as far off as I'd thought.

I was thrilled to observe a couple of women who were unmistakably pregnant, their round bellies accentuated by bright sashes of the type Kylie and I had admired in the marketplace. And there were children: the first Vardeshi children I had ever seen. They clung to their parents' hands or peered around from behind their legs at us, wary and shyly inquisitive. They were quieter than human children would have been, and so ethereally beautiful, with their brilliant eyes and drifts of pale hair, that I recalled another of our nicknames for their people: Ice Angels. I could hardly take my eyes off them.

After an hour or so, Zey abruptly drained his drink and set his glass down. "All right. Enough people-watching. Let's hit Downhelix and find some real bars."

"Downhelix? Is that a place?" I asked Sohra.

"It's a slang word for the lower levels of the starhaven, just above the docking bays. It's a little . . . edgier than the Atrium."

"If you're up for that," Zey said innocently.

Kylie finished her drink and slammed the empty glass down next to his. "We're up for anything."

As the four of us wandered through Downhelix, security personnel in tow, I looked around with eager interest. I hadn't believed that any place designed by the Vardeshi could rival the seedier and dingier quarters of a major Earth city, but in Downhelix they had made a credible attempt. The district was a maze of dimly lit bars that spilled unpredictably into each other. Some were walled off and uninviting, their interiors hidden behind grimy viewports. Others were bounded only by a half-wall and disgorged their seats and tables into the corridor, forcing us to pick our way around them. I peered into one doorway after another, seeing more of the unearthly blue and green lights I'd noticed on the docking levels. The clientele themselves looked unexpectedly well-dressed and sober. I didn't see anything that looked recognizably like a dance club, but we did pass by one purple-lit den in which shadowy bodies moved in an odd undulating pattern. A distinctly percussive thumping emanated from within. Zey quickened his pace. I looked over at Sohra. "Rana club," she said quietly.

"You mean everyone in there is high on rana? That's allowed?" In addition to facilitating participation in the Listening for latent telepaths, rana was also a mild intoxicant which clouded thinking and slowed reaction time. Due to its addictive properties, it was strictly controlled on Echelon ships. The Fleet took a more permissive approach, but excessive use was strongly discouraged. Rhevi Vethna, the *Pinion*'s engineer and one of my least favorite crewmates, had been cut off completely after one too many episodes of conspicuous overindulgence.

"Not exactly," Zey said. "The starhaven tries to close them down. But every time they shut one down, another one opens up somewhere else." His tone was contemptuous. I thought I understood why. It must be infuriating to see others making such perverted use of a substance meant to unlock a door forever closed to him as a Blank.

At a seemingly random establishment, he stopped and waved us inside. I looked at the illuminated sign beside the door. "The Gravity Well. Why this one?"

Sohra tapped the next line on the panel. "Why else? Cheap whiskey."

"Some things really are universal," Kylie said.

We entered and found an unoccupied length of bar to lean against. Zey went to order drinks for himself, Sohra, and Kylie. A little self-consciously, I took another beer out of my bag and opened it. The hiss of escaping carbonation turned a few heads. Someone a little farther down the bar said knowingly in Vardeshi to his companion, "Earth beer. She can't drink ours."

"I can tomorrow," I called back to him. He stared, then grinned wolfishly and saluted me with his glass.

When Zey returned, he had the drinks in one hand and a fistful of what looked like large sequins in the other. He distributed them carefully among us. "Is that money?" Kylie asked.

"Not really. They're bar coins. You get a couple whenever you buy food or drink somewhere that allows gaming." Zey indicated the table near us, where three men in Fleet uniforms were engaged in a game that involved stacking glass discs on long metal rods, one I'd seen my crewmates playing on the *Pinion*. "They're specifically for gambling. They're standard across the starhaven, so you can redeem them for food and drink anywhere that has game tables."

I turned the little metallic chip over curiously in my fingers. It was smooth and flat, a bit like a guitar pick. "Can you exchange them for units?"

"No, and they only work on Arkhati, so when people leave, they hand off any extras to someone who's just arriving."

"What's the point?"

"There's no point. They're just fun."

"They're poker chips," Kylie said.

This revelation confirmed something I had long suspected, which was that the Vardeshi, while in many ways highly conservative, were keen players of games. Players and spectators, it seemed; they drifted over to observe each other's prowess at the various tables as casually as denizens of a casino. Much like the free circulating movement I'd noted at the music concerts on the *Pinion*, social groups seemed to drift apart and reform, their members joining other tables at will. Zey and Sohra were almost immediately drawn into the rods-and-discs game. Kylie and I played a couple of rounds of the simple dice game I'd learned in my first days on the *Pinion*. Then she produced a deck of cards from her bag and began to shuffle them. Instantly our table was the focus of intense interest. Kylie looked up at the three strangers, two men and one woman, who had dropped onto stools around our table. Calmly she dealt them in. She proceeded to explain the rules of poker in English. I clarified a few points in Vardeshi. As I was talking, I saw several of the onlookers exchange knowing looks, which I took to mean they had identified me.

To my complete lack of surprise, I emerged as the worst player at the table. Looking back to the long-ago evening in the *Pinion*'s mess hall on which I had introduced Zey and Hathan to poker, I didn't think any of the others demonstrated Hathan's instant command of the game. There were frequent halts to discuss rules and strategy. However, all three of our Vardeshi challengers were quick learners with keen competitive instincts. I lost four successive hands and all of my bar coins. "No pressure, but the reputation of the human race rests with you," I said to Kylie as I trickled my last few coins through my fingers onto her stack.

She snorted. "It would be a sad day for humanity if that were true."

I vacated my stool, which was instantly claimed by one of the people who had been looking eagerly over my shoulder, and made my way to Zey's table. I watched his game for a while, finding it just as perplexing as I had the first time, before a young white-haired man in a Fleet uniform invited me to play a round of dice. "I don't have any coins left," I said apologetically.

"No problem. If you lose, you can get my next round." He smiled. His eyes were startlingly dark, like Zey's, beneath that bright hair.

I looked down at his right hand, noted the lack of a gold sigil, and realized that there was a distinct possibility that I had just been flirted with. When I met his eyes again, his smile had broadened. My sigil check hadn't been especially subtle. I grinned back a little self-consciously. "Sure. Why not?"

I didn't perform much better at dice than I had at poker, but it didn't seem to matter. The insignia on my opponent's collar told me he was a novi too, and we quickly fell to trading stories. I told him about my struggle to operate Vardeshi tech and the shock of stumbling upon a Listening for the first time. He told me about the bitter rivalry between the senior novis on his own ship and the coolant leak that had contaminated the remaining stock of senek several days out from Arkhati, rendering the entire crew twitchy and irritable. We commiserated about late officers' dinners that ran up against early briefings. I didn't ask him his name. He didn't ask me what it had been like to be demoted and imprisoned. He didn't let me buy him a drink either, although I reminded him that that had been our agreement. "I only said that to get you to play," he explained. I was grateful when Sohra came by and wordlessly deposited a glittering handful of her winnings on the table in front of me. I won the next few rounds, possibly by design, before my new friend claimed the entire stack with a lucky toss. "How long ago did you graduate from the Institute?" I said suspiciously.

"Six months."

I sighed. "I should have known. 'Dice at the Institute are as common as dust on Arideth,' right?"

He laughed. "Have you ever been to Arideth?"

"No, but I hear it's pretty dusty."

"So they say. I wouldn't know. I've never been there either."

I took a swig of my now unpleasantly warm beer. "Where are you headed?"

"Khivrik. It's one of the outlying planets. We're transporting personnel and medical supplies. Not quite as dramatic as your mission."

"Maybe not, but at least nobody's blowing holes in your ship."

"Not yet, anyway." He checked his flexscreen. "Well, I'm off. If I stay any longer I'll miss my launch." He stood up and jingled the coins in his hand.

Zey, who had been leaning against the wall looking on for the last couple of rounds, said hopefully, "Looking to offload those coins before you go?"

The young officer laughed. "Are you kidding? I won these off Novi Alkhat. I'm keeping them." He flashed his sigil at me in farewell, a sort of inverse wave. "Thanks for the company."

When he had disappeared through the doorway, Zey said, "He liked you."

"Only because I'm famous. You heard what he said. He'll probably be drinking on this story for the next month."

"No," he said firmly. "He liked you."

I gave him a skeptical look. "How could you even tell? What are the signs?"

"Did you notice his sigil?"

"I noticed that he only had the ink one. He's not engaged. Or married."

"Right. Did you see how quickly he dropped his hand when he said goodbye? That was a compliment. As a member of an unranked family, you should have been the first one to lower your hand."

"But I didn't even raise my hand. He didn't give me any time."

Zey nodded. "Exactly. I'm engaged, so if I saluted you like that, it would be a show of respect. But since he's unattached, it means something different. He was telling you he liked you."

Sohra came over with a brimming glass of beer. Glancing at the empty table in front of me, she said, "Eyvri, how did you lose all those coins I gave you in the time it took me to get one drink?"

"She's terrible at dice, but she's a winner in the game of love," Zey said, mimicking the quick farewell salute.

"Really?" Sohra said eagerly. "Who was he?"

I groaned. "Oh, by the nineteen ancient sigils. Don't encourage him."

Zey laughed. "You don't even know what the nineteen ancient sigils are."

"I know some of them," I said defensively.

"Prove it. You looked at his hand. Which one was he?"

"I . . ." I tried and failed to picture the design. "I have no idea."

"That's what I thought," Zey said smugly.

"Which one?" Sohra prompted.

"Kasrash."

Sohra's eyes widened. "An unattached Kasrash? That's quite a conquest, Eyvri. Kasrash is ranked second-highest. Just under Vadra."

I waved a careless hand. "Yeah, yeah. I'll get my matchmaker on the phone. In the meantime, what's next?"

The only discordant note in the evening occurred toward the end. We were sitting in various stages of intoxication in our third or fourth artfully run-down bar. Zey, too far gone on cheap whiskey for the gaming tables now, was absorbed in stacking his winnings in a perfectly aligned column. Kylie was equally engrossed in knocking it over. Sohra and I were playing a memory game with Kylie's deck of cards, mostly to keep ourselves awake. I was vaguely aware that the bar was emptying out around us. A dark-haired man in nondescript civilian clothing went by our table on his way to the door. I looked up from my cards, thinking he was passing a little closer to Zey's stool than necessary, in time to hear him mutter something containing the words "Vekesh House." By the time I fully turned my head to look at him, I had to peer through a virtual thicket of Vardeshi. Only two of them wore the black and red uniforms of starhaven security. It seemed that half the occupants of the room—including the woman with the shimmering teal bob who only an instant ago I had seen knock half a glass of beer into her companion's lap—were members of some kind of undercover protection detail. I caught only a fleeting second glimpse of the man who had spoken before he was forcibly but silently dragged out through the door. I turned to where Zey was sitting, or had been sitting. Both he and Sohra were on their feet. "What did he say?"

Zey repeated the sentence in an undertone. He sounded, and looked, considerably less drunk than I'd thought he was.

"'Vekesh House will be avenged,'" I repeated. My voice shook a little.

Sohra put a comforting hand on my arm. "It doesn't mean anything. He was just trying to scare you."

"It worked."

Zey swept his bar coins into a pile and pocketed them. "Sohra's right. It was just talk. No one likes Vekesh House enough to avenge it. Let's go."

We went. Most of our security detail went with us, all attempt at pretense abandoned. The teal-haired woman fell into step with me and introduced herself as Officer Jaiya Deyn, head of my personal security. "Let me guess," I said half-jokingly, "you're going to tell me I can't go back to Downhelix again."

"Not tonight," she said. "And not alone. Beyond that, we'll have to see."

Officer Nerev, evidently summoned from wherever she spent her off-duty hours, joined us at a corridor junction. She and Officer Deyn dropped back to walk together just behind Kylie and me, discussing the incident—or so I assumed—in voices pitched too low for me to overhear. We walked through hallways that were otherwise deserted, either because it was so late or because they were being deliberately cleared in advance of our passage, I wasn't sure which. Zey and Sohra were quartered with the rest of the crew on the helix below ours. When they diverged from our route, I was glad to see two of the security officers peel off to accompany them.

"It's all right, Eyvri," Sohra said reassuringly before they left. "You're safe here. You're protected. Try to forget about it."

Kylie and I waited in the corridor while our combined security teams did a thorough sweep of her rooms. When they emerged, one of them nodded to Officer Deyn, who had been among those standing guard in the hallway. "Your protective detail will be doubled while we investigate the man from the bar," she told me. "We'll inform you as soon as we know anything concrete. For now, try not to let the incident alarm you. Your friend was right. You're not on the *Pinion* anymore. You're in safe hands."

Once inside Kylie's rooms, I went around and methodically turned on every light I could find. Kylie watched for a while, then went into the galley. I climbed the narrow stairs to my bedroom, changed into pajamas, and went into the sanitation room to wash my face. When I came out again, Kylie was curled up on my bed beside a tray that held two cups of tea. I sat down on the other end of the bed and pulled a blanket over myself.

"Are you all right?" she asked.

"I'm fine."

"I'm not one of them. You don't have to pretend with me."

I said again, "I'm fine." When she didn't reply, I added, "I just . . . I thought it was over."

She looked at me steadily until I lifted my eyes to meet hers. I had never seen her face so serious. "Did you really think that?" she asked.

"Okay, I hoped it was over, is that better?"

"It's easier to believe." Kylie cradled her tea in her hands, but didn't drink it. "Your khavi is gone. That part is over. But he was just one man. The movement that put him on your ship and a gun in his hand is still out there. And it's not just the Vardeshi—there are anti-alliance movements on Earth too. And ours are likely to be a lot bigger and a lot uglier than theirs. At least most of them claim to have renounced violence. How many people on Earth can say the same? For every human and every Vardeshi working for the alliance, there's probably someone on the other side working against it. We can't change that. We just have to make sure we do our jobs better than they do theirs."

I nodded.

Kylie shifted the tea tray to her other side, slid closer to me, and put her arm around my shoulders. "I meant what I said before. You're tough. You had to be, to get this far. But don't lie to yourself. It won't get any easier from here. So if you're serious about going on, you'll have to get tougher. It's the only way you'll survive."

"I know," I whispered. She tightened her arm around me. I rested my head on her shoulder and pulled the soft gray blanket up over both of us. We sat like that, nestled together like animals, without speaking for a very long time.

* * *

I slept uneasily that night. My follow-up appointment with the doctor was scheduled for early evening of the next day. I passed the afternoon hours scrolling through Kylie's music and movies, downloading my selections onto her spare laptop and phone, and organizing them into playlists. The task was comforting, but it was also avoidance of a kind. Kylie kept me company until midafternoon, then went to have a prowl through the Atrium. When she asked me to join her, I demurred. "I'm a little tired. Tomorrow?"

Disappointment and compassion mingled in her face as she said, "Sure. Tomorrow's fine."

Officer Deyn escorted me to my appointment with the doctor, who examined my forearm closely, took several photographs on her flexscreen, and finally declared me free to sample the dozen or so foods and beverages on the approved list. "Use common sense," she instructed. "Don't try anything in large quantities or when you're alone, and make sure you have your allergy medication at hand at all times. What are you going try first?"

"Senek," I said without hesitation.

Just before leaving Kylie's quarters, I had received a message from Saresh inviting me to stop by the medical wing for a visit that evening. The time he'd proposed coincided with the hour of the evening senek ritual, which had given me an idea. I texted Zey to ask whether Saresh had any favorites among the Atrium's senek shops. He directed me to Stall 27, the Golden Leaf. I made my way there amid the crush of Vardeshi seeking an infusion of their preferred beverage. The line at Stall 27 was especially long, and my presence in it drew considerable interest—although it was difficult to tell whether people were looking at me or at Officer Deyn, who stood, defiantly blue-haired and in the strappiest of strappy tops, just behind me in line. I realized I was glad she was there.

To my relief, the shop's proprietor accepted both my appearance and my request without blinking, although he examined my thermos with interest before pouring in the steaming liquid. My crewmates on the *Pinion* had reacted in the same way to the turquoise enamel. I asked about disposable cups and was told that the Vardeshi didn't manufacture them, but that the simple glass cups used here were standard throughout the Atrium and could be returned to any establishment or deposited at an exit. I stacked two cups together and placed the sugar pellets carefully in the top one. I knew Saresh's preference without having to think about it; brewing the morning and evening senek was one of the novi duties Zey and I shared. As I turned to make my way out of the Atrium, I wondered how many of the people standing near us in line had been members of my security detail. I hadn't recognized any of them from last night.

We were met outside Saresh's room by a young man in a starhaven security uniform who spoke a code word to Officer Deyn, presumably giving the all-clear, since she waved me toward the door at once. I found Saresh sitting up in bed, looking alert and rested, though the blue undertones in his skin were more prominent than usual. Hathan was sitting on a stool beside the bed. He was still in uniform, having presumably come straight from a debriefing session. Both of them looked up in surprise when I entered; I had clearly interrupted a conversation. "I can come back," I said quickly, hoping they would ask me to stay.

"What's in the flask?" Hathan asked.

"Senek." I raised the thermos hopefully. "It's from the Golden Leaf."

Saresh smiled. "Oh, well, in that case, join us."

"You brought two cups," Hathan noted as I pulled over another stool and placed my offerings on the table next to the bed. "But you weren't expecting me. Who's the second one for?"

"For me." I displayed my unmarked forearm. "I passed my allergy screen."

"Have you tried it yet?"

"First time."

I tipped the sugar pellets out onto the bedside table and placed the two glass cups side by side. Then I unscrewed the cap of my thermos and set it with the other cups. Out of long habit, I pushed the thermos toward Hathan. He pushed it back toward me.

"Never mind the formalities. This is a historic occasion. Help yourself." His tone was light, his posture relaxed, but he had been tapping one foot restlessly on the floor since I arrived. Remembering that senek served a physiological as well as a cultural function, I filled my own cup and tried again to pass him the thermos. This time he took it.

As he poured, I looked at the sugar pellets in chagrin. "I didn't bring any sugar for you."

"This is good enough to drink straight," he assured me. He drained his own cup at once. I imagined I could see him relaxing as the calming effect took hold.

As he leaned over to serve his brother, Saresh said, "Only half for me. Any more and I'll fall asleep."

"You're in recovery," Hathan pointed out. "You should sleep." But he stopped pouring. Saresh took the cup, breathed in the steam appreciatively, and drank. Hathan nodded to me. "All right, Avery. It's your turn."

I looked dubiously at the sugar pellets. Saresh said, "Hathan was right. This is better than anything on the *Pinion*. You should try it on its own first."

I lifted my cup and took a tentative sip. The liquid was still steaming hot, which was how it was properly served, as I well knew. My first impression was of almost medicinal bitterness. That faded quickly, replaced by a mild nutty flavor like that of hazelnuts. The lingering aftertaste was faintly sweet, like anise. As I sat there, cup still in hand, trying to place the mingled flavors, I felt suffused with a deep tranquility. The drink had an effect akin to that of liquor, only it was a tingling coolness, rather than warmth, that radiated through my body. Until that instant, I hadn't known how tense I was. I sighed. "Wow. That's amazing. I see why you guys like it."

"How does it make you feel?" Hathan asked.

"Relaxed." I drank again.

"It's working, then."

"No, I mean really relaxed. I think . . . Let's just say I won't be drinking it at morning briefing."

Saresh laughed. "You mean it's intoxicating?"

"It would be, if I drank any more of it." I put my cup down carefully on the table. "So how was the surgery?"

"Perfectly routine. I'll be here another night, and I'll wear a brace for a few days, but I should be able to walk out of here on my own tomorrow morning." There was a blanket covering his legs, and as he spoke, he pulled it up to his left knee, exposing his lower leg. The skin was perfectly smooth save for a vertical white seam as narrow as a pencil line and about three inches long.

"That's it?" I said in disbelief.

"That's it. In a few months, you won't even be able to find the scar."

"That's incredible. Your medical tech is so far beyond ours."

"Our surgeons consider scars to be . . . messy. Inelegant."

"They're right." Even as I said the words, I felt a hollowness inside. Something that was shared had been lost. I had been wrong to think Saresh and I had both been permanently marked by Vekesh. In the end, it had only been me. I looked down at the right sleeve of my sweater, thinking of the scar it concealed: messy, inelegant, ineradicable. My eyes moved to the crescent of new skin between my thumb and forefinger, souvenir of an inattentive moment in the galley during the long days of my estrangement on the *Pinion*. The Vardeshi might not have to wear the traces of their accidents and errors on their bodies, but humans still did. It was just one more way in which we were inferior to them.

Saresh said gently, "Even our tech is no match for the second scar."

"The second scar?"

He touched two fingers to his temple. "Here."

And just like that, I knew the bond was still there, and that he felt it as strongly as I did. We had shared memories. More than that, we had traded them. Nothing could take that away from us. If the Echelon saw fit to assign us to different ships, though, I might lose his presence, his sensitivity and kindness, out of my life forever. The thought made me want to weep— or scream. To preempt either impulse, I took another long drink of senek. The calm that instantly washed over me pushed the despair back a little. I got up from my stool and went over to look out through the viewport. One wall of Saresh's room appeared to be a floor-to-ceiling portal looking onto the Arboretum from above. I looked down at the winding paths and the intermingled gray and blue and red foliage, which stirred gently in a breeze I couldn't feel. Then I looked back at the door through which I'd entered. My sense of direction on the starhaven was still imperfect, but I was fairly certain that the Arboretum was several levels above us. I turned back toward the others. "Is this a window?"

"It's a projection," Hathan answered. "It can be adjusted to show different views of the starhaven." He pressed a control on the bedside table. The view changed to an exterior view of Arkhati, taken from a nearby satellite, perhaps. At another touch of the control, the vista changed again to a scene from the Atrium. He cycled through a few more images, including one that had to be of hydroponics, then returned to the view of the Arboretum.

"There's no view of Downhelix," I noted.

"A conscious omission, no doubt," Saresh said. "The doctors probably felt it would be too stimulating."

Hathan glanced at his brother. "Speaking of stimulating, Zey told us about your encounter last night."

"He did? Why?" I tried to sound nonchalant, but I felt a rush of heat to my face.

"He must have thought we'd be interested."

"Well, I think he was imagining things. We were just talking."

Hathan looked perplexed. Then his expression cleared. "Ah. Yes. Zey told us about that encounter too. But since you're not actually wearing the sigil of Kasrash House, I assume he exaggerated a little."

"You checked?" Saresh said.

"Of course. I didn't want to use the wrong honorific. I'd hate to offend a Kasrash." His smile was brief and wry and included me and Saresh equally. He went on, "No, I meant the other encounter. The one that wasn't so friendly."

"Oh," I said. "That. It wasn't a big deal."

"It sounds like starhaven security thought otherwise."

"That was actually kind of amazing. I thought they were being generous to give us two security guards. It turns out we have a lot more than that."

"Still, you didn't know that at the time," Saresh said. "It must have been frightening."

"Maybe a little. It was all over before I knew what was happening. Mostly I was just surprised. Although Kylie said I should have been expecting something like that."

"How are things going with Kylie?" Saresh asked.

"They're good. She's a good friend."

Hathan said, "You must be glad to be with your own kind again."

"I am," I said, and stopped. I wasn't sure I could say what I wanted to say, which was that I was glad, but I was also anxious for a decision from the Echelon. The fate of the *Pinion*'s crew now rested in other hands than my own. Principally, it seemed, in Hathan's. His ability to persuade the Echelon of his fitness for command would dictate whether Zey and I ever had the chance to sit together in the lounge of another ship, joking about our late nights in Downhelix. And all three of us were perfectly aware of that fact without my drawing attention to it.

Hathan, as always, seemed to anticipate my thoughts. He poured himself another cup of senek and stirred one of the remaining sugar pellets into it. "Three days. That's what I've been told. The Echelon will make a decision within the next three days." He toggled through the images on the wall again, idly, I thought, but he stopped on a view of the docking bays. He went over to the wall and pointed out a ship that even to my untrained eyes bore a marked resemblance to the *Pinion,* though its lines were a bit sharper and its hull had a bronze rather than a silver sheen. "This is the ship they'll give us if we're lucky. Straight out of the Zenadir shipyards, built for a crew of fifteen. Top-of-the-line propulsion and navigation. Not a mark on the hull." There was something in his voice that was almost wistful. He wanted this as much as I did, I realized. His reasons, whatever they might be, had nothing to do with me. Maybe he liked being on a ship with his brothers. Maybe his brief taste of command had awoken a hunger for more. Maybe it was simply pride: having once been entrusted with an important task, he wanted to see it through to the end. Whatever the reason though, he wanted us all to go forward together, just like I did.

I went over for a closer look, careful not to stand too near him. "What's it called?"

"*Shavinakh*," Hathan said. "The *Ascendant*."

5

Hathan had said to expect word from the Echelon within three days. I resolved to put all questions about the future out of my mind until they made their decision. I was safely on Arkhati, one of the first of my kind ever to be granted that privilege, and I was determined to enjoy it. If these days were the last I spent with my crewmates, then they were doubly precious. Either way, I thought, I owed it to myself to make the most of my time here.

Kylie agreed. With the exception of that first formal dinner, her duties as Earth's designated cultural representative on Arkhati hadn't officially begun yet. We speculated that her handlers had been told to leave her schedule open for the duration of my visit. She offered herself as a willing second on all of my explorations. We spent the morning after my visit to Saresh wandering through the twisting alleys of the Atrium, shadowed but not impeded by a pair of the ever-present security guards. There we met up with Khiva, the *Pinion*'s chief of requisitions and my preferred source of wardrobe advice, who had just been released from her final debriefing session. As I'd expected, she had the answers to all of my sartorial questions.

"The hair colors you saw were artificial," she said as we browsed through a display of spiky metallic objects she said were hair ornaments. "If it's not black or gray or silver or white, it's fake. We don't use pastes or dyes. There's a radiation process that's harmless but permanent. Gold and red are the trendy colors right now, but it has nothing to do with what's popular on Earth. The different skin tones were real though. Some of our outlying worlds are exposed to different spectrums of light. The early settlers were worried about radiation damage, so they modified their skin pigments to increase their protection. When they had children, they passed on the altered colors. You'll see gray and blue and even purple. That one's pretty rare. Not a lot of people on that planet."

"They genetically engineered different skin tones for themselves?" I asked. "Just like that?"

Khiva shrugged. "It was practical. And our people have a deep respect for explorers. We don't all succumb to wanderlust, but we all feel it. Ask anyone working soilside and they'll tell you they're saving for a trip offworld."

"Ivri khedai," I said. Literally translated, the phrase meant "the longing for another sky." Its companion term, ivri avanshekh, meant "the longing for permanence." I thought of it as "homesickness."

"Exactly. So a unique skin tone is a good thing. It shows that your ancestors were pioneers. Of course, it helps that they picked attractive colors. Most of us find them glamorous."

Kylie, ever direct, said, "Meaning sexy?"

Khiva flashed her a grin. "That too."

A few stalls down I stopped, mystified, in front of a display of what were obviously House sigils, all rendered in deep indigo or gold on squares of what looked like gray canvas, each at least a foot across. I recognized the Takheri sigil, and some of the others looked familiar. I didn't think Vekesh was among them. "Is this artwork?" I asked. "Would you hang a picture of your sigil in your quarters?"

Khiva laughed. "No. These are just to show the quality of the artist's work. She paints actual sigils." She held up her right hand for emphasis.

"There's a market for that? Here?"

"Not a large one. But some people come of age when they're starside. The main demand here is for the gold ones though."

Kylie traced the sweeping lines of a gold sigil with her forefinger in a sequence that looked utterly haphazard to my Mandarin-trained eye. "People get engaged in space?"

"All the time. Lots of marriages are arranged long-distance. If my parents found me a match while I was between worlds, I'd get my sigil at the next starhaven."

"That's it?" I said. "You just go to a stall and buy it? I was picturing something a little more . . ."

"Romantic?" Kylie said. "What do you expect, when you let your parents pick a husband for you? They probably don't go down on one knee either. It's basically a business transaction."

"More or less," Khiva agreed, seeming unoffended by the analogy. "And it's important to get your new sigil as soon as possible, especially if you're marrying into a house that's ranked higher than your birth house. If someone greets you incorrectly, and then finds out that you outrank them, it's embarrassing for everyone."

"Practical," I said. "Again."

"So what do you say?" Khiva gestured to the display. "Want to join a house? This is your chance. If I were you, I'd choose one of the higher ones. Everyone says it doesn't matter, but it does."

"Where's Khiva House ranked?" Kylie asked.

Khiva smiled. "There is no Khiva House. We're subordinate to Garian. They're right in the middle."

Kylie looked thoughtfully at the back of her own right hand. "It would be a pretty great joke. Imagine the looks we'd get."

"If you really wanted to confuse people, you'd get a gold one," Khiva said. "An ink one would be an obvious lie, since you clearly weren't born into a Vardeshi house. But who's to say you aren't engaged to one of us? There are humans and Vardeshi sleeping together, so why not getting married? No one would know how seriously to take it. It would be hilarious."

"The joke would wear pretty thin after a while," I said. "Unlike the sigil. I think I'll pass."

Kylie said, "Maybe someday they'll design a twentieth one. For humans."

"I wonder what it would look like," I mused.

"I wonder where it would rank," Khiva said more pragmatically.

"Probably right at the bottom." I had meant it as a joke, but the look on Kylie's face told me it had fallen flat. I turned away, pretending to admire the brushwork on one of the sigil paintings, until I saw her move on to the next stall.

* * *

We fell into the habit of spending our mornings in the Atrium, our afternoons in Kylie's suite, and our nights in Downhclix. I checked my Vardeshi bank account, saw that it contained just under thirteen thousand units, and spent them lavishly. I saw no reason to restrain myself, given that my food and lodging were provided by the Fleet and that another twelve thousand units would have accumulated by the time we reached Vardesh Prime. I went back to the stall with the gray crystal whiskey glasses and bought them as a gift for Dr. Sawyer. I bought an embroidered wall tapestry for my mother and a senek set for my father, along with a canister of powdered senek leaves from Stall 27. I bought myself a memory crystal, more for the aesthetic appeal of the object itself than for its recording function, although I did have it encoded with an image of the *Pinion*. I wandered from one jewelry stand to another until I found a pendant that suited me, a faceted gemstone strung on a glimmering silver chain, its color the exact blue of the silk dress I had bought in Zurich for an unspecified formal occasion that had yet to materialize. The stone had been mined on Vardesh Prime, the shop owner told me. I weighed it in my palm: a tiny intact fragment of another planet. In taking it away with me from Arkhati I would be, at least temporarily, bringing it home. I liked the idea of wearing it together with the silk dress, two beautiful objects of identical hue from different worlds. I still wasn't sure I had the courage to wear the dress among the Vardeshi, after what Khiva had told me about the symbolism of that particular shade of blue, which was apparently a near match for their blood. To wrap my purchases for transport I bought filmy scarves in all the colors Arkhati's inhabitants seemed to favor:

white, orange, gray, indigo, purple.

When we tired of shopping, Kylie and I summoned our collective courage and went to get haircuts. The stall we chose, on Khiva's recommendation, was on a bustling commercial helix below the Atrium. It looked more like a spa than a salon; there were no mirrors that I could see, the dark walls were adorned with spiraling designs in silver and gold, and the lighting was so soft I wondered how the stylists could see their work. Hairdressers and patrons alike stared when we walked through the door. For an instant the silence was so oppressive that I wanted to flee, but Kylie held me in place with a firm hand on my elbow. After a brief murmured exchange, two of the stylists, a man and a woman, stepped away from their clients and approached us. The woman asked in halting and oddly inflected English how they could be of service. Finally, I thought, someone who didn't speak perfect English—although why a hairdresser on a starhaven three months' flight from Earth would need to speak a word of it was beyond my comprehension. I quickly explained why we were there. The relief that flooded her face and her companion's when they heard my Vardeshi was almost comical. They ushered us to two hastily positioned stools at the very front of the shop, where anyone passing by would be sure to notice us. So much for trying to be discreet, I thought, sitting down on the right-hand stool.

The woman spent a few moments running her fingers through my hair, making comments about its choppy styling. I said apologetically that I'd been trimming it myself in my quarters. She laughed. "It shows. Why didn't you just freeze it before you left your homeworld?"

"Freeze it?" I said.

"Have it treated to stop new growth."

Was that how Zey had maintained his perfect spikes for three months? I wondered. His hair certainly didn't look like he'd been cutting it in front of a sanitation-room mirror. "You can do that?"

"Of course."

"Permanently?"

"The effect lasts for about a year. I can do it for you today, if you like."

"I think I'd like to see how it looks first," I hedged.

She laughed again and began smoothing a fragrant oil onto her hands. "This will soften the texture of your hair. It's so coarse. Like a khanat's bristles. You should be treating it every day."

I didn't know what a khanat was, but I didn't think the description was meant as a compliment. I also didn't think my hair was especially coarse. It must seem that way to the Vardeshi though. Their hair was as fine and smooth as cornsilk, if I could generalize from Zey and Sohra, who had submitted cheerfully to a tactile investigation shortly after we left Earth. I glanced over at Kylie, who was receiving a similar treatment. "Do you think this is safe?"

"Soaps and lotions are supposed to be fine," she said dubiously. "Let's hope this oil stuff counts."

Kylie's shoulder-length hair needed only a straightforward trim, but at the last minute she gave in to her stylist's urging that she replace her grown-out blond highlights with platinum streaks. The result looked better than I would have predicted. Somehow the glints of silver brought out the darker gold of her natural hair color and the blueness of her eyes. "That's great," I said. "Very chic. You should freeze it like that."

For lack of a mirror, Kylie admired the effect by reversing

the camera on her phone, an object of instant fascination for both our stylists. "Maybe I will. There's no hurry. I have six months to think about it."

My own cut took a little longer, but when it was done, I was relieved to see that my hair looked more or less as it had when I launched, though perhaps a bit wispier and spikier. A little more like Zey's, in fact. I declined the offer of coppery highlights. The reflection I saw on Kylie's phone screen had begun to lose its alarming pallor, and now, the stylist's work completed, it was more familiar than it had been in weeks. I didn't want to do anything to disrupt that sense of recognition. We paid with our flexscreens and left. On my way out the door, I was flattered to hear an older woman inquiring whether the salon could match the shade of my hair. Human pigmentation might not be a fad yet, but maybe it was about to trend. I wondered how many salons on Earth were booked solid with requests for silver and gray and white tones. Most of them, probably. The glamour of the Vardeshi had been irresistible even on their first visit to Earth, and now that they were poised to become a fixture in our lives, their allure would only intensify. When next season's hottest looks arrived on the runways of Paris and Milan, I had no doubt that platinum hair and jumpsuits would figure prominently in them.

To celebrate the success of our venture, we went back to Kylie's suite for a beer. I had finally had my first taste of the cloudy Vardeshi beer, which I found to have a relatively mild grainy flavor with a slight sourness and an incongruous herbal aftertaste. It was highly carbonated and not especially strong. It didn't thrill me in the way senek had, but the satisfaction of being able to fill my own glass and Zey's from the same pitcher was tremendous.

He and Khiva were waiting for us outside Kylie's rooms. Her suite had become a popular afternoon hangout for my crewmates, most of whom had now finished their debriefings. They were fascinated by the casual displays of Earth culture scattered around. Kylie was traditionally feminine in a way I wasn't, and the common spaces were littered with shoes and stacks of fashion magazines and baskets of nail polish. Our most frequent visitors were Zey and Sohra and Khiva, but Ziral stopped by a couple of times, once with her fiancé, Ahnir, the *Pinion*'s cook, in tow. I had invited him specifically to witness my attempt to make popcorn on a camp stove. Corn was on the list of Earth foods approved for the Vardeshi, and I had been inspired when I discovered a bag of kernels among Kylie's food stores. I burnt the first batch, causing an embarrassing halt while my security team flooded into the galley to investigate the source of the smoke, but the second batch came out perfectly. Ahnir made no attempt to hide his shocked delight when I lifted the lid to reveal the fluffy white popcorn. He took a piece, crunched it thoughtfully, and nodded. When he asked me to teach him the preparation method, I knew I had won his approval. Stepping out into the lounge again, I felt sheer elation at the sight of Zey, gray beer in one hand, popcorn in the other, curled up in rapt contemplation of a movie on Kylie's laptop.

Daskar came by at one point to trade the mystery novel she had borrowed while we were still on the *Pinion* for another. I suspected her of using the book as a pretext to check on me. She stayed for a cup of senek, which she drank while flipping through one of Kylie's racier magazines, her expression so neutral I was sure it concealed some maternal disapproval. Even Vethna paid us a brief visit, mainly, it seemed, to drink our beer and make mocking comments while he watched Kylie paint Zey's fingernails. Zey had watched her giving Sohra and Khiva manicures the day before and had insisted on having his own turn next. He picked through the basket of little bottles for a long time before settling on jet black, which made him look more like a diminutive punk rocker than ever. The next day he gleefully reported that Hathan had condemned his cosmetic experiment. "He said I should take it off right away. It makes me look like a corpse."

"Tell him he has no appreciation for culture," Kylie said. "Anyway, it's part of your outfit for Earth Night."

Zey nodded. "That's what I said."

"Will he be there tonight?"

"Him and Saresh both. They said they wouldn't miss it."

"Good," Kylie said. "They'd better be in fancy dress."

Zey looked doubtful. "I can get them in the door. I can't promise anything more than that."

"Earth Night" was what Kylie had taken to calling the intercultural mixer she had arranged to throw in one of the Downhelix bars. There would be specialty cocktails (which we couldn't drink) and blaring pop music courtesy of Kylie's portable speaker. She was offering a prize for the best human impersonator, and although I doubted there would be many contenders, several of our friends had embraced the challenge. I had lent out half my wardrobe to members of the *Pinion*'s crew. I wasn't sure which I liked better, Zey in ripped jeans and a graphic tee or Khiva in tall black boots and a sequined miniskirt. Even Officer Deyn had gotten into the spirit of the thing, borrowing an embroidered denim jacket of Kylie's that clashed horribly with her hair. As judges, Kylie and I were going to have our work cut out for us.

When we arrived at the bar that night, I was surprised to

see that a considerable crowd had already gathered. There were a handful of uniformed security officers stationed throughout the room; no doubt several of their fellows mingled incognito in the throng. Kylie, who was taking her responsibility as DJ very seriously, experimented with a few locations for her speaker before settling in at the bar, phone in hand. Zey and I trailed after her. I ordered a beer for myself and an "Earth elixir," an unappetizing concoction of mottled blue and green liquor served in a globe-shaped cup, for him. He tasted it and grimaced. "That's disgusting."

"It's foreign," the bartender corrected him.

"Yeah. Very." Zey drank a little more. "Strong, though."

As the night progressed, I tried to keep my gaze from drifting too obviously toward the door. The music pulled in a steady stream of curious passersby. Few of them were in costume, and even fewer stayed for more than a couple of songs. It seemed that the novelty of the sound, or perhaps the volume, quickly lost its appeal. The energy in the room was good though, and the bartender was doing a brisk trade in Earth elixirs. I myself was having a better time than I'd anticipated. I had to credit Kylie for her inspiration. It had been fun to blast music and dance around in her suite. It was more fun to do it in a real bar.

And the entries in the costume contest were fascinating. I had been somewhat narrow-mindedly expecting to see imitations of Western dress, and there were a number of those. But several people arrived in flowing printed robes with a vaguely African flair, and in a surprise upset, the costume contest went to a tiny black-haired woman in a Japanese kimono and carefully pleated sash. She beamed with pride as Kylie presented her with the grand prize, which was a tote bag stuffed with relics of Earth fashion: magazines, bangles, lipstick. I could see Khiva looking on a little spitefully. I made a mental note to ask Kylie if she had anything else she'd be willing to pass along. My own wardrobe had been hit hard by the decompression of the cargo holds, and Kylie's things were more exciting anyway. Even when I wasn't in uniform, she was the flashier dresser.

"How do you know how to do this stuff?" I asked her when we found ourselves side by side in the drinks line a little later. "I never would have thought of throwing a party like this. And if I had, I would have assumed no one would come."

"That's because your crewmates weren't allowed to be curious about Earth culture," she said. "Mine were. So I knew the interest was there. Although your friends seem to be making up for lost time." She indicated Sohra and Ziral, who were gamely attempting to dance to a rap song when not incapacitated by laughter. We collected our drinks and went to join them.

Things had begun to wind down by the time Saresh and Hathan arrived. Kylie was arranging with the owner of the bar, who had been favorably impressed by the size of the crowd and the boost to his profit margin, to make Earth Night a monthly occurrence. I was sitting at the bar with Zey. He had spent the last hour taking hysterically amateur selfies on my borrowed phone and was eager to show them off. I was admiring the last picture, an angled shot of him and Sohra that was actually fairly good, when he said irritably, "It's about time." I looked up. Hathan and Saresh were making their way toward us. Both were in uniform. I was beginning to wonder if Hathan had brought anything else to wear. Maybe his suitcases had been stashed in the same cargo hold as mine. Even as I thought it, Kylie called over, "Unless you both decided to come as Avery, you're not in fancy dress."

"They didn't," said Zey. "Wrong insignia."

"We were just dismissed," Hathan said shortly.

Saresh smoothed things over with a smile and a nod toward Zey. "Fortunately, it looks like the family is well represented in spite of us."

"Not well enough to win," Zey said.

I patted his shoulder. "You had some tough competition."

Brightening, he held up my phone. "Check it out. Eyvri's been letting me play with her tech. It's like a museum piece. It doesn't even telescope." He tugged fruitlessly at the corners of the phone. "See? Nothing happens."

He held it out to Hathan, who reached for it, then hesitated, looking at me. "May I?" he asked.

I knew he was thinking about the fate of my previous phone. I was thinking about it too. I said quickly, "It's fine," and pressed the phone into his hand, trying to end our mutual embarrassment as quickly as possible.

I hadn't reckoned on Kylie, who said, "Are you sure you can trust him with that? I know what he did to your last phone. That's my only backup."

She spoke lightly, but I wasn't sure Hathan would catch the humor. I glanced at him, afraid he'd take offense. To my relief, he lifted his chin as if acknowledging the hit. "Don't worry. It's a long walk to the closest airlock. Although if the next song in your queue is as abrasive as this one, I may be willing to make the trip. That's your device there on the bar, isn't it?"

Kylie snatched it out of his reach. "Help, Avery! Abrasive is pretty much all I've got."

"Can I take a look?" Saresh inquired.

She gave him a skeptical look. "Do you know much about Earth music?"

"About as much as I do," I said.

Seeing her perplexity, Saresh began to explain the unforeseen side effect of the Listening we had shared. Hathan, to my surprise, shifted nearer to me along the bar. "It looks like your party was a success," he said.

I felt obliged to correct him. "It's really Kylie's party. But it's been great. Can I get you a beer? Or an Earth elixir?"

He cast a doubtful look at the drink in Zey's hand. "I think I'll stick with beer."

I asked for another glass and filled it for him from the pitcher I'd been sharing with Zey and Kylie, then topped off my own. "How are the hearings going?"

"They're done, as of tonight."

"Do you think they went well?"

He was silent for a long moment, drinking his beer. Then he said, "I'll put it this way. I hope you have your song ready."

It wasn't the answer I wanted to hear. I had promised to sing in front of the *Pinion*'s crew at some point before we all parted ways. I said staunchly, "I haven't been practicing at all."

"No? You're more confident than I am."

"Not confident. Just optimistic."

Hathan nodded. "Here's a cultural question for you. Do humans have a way of . . . invoking things they want to happen? When they're drinking?"

"Invoking? I'm not sure. Celebrating, definitely." I clinked my glass against his. "Here's to optimism."

"To optimism," he echoed. I drank, and he followed suit.

"How about you guys?" I asked. "What do you do?"

By way of reply, Hathan dipped a finger into his beer and wrote a complicated glyph on the surface of the bar. It gleamed faintly in the light, but I couldn't make the lines resolve into anything familiar. "What's that?" I asked.

"It's the tribute symbol. The liquid is a token offering to your ancestors, or to anyone else you think might be listening. Different people choose to invoke different powers. While you write, you hold a picture in your mind of the thing you want."

"Is there something you're supposed to say?"

"If you like, you can name the thing you're asking for. Or you can keep it to yourself."

Let me guess which one you prefer, I thought. I dipped my own forefinger into my glass, leaned forward until the damp traces of his writing caught the light, and copied the symbol as closely as I could. "The *Ascendant.*" I looked to him for approval. "Close enough?"

He said, "I forgot you could do that."

"What, copy a symbol the first time I see it? I took four years of Mandarin before Vardeshi came along. I'm just glad it's still good for something. Now what?"

Hathan emptied the pitcher into our glasses and signaled for a refill. "Now we wait. There's nothing else we can do."

"Except drink."

"Except that," he agreed.

We sat for a few minutes in contemplative stillness—*quiet* would have been the wrong word, as Kylie's speaker was still blasting—before he said, "I saw Vekesh today."

Alarmed, I said, "Where?"

"At his sentencing. I was asked to attend as a representative of the *Pinion*'s crew."

"How was it?"

"Brief," he said, and paused, "and that's the best thing I can say about it. He was convicted, to no one's surprise, of treason, attempted murder, and destruction of Fleet property."

"To the Vardeshi criminal justice system," I said, and knocked my glass against his. "What will happen to him now?"

"He'll remain in custody here on Arkhati for the present. Eventually he'll be transferred to a prison facility on one of the outlying worlds, where I expect he'll spend the rest of his life. He's not a very promising candidate for—" he used a word I didn't recognize, noted my confusion, and said, "you might translate it as . . . thought clemency."

"Thought clemency," I repeated.

Hathan nodded. "We believe in an individual's capacity for change. Prisoners convicted of non-fatal crimes are given opportunities to demonstrate remorse and personal growth such that they would be unlikely to repeat their offenses. Vekesh would have to prove those things telepathically, through a series of Listenings, before he could even be considered for reintegration with society. And, if released, he would be closely monitored and subject to regular—" he used another word unfamiliar to me, frowned slightly, and settled on "intention checks."

"Does this . . . thought clemency . . . happen often?"

"No. But it happens."

I thought about that. "What about Blanks?"

He turned his empty glass slowly around on the bar. "There, I'm afraid, our criminal justice system runs up against the same problem as yours: we can't read their minds."

"It's unfair," I said, and looked toward the dance floor, where Zey was leading Kylie through a set of modified ranshai forms in time to the music.

Hathan followed my gaze. "It is, yes, inherently unfair."

Some time later, Kylie and I walked back to her rooms. We were shadowed by the handful of security personnel who permitted us to see them and, I now knew, by many others who moved invisibly before and behind us. The dim corridors of Arkhati no longer felt quite as inimical as they had in the beginning, and I navigated them without difficulty, though I doubted they would take on the familiarity of the *Pinion*'s intuitive corkscrew design even if I stayed here six months. We'd been walking for a while when Kylie said abruptly, "Are you sure you're not in love with him?"

I knew an instant of sheer terror before the words *are you sure* registered. Of course. She was talking about Saresh. "I'm sure," I said firmly.

"I think I would be, if I were you. He's quite fit, isn't he?"

I couldn't resist teasing her a little. "I thought they were all creepily polite robots."

"At least Saresh smiles once in a while. Not like that brother of his." I knew she wasn't referring to Zey. She added, "They're quite different, aren't they?"

My mind offered up a picture of Hathan at the music concert on our last night on the *Pinion,* his face intent, Ahnir's mandolin cradled in his hands. "Not as different as you'd think."

* * *

It was with mingled dread and relief that I checked my flexscreen late the following morning to find a message awaiting me from Governor Tavri. The message itself was innocuous enough, an invitation to meet with her in the administrative wing that afternoon, but I knew what it signified. Within a few hours I would know whose instinct had been correct, Hathan's or my own, and whether our combined prayers of the night before had achieved anything.

Kylie got up from the table to make more toast. While she was gone, I used the gently cooling remnants of my tea to write the tribute symbol on the table. *Please,* I thought. *Give us another chance. We all deserve it.* I wasn't sure who to whom I was appealing. I heard Kylie's approaching steps and wiped away the marks with my napkin rather than explain them.

"Tavri wants to meet with me later," I said when she had rejoined me at the table.

She slid a piece of toast onto my plate. "That's it, then. What time?"

"Three."

"Want me to come along?"

"Of course."

"Good, because I want to hear this."

Reflexively I texted Zey. *Heard anything from the Echelon?*

No, he sent back immediately. *You?*

They want to see me later today.

Sigil to the stars, he wrote. I had to think about that one for a moment. Belatedly I placed it as the Vardeshi equivalent of crossing one's fingers.

Me too, I replied, hoping that would make him smile. *I'll let you know what I hear.*

* * *

I could read nothing in the polite neutrality of Governor Tavri's expression as she welcomed us into her office several hours later. She complimented my haircut and Kylie's silver highlights, as well as the success of Earth Night, which had apparently generated quite a buzz on the starhaven. The pleasantries concluded, she addressed her attention to me, but not, as I expected, to raise the subject of my departure from Arkhati. Instead she said, "I thought you might like to know that we've gathered fairly conclusive evidence that the man who threatened you in Downhelix has no clear ties either to Vekesh or its subordinate houses or to the most prominent anti-alliance groups. We believe that, like Reyjai Vekesh himself, he was paid to act as he did.

He claims to have been approached by an anonymous stranger in Downhelix who offered him a substantial advance payment to make the threat. He was paid in black-market rana, which carries no chemical signature, rendering it untraceable."

"Of course," Kylie said.

"Of course," the governor agreed. "As an explanation, I find it unsatisfying but credible. I'm afraid it doesn't offer much guidance as to how to prevent such incidents moving forward. We're continuing to process new arrivals on the starhaven thoroughly for possible anti-alliance affiliations. Your security team reports no incidents of concern in the past few days. Has either of you noticed anything out of the ordinary?"

Kylie and I looked at each other. Both of us shook our heads.

"Good. Then I'd say we're doing all we can. The best advice I can give you is to remain alert for anything that seems unusual or out of place. But I imagine you're both veterans at that by now."

"Avery certainly is," said Kylie.

"Good." The governor shifted a little in her chair and flicked to a different display on her flexscreen. Then she looked up and said with a kind of resolute brightness, "I have good news for you."

My heart leapt. "Really?"

"Yes. After a great deal of deliberation, the Echelon has made a decision. We've decided to place you on one of our ships for the remainder of your journey."

"An Echelon ship," I said.

"We feel you'll be safer in our hands. The events of the past few weeks have shown that this mission is far too important to be entrusted to a civilian organization. An Echelon officer would never have fallen victim to the kind of coercion that led Reyjai Vekesh to betray you, for the simple reason that they aren't susceptible to bribery. Echelon training incorporates rigorous ideological coaching. The success of the mission isn't just the primary objective for them—it's the only one."

"You want to put me on a ship with soldiers?"

"Technically they're officers of the interstellar navy, but yes. We feel that that's the wisest course."

Confused, I said, "But I signed a contract with the Fleet."

"A contract which is no longer valid." Tavri seemed to be on firmer ground here. Her words rang with authority. "You were assured safe working conditions, which the Fleet has spectacularly failed to provide. I think any legal expert on either of our worlds could attest to that fact. In consequence of their breach of contract, the Fleet owes you the remaining sum of your year's salary." *Such as it is,* her expression said. She concluded, "You owe them nothing."

"But I asked . . ." I couldn't seem to get the words out past the constriction in my throat.

"I heard your request, and I can assure you that the Echelon gave it due consideration. You're the first representative of an alien world ever to travel to our home planet. Simply put, you're precious cargo. You've already had one incredibly close escape. If anything were to happen to you, it could have a catastrophic outcome for the alliance. It's just too risky."

"What about my crew? Can they come with me?" Even as I asked the question, I knew it was impossible.

"Unfortunately, the *Pinion*'s crew wouldn't integrate well with the crew of an Echelon ship. There are differences of training, procedure, and, if you'll forgive my bluntness, professionalism. And I don't think they would enjoy the experience. Could the crew of a commercial freighter on Earth walk onto a navy vessel and expect to be welcomed?"

"No," I whispered.

"The *Izdarith* is scheduled to dock with us tomorrow morning. It's an Echelon ship with a crew of thirty-six, all veteran officers whose records and affiliations are above reproach. It would need minimal refueling and resupplying, but it could be ready to launch again within another three or four days."

"The *Ascendant* is ready now," I said. "So is the *Pinion*'s crew." I was surprised by my own persistence. So, to judge by the sidelong look she gave me, was Kylie.

The governor's tone was as mild as ever, but her next words were clipped. "Let me be clear. As things stand now, there is virtually no chance of your continuing on to Vardesh Prime with your original crew. On any ship."

"Then send us somewhere else!" The words were out of my mouth before I realized what I was saying.

Tavri said, "Forgive the repetition, but this is an important matter, and I need to be sure I'm understanding you correctly. Are you telling me you no longer wish to go to Vardesh Prime?"

I could feel Kylie's intent listening stillness beside me. I took a deep, steadying breath. "Of course I want to go to Vardesh Prime. That hasn't changed. But even more than that, I want to be with the people I know. I've spent months building connections with them. I trust them. I understand that I might be safer on an Echelon ship, and I appreciate that you're trying to act in my best interest. But I'd rather take my chances with the Fleet. If that means someone else gets to go to Vardesh Prime in my place, then so be it."

"You would abandon your mission?"

"As far as I'm concerned, my mission is about building connections. I don't see this as abandoning it. Just taking it in a different direction."

Tavri nodded. Her blue eyes studied my face with intensity and no discernible warmth. "Your official position, then, is that you'd rather stay with some or all of the *Pinion*'s crew, regardless of the destination, than travel to Vardesh Prime with an Echelon escort."

"That's right."

She reached for her flexscreen. "I'll have to see what can be arranged. It may be some time before I have a response for you. I'd advise you to spend that time seriously considering whether your request is in the best interests of your people and the alliance. Try to remember that there's more at stake here than your personal happiness. You can speak lightly about taking your chances with the Fleet, but you're not just an ordinary citizen anymore. What happens to you has a direct impact on two worlds. To lose sight of that fact would be not only irresponsible but, frankly, selfish."

Out in the hallway, I turned automatically toward the guest wing, but Kylie said, "This way," and started off in the opposite direction. I went after her. Officer Deyn and her companion, who had moved to follow me, did likewise. I realized almost at once that Kylie was steering us toward the Atrium. She didn't say anything more until she'd found us seats on the upper refreshment tier and placed a foamy gray beer in front of each of us. She took a long pull of hers. Then she said, "You know, Avery, you're a terrible poker player, but that was one hell of a bluff."

"It wasn't a bluff."

She stared at me. "You were serious about giving up Vardesh Prime? Why?"

"I want to be with my friends."

Kylie traced a pattern that looked vaguely like a sigil in the condensation on her glass. "I've met your friends. I liked them. I can see why you like them. But you've been offered a chance to be the first human on another planet. And not just any planet—the Vardeshi homeworld. I can't believe you'd just walk away from that."

"Believe it."

"And what about your crew? What if they don't feel the same way you do? The Echelon might take you at your word, you know. We don't know how vindictive they are. They might ship you off to some backwater starhaven or frozen asteroid. It's not fair to drag everyone else along without even asking them what they want. For all you know, they might like their new assignments better. At the very least, they might appreciate being given a choice."

I stared at her, appalled. "I didn't think of that."

"You'd better talk to them. If it's not already too late."

I stood up, fumbling for my flexscreen. Deftly she tipped the remaining beer from my glass into hers. "Hurry. I have a feeling it won't take Tavri all that long to make her calls."

I called Zey while en route to his quarters to ask if I could stop by for a visit. He opened the door looking tired but cheerful, his hair still tousled from sleep. I followed Officer Deyn inside and waited while she did a perfunctory sweep of his rooms. Once we were alone, I began a rapid-fire recitation of the meeting that had just concluded. Zey's cheerfulness faded as I spoke. When I was done he said incredulously, "You said that? To the governor?"

"Yes, I said it, and now I'm afraid I made a huge mistake. Kylie thinks I shouldn't have spoken for the rest of you. And she thinks the Echelon could punish me by sending us somewhere really terrible."

We had been standing in his front room, which was significantly less opulent than anything in Kylie's suite. Now I followed him into the tiny adjoining galley, where he unscrewed the cap on a flask of what was obviously last night's senek, sniffed it judiciously, and poured some into a cup. Before drinking, he waved the flask inquiringly in my direction. I shook my head. He drained his own cup, rubbed a hand over his face, and said, "I wouldn't worry too much about that. The thing that drew most of us to this mission was the chance to visit Earth. If we stick by you, we get three weeks of leave there after we drop you off at your front door. And anyway, what's the worst they can do? They have to have you soilside again within nine months. Most of the really bad places are a longer haul than that. Six months or a year in the wrong direction. Hathan would know better than I would. He could probably tell you all the options without even looking at a star chart. Besides, the Echelon has their own image to think of. They're not going to send the heroine of the *Pinion* off to the ice mines of Zarakhat after she nobly stood by her disgraced crew. As much as they might like to dump the rest of us there." He swirled the dregs of the senek in his cup, wrinkled his nose at the dark sediment of powdered leaves at the bottom, and drank it anyway. "Ahh. It's no good cold."

"I should have brought you some from the Atrium. I wish I'd thought of it." I didn't point out that it was almost four in the afternoon and even the late risers among the Vardeshi had had their morning senek several hours ago. Zey had still been going strong, fueled by trashy pop music and Earth elixirs, when Kylie and I left Downhelix the night before.

"Only Saresh gets that kind of special treatment, am I right?" He grinned. "So what did Tavri say, in the end?"

"They're going to reevaluate. She didn't look pleased."

"Of course she's not pleased. You just made her job harder. She's trying to keep the exchange running smoothly. And to be fair, she's right. You probably would be safer on an Echelon ship."

"I don't care," I said stubbornly. "It sounds lonely. Me and a bunch of military commandos. I'm not just some package to be delivered."

"It sounds like you made that point pretty effectively."

"Emphatically, for sure," I said. "Effectively remains to be seen."

6

I wasn't in the mood to pace around Kylie's suite obsessively checking my flexscreen, and I'd spent all the units I could decently afford to spend in the Atrium, so I went from Zey's quarters to the largest of the starhaven's hydroponics bays. It wasn't on the scale of the Arboretum, but it was a generously sized room. The brilliant blue-white radiance I now knew to be simulated sunlight poured down from the ceiling panels. The walk to hydroponics had given Officer Deyn sufficient time to put her team in place; two uniformed security officers guarded the entrance, and as we went in, I saw a third escorting two workers in drab gray uniforms toward a door at the far end of the room. Abandoned on the ground behind them lay a basket half-full of purple gourds, evidently an incomplete harvest. I felt a twinge of guilt at having interrupted their labor.

I wandered for a while among the rows of meticulously tended crops. Just as in the *Pinion*'s tiny hydroponics bay, every available inch of space was carefully utilized. I still didn't recognize most of the plants, but I could identify one or two. I paused to look at a silver trellis covered in the cobalt-blue vines and star-shaped leaves Zey had noted as belonging to the senek plant, and again beside a stunted tree with narrow crimson leaves that Ziral had said proliferated on her homeworld of Rikasa. Standing there in the warm, heavily perfumed air, I wondered if this was as close as I would ever come to walking on a Vardeshi world. Had I just torpedoed my only chance of seeing Vardesh Prime?

Try as I might, I couldn't seem to make myself regret it. I could see exactly how my remaining days among the Vardeshi would go if I submitted to the Echelon's urging. There would be no more movie nights or raucous dice games in the lounge. Instead there would be stilted officers' dinners and sparsely attended lectures on history and culture. I wouldn't be a crew member. I wouldn't belong. I would spend three lonely months on the *Izdarith,* two lonely weeks in Khezendri, the capital city of Vardesh Prime, and six more lonely months on another Echelon ship before I was deposited on Earth, neat and intact, like the parcel I was. It was still a generous offer. There was a time when it would have been enough. It didn't feel like enough now.

"Eyvri," Officer Deyn said behind me.

Startled out of my thoughts, I turned around. She wasn't alone; just behind her stood Councilor Zirian.

"May I join you?" he asked. "I've just been speaking to Governor Tavri."

I nodded to Officer Deyn, who retreated to stand near the door. To Zirian I said, "Something tells me I'm not her favorite person right now."

"No," he agreed mildly. "You would have made things

much easier on her—and me—if you'd simply smiled and complied with our request. That's what usually happens in politics, you know."

I looked at him suspiciously. Had that been a joke?

He smiled slightly. "You weren't expecting humor from the Echelon."

"Not humor I can understand," I said. "Not from anyone."

"Humor is an elusive concept, isn't it? It's all about expectations. To truly understand a joke, you have to understand how it diverges from what's expected. And why."

The parallel was obvious. "I guess that's what I'm doing. Diverging from what's expected." I stopped to consider my words. "I'm not trying to make things harder for the Echelon. I know you're just trying to keep me safe. I'm grateful for that. And I'm sorry if my request sounds unreasonable. But I stand by it."

He nodded. "It may surprise you to hear this, but it doesn't sound unreasonable to me. I spent fifteen years in the Fleet. I think I understand your position a little better than the governor does. There is a special quality to the relationships that you build when you're working in close quarters in deep space. I maintain a number of friends from that time in my present life. One of them is Novak Takheri."

"I didn't know he was in the Fleet," I said.

"It was a long time ago." Zirian reached up to an overhanging branch, which trailed its feathery leaves in long gray tassels, and plucked a pale blue bud. He crushed it between his fingers and breathed in its scent. "You're right to think that your life on the *Izdarith* would be materially different from what you knew on the *Pinion*. In some ways, that would be a good thing. Tighter discipline, fewer opportunities for things to go as disastrously wrong as they did for you. But you would lose things as well. The collaboration. The closeness." Wryly he added, "You wouldn't find yourself roaming Downhelix at all hours of the night with the officers of the *Izdarith*."

"Those are the things that matter to me," I said.

"So I see. Tell me, then, would you consider a compromise?"

"What kind of compromise?"

"You launch for Vardesh Prime as planned, on the *Ascendant*, with the addition of an Echelon officer to serve as second-in-command. Hathan Takheri continues as khavi, Athra Ziral resumes her original rank of rhevi. All other crew assignments are unchanged, with the obvious exception of Reyjai Vekesh. You reprise your role as Novi Alkhat."

I stared at him in disbelief. "That's hardly even a compromise. That sounds . . . perfect."

"It might not be as idyllic as it seems at first glance. The addition of an Echelon officer would alter the power structure on the ship. Your crewmates might resent a new presence among them. They might resist his authority. There are understandable tensions between the Fleet and the Echelon navy. Life wouldn't be exactly as it was before."

I had to smile at that. "Believe me, I don't think anyone wants it to be exactly the way it was before. But would that be enough to satisfy the Echelon? One new officer?"

Zirian's answer made it clear that he had been considering the question. "It would mean a direct line to the inner workings of the ship. We would have a perspective on events that we didn't have before, and a source of information we implicitly trusted. All our officers undergo rigorous martial-arts training, so he would be prepared to physically defend you if your safety were threatened. And, as second-in-command, he would be well placed to assume control of the ship if needed. It helps, of course, that three of your crewmates are sons of Senator Takheri, a known and respected member of the Echelon. Taken together, I think the arguments might be compelling."

"Governor Tavri thought it would be difficult to integrate two crews together," I said.

"And she was undoubtedly correct. But the smaller the numbers involved, the more straightforward the integration. I think one Echelon officer with a flexible mindset could assimilate into a small Fleet crew without difficulty. I can't make any promises, of course. But if you like, I'll speak to the governor and see what can be achieved."

"Thank you," I said. "Thank you so much."

"I'm glad to be of service," he said.

As he walked away, I remembered that Daskar had advised me to identify my allies. Evidently I hadn't done a very good job; here was one I hadn't even known I had.

* * *

That night Kylie and I found ourselves united in our desire for a quiet evening. We made our way to a senek room we had visited a few nights before with Zey and Sohra. "Good choice," Officer Nerev murmured as we filed past her through the door, and it occurred to me that our security personnel must be grateful for the respite as well.

The senek room was the Vardeshi equivalent of a café, complete with mood lighting and a young woman with long silver hair plucking soulfully away at a mandolin in one corner. Kylie and I installed ourselves in one of the recessed seating areas and ordered senek and tea. There was only one variety of tea on the list of approved beverages, and I liked it more for its aura of authenticity than for its flavor, which was insipid and blandly floral. We'd each brought a project with us—unedited Earth Night publicity photos for her, a backlog of messages from home for me—and we worked in companionable silence. I was vaguely aware of the *Pinion*'s crew members drifting in by ones and twos to claim the other seats in our recess and the one adjoining it. I hadn't told anyone other than Kylie and Zey about my conversations with Tavri and Zirian, but word seemed to have gotten around. When Sohra slid into the seat beside me, I took it as a cue to collapse my flexscreen. With a sigh of relief, I curled my legs under me and reached for my senek.

"Any word?" Sohra asked.

"From the Echelon? Not yet."

"It won't be long though," Zey said from her other side. "We'll know tonight."

"You think so?"

"Why else do you think everyone's here? It's just a question of who they tell first, you or Hathan."

I looked over at the other alcove, where Hathan and Saresh sat studying a display they had called up on one side of the seating area's low table. They looked relaxed, although I noticed that both their flexscreens were in easy reach. For that matter, I realized, I felt perfectly at ease myself. It might have been only the effect of the senek, but there was a sense of inevitability about the moment that was almost comforting. I knew Zey was right. Either way, we were going to know tonight.

"What are they doing?" I asked Zey.

He turned to look. "Probably mapping out possible

destinations. Places the Echelon could send us if they decide to call your bluff."

"Do you think they'd mind if I looked?"

As always I was grateful for the transparency of Zey's expression. He looked at me blankly. "They're here, aren't they? If they wanted to sit by themselves looking at a star chart, they wouldn't do it in a senek room."

I picked up my tea and went over to take the empty seat next to Hathan. He was finally in civilian wear. I liked the vest he was wearing. It was the color of rust, with silver embroidery, and I didn't think I'd seen him wear it before. His hair looked a bit shorter too, although the style was unchanged. Maybe he'd finally found time to visit the Atrium. After the obligatory greetings, he said, "Eyvri, I think it's time you learned some stellar cartography. This is a map of the region surrounding Arkhati. Can you find Earth?"

I studied the map carefully, then pointed to a glowing blue triangle labeled *Earth* in Vardeshi script.

He nodded. "Good. Starhavens are marked in orange. Naturally occurring bodies—that's planets, moons, asteroids—are in blue. I've rotated the map so that Earth, Arkhati, and Vardesh Prime appear more or less in alignment." He waited while I hunted for the orange icon labeled *Arkhati* and the blue one marked simply *Prime*. "In three dimensions, of course, the configuration isn't quite so neat, but it's helpful to visualize them this way. The lines marked in gold are potential routes. This is our original flight path." He traced the connector that ran with umbilical directness from Earth to Arkhati to Vardesh Prime, its thickness doubled to indicate a round trip. It was the only straight line on the chart. The other routes spiderwebbed around it, each one originating on Arkhati and terminating on Earth. "Presuming a ship with the *Ascendant*'s capabilities, these are all the other places of interest that we could visit and still return to Earth within about nine months. I don't know exactly what the Echelon's criteria are, but I've ruled out the smaller starhavens and the planets with no biological or cultural significance."

"That still leaves a lot of possibilities," I said.

Hathan said simply, "We build fast ships."

"Are there routes you like better than others?"

He touched a control on the bottom of the display. Most of the gold lines vanished, leaving only six or seven in addition to our original route. "Saresh and I have been picking out our favorites. This one would be interesting. This moon, Veynir, doesn't look like much on the surface, but it's honeycombed with natural rock caves full of bioluminescent organisms."

"Like algae?"

"Not just algae. Trees, flowers, even insects and birds."

"The Dream Forests," Saresh said. "Veynir is a site of pilgrimage for artists and anyone else seeking inspiration."

"And we'd pass by Evrathi Starhaven, where the ranshai competitions are held, on the way back to Earth. Khiva would like that. If the timing was right, she'd get to see her fiancé compete. Elteni to Rikasa would be another good one. That would give Ziral a chance to see her family. She hasn't been home in a few years."

"Where's the place with the ice mines?" I asked.

Saresh laughed. "You've been talking to Zey."

Hathan rested a finger on the extreme edge of the map. "He needs to brush up on his navigation. Zarakhat is well out of range."

"Luckily for us," murmured Daskar, who was watching the lesson with interest.

At that moment Hathan's flexscreen chimed: an incoming call, not a message. Without a word he rose, picked it up, and headed for the door. The conversations around us dropped into silence, and I knew the others had noted his departure as well. I didn't look at Saresh or anyone else. Instead I stared down at the map, concentrating all my attention on the gold line that bisected it. *Arkhati, Vardesh Prime, Earth.* I whispered the Vardeshi translations in my mind, over and over again, like an incantation.

Several long minutes elapsed before Hathan returned. When he did, he sat down again and studied the map another moment before touching a control on the tabletop display. The glimmering golden tracery vanished, leaving one line remaining. Arkhati, Vardesh Prime, Earth. Saresh lifted his senek cup in a reserved salute. Hathan inclined his head slightly, acknowledging the gesture. I tried to imitate their calm, but I could feel an irrepressible grin spreading across my face. The Echelon was giving me everything I wanted.

"Sigils and emblems," Saresh said. "They went for Zirian's compromise?"

"They did. We launch for Prime in two days. Along with"—Hathan consulted his flexscreen—"one Reyna Ekhran, formerly of the *Izdarith,* now suvi of the *Ascendant.*"

I felt a sudden illogical stab of jealousy. Without thinking I said, "Reyna? Isn't that a woman's name?"

Saresh gave me an odd look. Hathan said, "Does that surprise you?"

I fumbled for a credible response. "It's just that, when we were talking, Councilor Zirian made it sound like the Echelon officer was going to be a man."

Hathan said, "Considering that they wanted to put you with a crew of thirty-six, I'm sure the debate over officer selection was fairly heated. Zirian may have had someone in mind who was ultimately passed over."

"Ah, well," Saresh said with a philosophical air. "It looks like the Dream Forests will have to wait a little longer for me." He smiled at me. "Congratulations, Novi. You're going to Vardesh Prime. Again."

"And you're going to Earth. Again. We may not have any dream forests, but I promise I'll find you something equally amazing."

"I'll hold you to that," he said.

"I'm sorry about Rikasa," I said to Ziral. "I would have liked to see it."

Her smile seemed unforced. "It's all right. I'll try to visit on the way back from Earth."

"One more year," Daskar said.

"One more year," Ziral agreed. The phrase sounded formulaic. I wondered if it was a mantra of long-range space travelers. From what I understood about the Fleet, reassignments and sudden route changes were commonplace, especially for those in the lower ranks. It wasn't an unusual thing to have a planned trip home delayed by months or years. Someone was always going to be disappointed, I reminded myself. No one had been absolutely guaranteed a trip home on this journey. Except me.

Zey hung over the back of his seat to peer over at the star chart. "All right, you've kept us waiting long enough. Where are we going?"

"Home," said Saresh. "And then back to Earth."

"Earth!" Zey shouted and downed his senek. There was laughter from the *Pinion*'s crew—no, I corrected myself, the *Ascendant*'s crew—and most of them followed suit.

Khiva got to her feet. "Crew of the *Ascendant!*" she called.

"And friends, obviously. Our careers are saved, our mission has been extended, and the Echelon's giving us a shiny new ship. We're going drinking in Downhelix. First round is on me."

Amid the ensuing commotion, Saresh looked over at Hathan. "What do you say, Khavi?"

Hathan raised a hand in demurral. "I'm out. I'm meeting with Suvi Ekhran as soon as the *Izdarith* docks in the morning. We have a lot of work to do if we're going to be ready to launch in two days."

"You haven't had much of a holiday," I said. "You got, what, one day off?"

He smiled faintly. "It's more than I expected. My mission doesn't end until you're safely back on Earth. I'll take my vacation then."

"Well," I said, "you couldn't pick a better place for it. Relaxing is one thing humans do really, really well."

Kylie leaned over the back of her own seat. "Speaking of which. How about it, Novi? Up for another night in Downhelix?"

I hesitated. "I don't know. It's pretty late."

"Come on," Zey urged. "We'll drink to your victory over the Echelon."

"I think you probably shouldn't call it that," I said.

"Well, not in front of Suvi Ekhran, for sure." He winked, a mannerism that invariably made me laugh, it was so exaggerated. He'd learned it from my TV shows and Kylie's movies, and he couldn't seem to do it without contorting his entire face.

Reluctantly I said, "You guys go ahead. Have an extra drink for me. Maybe I'll stop by later."

"Yeah, sure. I know what that means," Kylie said good-naturedly. She passed me my senek cup, which I'd abandoned on the other table. "Finish this, at least. It's probably bad luck to leave it half full." I took the cup. "Wait," she said before I could drink. She clinked her own cup against mine. "A toast to your success."

"To Councilor Zirian's success," I corrected, and drank.

When everyone else had departed for Downhelix or the residential wing, I found myself sitting alone with Saresh in the sudden enveloping quiet. He reached over and touched a final control on the table, darkening the display until all that remained were the soft yellow globes of the senek room's lights, reflected in the polished surface. Then he rested his hand lightly on my shoulder. He didn't say anything, but he didn't have to. He alone knew what this moment meant to me. I wouldn't have cared if the Echelon had sent us to Veynir, or Rikasa, or to any of the other blue or orange icons I had seen on the chart. The important thing was that they had kept the *Pinion*'s crew together. They had given me nine more months with Hathan.

"What are you going to do now?" he asked.

"I'd like to go to sleep. But first, I should probably send a message to my parents."

"Not an appealing thought?"

I sighed. "They're not going to be happy about this news. They want me to come home. I tried to tell them about Arkhati, about how cool and exotic it was, and they took it all wrong. In their eyes, I've had my taste of alien culture, I've gotten what I came for, and it's time to turn around. Now I have to tell them I'm going in completely the wrong direction. Farther out. And they're going to like it even less when they hear about the offer I turned down. They would have been thrilled to have me on an Echelon ship. Why settle for scrubbing toilets in coach when you could be sipping champagne on Air Force One?"

I said the last sentence in English. Saresh frowned. "I followed most of that. Of course they'd rather have you on an Echelon ship. They're your parents. They want you to be safe."

"I know. And I also know that, whatever they say, they won't be really happy until I'm soilside on Earth again. So it doesn't actually matter what ship I'm on. Hey, but at least you get to send some good news home. You'll be seeing your family again in three months, right? You and Zey and . . ."

I still couldn't bring myself to say Hathan's name. Saresh didn't even blink at the omission. "We'll see our father, yes. Our mother isn't on Vardesh Prime. She's working on a research station on one of the outlying planets. She was home for Zey's Institute graduation, but I doubt she'll visit again for another few years. Probably not until one of us gets married."

"When," I said, and stopped. "I want to hear more about that. But not tonight."

"We'll have plenty of nights on the *Ascendant,*" he said reassuringly. "And no Khavi Vekesh to stop us from talking to each other. There will be time for all your questions."

"That's what you think," I said. "You don't know how many I have."

Back in my room, I made a couple of abortive attempts to record a message for my parents that was equal parts firm and contrite. In the end, I left it for the morning. There was really nothing I could say to make things better. The only words they actually wanted to hear from me were "I'm coming home," and I wasn't ready to say them. Not yet.

* * *

The next two days were a whirl of pre-departure activity. The Council had sent a long list of the gear I would require to be considered fully prepared for nine additional months in deep space, given how many of my redundancies had been lost in the damage to the *Pinion*. Kylie and I spent several hours sorting through my provisions and checking things off, then supplementing where necessary from her equipment. I took another pass through her media files to make sure there weren't any songs or shows I couldn't live without. I did find one newish Vardrama I thought Zey would enjoy, although we'd have to wait until Earth to finish *Divided by Stars,* the show we had started before Hathan spaced all my tech. I had another complete physical examination, at the end of which the doctor (whose name I was now too embarrassed to ask) confirmed that my readings were now within acceptable parameters, although they hadn't improved as much as she would have liked. I made a final trip to the Atrium for last-minute gifts and souvenirs, and another to the Arboretum to luxuriate in the feeling of standing beneath real trees, albeit ones enclosed by metal walls. I packed my duffel bag and persuaded Kylie to part with a couple of things for Khiva and a few more for me. I really needed another pair of jeans, and since we were exactly the same size, it seemed only fair.

"You can get more," I pointed out. "I can't." She yielded with bad grace.

I'd had my eye on another item from her closet, a strappy black dress decorated with geometric designs picked out in tiny gold beads. She went so far as to permit me to try it on, but refused to consider parting with it. Three months ago I wouldn't have even bothered to ask; it was too flimsy and unstructured. Now, however, it draped perfectly on my slightly leaner frame. I observed as much to Kylie, who said quellingly, "That's not a good thing. You heard the doctor. You were supposed to be back at your original weight by this point."

I turned to admire the dress from another angle. "Well, you can't say I haven't tried. I must have eaten my weight in chocolate in the last week. Can I wear it tonight, at least?"

"Tonight is fine. I had something else picked out anyway."

It was early evening of my last day on Arkhati. We had been invited, along with my crewmates, to a farewell banquet in honor of the *Ascendant*'s launch. The invitation had specified civilian formal wear, which I thought might be a dig at me from Governor Tavri for wearing my uniform to the welcome dinner. As little as I liked to be on display, I found myself actually looking forward to the occasion. I was eager to meet Reyna Ekhran, who had been closeted with Hathan since the *Izdarith* docked the previous morning, and to thank Councilor Zirian for speaking in my defense. Still, the thought of coming face-to-face with Tavri again dampened my enthusiasm a little.

"You should be nervous," Kylie said darkly. "After all, you basically gave her an ultimatum. If I were her, I'd be looking for a way to punish you. Nothing too obvious, of course. Maybe she'll ask you to perform a ceremonial dance from Earth. Or translate something on the fly. That's what I'd do."

"She wouldn't," I said, alarmed at the thought.

"She might. If I were you, I'd keep my wits about me."

I finished dressing and watched while Kylie saw to her own toilette, a process considerably more involved than mine. At the last moment she rejected the dress she'd laid out in favor of a sleek black jumpsuit. When she'd finished her preparations, I held obediently still while she applied my eye makeup, a skill I'd never acquired. I hadn't intended to wear any, but she insisted, and as I gauged the effect in the mirror, I thought she was right. Between the borrowed dress, my new haircut, and Kylie's ministrations, I looked better than I had in a while. That fact pleased me for a reason that had nothing to do with personal vanity. When the publicity photos from tonight made their way back to Earth, Anton, my physician at the Villiger Center, and Dr. Okoye would see a different person from the hollow-eyed waif who had stumbled off the *Pinion* a week ago. Hopefully the pictures would lay to rest any lingering misgivings about my physical condition. As far as I was concerned, my recovery was complete.

In the privacy of my own thoughts, though, I had to admit that there was another reason for my eagerness to depart. The Echelon had accepted the compromise proposed by Councilor Zirian, but their agreement had the feel of a concession, and I knew it could be snatched away as quickly as it had been given. I didn't want to hang around waiting for them to change their minds. Some part of me wouldn't feel completely secure until the *Ascendant* was well away, with Arkhati dwindling safely behind it in the viewport.

We had arranged to meet Saresh and Sohra for a last drink at the Atrium. As we walked over, Kylie said, "If anyone asks you if we're going out after dinner, the answer is no. I've got a surprise for you, but it's strictly humans only. No Vardeshi allowed."

I eyed her warily. "What kind of surprise? You didn't hire a stripper or something, did you?"

"I said no Vardeshi allowed. This is just for the two of us. And that's the only hint you'll get. But"—she grinned—"I think you're going to like it."

The four of us spent a leisurely hour watching the early evening traffic in the Atrium. Our companions were as undemanding as ever. After a while, the talk turned to the newest member of the *Ascendant*'s crew.

"Have you met her?" I asked.

Sohra shook her head. "Not yet."

"I have," said Saresh.

When he didn't elaborate, I exchanged an exasperated look with Sohra, who prompted, "And? What did you think?"

"I think I should let you form your own opinions."

"As if you could stop them," Kylie retorted.

He gave her an amused look. "All right, I'll say this much. I think she's been sent to us with an objective, and she means to achieve it. I think she views the *Ascendant* as an assignment like any other. Perhaps with slightly higher stakes. I don't think she's passionate about Earth or English or the alliance. She's a soldier, and she's been sent among civilians to do what I, in her place, would fully expect to be a difficult and rather thankless job

"You didn't like her," Kylie said.

"Actually I did." The swiftness of his answer surprised me.

I hadn't exactly formed an image of Reyna Ekhran in my mind, before or after Saresh's assessment, but I had tentatively pictured her as a sort of female version of him: tall, silver-haired, competent. When I met her in person a few minutes later, I saw that she looked nothing like him at all. The aura of quiet competence seemed to be the only trait they shared. Firstly, she was petite. The top of her head barely came to my chin, and she was slim. Her movements had the grace of a fighter or a dancer. I felt more elephantine than usual as I returned her Vardeshi salute. If I lived among these people any longer, I was going to develop a complex about tiny women. She had dark chin-length hair and dark wide-set eyes and a perfectly pointed chin. Her coloring, added to the flatness of her features, made her appear more Asian than alien. She was in civilian wear, per the invitation, but I thought the ensemble she had chosen—black and white with touches of indigo—might be a nod to Echelon colors. She greeted me matter-of-factly in her own language, addressing me as "Novi Alkhat," two immediate points in her favor.

"Suvi," I said. "I hope your voyage on the *Izdarith* was untroubled." Zey had taught me that it was proper protocol on meeting a fellow Fleet employee to inquire about the success of her previous mission. I prayed that the same held true for the Echelon, or, barring that, Suvi Ekhran would recognize the attempt at courtesy for what it was.

"It was routine, which is more than can be said for your time on the *Pinion*." As she spoke, I studied her face in fascination. She spoke without inflection beyond the inevitable rise and fall of Vardeshi tones. The flatness of her affect was so complete I knew it must be intentional. She reminded me of Tristan, my trainer in covert signaling. Next to her, I thought, Hathan would look positively demonstrative. I wondered what she would sound like speaking English.

"We had a few surprises," I said. "I'm hoping for smoother sailing from here to Vardesh Prime."

"An Echelon ship would have been your best guarantee of safe passage. And yet you turned down a placement on the *Izdarith*. Why?"

Taken aback at her bluntness, I fought my instinct to go on the defensive. I dredged up an expression I'd acquired in my trade with Saresh: "The horizon looks emptiest from the bow of a one-man craft."

Instead of acknowledging the point I was trying to make, she fixed on the phrase itself. "That idiom is in the archaic form. You must have learned it from Saresh Takheri. How much of his knowledge was left in your mind after the Listening?"

Again the directness of the question surprised me into honesty. "Not much. Just a couple of idioms."

"Ah. The rumors indicated it was closer to a complete memory transfer."

"Rumors tend to be overblown. At least where I come from."

Before she could respond, we were invited to take our seats. As I looked for my place, I found that the seat assignments had been laid out according to formal Fleet protocol, in descending order of rank. I was clustered with Zey, Sohra, and Khiva at one end of a long table, while Kylie was seated with Zirian, Tavri, Hathan, Suvi Ekhran, and Saresh at the other. I wondered if the ordering was intended as a slight. Depending on which of my two identities one considered, I was either one of the highest-ranked people in the room or the single most inferior. Tavri—I was sure it had been her— had placed me according to the latter designation. I didn't care. Being with my friends meant I didn't have to perform for anyone. And it wasn't an insult to me to be identified as Novi Alkhat. On the contrary, it was exactly what I wanted— and what the Echelon had almost taken away from me.

The energy at our end of the table was high. Everyone was giddy with excitement about the upcoming launch. Khiva was looking forward to going home, Zey was relieved that his three weeks of leave on Earth had been reinstated, and Sohra was eager to investigate some of the newer systems on the *Ascendant*. "And Eyvri is excited to do more laundry," Sohra teased me. "You must really miss the smell of our cleaning solvents. You know you wouldn't have had to do any work on the *Izdarith*, right? You would have been an honored guest. A luminary."

"I would have been a package. They probably would have listed me on the cargo manifest. Special delivery, one human female. Weight: fifty-four kilograms. Destination: Khezendri."

"Contents under pressure," Khiva murmured. I grinned at her.

"Well, you're still that, at least to one of us," said Zey. "The ahtziri is coming with us, remember?"

The ahtziri was Vethna's sardonic nickname for Suvi Ekhran. Sohra had shown me pictures of the animal on her flexscreen. It was a lithe silver-furred creature that looked like a cross between a fox and a cat. I had to admit the resemblance was striking; the cold black eyes and haughtily upright bearing were the same. Still, I didn't like the idea that Suvi Ekhran was already an object of ridicule. It was my fault she had been placed on the *Ascendant,* and I wanted her to be given a fighting chance. And I had been on the receiving end of a nickname from Vethna too recently to have forgotten its sting. "Don't call her that," I hissed.

Zey sent an unconcerned look down the length of the table. Tavri was saying something to Suvi Ekhran. Neither of them was looking in our direction. "Why not? They can't hear us. And it's over. Everything's been settled. The Echelon's not going to change the plan now. Stop worrying."

"I'll stop worrying when we've launched. Until then, could you try not to annoy them more than you absolutely have to?"

"You're the one who rejected them, Eyvri," Khiva said

dryly. "You practically begged not to be put on their ship. I think the damage is probably done."

I knew she was right. Even so, I put on my best political face for the drinks course that succeeded the main meal. The senek, brandy, and savory plates were served in a long gallery adjacent to the dining room. Floor-to-ceiling viewports like the ones in Kylie's suite offered a stunning view of the starhaven. I downed a fortifying cup of senek, steeled myself, and made straight for Governor Tavri, who was talking to Suvi Ekhran near the viewports.

"Novi," Tavri said smoothly as I approached. "Join us. We were just discussing the latest news of the exchange." She spoke in Vardeshi, which I thought was generous of her. She went on, "There have been reports that another one of your cohort is drawing considerable praise for his linguistic prowess. He's apparently quite gifted. If the accounts are credible, his Vardeshi is near-native after only three months. You've been studying for how long—a year?"

"Fifteen months now," I said.

"Ah. And how would you describe your own skill level?"

This, I realized, was why we were speaking Vardeshi. It had nothing to do with courtesy. Tavri was trying to trap me into an embarrassing overestimation of my own abilities. I said, "Proficient." I waited for her next sally, but it didn't come. She seemed to be waiting for me to say more. Channeling Saresh, I assumed an expression of mild interest and said nothing. At Tavri's side, Reyna Ekhran watched me dispassionately.

When I didn't expand on my answer, Tavri pressed, "You wouldn't call yourself fluent?"

"I wouldn't go that far. I still have a lot to learn." A server passed by us carrying steaming cups of senek on a tray. I flagged him down for a refill. It took all my restraint not to snatch the cup out of his hand.

"Admirably modest," said Tavri.

Suvi Ekhran asked, "What's his name? The other human?"

After what I knew had to be a manufactured pause to retrieve it, Tavri said, "I think he was called . . . Simon?"

I drank some of my senek, which helped to settle my mind a little, and thought back to the night before my launch from the Villiger Center and the list of placements taped to the wall. It felt like a such long time ago. The name was familiar though. Hadn't I heard Scott and Rajani talking about him? "There was someone named Fletcher Simon who trained with me and Kylie. I didn't have a chance to meet him."

While I was speaking, Hathan made his way over to join our little group, senek cup in hand. I wondered what had drawn his attention. Had he noticed that I was outnumbered by the Echelon and come to lend his support, or was he simply hoping to prevent me from offending Governor Tavri again? I could have assured him that I had no such intention. I had sought her out in the hope of smoothing over any lingering tension between us. The antagonism was all on her side.

"How lucky for you that this Fletcher Simon didn't have the advantage of your early exposure to our language," Tavri said. "If he had, things might have been very different. He might be on his way to Vardesh Prime right now instead of you."

Was this the best she could do? I wondered. Vague hints that someone else was better at her language than I was? She had tapped into a vein of anxiety, it was true, but it was one that no longer had any power over me. Unless the Echelon was giving Fletcher Simon my berth on the *Ascendant,* I didn't care in the slightest if he had mastered the North Continent dialect, the South Continent dialect, the Khivrik accent, and Hebrew. While I was searching for a less sarcastic response, Hathan came unexpectedly to my defense.

"A story has a thousand beginnings, but only one ending," he said. "It's pointless to speculate on how things could have gone. The slightest shift at any stage would have led to a different outcome. In any case, I was one of the people who interviewed Eyvri, and I stand by my choice." And, with no warning at all, he put an encouraging hand on my shoulder.

Under any other circumstances it would have been a mere comradely gesture. Tonight, however, I wasn't wearing a uniform or a sweatshirt. I was wearing Kylie's strappy dress. There was nothing under his hand, no protective layer of fabric between his skin and mine. My entire awareness was instantly concentrated on the light pressure of his fingers on my bare shoulder. A feeling like the aftereffect of senek, exquisitely cool and soothing, spread outward from that single point of contact. After a few moments he took his hand away. I fought the urge to lift my own hand to cover the place where his had rested. What was Suvi Ekhran saying? Something about the relative difficulties of Vardeshi and English. I was trying desperately to remember if Hathan had ever touched me like that before. He had grabbed my arm in the corridor during my argument with Vethna to keep me from falling. And, I recalled with a fresh surge of mortification, he had carried me unconscious to the *Pinion*'s medical clinic after the shooting. But this . . . Others had offered as much. I didn't think he had.

Tavri was talking now. I blinked and made a supreme effort to engage with her words. "The Echelon is considering inviting him to Vardesh Prime as well." It took me a moment to place *him* as Fletcher Simon. "Perhaps very soon. Elteni Starhaven is only a month away from our world. You may not hold the title of the only human to visit it for very long. It's possible that his tenure could even overlap with yours."

If that was true, I thought, then this was the retaliation Kylie had cautioned me to expect. The Echelon had found an unobtrusive way to punish me for declining their escort, and it was far worse than any fleeting personal humiliation. They were trying to dilute my importance in the exchange. I was supposed to be the first human on Vardesh Prime. The first, singular, not one of the first. I felt an automatic twinge of resentment at the thought, but I wasn't about to give Tavri the satisfaction of showing it. I put on the brightest smile I could manage. "Good. It's been wonderful to explore Arkhati with Kylie. I'd love to cross paths with another Stranger. And it's a big step forward for the alliance. There are a hundred Vardeshi on Earth. Why should I be the only human on Vardesh Prime?"

Tavri said, "You won't mind sharing the spotlight, then?"

Suvi Ekhran said, "She was willing to give it up before. For the *Ascendant*."

If Hathan's words in my defense had been unexpected, hers were doubly so. I looked at her in surprise. She gazed coolly back at me, her dark eyes unreadable. I wondered if she had decided to give me a fighting chance too.

After a little while, Tavri excused herself and left the group. Suvi Ekhran drifted away. Left alone with Hathan, I said, "You didn't choose me."

He frowned. "What do you mean?"

"In the interview. You didn't choose me." I could feel myself growing flustered. Why had I even brought it up?

"You told Vekesh to pick someone else."

"In the interview," he repeated.

"Yes. At the Villiger Center. You said I had no technical skills."

His eyebrows lifted slightly. "You still remember that?"

"It was a pretty important conversation," I said defensively. "Life-changing, in fact. Of course I remember it."

"I see. Well, let's just say I gave Tavri a revised version of the facts." He nodded to where the Echelon representatives had formed a small knot near the door. "You really don't mind that you might not be the only human on Vardesh Prime?"

"I mind a little," I admitted. "I was pretty excited about being the first one. I just didn't want Tavri to know that."

"I thought as much. Well, it's not too late. Find out which ship is hosting Fletcher Simon. Odds are it's no match for the *Ascendant* at top speed. If I can get you there before him, I will."

I smiled. "Thanks. And not just for that. For standing up for me."

"You stood up for us," he said. "It seemed only fair."

After a little more mingling time and a few ceremonial speeches—none of them, mercifully, either given or translated by myself—the evening concluded. I said my formal farewells to Tavri and Zirian, taking advantage of a moment alone with the councilor to thank him for his intervention on my behalf. As Kylie and I left the gallery, I saw a few of the *Ascendant*'s crew clustered in the corridor, making plans for a final night in Downhelix. Per her instructions, I declined the invitation to join them. "Have fun," I told Zey. "Not too much though. Don't do anything to get us in trouble."

"No bar fights, you mean?" He grinned. "Don't worry.

The interesting stuff only happens when you're around."

As we walked away I asked Kylie, "Do you remember that guy who took the second-place spot on the List?"

She nodded. "Of course. Fletcher Simon. He launched with me. He's on his way to Elteni right now. Why?"

"Tavri was talking about him. About how great he is. Supposedly his Vardeshi is perfect. Already. She says the Echelon may be asking him to go to Vardesh Prime too."

"I told you she would try to rattle you."

I sighed. "Yeah."

"So don't let her," Kylie said firmly. "You won. You got the *Ascendant.* She can't take that away from you, so she's looking for something she can take. And for my money, it's not much. You've already made history. With or without Vardesh Prime."

"I know. I just wanted you to know you were right about her." Casting around for a lighter subject, I said, "So what's this surprise you were hinting at before?"

"That's our next stop. But we'll need to swing by my rooms first to change."

"Into what?" I said warily.

She laughed. "Whatever you want. But wear a bikini underneath. And bring a bottle of water and a towel."

"A bikini? Are we going swimming?"

"The faster you change, the sooner you'll find out."

We had reached her suite. Kylie went in first, tossed her bag onto a side table, and headed for her bedroom. Mystified, I went up to my own room and changed into a bathing suit. I almost hadn't brought one. When, shortly before docking with Arkhati, I had inquired about the likelihood of finding a swimming pool on the starhaven, Zey had given me a look of pure horror. It seemed that, barring a handful of localized traditions on outlying worlds, most Vardeshi found the idea of swimming deeply distasteful. I disagreed. My philosophy during college had been "Never pass up a chance to swim," and I'd never quite gotten out of the habit of tucking a swimsuit into every overnight bag I packed. Now I was glad I hadn't. I put on jeans, a short-sleeved shirt, and sandals, tossed water and a towel into a tote bag, and headed downstairs. I stopped by Kylie's room on the way and draped the black and gold dress carefully across her bed. I felt a pang of regret as I turned away from it. I would have liked to keep it.

Kylie met me in the entryway and we set out again, shepherded as always by our security team, which I found comforting. Whatever surprise she had concocted, if it had been sanctioned by our handlers, it couldn't be too outrageous.

"Medical helix," I said in surprise as we stepped off the elevator. "What are we doing here? Getting a massage? Or . . . a tattoo?"

"Not quite." Kylie led me into a room that resembled the shower room in her suite. It had the same round-tiled floor and oceanic lighting. However, I didn't see the familiar sleek shower fixture suspended above a shallow well in the floor. Instead, a raised platform held a hip-high structure that was unquestionably a tub. In keeping with the Vardeshi penchant for natural materials, it appeared to be made of bamboo. It was full nearly to the brim. The water steamed gently in the cool air, giving off an unfamiliar fragrance, possibly one of the Vardeshi soaps Kylie had admired. I went closer and dipped a tentative hand in. "It's a hot tub!"

"For tonight it is," Kylie agreed. "It's actually meant for hydrotherapy."

"I didn't even know they had bathtubs. I've never seen

one. How did you find out about it?"

Kylie had begun to arrange her phone and speaker. I recognized the opening notes from one of my favorite albums. "I was asking Saresh about the recovery process for his leg," she explained. "He mentioned hydrotherapy, and that gave me the idea. Your doctor from the *Pinion* helped me make the arrangements. There's only one room like this on Arkhati, and I had to formally request to be allowed to use it for recreational purposes. Our hosts don't take baths—or swim, apparently. I told them immersion in water was a ritual that had cultural significance for humans."

"Well, it is." I kicked off my sandals, stripped down to my bikini, and eased into the water. It was cooler than a hot tub on Earth would have been, but warm enough to be instantly soothing.

"This is as hot as it would go," Kylie said, slipping in beside me. "The Vardeshi do their therapy in cold water."

"Oh, of course they do." I leaned my elbows on the edge of the tub and sighed. "This is perfect."

"It's almost perfect." Kylie leaned out to extract something from her purse, which she'd dropped on the floor next to the tub. She held it up for me to see. "Now it's perfect."

I stared at the object in her hand. "Is that what I think it is?"

"What do you think it is?"

"A joint," I said.

"Right in one."

She held out the tiny pink and white cylinder, and I took it. It looked like a cheap ballpoint pen. If I'd seen it jumbled among her lipsticks in a drawer back on Earth, I wouldn't have looked at it twice. Still, it was hard to credit its appearance here on Arkhati. "I don't get it," I said. "All our gear was searched twice. First by the humans, then by the Vardeshi. How in the world did you get it through?"

"Max knew," Kylie said calmly. "I never would have gotten it past him. He tucked it into one of the medical crates, along with the pain relievers, and the Vardeshi didn't flag it."

"Unbelievable." I tried to picture the weathered gear specialist conspiring with Kylie to sneak contraband drugs into her luggage.

"Max and I have an understanding. He looked the other way provided I promised not to offer it to the Vardeshi—which I would never do; I'm not a total idiot—and I promised to bring him back any interesting substances I ran across on the way. I already have a canister of senek with his name on it. And a bottle of Vardeshi whiskey. He's not worried about an upset stomach. Small price to pay for a taste of—what did he call it?—alien hooch."

I shook my head. "It would never even have occurred to me to try to bring something like this on board. And if it had, I never would have asked Max for help."

"I know. You're too innocent."

"How did you know he was the right one to ask?"

She waved a hand, wafting perfumed steam toward me. "I saw him smoking a joint in the gardens during the first week of training."

"Still, weren't you afraid you'd be thrown out of the program if they found it?"

She laughed. "You were always worrying about that. It's a lot less likely than you think. Remember, we were selected for this mission over everyone else on Earth. All seven billion of them. Do you have any idea how much it cost to train us? The worst anyone would have done was give me a light scolding. And pocket it for themselves. So are you just going to hold that thing, or are you going to smoke it?"

I looked doubtfully at the vaporizer pen. Kylie laughed again. "You do realize, don't you, that you'd have to travel for three months to reach a place where smoking it is illegal? You'll never have a better chance than right now."

My final objection was halfhearted. "What if it triggers some kind of environmental alarm? Like when we burned the popcorn?"

"It won't."

She spoke so coolly that I had to laugh. "You've already tried it?"

"Once. I had to be sure it worked. Didn't want to disappoint you."

"Believe me, you haven't."

I'd been high a few times in college and once or twice in grad school, but it had been a while. My first drag resulted in a paroxysm of coughing. Kylie, watching me, laughed until tears came to her eyes. I laughed too, when I got my breath back. I only took a couple of hits: enough to relax, not enough to dim the lucidity of my thoughts. Then I lay back in the warm water and closed my eyes, giving in to the heightened sense of awareness conferred by the drug. Here we were, the two of us, humans together, impossibly far from home. I'd resented Kylie a little at first for taking away my uniqueness. I'd known even then how irrational that was. Now I found myself realizing how lonely I would be without her. All the references effortlessly understood, all the shared laughs and eloquent looks. When would I be in the company of another human? I found myself almost hoping I would encounter Fletcher Simon on Vardesh Prime. There was a profound solitude in being the only one of my kind among aliens, even ones as familiar as Zey and the others now were to me. I couldn't ever be known by them as deeply and completely as I was right now. At least, I amended, not until the Council rescinded its ban on human participation in the Listening.

The first album had ended and the water was beginning to cool down when Kylie asked, "Are you afraid?"

"Of what?"

"Of going out there again. Of being alone with them."

I had to smile, so precisely did her question parallel my thoughts. "I'm not afraid of them. But yeah, I'm afraid of going out there again. When I launched the first time, I thought I knew what to expect. Now I know I don't."

"Good," she said. "If you thought anything else, you'd be an idiot." She hesitated. "You're sure you made the right decision? Turning down the Echelon ship? I know what you told Tavri. But this is me asking."

"Yeah, I'm sure."

"You know I would have gone with you. If you'd asked."

I looked at her. She went on, "You think I'm still angling for Vardesh Prime. I'm not. I would have gone home with you too, if you needed me to. If you had asked."

"Thank you," I said.

After another brief silence I asked her, "So what about you? Are you going to be all right here on your own?"

"It's different for me. There will be other Strangers passing through Arkhati. The next wave will be here in a couple of weeks. I won't be alone, not like you."

"I won't be alone," I said. "Not like I was before." I knew I was reassuring myself as much as her.

I slept in Kylie's bed that night. I didn't explicitly ask if I could, but she didn't look surprised when I appeared in her doorway holding my pillow and blanket. She simply shifted over in the bed to make room for me. Attempting to settle down in my own room, I had been surprised by a longing for her that was intensely physical while at the same time being completely nonsexual. We didn't talk to each other. We didn't even touch. I simply lay beside her in the shared warmth under the blankets until the rhythm of her breathing lulled me to sleep. My rest that night was more refreshing than it had been in a long time. There was a strangeness to Vardeshi bodies, a composite of their slightly different odors and temperatures and breathing rates, which was so faint as to be almost imperceptible. I wasn't consciously aware of it, but it seemed that my body was. Even in repose, I had been ever so slightly on the alert every night that I spent on my own. With Kylie there, no more than an arm's length away, I could finally relax. It was my animal self, as Dr. Okoye would have called it, recognizing one of its own kind at long last.

7

Life on the *Ascendant* was different from life on the *Pinion*. Suvi Ekhran—or Reyna, as she insisted I call her outside of duty hours—made sure of that. If I had expected her to abandon her Echelon practices wholesale for those of the Fleet, I quickly learned the error of my ways. She lost no time in implementing a number of new and stricter protocols. At the end of the first month, Zey and Sohra and I sat in the *Ascendant*'s lounge and tallied up all the changes. "No more free access to rana," Sohra said. "I think that's an improvement." The *Ascendant*'s supply of rana was now locked securely away in the medical clinic, a shift at which Khiva took personal offense. So, bizarrely, did Zey. "But you don't even use it," Sohra pointed out. "Why should you care where it's kept?"

"It's the principle. The new policy is patronizing. Typical Echelon. At least the Fleet gives us credit for a little self-control."

"That didn't work so well for Vethna, did it?"

There was a tightness in Sohra's voice. I glanced at Zey. He must have heard it as well, because when he spoke again, it was in a softer tone. "I know you're thinking about your brother. But this policy wouldn't have helped him. Even on an Echelon ship, he could have gotten rana anytime he wanted it. They were selling it in Downhelix. Hell, they were selling it in the Atrium."

"I know. Still, this makes me feel safer."

"In that case, you must love the mandatory ranshai practices."

The accusation drew a reluctant smile from Sohra. "I'd like them more if they were a little later," she admitted.

Echelon officers were required to be in a state of perpetual combat readiness. Reyna had assessed the crew's ranshai skills and declared them sadly out of practice, with the predictable exceptions of Hathan and Ziral. "What about me?" Zey had said indignantly after she gave her verdict. "I took down Khavi Vekesh. That has to count for something."

"Well, how was your individual session with her?" Sohra asked.

"Not good," he admitted. "She's even smaller than I am. You wouldn't think she'd be so strong. Or fast."

All crew members were now required to attend daily ranshai practice for an hour beginning at five-thirty in the morning. The policy had initially included rest days, but the outcry from the crew had been so strident that the rule had been hastily amended to allow two absences per eight-day week. I was sure the amendment was Hathan's touch, though the announcement had come from Reyna herself. I had begged to be exempted from the drills. "I'm clumsier than you can possibly imagine. Clumsy even for a human, I mean. I have no coordination and no fighting skills. So unless you really want to embarrass me, please don't make me go. I'll work out in the fitness center at five-thirty every day. I'll do whatever you want. Just, please, not ranshai.''

Reyna had replied coolly, "There's no question of your participating. As a complete novice, you would only be an impediment to our drills. And you could be seriously hurt. It's stipulated in your contract that we can't make unreasonable demands on your time or energy. I'll leave it to you to decide whether you want to show solidarity by scheduling your own workouts to coincide with our practices."

As far as I was concerned, I had already done my part for solidarity by securing us the *Ascendant*. The thought of committing to a regular five o'clock wake-up call was hardly enticing. However, it was the perfect pretext for watching the drills, so I gritted my teeth and set my alarm back another hour. I was instantly rewarded. Watching Reyna in action was riveting. She was the smallest figure on the practice mats, but unquestionably the most powerful. Her slightest movement conveyed skill and confidence. If she had been matched against Vekesh, she would have beaten him handily. As I watched her fling Saresh across the room without perceptible effort, I felt a grudging respect for the Echelon. Their training methods were clearly effective. And I couldn't deny that I felt safer knowing she was on board expressly for my protection. The crew continued to complain about the mandatory workouts, the more so when they began sporting purple and gray bruises, but even I could see that they were improving.

The unfortunate side effect of the mandatory group practices was an increased demand for the *Ascendant*'s two showers in advance of morning briefing. This was particularly hard on the lower-ranking crew, because even when we took care to reserve slots ahead of time, a higher-ranked officer's request took precedence. More than one junior crew member was written up for tardiness after being unexpectedly bumped down the shower queue. When Sohra and Khiva brought the unfairness of the system to Reyna's attention, she said dismissively, "Take shorter showers. On an Echelon ship the slots are eight minutes long."

"That explains the smell," Zey had muttered when Sohra recounted the exchange. He had taken an immediate and wholehearted dislike to Suvi Ekhran. She had singled him out for a uniform violation the day after we launched from Arkhati, and he was convinced that she felt some animus for him in particular. Sohra and I pointed out that he was hardly alone in being reprimanded. I myself had been admonished twice, for formatting a report incorrectly and for arriving late to evening briefing. My lateness had nothing to do with the shower schedule. I was still learning to navigate the *Ascendant*'s unfamiliar passageways, and I'd simply gotten lost. Our reassurances had no effect. Zey insisted that the ahtziri had it in for him, and after a few attempts to persuade him otherwise, Sohra and I mutually decided to let it go.

"All right," he said now, with an air of finality. "The night-duty schedule. That's one change you can't say anything good about, so don't even try."

"I won't," Sohra assured him. "I don't like it any more than you do."

The night-duty schedule was Reyna's least-popular innovation. To her military-trained mind, it was beyond reckless that we all kept the same hours and that there was no designated crew member on duty during the nights. She immediately instituted a watch system that assigned everyone on board a seven-hour overnight duty shift roughly twice a week. The on-duty crew member was required to be awake and in the axis chamber, the command hub of the ship, for the duration of the shift. Everyone else was annoyed at having to do it. I was annoyed because she wouldn't put my name on the roster. "Let me take my turn," I pleaded. "Everyone else has to."

"No," Reyna said immovably. "I've seen your medical reports. The others can do without a few hours of sleep here and there. You can't. Rhevi Daskar agrees with me, and so do your Earth physicians. There's no use in arguing."

"But it's not fair," I said lamely.

"It's perfectly fair." She tilted her head and looked at me in puzzlement. "I don't understand you. You're already wasting hours every day cleaning a starship. You've made yourself subservient to us in a way you had no need to do. Isn't that enough? Why torture yourself more?"

This was a common theme of our conversations. I quickly discovered, or rather Reyna informed me, that her mission on board wasn't only to keep me safe. The Echelon had agreed to send me to Vardesh Prime on a Fleet ship, but there was still the return trip to Earth to consider, and while they might not be able to force me onto one of their own ships, they could conceivably still talk me onto one. Reyna was under explicit orders to win me over to the Echelon's way of thinking if she possibly could. Twice in our first week on the *Ascendant,* she cornered me and interrogated me about what she considered my inexplicable devotion to the Fleet. "Can't you see that the Echelon is offering you an opportunity to make a real and lasting contribution to the alliance?"

I said defensively, "I think I'm already making an important contribution."

She took my objection entirely in stride. "You're right. You are. Or, rather, you have. When Reyjai Vekesh first suggested that the Fleet take you on as an employee, even at the lowest level, everyone in our territories thought he was joking. Three months later, no one is laughing. You've proven that your kind is compatible with mine. No rational person still questions the ability of humans and Vardeshi to work side by side. You've accomplished what you set out to do. So why spend another minute folding uniforms and scrubbing the galley? Any Vardeshi with a pulse can do novi work."

"I've learned more about your culture in three months of novi work than I would have in a year as a passenger on an Echelon ship," I said. "I don't want to sit around watching other people work. I want to help them. And so do you, or you wouldn't be in the Echelon."

"That's different. I'm a soldier. This is my work. You're a cultural ambassador. Talking and thinking and writing is yours. Or it would be, if you weren't spending all your time washing dishes and cleaning floors."

I shrugged. "I'd rather wash dishes and clean floors on a ship with my friends than go to dinners and give lectures on a ship full of strangers."

"Yes, you've made that clear," Reyna said dryly.

"Then why are you still trying to change my mind?"

"Because you're a major player in the alliance. For now. The exchange will be over in nine months, and things are going to move very quickly after that. The Echelon can help you position yourself to take advantage of those changes, if you let us. But we can't help you if you insist on clinging to the Fleet."

"I'm not a major player in the alliance," I protested.

"Tavri said you were modest. She didn't say you were ignorant. You must know how important you are."

I didn't feel like contesting the point further, and anyway I had a sneaking suspicion that she was right. I tried a different argument. "You're talking like the alliance is a done deal. Like it's sure to go forward. But we're only a couple of months into the exchange. And Earth was on the verge of pulling out just a few weeks ago."

"That was posturing," Reyna said dismissively. "Your people never would have gone through with that threat. If you'd been killed, it would have slowed the progression of events, not stopped them. It's a lonely universe. Neither of our races wants to go back to being the only ones in the room. We have too much to offer each other. The technological advances may be all on our side, but you have a myriad of cultures, a planet rich in resources, and several billion laborers and consumers. No, the alliance will go forward. The Echelon is certain of it. You should be looking ahead to the next stage in your diplomatic career. I can guarantee that the rest of your peers are doing exactly that. Your friend Kylie included."

"I hope so," I said. "I can't think of anyone better qualified than Kylie. She'll probably be ambassador to Vardesh Prime one day."

Reyna studied me, her black eyes quizzical. "You have no ambition."

"Not the kind you're talking about, no."

"Are there other kinds?" she asked seriously.

I wanted to dislike her. It should have been easy. She was a harsh critic, ready to point out with cold precision any error, however slight, in my execution of my duties. But whatever Zey might claim, I found her treatment of the *Ascendant*'s crew to be remarkably fair. Clear rules and predictable consequences were a welcome change from the poisonous atmosphere of fear I remembered from Khavi Vekesh. I couldn't even find fault with her dogged attempts to talk me out of staying on the *Ascendant*. There was no malice in them. She was simply carrying out the task she had been assigned.

And she was assiduous in her attention to the other areas of my work as well. When she discovered how pathetically little I actually knew about the structure of the Fleet or the operations of its ships, she declared herself my tutor. My afternoons, which had previously been spent working on vocabulary notes or writing reports home, were now devoted to slogging through excerpts from a document I suspected was the foundational text on Fleet history assigned to incoming Institute students. After months in an immersion environment that required constant verbal interaction and minimal writing, my speaking and listening skills far outstripped my reading. For anyone else on board, the texts would have been elementary. For me, they were impenetrable. I would have given anything for a printer; I ached to highlight and scrawl notes and draw arrows. I could do all those things on the flexscreen, but it wasn't the same. Every passage took hours to decode. Despite what I had told Governor Tavri, I had been beginning to feel somewhat more than proficient in Vardeshi. Now I was confronted yet again with proof of my incompetence. It was a humbling reminder of exactly how much I still didn't know.

When I finally completed a segment of the readings, Reyna and I would meet to discuss it. After I read the complete text aloud, she would question me about the content until she was satisfied that I fully understood it. I dreaded my first meeting with her, but I found her to be a surprisingly patient teacher. She didn't mind being asked for the definition of six or seven words out of every ten. She didn't object to spending three hours discussing a single page of text. If anything, the reverse was true. The surest way to irritate her was to gloss over gaps in my understanding—or to reveal my frustration with my slow progress. I quickly learned not to give voice to my irritation in front of her. As befitted her military background, she had no sympathy for complaining.

She took my role as cultural emissary seriously too. At her instigation I began offering a weekly lesson on colloquial English. This event, held in the lounge during the senek hour, was surprisingly popular. My crewmates' English, while generally superb, tended toward the formal. Apparently that fact had struck several of them while listening to my conversations with Kylie on Arkhati.

"I would have been fine if you'd just used a little less slang," Khiva said critically, which made me laugh.

"I will if you will," I told her.

The nature of the class was directly dependent on who was in attendance on a given night. Daskar was interested in idioms, Zey liked to analyze sitcom dialogue, and Vethna's sole purpose seemed to be to expand his repertoire of English profanity. On one memorable night, the lesson was just concluding when Sohra asked, "Why do you have so many metaphors about sex?"

"Probably because they're all trying to sleep with each other all the time," Ziral said.

"Not all the time," I protested.

"Compared to us," Ziral said with inarguable logic.

Zey asked, "Do you have a word for a human who wants to sleep with a Vardeshi?"

I tried to dodge the question. "Well, a human who's weirdly obsessed with the Vardeshi is called a Vaku."

He waved his hand. "We know that one already. I mean a word for a human who wants to . . ." He frowned, obviously trying to dredge up one of the slang words for sex we'd catalogued on previous nights.

I cut him off before he could come up with anything. "I know what you mean. And yes, we have a word for it. It's just not that flattering. It's called ice-fishing. Because of your cooler body temperatures. And because we don't read your facial expressions very well, so we think of you as emotionally cold. Oh, and before you ask, we don't have a word for a human who actually sleeps with your people yet, because it's only happened once. That we know of, anyway."

"Eyvri's embarrassed," Khiva said gleefully. "Look, she's the color of a kina fruit."

Even if I hadn't seen kina trees laden with crimson fruit in the hydroponics bay on Arkhati, I would have known from the heat in my face how deeply I was blushing. Wishing Hathan weren't in the room, I tried to deflect the attention from myself. "So what about you guys? Do you have a word for a Vardeshi who's into humans?"

They exchanged considering looks. "Not really," Ziral said.

"Not yet," Zey corrected. "I bet we'll have one soon. It's rare, but it's not that rare."

"It's a lonely universe," I said, wondering if Reyna would recognize her own words. Glancing her way, I thought I saw the shadow of a smile.

Equally well attended, if less salacious in its content, was the other class Reyna suggested. This one, which I thought of as "topics in Earth studies," consisted of a brief lecture followed by questions. My crewmates suggested the lecture topics. We had talked about food (at Ahnir's request) and fashion (at Khiva's) and a few other subjects before Reyna herself suggested a lecture on geography. On arriving at the lounge that night, I was startled to see the entire crew expectantly assembled.

"Of course everyone came," Zey said afterward, in the tone of one stating the obvious. "We have three weeks of leave on Earth coming up, and nobody has any idea where to go."

I immediately began an extended series on the many and varied tourist destinations of Earth. It was surprising and fascinating to see which places caught my crewmates' interest. I was reasonably sure that Ziral and Ahnir would be spending their leave lying on a tropical beach somewhere, while Daskar and Sohra seemed inclined toward India. I did an hour on Japan for Saresh, and one on New York and Los Angeles for Zey. "You're just trying to get your acting career started," I teased him.

"Obviously," he agreed. "If I'm going to star in a Vardrama, I have to be—what do you call it? Discovered."

As I fielded my crewmates' questions about climate and etiquette and custom, I had to admit that the role reversal was enjoyable. For once, I was dispensing knowledge rather than receiving it. I savored those conversations almost as much as I had savored the preceding discussions of the Vardeshi worlds. It helped that geography was a safe subject. I could describe the natural beauty of my home with undiluted pride. How my fellow humans would represent themselves to our visitors—how, for that matter, they were already representing themselves to the hundred Vardeshi stationed at various points around the globe—was another question, but I didn't allow my thoughts to linger on it. It was pointless to worry about something so entirely beyond my control. I couldn't curate all of humanity for Vardeshi consumption. And if, as Reyna asserted, the alliance was going to go forward, it was probably better that they know as early as possible what they were signing on for. I hoped that they could forgive us for a little ignorance and bigotry. It didn't seem like too much to ask. After all, I had forgiven them for Vekesh.

It didn't escape my notice that when my crewmates and I inventoried the changes that had taken place since the launch of the *Ascendant,* for the most part we were talking about Reyna. Her impact on our lives was instantly visible. For me, there were the classes and the readings and the tactful but persistent attempts to win me away from the Fleet. For the others, there were the ranshai practices and the night-duty shifts and the room inspections. Hers was the voice we heard at morning and evening briefings. As for Hathan in his new role as khavi, his touch on the reins was either remarkably light or invisible to me. I thought he must be deliberately holding back to see how Reyna integrated into the life of the ship. I watched for signs of tension between them, but saw none. If they had disagreements, they settled them in private. I had to admire their professionalism, even while I wished it were a little less airtight.

They were constantly together. I knew it was only a function of their roles—Hathan and Vekesh had been equally inseparable—but I was ferociously jealous. I couldn't help it, even while I knew it was absurd. I never felt more out of place or more ploddingly human than when I watched the two of them at work, his gray head and her dark one bent together over one of their flexscreens. They were so perfectly suited, those two slim upright figures, two inscrutable faces, two un-inflected voices. During briefings I forced myself to stare at each of their right hands, reminding myself of the significance of the gold sigil. They were engaged. To other people. Just because they looked ideally matched to me didn't mean they actually were.

And what did I know about what constituted a good match among the Vardeshi, anyway? Sohra was the only one who had ever talked to me about her fiancé. The rest of them seemed to glide along in the calm certainty that someone else who had been judged tolerably compatible was out there as well, going through the round of his or her own days, looking ahead without visible anticipation to the day when they would eventually be united for life. To me it was impossibly foreign. No—the correct word was the one I had sidestepped ever since I realized how profound a hold the Vardeshi had on me. It was alien. Hathan and Reyna weren't flirting. They weren't falling in love. The thought probably never even crossed either of their minds. They didn't look for perfect compatibility, as I did, in the serendipitous crossing of paths that occurred in a random universe. Their minds simply didn't work that way.

Mine did. And while Hathan and I weren't flirting either, the part of me that kept tabs on whatever connection existed between us was convinced that it was slowly strengthening. I was still hesitant to call it friendship. He never sought me out, and I continued to treat him with the same bright cool impersonal courtesy I had drawn around myself like a shell when I first recognized my true feelings for him. Still, the tentative sharings of culture we had begun on Arkhati had laid the groundwork for more of the same. I gave silent thanks to Reyna for her insistence on the Earth culture lectures, as they bore unexpected fruit. During the final lecture of the travel series, Hathan expressed interest in exploring the mountain ranges of Earth. I lost no time in requesting electronic versions of a few different hiking guides and trail maps from home. Wary of betraying myself, I mentioned to him in an offhand manner that the documents had arrived and that he might want to look them over.

"Let's look at them together," he said at once. "Without your help, they won't mean much more to me than our star charts do to you."

I thought that was overstating things a little, but I wasn't about to pass up the invitation. The evening we spent alone in the lounge, mapping out possible routes and trading backpacking stories from my college days and his Institute training, was one of the most precious of the journey for me. It was made inexpressibly sweeter by the fantasy it allowed me to entertain of our one day taking such a trip together. I knew it could only be a fantasy. I wasn't about to invite myself along on his vacation, and despite my best efforts to subtly sway him toward spending at least some of it in my native New England, where we might plausibly run into each other, I had the distinct impression that he was leaning toward Patagonia.

Two of the three months that separated Arkhati from Vardesh Prime passed with astonishing speed. My life on the *Ascendant* was full and rewarding. My novi duties were second nature now. The afternoon readings were still frustratingly difficult, but I was conscious of making steady, incremental progress under Reyna's tutelage. I was no closer to understanding Vardeshi propulsion or navigation than I had ever been, but I had now read nearly a full chapter of the introductory Fleet textbook, and I knew a little about the first tentative forays of the Vardeshi beyond their homeworld's atmosphere. The evening English and culture lectures were an undeniable success.

And, always, there was Hathan. In the inevitable way of travelers sharing tight quarters, we were in constant proximity, close without being close. On a ship built for fifteen, I was never more than a few minutes away from the sound of his voice. There were briefings and officers' dinners and ranshai practices and chance corridor passings to look forward to. And there was the knowledge of months of such encounters still ahead. And, drawing ever closer, Vardesh Prime. Already in my dreams I walked among the glass spires of Khezendri or the burnished forests of Nasthav Province. At the final evening briefing of each week, I waited impatiently for the moment when Hathan would call up the navigation chart with the blue triangle labeled "Prime" and the blinking white pinpoint marking the *Ascendant*'s current position. Every week, the two were fractionally closer together. I had crossed the darkness to find a new world, and I was almost there.

As I had done once before, I allowed myself to drift into a sense of complacency. And once again I discovered the futility—or, worse, hubris—of believing that my life among the Vardeshi could ever be predictable. We were just under a month out from Vardesh Prime when it happened. The day in question began in utterly prosaic fashion. It had been Zey's turn to brew the morning senek. Arriving just prior to the start of the briefing, I settled myself on my stool and logged into the tabletop display. Seeing no new messages worthy of note, I pulled up the agenda for the briefing and scanned it. Suvi Ekhran was listed as the first to speak. As she began her report on the night-duty rotation, I stifled a yawn. The fivethirty workouts didn't seem to be getting any easier, and as I was scheduled to serve at officers' dinner that night, it was going to be a very long day. Luckily, I had the next day free. Knowing I should be paying attention, I dragged my thoughts back to the present.

"If you're planning to trade night-duty shifts," Reyna was

saying, "it's essential that you inform me so that the change can be listed on the official roster. In an emergency, we could lose valuable time contacting the wrong—"

"What's this?" said Saresh.

I glanced at him in surprise. I couldn't recall ever hearing him interrupt anyone before, and certainly not in the middle of an official report. He was frowning down at the senek cup in his hand. I saw that the silver senek pot was still at his elbow. He hadn't passed it on yet.

Zey and I looked at each other blankly. Both of us had prepared senek so many times the process had long since become automatic. I didn't think anyone had voiced a complaint since the era of Khavi Vekesh, and even then, the offender had typically been me, not Zey.

"Is there something wrong with the senek?" he asked.

Saresh raised an eyebrow. "Is that what you call this?"

Zey blinked. "I—"

"This isn't senek," Saresh said, slowly and clearly. "This is trash."

By this time everyone in the room was watching the exchange in appalled fascination. Out of the corner of my eye I saw Hathan, who as khavi had been the first to serve himself, pick up his own cup and taste the liquid within. He set the cup down slowly. He and Reyna exchanged a look.

"I—I'll make it again," Zey stammered.

"Don't bother. The next batch will be trash as well, just like everything else you touch."

"Hadazi," Reyna said quietly.

Saresh didn't even look at her. He reached out and swept the cup, saucer, tray, and senek vessel off the table and onto the floor. There was a tinkling sound as the crockery shattered. "There. More trash for you to clean up. That's all you're good for anyway. I thought you might be able to manage one simple task, but apparently even that's asking too much from a Blank."

Zey flinched. Saresh laughed. The sound was low and mocking and cruel. Hearing it, I shivered. Something was terribly wrong. It had to be, for him to make a sound like that.

Hathan leaned toward his elder brother. "What the hell is your problem?" he asked in a low voice that nonetheless carried clearly in the shocked silence.

"My problem?" Saresh said coldly. "He's the one with the problem. And I think we all know what it is. But since I seem to be the only one willing to name it, let me say it again. He's a Blank, and he's just as worthless as all the rest of them. It was better in the old days. They used to be strangled at birth, you know."

There was another horrified pause while everyone stared at Saresh. The first to speak was Ahnir. "Sigils of our fathers," he murmured, "today we are truly alone in the dark."

"What are you talking about?" Hathan said.

It was Daskar who answered. "Azdreth," she whispered.

I hadn't heard the word for months, but I knew it at once. It meant the madness that lay between the stars, the specter of irrational rage that haunted all spacefaring Vardeshi.

Somehow, against all probability, the *Ascendant* had been infected by the Flare.

PART TWO: AZDRETH

8

In an instant everyone in the room was on their feet. No one moved more swiftly than Reyna. She caught my arm in a steely grip and shoved me in front of her out the door to the hallway. I looked back over my shoulder in time to see Saresh hurl himself at Zey, his weight carrying them both to the floor. Hathan and Ahnir lunged after him. Then the door slid shut, concealing the ugliness within.

I tried unsuccessfully to pull free of Reyna's grip. "What's going on? Where are you taking me?"

"The galley. You need to pack food and water for three days as quickly as possible."

"Three days? Why?"

"The Echelon has a protocol for the Flare. All crew members are to be confined in separate areas of the ship with sufficient food and water for a three-day quarantine period. Two days is the longest a recorded outbreak has ever lasted, so if you can make it through three days, you should be safe." She keyed open the door to the mess hall and shoved me in. "You have two minutes. Go."

After the door closed, I stood immobile for a moment, locked in place by fear and disbelief. Was this really happening? Could it be possible that a terror that struck perhaps once in a generation had taken root on the *Ascendant?* I heard again that low, grating laugh from Saresh. That was the sound of madness. There could be no mistaking it. A wash of sick fear propelled me into action. I ran into the galley, grabbed an empty dish tray, and loaded it with random food items. Then I found a large water jug and filled it. When I stepped out through the door, Reyna grabbed the jug in one hand and my arm in the other and drew me down the corridor.

"This isn't the way to my quarters," I said.

"I'm not taking you to your quarters. It's too obvious. If anyone goes looking for you, that's the first place they'll look." I stumbled after her until we reached the maze of storage rooms on helix one. She opened a door seemingly at random. "In here. I'm going to lock you in. The door will be programmed with a time lock. It won't open for anyone for three full days. Turn off your flexscreen and leave it off. If anyone hails you through the ship's comm system, don't answer. From this moment forward, no one is trustworthy. Anyone could be infected. Including me. The only way to stay safe is to stay in this room. Alone. Good luck."

"This isn't really happening," I said, hoping for reassurance even while I knew there was none to be found. "Is it?"

"You know Saresh. You've seen his mind. You heard how he spoke to Zey just now. Was that the man you know?"

"No," I admitted. "But aren't there rumors about the Flare, every now and then? Don't they usually turn out to be false? Maybe Daskar was wrong."

"I hope so. But we need to act as if she wasn't." She turned to leave.

"Wait!" I cried. "You can't just leave me here."

"It's the safest place for you," she said firmly.

"But I want to help. My friends are still out there. Zey's out there."

Reyna turned back toward me and set her hands on my shoulders, her gaze boring into mine. "Eyvri, listen to me. There's nothing you can do for him now. You're not strong enough. If you go out there again, you'll only endanger yourself. I can't protect you and help the others at the same time."

"I can't just sit here," I insisted.

"You can't do anything else. Anyone could be infected by now. The theory is that the Flare is spread through physical contact. Every single member of the crew was at ranshai practice this morning. We have to assume everyone was exposed. The sooner you let me get back to the axis chamber, the sooner I can get control of the situation."

"But what if you can't? What if too many people are infected?"

"Then I'll die," she said, with a stark simplicity that snuffed out my remaining protests. "Along with everyone else. It wouldn't be the first time the Fleet or the Echelon has lost an entire crew to the Flare." She paused while I took that in. "But as long as you're in here, you'll be safe. That's my primary objective, and I haven't achieved it until I'm on the other side of that door. So are you going to keep arguing with me, or are you going to let me go?"

"Go," I said, knowing no other response was possible.

After the door closed behind her, I wheeled around, made my way to the far end of the storeroom, leaned against the wall, and slid slowly down it to the floor. There was a horrible familiarity to my predicament. In a storeroom just like this one on the *Pinion* I had waited for Hathan to find Saresh and ask him to perform the Listening, or to turn me over to Vekesh. I hadn't known then whether I could trust him. I knew now that I couldn't trust anyone. Whatever gruesome drama was unfolding beyond the locked door, my role in it was to wait passively until the quarantine period expired.

What scene would greet me when I emerged three interminable days from now? Images chased each other through my mind, each one more vivid and twisted than the last. What would Reyna see when she returned to the axis chamber? Had the others managed to subdue Saresh, or had the madness already claimed new victims? Even in the absolute best case, in which Reyna was able to execute the Echelon's protocol perfectly and place each member of the crew in isolation, the Flare had already set its stamp on us. I had seen one brother attack another. There was no way Saresh could take back the violence and cruelty he had shown Zey. Something precious had already been broken.

The silence pressed in on me like the stifling hush before a thunderstorm. I looked around my new prison. In one corner a few empty packing crates were stacked beside a hoverlifter. There was nothing else in the room, no furniture of any kind. It was going to be a miserable three days, physically as well as emotionally. I sat with my arms around my knees for a while, seeing in my mind the look on Zey's face when Saresh called him a Blank. Then I took out my flexscreen and set it down on the floor beside me. Reyna had told me to turn it off. Nothing good could come of leaving it on; any message I received in the quarantine period would most likely be a ruse meant to lure me out of hiding. I knew Reyna was right. I also knew that I wasn't going to follow her instructions. The flexscreen was my only conduit to the events taking place beyond the storeroom walls. I couldn't bring myself to turn it off. Any message, however troubling, would be preferable to silence. At the very least, if anyone messaged me, I would know I wasn't the only one left alive.

I sat for a long time in a kind of trance of horror, oblivious to the passage of time. The dark truth of what had befallen us was slowly sinking in. At first glance it had seemed—like the last days under Khavi Vekesh on the *Pinion*—too far-fetched to be credible. A sickness that drove its victims into homicidal rage? If such a thing had occurred on *Divided by Stars,* Zey and I would have dismissed it with laughter and derision. Yet this was real. I remembered Reyna's words: entire crews had been lost to the Flare. It might surface only once in a generation, but the Echelon took it seriously enough to have a detailed protocol in place. And the more I thought about it, the less impossible it seemed. I was no medical expert, but I could call to mind a handful of analogous diseases on Earth. Syphilis produced psychosis in its later stages. A better comparison was rabies, in which aggression was the mechanism that facilitated transmission. What distinguished the Flare was its seemingly instantaneous rate of infection. Even the most virulent pathogens known to humans had incubation periods of days, not hours. Certainly not minutes. Perhaps that was what made the Flare so terrifying: the idea of an illness that leapt from one host to another like fire in a summer forest. By the time the first symptoms were recognized, the damage was already done.

Were humans susceptible? I wondered. If so, then by dragging me down the corridor, Reyna had effectively exposed me. Surely that thought had occurred to her as well. She must have decided that the need to isolate me from the others outweighed the risk of infection. And as the minutes dragged past, I felt more and more certain that either I hadn't been infected, or the Flare didn't affect humans. I felt sad and frightened. I didn't feel angry or paranoid. I didn't want to claw the walls or howl like a caged animal. I didn't want to attack my crewmates. All I wanted, desperately, was for all of them to be safe.

Hours had passed, and I was growing cold and stiff on the metal floor, when my flexscreen chimed. I started. The signal indicated an incoming message, text only. I stared down at the little device like it was a venomous insect poised to strike. Instead of reaching for it, I brushed my fingers across the floor, opening an interface with the ship's computer. The time stamp told me only six hours had elapsed since Reyna locked me into the storeroom. It was too soon. Whatever message I had just received, it was nothing good.

Still avoiding the flexscreen, I got up and walked a few circuits of the storeroom to stretch my legs and warm up a little. There was no internal temperature control in the tiny chamber. I didn't think it was cool enough to present a hypothermia risk, but I was going to be chilled to the bone by the time I got out of here. I looked through the tray of food I had assembled in the galley, picked out a granola bar, and ate half of it. I contemplated the jug of water but didn't drink any. I already felt the need to visit the sanitation room, and there wasn't one. I decided to postpone that particular unpleasantness a little longer.

Having exhausted all the stalling tactics I could readily call to mind, I sat down cross-legged in front of the flexscreen again. With great reluctance I reached out and touched the edge of the screen with one fingertip. The orange letters that glimmered into visibility informed me that the message was from Zey. I took a deep, shaky breath. He was alive. It was more than I had known before. I forced myself to get up and walk away again.

I lasted another hour before curiosity drew me back to the flexscreen. Cradling it in both hands, I forced myself to confront the question: Beyond satisfying my morbid curiosity, what could I gain from reading the message? If Zey was infected, the content would be either disturbing or deliberately misleading. If he was genuinely in trouble and needed help, not that I had any way of distinguishing a real cry for assistance from a ploy, there was nothing I could do in any case. Reyna was right: set against even the weakest of my crewmates, I was hopelessly outmatched. If I stepped outside the confines of the storeroom, I would be putting my own life at risk to no purpose. And the alternative, to sit here and watch an unthinkable tragedy unfold via text message, would be a drawn-out and pointless form of self-torture. The most prudent course of action would be the one Reyna had advised in the first place: to turn off the flexscreen.

I wasn't entirely powerless though. I might not be able to hold my own in a fight, but there were things I could do without leaving the storeroom. I wasn't quite as inept at navigating Vardeshi computers as I had been when I arrived on the *Pinion* five months ago. I might be able to create a diversion of some kind. If there was any chance that I could offer Zey some kind of help, I owed it to him to try. In my place he would unhesitatingly have done the same.

I had made my decision, but even so, I felt deeply uneasy as I keyed in my code and read the waiting message. *Eyvri,* it said. *I know you're not allowed to tell me where you are. But are you safe?*

He didn't sound like someone in the grip of a hallucinatory rage. Still, I knew I had to be careful. *I'm safe,* I wrote back. *You?*

For now. I'm in an empty conference room on helix three. The next message gave the specific room designation. *I hope your hiding place is more comfortable than mine. I think the ahtziri would have stuck me in the galley freezer compartment if she thought she could get away with it.*

I'd grown accustomed to the nickname, but I found his use of it now somehow off-putting. *Give her a break,* I wrote. *She's just trying to keep us safe.*

Sorry. I'm a little punchy. Weird day.

Yeah. After I had sent the word, I stared down at it. It was perhaps the most utterly banal syllable to which I had ever given voice, electronically or otherwise. But the things I wanted to say to him needed to be said in person. He had been degraded and viciously attacked by his own brother. Now he was sitting, like I was, alone in a locked room, waiting for the tide of inexplicable anger to run its course. There was no way to distill my shocked sympathy into a string of characters on a screen.

After a brief silence I wrote, *Do you know who else is infected?*

I had scarcely pressed the "send" command when his reply arrived. *Hang on. Something's wrong.*

What? I sent back at once.

There was a long, ominous pause. Then he said, *I think someone's trying to force the door.*

And at that instant, with uncannily precise timing, the door to my own prison hissed open.

I leapt to my feet. The flexscreen slipped out of my fingers and clattered to the floor. The corridor outside was dark, and I cursed myself for my thoughtlessness in leaving the storeroom lights on. I couldn't see anything beyond the doorway. Hurriedly I turned off the light. Then I backed toward the corner of the storeroom, bent down beside my food tray, and picked up a steel canister of peanut butter, the only vaguely weaponlike object to hand. I crouched there for some moments longer, clutching my makeshift club and feeling absurdly primitive, while my eyes adjusted to the gloom.

Finally I was able to make out the section of hallway visible through the door. There was no one there. I went to the threshold, pausing to scoop up my flexscreen on the way, and tapped the control panel beside the door. Nothing happened. Cautiously I stepped out into the hallway. The doors on either side of mine were open too. A malfunction? I didn't think so. Zey had said someone was trying to force his door. Maybe whatever that person had done had caused every door on the ship to open simultaneously. Whatever the cause, it was clear that my safety had been compromised. Squatting in plain sight in front of an open door didn't strike me as a very good survival strategy. If nothing else, I should find a room with some furniture to hide behind. Or some better weapons.

I knew I had to move, and quickly. The question was where to go. If every door on the ship was open—as a quick glance up and down the corridor suggested they were—then I would be in danger no matter where I went. For whatever reason, Reyna's protocol had failed. I was equally likely to run into an infected crewmate on my way to the cargo holds or the conference rooms. At least there was a chance that I had an ally waiting on helix three. My choice was no longer one between action and inaction, but between trust and suspicion. My instincts told me to err on the side of trust. I activated my flexscreen again and scrolled through the chain of messages. It certainly sounded like Zey, and Zey in his right mind, at that. I decided to head for the room he had specified. I didn't have to go in. If the doors on helix three were open, I would hear the sounds of a struggle long before anyone there became aware of my presence. If the room was silent, I would assume that either it was a trap or I had arrived too late, and seek shelter elsewhere.

I disabled the sound on my flexscreen, went to slip it into my pocket, then hesitated. Should I call Reyna and tell her where I was going? Her mandate was to protect me. But we were more than seven hours into the outbreak. She herself might be infected. I decided the safest course was to keep silent for now. I turned in the direction of helix three and began to walk. After a few steps I stopped, took off my shoes, set them down in a recess where no one was likely to trip over them, and went on nearly silently in my socks.

At the first junction, I ducked into the secondary passageways. The *Ascendant* had these, just like the *Pinion,* and I had lost no time in committing their twists and turns to memory. As I made my way through the ship, pausing every so often to listen for voices or footsteps, I was forcibly reminded of my similar flight through the *Pinion* in search of Saresh. At least on that day, terrible though it had been, I had feared only imprisonment and a quick clean death. I hadn't been afraid my companions would tear me apart with their bare hands.

I reached the entrance to helix three unscathed. Apart from the airlocks, I had not seen a single closed door. I knew the general location of the room Zey had named, and I got as close to it as I could via the secondary tunnels, but I would have to navigate a final open stretch of main corridor to approach the room itself. The thought of such total exposure was unsettling. Before moving out into the open, I hefted the peanut-butter canister thoughtfully, weighing it in my hand. Something said by Davnah, my Krav-Maga instructor, during my two brief weeks of training came back to me: a weapon in the hands of an unskilled fighter was more likely to be a liability than an advantage. The probability of my successfully landing a blow on one of my crewmates was minimal, while the probability of someone ripping it out of my grasp and clubbing me to death with it was exceedingly high. I bent down and placed the canister carefully on the floor. Then I took a deep breath and moved forward into the open.

I'd overshot a little and had to backtrack to find the correct room. I approached it slowly. When I'd gotten as close as I could without being visible from within, I stopped and listened. Silence. No voices, no sounds of a struggle. Zey was gone—if he had ever been here. Fear sent a cold prickle down my spine. I checked my flexscreen: no recent messages. Without hesitation, I turned and began to retrace my steps to the entrance to the secondary passages. Just before I reached it, my flexscreen buzzed. I nearly dropped it in surprise. The display showed an incoming call from Reyna. I stepped into the darkened room nearest me, picked my way through the workstations and stools until I was some distance away from the door, and answered the call in a whisper.

"I'm on helix one," said Reyna. "Your room is empty. Where are you?"

Her tone of crisp command, together with my mounting apprehension, compelled me to tell her the truth. "On helix three. Zey messaged me. I think he's in trouble."

"Zey is asleep in his quarters. I checked on him on my way to you." Her voice sharpened. "Eyvri, get out of there. Meet me on helix two near engineering."

I pocketed the flexscreen and took one step toward the door. The lights snapped on. Blinking in the sudden brightness, I saw, standing in the doorway, the one person above all others I would have given anything to avoid.

His gaze swept the room and stopped on me. Something altered in his expression. There was a trace of a smile, but it didn't reach his eyes. He came fully into the room, paused, and tapped a command into the door panel. The door hissed shut. Two facts struck me at once. The first was that he had been able to close the door, while the panel in my storeroom hadn't activated in response to my touch. Did he have some kind of special code or override? The second fact was that we were now alone in a room together. There was no doubt in my mind that he had locked the door.

He moved toward me, and my sense of wrongness intensified. After all those days and weeks and months of working so closely with him, I knew his presence, the way a room felt with him in it. This was instantly different. His stride was normally brisk and purposeful, but his pace now was languid, almost a saunter. I reached into my pocket and took out my flexscreen. As casually as possible, I began to key in my code.

"What are you doing?" Hathan asked. His voice was level and quiet, no edge to it yet, nothing amiss other than the fact of the question itself.

Never quick to improvise, I searched for a plausible lie. "Texting Zey. I think . . . he might be in trouble." My voice shook. I didn't look up from my flexscreen, but my hands were shaking too, and he had closed the gap between us and drawn the device smoothly out of my hand before I had accessed the messaging menu.

"I'll do it," he said.

"Thanks." I swallowed, staring at my flexscreen in his hand. He was doing something, typing, or appearing to type, with one hand. I took a slow step backward, then another, putting the nearest table between us.

"Done," he said, and set the flexscreen down on the table,

well out of my reach.

We were both still for a moment. I could feel his eyes on me, but I couldn't return the look. Instead, I glanced at the door. I couldn't stop myself. I needed to get out of here. Even without a message from me, Reyna would know when I failed to appear at engineering that something had gone wrong. She would come looking for me. I had told her I was on helix three. But she had no idea which room I was in. And even if she stumbled onto the closed door and understood its meaning, assuming my conjecture was right and Hathan had found a way to override the door controls, there was nothing she or anyone else could do to help me from outside. I was on my own.

He followed my look, and I saw it again, that glint of chilly amusement. "Something wrong?"

"No."

He frowned slightly. "What did you say?"

I hesitated. "I said no."

"That's what I thought." He studied my face. "You've always had it. Ever since you arrived. This . . . insubordinate air." His tone was still light, but I could feel the anger gathering behind it.

"I don't know what you mean," I said.

"Sir."

"What?"

"I don't know what you mean . . . sir." He spoke slowly, drawing the words out. "I can never tell how much is deafness, with you humans, and how much is just stupidity. What do you think?"

"What?" I cringed at the word as it left my mouth, but I couldn't contain it.

He placed his hands on the table and leaned forward. "Are

you deaf? Or are you stupid?"

"Neither. Sir."

He raised his eyebrows. "Deaf, stupid, and a liar, then."

I said nothing.

"We made the right choice the first time," he went on, as if to himself. "We never should have gone back to Earth. We should have left you to tear yourselves apart like the savages you are."

"Yeah, we're clearly the savages in this scenario."

I knew the words were reckless, but I couldn't keep them in. A tiny flame of anger had flickered to life inside me, deep down, below the terror. This was ridiculous. It was a ludicrous, tragic waste, what was going to happen in this room, very soon now, as I knew with total certainty. And it was my own fault. What could have possessed me to ignore Reyna's directions? I had fallen into what I now recognized as an utterly transparent trap. I had made a stupid mistake, and I was going to pay for it with my life.

"I don't know from where you get the presumption to speak to me like that," Hathan said, each word falling sharp and clear, like needles onto a tile floor. "Your kind are worthless. We should have ground you into dust when we had the chance. We should have taken the knife to every last one of you. Instead, here you are, breathing my air, drinking my water, eating my food. Contaminating everything you touch. Do you have any idea how much we despise you? How miserable it is to be in the same room with you? Your smell. The sound of your voice. It makes me sick to look at you. Did you know that?"

"No," I whispered.

"Don't speak to me!" he shouted. He caught the edge of the table and threw it sideways into the wall. My flexscreen smashed against the wall and shattered, cascading onto the floor in glittering shards.

I started to cry.

"Did you think we wanted you here?" he said, quiet again. "Did you think you could work with us as an equal? As a friend? Is that really what you believed?"

I crossed my arms tightly across my chest, hands wrapped around my elbows, trying to hold myself together.

"Look at me." His voice was soft.

I stared at the ground.

"Look at me," he ordered again.

I looked up at him.

"Are you afraid of me now?" he said.

I nodded.

"Say it."

"Yes," I whispered.

"You're a slow learner. Yes, what?"

"Yes, sir." My throat closed on the words. I could barely get them out. If I could have saved myself at that moment by shouting for help, I wouldn't have been able to do it.

"You should have been afraid of me all along," he said. "Because this is who I was all along. Under the surface. I never wanted you here. Wearing our uniform. Speaking our language—or trying to. I should have gotten rid of you any way I could. Vekesh had the right idea. If he'd been a better shot, I wouldn't have to finish his work for him. But better late than never."

"Stop it," I said.

He went still. "What?"

"Stop it." My voice was a thread of sound, and it broke on the second word, but I pushed on. "Please. Please stop and think about what you're doing. This is not who you are.

The Hathan I know—"

There was a crack and a blinding flash of white, and I fell backward over a chair I hadn't known was there. I hit the floor hard, and wrong; one of my wrists bent sickeningly backward. The right side of my face was numb. I had been looking directly at him, and I hadn't seen the blow coming. My vision was blurred, and there was a deafening roar in my ears. I tried to breathe, tried to gather myself back together. My face and my wrist already hurt more than anything in my life had ever hurt. I got my hands and knees under me and started to crawl forward, with no orientation other than the drive to escape. Where was he? I didn't dare look around. My sight was a dark tunnel with a queasily bright patch of clarity at the center. My hands found a wall, and I dragged myself upward. Somehow I was next to the door. I fumbled for the control panel.

His hand closed on my wrist—the injured one—and twisted hard. I screamed. The spike of pain forced me to my knees, and I would have fallen if he hadn't still been holding onto my wrist. Nausea and terror rolled over me in black waves.

The pressure on my wrist relented, enough for me to swim back up toward awareness, but he hadn't released me. "Can you hear me?" he asked quietly.

I nodded. My breath sobbed in my throat.

"Don't ever use my name again," he said. "Names are for equals. You are not my equal. Do you understand?"

I nodded again.

Hathan said, "No. You don't. But you will. I'm going to make an example of you for the rest of them. Get up." He waited while I got unsteadily to my feet, my wrist and face still throbbing. Then he reached out with his free hand and unlocked the door. "Let's go." He shoved me forward through the doorway, one hand between my shoulder blades, the other hand still bending my wrist up behind me. "Where are the others?"

"I—"

He twisted my wrist again.

"Engineering," I whispered, when the darkness had receded again.

He shoved me ahead of him down the corridor.

We had gone only a few steps when the overhead lights blinked on. There was a rush of movement on each side of us. I heard him cry out. He pulled on my wrist, dragging me backward a step, then abruptly let go. Not knowing what was happening, I stumbled over to the wall, slid down it, and sat with my knees pulled up to my chest, cradling my injured wrist. I tried to concentrate on breathing in and out. Gradually the racing of my heart subsided. The roaring in my ears began to fade. I put my head down on my knees and closed my eyes. It was over. I had endured it, and it was over.

9

After a time I heard two sets of approaching footsteps. I didn't lift my head. The footsteps stopped beside me. I felt a gentle touch on my arm. "Eyvri?" said a voice. I looked up in surprise. It was Sohra. Ahnir was standing beside her.

"Where's Reyna?" I asked. Moisture tickled my upper lip. I dabbed at it with the back of my wrist and saw with a sense of unreality that there was blood on my sleeve. My nose was bleeding.

"Trying to find someplace to put Hathan," Ahnir said grimly. "Not an easy task when none of the doors will close. She sent us to help you. I'm trained as a medic. Do you have an emergency kit in your quarters?"

I nodded. "Under my bed." Slowly I processed what he was saying. "Where's Daskar?"

"She's unconscious in the clinic. We think she may have felt the symptoms of the Flare coming on and dosed herself with a sedative."

"Come on," Sohra said. "Let's get you back to your quarters."

I let her help me to my feet. "Is anyone else hurt?"

Ahnir said, "Zey has some bruising, but nothing serious. Ziral has a broken nose and, I think, some fractured ribs."

"How?"

"Khiva. Fortunately, Ziral is the better fighter, even when taken by surprise. Khiva herself has a mild concussion and some bruises."

"Who else is infected?"

"Only the three," Sohra said. "It looks like it may have run its course. But just to be safe, we're working in pairs as much as possible, and checking in with Suvi Ekhran every twenty minutes."

"Run its course," I repeated. "Already?"

"There are only ten of us," Ahnir said. "It's possible that there's simply no one left to infect."

We had reached my quarters. I was sure there were more questions I ought to be asking, but I was too tired to think of them. I went inside—the door, of course, was open—and sat down on the edge of the bed. Ahnir followed me in, knelt down beside the bed, and drew the medical kit from underneath it. "May I perform an examination?" he asked. I nodded. His fingers were cool on my skin as he traced the line of my jaw and cheekbone, then the orbit of my eye all the way to my eyebrow. After the manual examination, he performed a scan using an instrument I didn't recognize. Studying the readout, he nodded as if it confirmed his expectations. "I don't think anything's broken. The bones are intact, and your eye is fine. I'm afraid the bruising will only get worse though. Are you hurt anywhere else?"

"My wrist."

"Let me see." Exhibiting a surprising gentleness of touch, he examined my wrist, concluding that it was sprained, not

broken. "Obviously we'll have Daskar perform her own examination as soon as possible," he assured me. He applied a
Vardeshi cooling salve, then produced a silver brace, a more
delicate version of the one I had seen Saresh wear, which he
fastened around my wrist. He made a few careful adjustments
to the fit before touching a control. Instantly the brace tightened into place, matching the contours of my hand and arm
as if it had been crafted for me. I moved my right hand ex-
perimentally. The brace was so light I could scarcely feel it,
but it immobilized my wrist. Ahnir watched me flex my fingers and nodded in satisfaction. "It looks like it's fitted
correctly. Are there any other injuries I should be aware of?"

I shook my head.

"In that case, you should try to get some rest. I'll go get
your food and water from the storeroom. Do you remember
which room it was?"

"Reyna knows," I whispered. He nodded and left. When
he had gone, I picked through the open medical kit until I
found the packets of ibuprofen. I took out two of the little
envelopes, tore them open with my teeth, and swallowed the
pills. Then I leaned back against the wall and closed my eyes.
Sohra's and Vethna's voices drifted in from the corridor.
From what I could hear, they were cobbling together a makeshift door from a spare deck plate and some magnetic bolts.
I was glad they were there. The very ordinariness of their dialogue was a comfort. I could almost pretend that things were
as they should be, that my world hadn't tilted and slid sideways into some dark parody of itself the moment Hathan
took the flexscreen out of my hand.

I sat without moving until Ahnir returned. I was cold, but
I was too tired to reach for a blanket. Finally I heard the thud
and scrape of heavy objects being set down. I opened my

eyes. Ahnir finished arranging the food tray and water jug on my table and straightened up. "All right, I think you should have everything you need for now. Sohra, how's the door coming?"

"It's done," she said, stepping into the room. "I'm sorry, Eyvri, it's not a very elegant fix. We're effectively locking you in again. You'll have to call one of us to remove the bolts when you want to come out. But at least you'll be safe. Suvi Ekhran wants you to stay in isolation for another day anyway."

"One day," I said faintly.

Ahnir said, "If no one else is showing symptoms by tomorrow night, she's going to call off the quarantine."

I nodded.

"Get some sleep," Sohra said. "Let us know if you need anything."

Not until they had left and I heard the metallic click of the magnetic bolts snapping into place did I realize that, once again, I had been left without a flexscreen. It didn't matter. As far as I knew, the *Ascendant*'s communications network was intact. I would have no difficulty calling for help if I needed it. I closed my eyes again. The throbbing in my face and wrist eased by degrees as the painkillers took effect. I realized I was shivering. With a great effort I roused myself to increase the temperature in my room using the controls on the bedside panel. Then I turned off the overhead light, lowered myself down onto my bunk, and pulled the blankets up. I was asleep in an instant.

Some time later I lurched awake in a dizzying surge of panic, certain I had heard his voice in the dark. I fumbled for the light control with fingers made clumsy by panic. When the light came on, I sat tensely in the bed, listening to the stillness with its underlying hum of distant propulsion systems. At length I forced myself to climb out onto the chilly floor. Heart hammering in my chest, I checked the closet and the sanitation room. Then I went to the doorway and pushed on the deck plate. It was still secure. I got back into bed, but I couldn't bring myself to turn off the light again, so I just sat in the warm nest of blankets until I finally relaxed enough to doze upright against the wall in full simulated daylight.

* * *

Waking again, hours later, I reached instinctively for a flexscreen that wasn't there. I fumbled along the wall shelf where it normally sat until my sleep-dulled mind presented an image of it in fragments on the conference-room floor. I activated the wall display next to the bed. It was almost noon. There were no messages for me. I pushed away the blankets and climbed out of bed. My right arm ached fiercely all the way up to the shoulder, and my neck was so stiff I could barely turn my head. The pain in my temple had returned in full force. I fumbled through the medical kit, which I had shifted onto the floor before collapsing the previous night, for more ibuprofen. Pills in hand, I shuffled into the sanitation room for a glass of water.

The sight of my reflection stopped me. The lighting in the sanitation room was harsh and unflattering, designed to complement blue-toned Vardeshi skin. It had never done me any favors. It hid nothing now. I looked pale and tired. My hair was lank, my slept-in uniform disheveled, the bruising around my eye grotesque. Ahnir had said it would get worse, but how was that possible? I felt sick at the sight of it. Before turning away, I sent one quick piercing look into the eyes of my reflection. She looked fierce and sad, and somehow defeated, in a way she hadn't before. I looked away quickly.

I began running hot water into the basin. At that instant I would have given anything for a private shower like the one in Kylie's suite on Arkhati. I knew showering was out of the question until the quarantine expired, so I cleaned myself up as best I could, given the constraints of my sprained wrist and the tiny sanitation-room basin. Then I went to examine the contents of my food tray. I had slept through the early stages of hunger, and now that I was fully awake, my body was demanding food with a panicked, slightly nauseous urgency. I added a hot meal to the list of comforts that would have to be deferred until I regained access to the rest of the ship. Even a hot drink would have gone a long way toward restoring my sense of well-being. As it was, I had to settle for granola, dried fruit, and powdered milk. I felt a little better after I'd eaten. I found my laptop and hard drive, arranged them on a stool next to the bed, scrolled through Kylie's sitcoms, and selected an episode so familiar I could practically recite it. Then I lay down on my bunk again.

For the rest of that day I alternately slept and watched episodes of old sitcoms. When I was hungry, I ate something from the tray. When the ache in my wrist and face reasserted itself, I took more painkillers. Addressing each immediate physical need as it arose cost me all the energy I could muster. I didn't think about the Flare. I couldn't. I knew the memory was there, every word and glance and blow preserved as if in amber, but my waking mind shied away from it. My quarters were a safe haven. I had food and privacy and a soft bed, and for the moment, those were the only things I needed. About the fate of the others I felt only occasional muted stirrings of curiosity. I forced myself to check my messages every couple of hours and sighed in relief each time the screen displayed an empty inbox. I was grateful for the silence from my crewmates. It demanded nothing from me. I didn't have to think about how I was going to face them again. I didn't have to think about anything. I lay in a cocoon of warm numbing quiet, blessedly free from thought.

At ten o'clock that night I finally received a message from Reyna. It was brief and general, directed at the entire crew, and said only that the quarantine would be lifted at midnight and that there would be a mandatory meeting in the mess hall tomorrow morning. I checked the time, saw that there were still a couple of hours left before the quarantine was due to lift, put my head down again, and went back to sleep.

I woke to a series of clunks, which I placed after the first startled moment as the sound of magnetic bolts hitting the floor one by one. Someone was dismantling my improvised door. I went over to see who it was, hoping for a friendly face. To my profound disappointment, the deck plate shifted aside to reveal Vethna standing outside my quarters. "Quarantine's over," he said over his shoulder as he eased the heavy plate to the floor and leaned it against the wall. Straightening, he took a look at my face and winced. "You look like shit. Hathan must have one hell of a backhand."

I waved at the deck plate. "How am I supposed to close my door now?"

"The controls are working again."

"Perfect." I closed the door in his face. Then I stood in front of it and trembled for a long time. Finally I went to look for clean pajamas and a towel. I wanted to curl up on my bunk and stay there forever, but I wanted a shower more. I knew, too, that the longer I delayed my first departure from my quarters, the harder it would be. I collected the things I needed and put them in a bag to keep my left hand free for keying in door codes. Quickly, before I could reconsider, I opened my door and ventured out into the hallway.

Vethna and the deck plate had both vanished. The residential corridor was empty, but as I stood in front of the shower room, checking to see that it was unoccupied, I saw Reyna approaching from the direction of helix three. Her quick assessing look moved from my bruised face and braced wrist to the bag slung over my shoulder. "Take your time in the shower," she said. "The water restriction's been lifted temporarily. You saw the message about tomorrow's meeting?"

I nodded.

"Will you attend it?"

I didn't want to commit myself, so I said, "I'll try."

"Good. I hope you can get some rest tonight. The worst is over."

She turned to leave, but I called her back. "Reyna?"

"Yes?"

"Why . . ." I tried to meet her eyes, but my gaze faltered before the directness of hers. "Why did you say that? About the shower?"

"What did I say?"

"That I should take my time."

She looked faintly surprised. "Humans enjoy their cleansing rites, don't they? I heard about your ritual bath on Arkhati. I thought you'd be glad to hear the water restriction had been removed. Everyone else was."

"Oh."

"What did you think I meant?"

"Nothing. I don't know." Quickly I keyed in the code and stepped into the shower room, afraid that if I stood there any longer, my thin veneer of self-control might crack under her scrutiny.

Safely inside the shower room, I turned on the water, methodically stripped off my uniform and underwear, and dropped them on the floor. I was shivering as I stepped under the cascade. Even with the water as hot as it would go, it was several minutes before the shivering stopped. I soaped my hair and rinsed it awkwardly, my right wrist stiff in the brace. I scrubbed my body until my skin was raw and pink. *Your smell,* he had said. Did I still smell like a human, standing here under the rush of water? When all the sweat and dust had been washed away, was the contamination still there? I pressed my forehead against the cool wall of the shower and finally, belatedly, let the tears come.

When I had cried myself out, I turned the shower off, dried myself, and put on my pajamas. I went back to my quarters, glad to find the hallway once again deserted. I lay down on my bunk and turned off the lights, hoping for the oblivion of sleep.

It had obliged me earlier. It eluded me now. It was as though Reyna's harmless comment about the shower had broken a spell. I lay wide-eyed in the dark, racked by wave after wave of guilt and mortification. It suddenly became clear to me that everything that had happened over the last two days had been my fault. I had been the one who pushed for keeping the *Pinion*'s crew together. I had singlehandedly brought us all here, to the *Ascendant,* and to a place and a time where we could be exposed to the Flare. I was to blame for every injury my companions had suffered, from Ziral's broken bones to Zey's bruises and the more insidious damage to his trust in Saresh. Seen in hindsight, the choices I had made since the beginning of the Flare unspooled in a clear chain of errors. I had ignored Reyna's directions, left my flexscreen active, trusted a message I should have known was false. With the most minimal cajoling, I had put myself squarely in Hathan's path. I had placed myself in danger as surely as if I had loaded a gun and set it in his hand. He wasn't to blame for what had happened in the conference room. He had been crazed, delirious, whereas I had been fully capable of thinking clearly. I just hadn't done it.

No wonder he despised me.

There was no question in my mind that he did. I thought back to the morning months ago when I first questioned Daskar about the nature of the Flare. She had described it as temporary insanity, but that wasn't right. It wasn't madness. It was sheer uncompromising honesty. Hathan had turned on me yesterday, not in an explosion of spontaneous violence, but in an outpouring of pent-up rage and loathing. I had heard the venom in his words. What the disease did, I saw now, was strip away the inhibitions of those it infected until only the raw truth was left. It had shattered Hathan's reserve like a hammer on glass. I cringed now at the thought of the fabricated courtesy he had shown me for so many months. He had feigned respect, even curiosity, so artfully that I might never have known it was all an act. Only once, on that horrible day when I had entreated his help against Vekesh and been flatly rejected, had I caught a glimpse of the contempt underlying his cool politeness. I had thought then that his behavior was an aberration. Now I knew the truth: he had been stung by anger and worry about Zey into disclosing his real feelings. He hated me. He had all along.

In an odd way, I was almost grateful for the Flare. Without it, I might have gone on unwittingly inflicting my humanity on him for months. That wouldn't happen now. I wouldn't let it. I would board the first Echelon ship that would take me, on Vardesh Prime, if not before. The solitude that had seemed so repellent before seemed positively enticing now. I would welcome the frosty silence of an Echelon crew. If nothing else, it was honest.

My decision made, I rearranged my position in the blankets and sank into a fitful sleep. An hour or two later, my alarm jarred me awake. I had been dreaming I was locked in the conference room with Hathan again. I rose to prepare for the meeting with his caustic words still echoing in my ears. In the sanitation room I splashed cold water on my face, then attempted to neaten my sleep-tousled hair, hampered as before by the wrist brace. I tried not to look at the bruising around my eye. Ahnir had been right. It was worse. When I had made myself as presentable as I could, I went to my closet and stood staring at the clean uniform hanging inside for five excruciating minutes. Then I struggled out of my pajamas and into jeans and a sweatshirt.

I was among the last to arrive at the mess hall. As the door opened, I cast a quick look around, located Zey, then fixed my eyes on the floor again. I couldn't bring myself to look into my crewmates' faces. I was reasonably sure I knew what I would see there—shock, pity, revulsion—and I wanted no part of it. I particularly avoided looking toward Hathan, though I knew he was there, standing absolutely still beside the higher-ranking table. I could imagine, without having to look at it, the perfectly calibrated mix of remorse and concern in his expression. He could have saved himself the trouble. I'd seen behind the mask now, and I knew it for what it was.

I made my way over to Zey. He was sitting as far away from the higher-ranking table as he could get, at the end of an empty table, with a wall at his back. His arms were folded across his chest, his expression mutinous. On the table in front of him was a small ceramic pot, of the type used to brew senek for one or two people, and a single cup. That was an act of rebellion, I thought, albeit a small one. After what had happened the last time he'd made senek for the entire crew, I couldn't blame him for letting them fend for themselves this morning.

I sat down next to him and leaned my elbows on the table. Neither of us spoke for a little while. Then I asked, "How are you feeling?"

"Like a three-day-old khanat carcass," he said hoarsely. "But at least I don't look like one. Which is more than I can say for you."

I studied the dark bruises on his throat. "I don't know, I think we're kind of a matched set right now."

"We would be, if you were wearing your uniform. What happened, are yours all in the laundry or something?"

I didn't say anything.

"Eyvri?"

I stared down at the tabletop. I couldn't look at him.

"You're leaving, aren't you." It wasn't a question.

"I think I might have to," I said.

"Have you even—" he broke off as Reyna raised her voice to call the crew to attention. I was glad of the interruption. I didn't want to discuss my decision with Zey until it was official. I was afraid he'd find some way to talk me out of it.

Reyna commenced with a brief, dry summary of the events of the preceding three days. Eschewing a list of those afflicted by the Flare, presumably because no one needed reminding, she catalogued the injuries suffered by the crew. Almost no one had escaped unharmed. Saresh, Hathan, Khiva, and Ziral were all on the list, as was Vethna, who must have been hurt while attempting to subdue the others. I wondered who had taken Hathan down. Reyna, probably. I wasn't sure anyone else could have done it. Reduced to bare facts, our casualties sounded relatively minor: bruises, a few broken ribs, a sprained wrist. At the mention of my wrist, I flexed my hand in the brace, then stopped when I saw Zey looking at it.

As Reyna was speaking, I gathered my courage and lifted my eyes to examine each of my crewmates in turn. I had never seen them so visibly demoralized, not even after the revelation of Vekesh's treachery, although of course I had been unconscious in the clinic during the immediate aftermath of that incident. The mood in the room was one of mingled weariness and tension. Ahnir was resting his head on his hand. Ziral's fingers clenched her water cup so tightly her knuckles were white. I looked at Reyna and was comforted by her air of cool assurance. She might have been running a perfectly routine morning briefing for all the evidence she gave of stress or fatigue. Another point to the Echelon, I thought: their officers were tough. My eyes strayed to Saresh, beside her, who was staring down at his interlaced fingers. As if he felt my glance, he lifted his eyes to meet mine. Instantly I recoiled, unable to hold his gaze, stunned by the depth of pain and sorrow I saw there.

"For the present, you should continue directing your medical inquiries to Rhevi Ahnir," Reyna was saying. "Rhevi Daskar has yet to regain consciousness. She appears to have self-administered a sedative at the start of the outbreak, and it's possible she may have misjudged the dose. Rhevi Ahnir is monitoring her condition."

I scanned the room for Sohra and realized that she was missing. "How's Sohra doing?" I whispered.

Zey shook his head. "She hasn't the left the clinic since

the quarantine ended."

I felt a stab of guilt at my own self-absorption. I had spent the last two days utterly blinded by my own problems while a friend's mother hovered between life and death. For the first time it struck me how uniquely devastating the Flare must be for a spacefaring culture that preferentially shipped families out together. And then that thought was gone, scattered with all the others like leaves before the wind, because Reyna had fallen silent, and Hathan was speaking.

Still unwilling to look at his face, I inspected a frayed spot on my sweatshirt cuff while I listened. I hadn't known what I would feel upon hearing his voice. My first reaction was relief. He was himself again. There could be no mistaking it. I thought I could detect a certain brittle quality to his composure, but the icy derision of two days ago was gone without a trace. This was the man who had sat beside me in the lounge last week and talked about losing a glove on a midwinter survival exercise and spending three days with a sock taped to his hand. He had made me laugh. Why had he done that? At once the relief gave way to anger. Why had he done any of it? Why had he put his hand on my shoulder at the farewell dinner on Arkhati? Why had he sung me an apology song on our last night on the *Pinion*? It was all meaningless. I clenched my fists so tightly my fingernails dug into my palms.

"First," he said, "I'd like to commend Suvi Ekhran for her courageous efforts to preserve the safety and sanity of this crew. She executed her duty perfectly. It was through no fault of hers that the quarantine failed."

"Why did it fail?" The question was Ahnir's.

Hathan said, "I compromised it by opening every door on the ship."

The muted stirring of surprise that followed this

announcement was the equivalent of a shocked outcry from a human crew. I felt numb. *I think someone's trying to force the door.* He had sent me that message from Zey's flexscreen only moments before he opened the doors himself. How could I have been so gullible?

"How?" Vethna asked.

"Just after we launched from Arkhati, I programmed in an override protocol. It was intended to help me maintain control of the ship should anyone else attempt a takeover." He paused. "Please don't think the irony is lost on me." At those words, which betrayed a little of the strain he had been working to conceal, I forced myself to look at him. Outwardly he looked much the same as ever, possibly a bit paler than usual. I couldn't see any obvious bruises. His posture was relaxed, and I thought he must be trying to project the same air of aloof confidence as Reyna. To my eyes he didn't do it quite as well as she did. He was studying his flexscreen. I wondered if he was doing it to avoid everyone's gaze, or just mine.

"Was that sanctioned by the Fleet?" Ziral said. There was a note of challenge in her voice.

"No. I was acting on my own initiative." Hathan stopped and cleared his throat. "It was an error in judgment, and I take full responsibility for the consequences."

"I'm not sure you can take personal credit for the Flare," Reyna said, "much as the Echelon would love to pin it on the Fleet." She spoke in a lightly ironic tone perfectly pitched to cut through the mounting tension in the room. I looked at her again, wondering if her equanimity was as complete as it seemed.

"She's so calm," I said in an undertone to Zey.

"Yeah, well, I'd be a lot calmer if I'd gotten to punch him a couple of times," he said darkly, confirming my suspicion that it was Reyna who had come to my rescue in the corridor. I marveled that she could step so neatly into the subordinate role again mere hours after coming to blows with her commander. What must their first post-quarantine meeting have been like? And did it mean anything that she had been willing to relinquish control to him? Or was she merely awaiting her inevitable promotion to khavi once the Echelon had had time to process our transmissions?

"So what happens now?" Ziral asked.

Hathan nodded at Reyna, who said, "Given our position, I expect we'll be diverted to Elteni for processing."

"More debriefing," Zey said in a low voice.

"Elteni is a month away," Khiva pointed out. "Farther than Prime at this point. Why the change of course?"

"Typically, in clear instances of the Flare, the Echelon will process the survivors at a starhaven before sending them soilside," Reyna said. "It's an extra measure of safety in case of lingering contagion. Elteni is the closest starhaven with a substantial Echelon presence." She turned to Saresh. "Hadazi, any communications updates?"

"Nothing beyond acknowledgments of messages received. I've been updating the Echelon, the Fleet, and Earth every few hours since I . . . recovered." I wondered if I would have noted the hesitation if I didn't know Saresh so well. To Vardeshi ears it must have been conspicuous. He went on, "We should be receiving orders within the next day or two."

"Good," Hathan said. "For now, our priorities are to heal ourselves and try to return to normal operations. Anyone in need of counseling should see Rhevi Ahnir or the hadazi. If you're not prepared to resume your duties, please speak to Suvi Ekhran or myself. We'll be as flexible as we can."

"That's everything for now," Reyna said. "Evening

briefing will be in the axis chamber."

There was a rising murmur as people resumed their meals and private conversations. I got up and threaded my way through the tables to the galley. My head was pounding, and I was desperate for a cup of coffee. The preparation took longer than usual, and I idled in the galley afterward, trying to extend my isolation for a few more minutes. It didn't work. Khiva came in presently to deposit her breakfast dishes, followed by Reyna, who was looking for me. "Khavi Takheri would like a word with you in his office," she said.

"Alone?" My voice sounded high and thin. I was aware of Khiva, quietly stacking dishes in the cleansing machine, listening for all she was worth.

"I can accompany you, if you like."

"Would you? I don't think I'm ready . . ."

"It's fine," she said briskly. "Shall we go?"

I looked down at my half-empty cup. Reyna said, "Bring it."

Still undecided, I said, "You guys hate the smell of coffee, don't you?"

"Eyvri, after what you just lived through, what do you care?" She took the cup and sniffed it. "I wouldn't drink it, but no one's asking me to. And as for Hathan, he should be grateful you're not throwing it at him."

"No promises," I said, and had the satisfaction of seeing her smile.

I followed her into Hathan's office. As I stepped over the threshold, the smallness of the room forced itself on my attention. The hiss of the door closing made me start. I stood frozen just across the threshold while Reyna seated herself on one of the stools in front of the table and took out her flexscreen. Hathan was sitting on the other side of the table.

His hands were flat on the tabletop, and I knew he was trying to present a nonthreatening image. As if that were possible. I wanted to laugh. I had seen him lift a table just like that one and throw it into the wall with one hand as if it weighed no more than a sheet of paper. I looked up to find that he was watching me, his gray eyes as serious as I had ever seen them. I held the look for only a moment before a wave of inexplicable shame forced my gaze down.

He gestured to the empty stool beside Reyna. "Please sit down, novi."

"Avery," I said. "Just Avery."

"Do you mean—"

I cut him off. "Look, you don't have to pretend anymore, okay? I know how you feel. You want me off your ship. It's fine. I'll go." I looked at Reyna, who had given up the pretense of absorption in her work and was looking at me, her expression one of mild perplexity. "Tell the Echelon I'll give them what they want. I'll transfer to one of their ships. As soon as we get to Elteni or Vardesh Prime or wherever we're going. I'd do it sooner if I could."

Hathan said, "Avery, I'm not sure you understand—"

Once again I interrupted him. "Believe it or not, you made yourself clear enough that even I got the point. I'm just sorry it took me so long. Better late than never, though, isn't that how you'd put it? Although I have to say, I would have figured it out a hell of a lot faster if you'd just told me the truth. And I'm not sure why you volunteered for this mission in the first place, if you hate humans so much. It's a big universe. It seems to me you could go pretty much anywhere to get away from us. But if you won't leave, I will. Right now, actually." I took a step toward the door.

He raised a hand to stop me. "Avery, wait—"

"I think we're done here," I said, and walked out.

10

I left Hathan's office with no direction beyond the drive to put as much distance as possible between myself and that tiny room. The panic I had been fighting to suppress had broken free, and it raged within me like a wild creature. My breath came in gasps, my heart slammed in my chest, and I could hear the blood rushing in my ears. I had been in a small sealed room with a man who had attacked me only days before. The rational side of my mind knew that the Flare no longer possessed him, but my animal self had been screaming at me to run from the moment I stepped through the door. The worst part—the part that made me feel even more powerless than the knowledge of my own vulnerability—was that I didn't hate him. I was afraid of him, but I didn't hate him. I wanted to. It would have been so much easier. My parting words, *I think we're done here,* were the same ones he had used to dismiss me on the long-ago day when I had begged for his help against Vekesh. I had flung them back at him in the hope that wounding him would bring me some relief. It hadn't. The dismay in his eyes as he recognized my chilly dismissal as his own had triggered another rush of shame. I didn't want to hurt him. Even knowing that he despised me, I couldn't bear to think that I had caused him pain.

I walked for a few minutes, trying to take deep steadying breaths, oblivious to my surroundings. Eventually my steps slowed. The throbbing in my head and wrist subsided to a dull buzzing. I looked around and saw that I had made my way to the medical clinic. Peering in through the windows that faced the corridor, I saw that the lights were off in the main chamber, but the rear alcove with its two narrow recovery cots was dimly illuminated. I tried the door and found it unlocked.

Inside, Sohra was kneeling beside one of the cots, her head bowed. She held her mother's limp hand in both of hers. The sight of Daskar shocked me. She had always appeared ageless to my eyes. Now it was as if she had aged decades in her two days of unconsciousness. Her face was gray and sunken. Fear robbed me of breath for an instant. I watched until I was certain of the subtle rise and fall of her chest. Then I sat down cross-legged on the floor next to Sohra. I didn't say anything, but without lifting her head, she murmured, "Eyvri?"

"If you don't want company, I'll leave," I said.

To my surprise she said, "Stay."

"Have you been here since the end of the quarantine?" I asked.

Sohra nodded.

"And she's been like this the whole time?"

"A few hours ago she stirred. I thought she was going to wake up, but . . ." She didn't finish the thought.

"Has Ahnir tried anything to bring her out of it?"

"He's afraid to, since he's not sure what she took. He says

the safest thing is to watch and wait. The doctors on Prime and Elteni should have some advice, but we won't hear back from them for another day."

I frowned. "But aren't there doctors on other ships nearby? We can't be alone out here. This is one of the busiest regions of Vardeshi space, isn't it?"

"There are other ships, but they're forbidden to communicate with us. It's one of the safeguards when there's been an outbreak of the Flare. No contact of any kind until the crew has been processed and cleared."

"What if our ship were damaged? Or someone needed surgery?"

She shook her head.

"That's a pretty harsh protocol," I said.

"We don't take chances with the Flare. You of all people should understand that."

I sighed and leaned my head back against the side of the cot. "Yeah. I guess I do."

"Do you hate us now?" Sohra asked.

"No."

"But you're afraid of us."

I didn't want to lie to her. "Yes," I said. In my mind I heard Hathan's voice. *You should have been afraid of me all along.*

"And you're leaving."

I turned my head to look at her. "How did you know that?"

"It's what I'd do. We said we'd keep you safe, and we haven't."

"There was always a risk." Even as I said the words, I wondered why I felt the need to say them.

"Anyway, Earth is bound to recall you after they hear about this. How could they not? That's twice now you've almost been killed. Two different commanders. They're not going to give us a third chance."

That possibility hadn't occurred to me. I had been assuming that, even if the Echelon rerouted us to Elteni for processing as Reyna had predicted, one of their ships would take me the remainder of the way to Vardesh Prime. The Council hadn't factored into my thoughts at all. Was Sohra right? Would Earth pull me back now, a scant month from my destination? They knew nothing of the Flare. Would they be able to see anything past the fact that a second Vardeshi commander had tried to kill me and nearly succeeded? Did the fact that he had been infected with a mysterious disease at the time make the picture better or worse? Finishing my journey on an Echelon vessel would be anticlimactic, but it would still be better than being turned back like an Everest climber within a few steps of the summit.

After a pause Sohra asked, "Do you think this will be the end of the alliance?"

I remembered Reyna's matter-of-fact assertion that even if Vekesh had killed me, it would only have slowed things down a little. "No. But I think it's probably the end of the exchange for all of us."

There was a longer silence. Finally she said, "You know, I really did want to see Earth."

Awkwardly I shifted onto my knees and put my arm around her. She didn't let go of her mother's hand, but she rested her head against mine, her silky black hair falling against my cheek.

After I left the clinic, I drifted around some more, trying to avoid running into either Reyna or Hathan, although I had calmed down sufficiently to recognize that my abrupt exit had left a number of issues unresolved. Sooner or later I was going to have to face one of them, if only to find out whether I was still a member of the *Ascendant*'s crew. Which would be worse, going through the daily round of my novi duties while resolutely avoiding Hathan's eyes, or idling in my quarters as a passenger? I wasn't sure. The excruciating awkwardness of the first scenario probably trumped the boredom of the second. But I had spent two long weeks on the *Pinion* sequestered away from my friends, and on the whole I thought I would rather be uncomfortable than lonely.

I had wandered as far as hydroponics, which was no longer a forbidden zone, though only a handful of the edible plants within had been approved for human consumption. I walked along one narrow row and then another with no real aim in mind except to breathe air perfumed by growing things. I heard Sohra's question again in my mind. *Do you hate us now?* I had answered honestly, or I thought I had. But now I started to doubt myself. Could a question of that magnitude be reduced to a simple yes or no? I didn't think I had it in me to hate the Vardeshi. I had given them too much of myself. But I was disappointed in them. Growing up in the years of their silence, I had imagined them as enlightened, cerebral, inhabiting a realm of celestial calm to which humanity could only aspire. When they had come into my life for real, I had seen the hundred tiny ways in which my fantasy was flawed. But that benevolence, their defining quality in my eyes, had been real. Vekesh's betrayal and the revelation of the anti-alliance factions had shaken my faith in them, but it hadn't destroyed it. I was only too conscious of humanity's failings. What right-thinking civilized race would want to prolong its acquaintance with us?

Now, however, everything was different. The ground had shifted under my feet. The Flare had uncovered a current of violence as dark and potent as any that ran through human veins. The Vardeshi weren't angels or emissaries. They were guilty of the same bigotry and malice as we were; they just hid it better. And it wasn't only in the abstract that they had fallen short of my vision of them. I was still reeling from the knowledge of Hathan's true feelings toward me, but he wasn't the only one who had been indicted. What about Saresh? I had been trying not to think about him, but I didn't think I could put it off any longer. Had I been wrong about him from the beginning? Were the things that drew me to him—his empathy, his kindness, his patience—all lies? And what about the Listening? Had that been just another elaborate deception? If the Flare exposed its victims' secret intolerances, then the casual cruelty Saresh had shown Zey was his true self. I hadn't just lost Hathan. I had lost them both.

The door opened. I looked up to see Saresh stepping through, almost as if he had heard his name in my thoughts. I watched him approach. He moved stiffly, no doubt due to the bruises Reyna had mentioned. I could have gone toward him, to shorten the distance between us. I didn't. He stopped in front of me. When we'd first met, I had been too dazzled by his good looks to see beyond them. Now all I could see was tiredness and strain. I felt the sympathy rising in me and forced it down. He wasn't my friend. He wasn't who I'd thought he was at all.

"Can we talk?" he asked quietly.

"I don't think there's anything to say."

He winced ever so slightly. "I can understand that. I've spoken to Reyna. She thinks you may have some . . . misconceptions about what the Flare is."

"I think I had misconceptions before," I said. "A lot of them. Now I think I'm finally seeing things clearly."

He nodded slowly. "Then you believe that everything you saw and heard was true. You believe Hathan hates you."

"He does," I whispered.

"And me? You believe that I hate Zey? My own brother?"

Tears stung my eyes. "I don't want to think that."

"But you do." His tone was gentle, with no recrimination in it.

"I know what I heard. The things you said . . . Those words came from somewhere. Some part of you was storing them up. A disease can't do that."

"It doesn't have to. Our minds do it all on their own. How much petty, small-minded bigotry does any of us witness in a lifetime? I'm a Vox. You'd better believe I've heard plenty of slurs against Blanks, spoken by people who assumed I would agree with them. And Hathan was the son of Novak Takheri even before he was second-in-command on the ship bringing the first human to Vardesh Prime. Our people have called yours a thousand different names, and he's heard them all. Some of the anti-alliance factions openly courted him after he was posted to the *Pinion*. And that was even before Vekesh went to work on him. You don't have to believe something to remember it."

"He did though," I said.

"He believed it when he said it. He doesn't believe it now."

"How can you be sure?"

"Because he's my brother, and I know him. And because Zey is my brother, and I love him. I didn't, though, for the eight hours that I was infected. Those were the worst hours of my life." He waited until I looked at him, then said firmly, "It was true in that moment. But it isn't true now. Hathan doesn't hate humans. He doesn't hate you. He didn't mean any of the things he said. Or did."

"But he did them," I choked. Something in me broke loose at the words. As he had done in the past, Saresh seemed to sense the tears coming before I did. He stepped forward and held me against his shoulder while I cried in great, racking sobs that shook my entire body. In that moment I despised myself for my weakness. Saresh hadn't proven his innocence or Hathan's in any conclusive way. As desperately as I wanted to trust his assurances, both for Zey's sake and my own, I knew I couldn't. But of everyone on the *Ascendant,* he was the only one who understood what it meant to me to have been attacked, not just by any Vardeshi, but by Hathan. He was the only one with whom I could be honest in my grief. I needed his compassion, even if I failed Zey as a friend by accepting it.

The storm of tears had subsided and I was pulling back, wiping my eyes on my sweatshirt sleeve, when I heard the scrape of a footstep behind me. I turned around. Zey was standing a few paces away from us in the same narrow aisle. I jerked away from Saresh as guiltily if we'd been caught kissing, knowing even as I did so that the damage was already done. There was no way to justify or explain away what I'd been doing. The betrayal was clear.

Zey looked from one of us to the other. I braced myself for his anger. To my surprise, though, he just sighed and said, "You're probably sick of hearing this, but I'm going to say it anyway, just in case the person you need to hear it from is me. Eyvri, the Flare doesn't mean anything. It's not real."

"Not real," I repeated.

"That's right."

"How can you say that? You still have the—" I gestured to the lingering bruises on his neck.

He brushed his fingers across them. "These? Oh, the attack was real. No one's denying that. But the feelings weren't. Saresh doesn't hate me."

"How—" The word scraped like broken glass in my throat. "How do you know?"

Zey looked at me incredulously. "What do you mean, how do I know? I know him. I've known him my whole life. And if that weren't enough, there are hundreds of firsthand accounts of the Flare written by ordinary, ethical people trying to come to grips with the horrifically violent things they've just done. Don't get me wrong, it was awful. But it's over, and if you read the histories, you'll see that the *Ascendant* got off pretty easy." He paused. "On second thought, don't read the histories."

I stared from one of them to the other. "So you're just . . . over it? You're fine. Both of you. You're cool now."

"No," Saresh said.

Zey said, "We're a long way from cool. He knows I'm pissed at him. But not that much more pissed than I'd be if we'd been out in Downhelix and someone slipped something into his drink that made him take a swing at me. The action is separate from the intent."

"It's not the same," I whispered.

They exchanged a look. Then Zey said, his tone surprisingly gentle, "Why not?"

"You weren't … alone … He didn't have … as much time …" I couldn't seem to find the right words. It was impossibly strange to be fumbling for them with Saresh and Zey standing shoulder to shoulder in front of me, for all the world as if one of them hadn't, mere hours ago, laid killing hands on the other's throat. The bruises were still there. How could it be that Zey and I had emerged from nearly identical experiences with opposite perspectives on them? How could he assert one brother's innocence, and by extension the other's, with such easy confidence? Hadn't he heard the venom in Saresh's voice when he belittled him for being a Blank, a condition I knew caused Zey deep frustration and insecurity? Not since the moment on the *Pinion* when I stumbled across my crewmates silent and still, immersed in a group Listening, had I felt so unsettled. I said tonelessly, "You weren't there. You don't know what you're talking about."

Zey said steadily, "I didn't say it didn't hurt. I just said it wasn't true."

I could feel the tears starting behind my eyes again. He was wrong, but I had no idea how to tell him so. I turned to leave. His voice stopped me. "Wait. This is for you. From Khiva." He held out a new flexscreen. I went back to him and took it, then left without another word.

The only bright spot in the rest of that day was Ahnir's announcement at evening briefing that Daskar had awakened and seemed to have suffered no ill effects from her long bout of unconsciousness. After the briefing, I ate a quiet dinner with Sohra, who was visibly relieved when I didn't press her to talk. I didn't mind the silence. It wasn't in me to make light, incidental conversation. Zey was at a different table with Ziral and Ahnir. Hathan and Reyna sat together, their food pushed to the sides to make space for their tabletop display. I couldn't tell from my angle what they were looking at. I wasn't sure I wanted to know.

After dinner I went directly back to my quarters. Shortly after the senek hour, Reyna messaged me to ask if we could talk. I would have liked to refuse, but I couldn't think of a reason that didn't sound like an excuse. We met in the lounge, on the balcony level, a luxury afforded by the *Ascendant*'s larger proportions. As I sat down she said, "Thank you for meeting me. I won't keep you long, but there's something I need to say. I think you should stay on the *Ascendant.*"

I stared at her. "You're joking, right? You've been trying to talk me onto an Echelon ship for two months. I thought you'd be thrilled."

"I was speaking for the Echelon then. I'm not speaking for them now."

I glanced down through the transparent railing to where Saresh and Hathan sat half-hidden in one of the raised platforms. Reyna followed my gaze. "I'm not speaking for him either. These are my words, no one else's. I think you should stay."

"Why?"

"Because I've seen what this ship and this crew mean to you. You would have been miserable on the *Izdarith.* This is your mission. This is where you want to be."

"Not right now, it isn't."

"This isn't where anyone wants to be right now. But this ship was your home. If you think it can ever be that again, you should stay."

"What makes you think I'd be allowed to do that, even if I wanted to? Isn't this exactly the kind of thing the Echelon was hoping would happen? Now they can say that if I'd been on one of their ships, the outbreak would have been contained immediately, and I never would have gotten hurt."

Reyna tilted her head a little, her eyes narrowed in thought. "I think you may be surprised by their response. Fear of the Flare runs as deep in the Echelon as it does in the Fleet. It's like fire on one of your old wooden ships—an instant killer. Our protocols are good, but they aren't airtight. We've seen our share of devastation too. Every other ship out there right now is thanking their sigils that it happened to us instead of them. No one with any political sense would claim outright that they would have handled it better. The Echelon may think that, but they won't say it."

"They won't have to," I said glumly. "Earth will say it for them."

"You may be right. But of all the powers in play, the Council is the most likely to listen to what you have to say. They trust your judgment. They have to. Right now, you represent the sum total of all human knowledge of the Flare. I'm not a counselor. I don't have any idea how your people process trauma. I do know that you've been through an experience more harrowing than anything I've ever endured. If the memory of the Flare is so terrible that it pollutes everything and everyone on the *Ascendant,* then I won't fault you for leaving. But if the only reason you're going is that you think Khavi Takheri hates you, then don't. At least give him a chance to defend himself."

"He didn't give me a chance," I muttered.

"That's a cheap shot and you know it," Reyna snapped.

The rebuke was like a slap in the face. I looked away to hide my consternation as she went on. "This isn't any easier for the khavi than it is for you. Talk to him. If you can't do that, listen to him. He's just as much a victim of the Flare as you are." She rose to leave. "I expect to see you in uniform at morning briefing. No more hiding in your quarters. This is a ship in crisis, and there's no room for passengers."

As she left, I looked again at the alcove below, where Hathan's outline was dimly visible through the sheer hanging. It had been one thing for Zey to insist on his brothers' innocence. It meant something else coming from Reyna. She had no motivation to lie about how the Flare worked. If anything, the opposite was true. I wondered if she had just laid her career on the line by urging me to stay when her orders directed her to do the opposite. Why take the risk? We weren't friends. I knew she saw the *Ascendant* as just another posting, more prestigious than some, more tedious than most. What did she care whether I stayed or went? I didn't know what to make of her interference. I wanted to be angry with her, for second-guessing me and for dismissing my pain so callously, but I couldn't. I owed her too much. She had saved my life, and when I had nearly tossed it away, she had saved it again, without a word of recrimination. She might not be my friend, but she had earned the right to speak to me like one. I would think about what she'd said. I might even talk to Hathan. Not tonight though. I didn't think I owed her that much.

* * *

The next morning I presented myself at the briefing as ordered. I caught Reyna's eye, and she lifted her chin in a reserved acknowledgment of my presence. I sat down next to Zey, who murmured a greeting but didn't look up from his flexscreen until Saresh announced that transmissions from Earth and Vardesh Prime had arrived during the night.

"As expected, we're being redirected to Elteni Starhaven for debriefing," he began. "We should arrive in a little over three weeks. We'll be quarantined in an outlying wing of the starhaven until the medical crew at Elteni clears us for entry. We should expect to be there for at least two weeks. Once we've been processed and cleared, anyone who wants to leave the *Ascendant* will be free to do so. The Echelon asks that anyone requesting a different posting do so as soon as possible. Novi Alkhat . . ." Saresh pressed his lips together, his eyes on his flexscreen, and I knew before he said them what his next words would be. "The Council and the Echelon are unanimous in their decision. Novi Alkhat is being recalled to Earth. The Council's precise words were 'unacceptable levels of physical and emotional trauma.'"

"So that's it," I said. "I'm not going to Vardesh Prime."

Saresh said gently, "Not on this trip, I'm afraid."

I didn't hear anything he said after that. When the meeting was over, I stumbled back to my quarters, sat down on my bed, and put my head in my hands. I didn't cry. I'd cried enough. After a while I lay down on my side and curled myself around the hollow ache in my chest. Why did I feel like this? I had already decided to leave the *Ascendant*. My mission was over. It had been over when Hathan knocked me to the floor, or even before that, when Saresh hurled himself at Zey. The shining path I had followed from California had ended somewhere behind us in the vast darkness between Arkhati and Vardesh Prime. I would never see another world. Never feel the pull of gravity on a new planet. The crystal spires of Khezendri, the Dream Forests of Veynir, the twin moons of Rikasa receded before my eyes into the realm of the imagined. I was nothing more than a parcel after all, something too delicate broken in transit, now to be taped up and shipped ignominiously home. I was a failure, and I was lonelier than I had ever been.

I lay on my bunk for the next few hours, drifting between sleep and a sort of listless, despairing trance. Reyna was going to be annoyed with me, I thought dully. I was shirking my novi duties. As if that mattered. Early in the afternoon my door chime sounded. I went to the door and opened it. Zey stood in the corridor outside. He was holding a large metal canister of the type used to store dry goods in the galley. I made a halfhearted joke. "Are you going to hit me with that?"

"What?" He looked down. "No. I made popcorn. I was hoping we could watch something. I'm supposed to be working with Ziral, but she cancelled. I don't feel like being alone right now."

"Me either," I said. "But I don't want to argue about the Flare."

"Neither do I."

"Okay." I stepped back to let him in. "You made popcorn all by yourself?"

"Yeah. And it's good. Not as good as Ahnir's, but close." He settled himself on the bed and nodded to my laptop. "What are we watching?"

"*Galactic Drift*. The crossover episodes."

Galactic Drift was a second-tier spinoff of *Divided by Stars*. It took place in London, as opposed to the original's California, which presumably explained Kylie's fondness for it. It was one of the only Vardramas I'd found among her video files. A handful of early episodes featured drop-ins by major characters from the earlier and more popular show. Zey nodded and reached for the 'play' control. I sat down next to him, pulled my blanket up over us, and helped myself to a handful of popcorn.

It was, in a way, exactly like the last night on Arkhati, when I had crawled into Kylie's bed to share her warmth. Zey and I were two animals breathing together in the tiny pocket of safety that was my room. Just that. I closed my eyes and let the various sounds wash over me: the predictable dialogue, the jokily pronounced musical cues, the occasional soft laugh from my best friend, the rustle of popcorn in the canister. Those noises were underpinned by another: the hum of the *Ascendant's* engines as the ship sped onward into the dark.

With my eyes closed, I could forget about Zey's bruises and the brace on my own wrist. I could float on the surface of the moment, untethered to memory. I could choose not to think about what happened next.

We watched two episodes. After the second one, Zey paused the show, pushed the blanket back, and stood up. "I have to go." He hesitated, then went on, "I know I said I didn't want to fight with you, and I don't. But I need to tell you something, as a friend. That's what we are, right? Friends?"

"Of course," I said, surprised.

"Then listen to me. You're wrong about the Flare. And you're wrong about Hathan. I know you don't know him well. But you know me, and I'm telling you the person you saw that day wasn't him. Remember what happened on the *Pinion*? He was wrong about you, right? And I kept trying to tell him, and he wouldn't listen. I won't let that happen again." He took a deep breath. "I'm right, and friends trust each other. So you should trust me."

"I do," I said.

"But you don't believe me."

"No."

He asked, more curious than angry, "Why not?"

"I . . . I can't explain it. It's just not enough."

"Have you talked to Hathan about it? Given him a chance to defend himself, or at least tell you what it was like from his side?"

"No," I admitted.

Zey stared at me from the doorway, frustration warring with sympathy in his face. At last he said, "Eyvri, you don't get to pick. You can't tell yourself that Saresh and Khiva didn't mean it but Hathan did. That's not fair to him. If you've decided to hate him for the Flare, then go ahead and hate him. But you have to hate the rest of us with him, because it could have been any one of us in that room with you. Even me."

"You're wrong," I whispered.

"No," he said quietly. "I'm not. I'm going to leave now. When you're ready to talk about it again, let me know."

He left. I sank down onto the bed and dragged the blanket over me again.

Zey's popcorn had been delicious, but it was meager fuel for hibernation. Late in the afternoon hunger drove me to the mess hall. I made soup and a sandwich and brought them on a tray to the lower-ranking table. Evening briefing had started a few minutes before, and I was certain of having the place to myself, but as I was finishing my meal, the door slid open to reveal Hathan. The sight of him triggered a lurch in my stomach that was half-excitement, half-fear. I wondered if the fear would fade with time. I would never know. We would part ways at Elteni, and I would never see him again.

He raised his hands slowly and waited for my reluctant nod before stepping inside. His first act was to fix the door in the open position. Marginally reassured, I turned back to my food. He went through to the galley and came back with two glasses of beer. He carried them to within a few paces of my table, stopped, and waited for me to look up before he asked, "Can I sit?"

My mouth was full, so in lieu of answering, I jerked my chin at the empty seat to my right. He placed the beers on the table and sat down. I took another bite and chewed methodically, glancing every so often at the open doorway. Leaving it open had been a symbolic rather than a practical choice. I knew how fast his kind could move. He would have trapped me in the conference room even with the door wide open.

"I left the briefing," he said in response to my unspoken question. "I was planning to speak to you afterward, but when I saw that you weren't there, I went looking for you."

"You found me," I said.

"I'm sorry about Vardesh Prime. I know how much that meant to you."

I nodded.

"I'm not going to try to talk you out of leaving the *Ascendant*. I have no right to keep you here. I have no right to ask you to listen to me either, but I think you'll want to hear what I have to say."

I finished my sandwich and washed it down with a swallow of beer. "Say it."

"Am I right in thinking that you don't want to talk to me about the Flare because you don't think talking will make any difference? You saw what you saw, and nothing I can say will convince you that that's not who I am?"

"Pretty much." I was aware that my curt answers, which would have been ungracious even in English, must be blatantly offensive to Vardeshi ears. I didn't care. The only way I could keep him from hearing the tremor in my voice was to use it as little as possible.

Hathan said slowly, "What if I didn't have to tell you? What if I could show you?"

"Show me? How?"

He didn't say anything. I looked at him in puzzlement. He held my gaze, his eyebrows raised slightly, as if he were waiting for me to reach an obvious conclusion. I had, but it was too absurd to contemplate.

The silence grew protracted. Finally I forced myself to break it. "You can't be serious."

"I am."

"A Listening?" I said incredulously. "That's your idea?"

"It worked for you once. It could work again."

I didn't even hesitate. "Nope. Out of the question."

"Because of what I did to you."

"No, because—" I fumbled for a credible reason. "Because you're not a Vox. There's no way it would work, unless rana works on humans, and I'm not about to try it. In case you've forgotten, it's a five-month trip to the nearest emergency room."

"Of course not," Hathan said swiftly. "I would never condone that. The drug is untested in humans. We have no idea what it would do to you. But Saresh thinks he might be able to serve as a conduit. A bridge between our minds. No rana needed on either side."

"Saresh knows?"

"It was his idea."

If Saresh had suggested it, I thought, it must mean he was confident that he would be able to screen my thoughts from Hathan. I asked the question anyway. "So would this be a two-way exchange, or . . ."

"No. You would see my memories. I wouldn't see yours."

If it failed, I thought, if Saresh overestimated his ability to control the flow of information, the consequences would be disastrous. But if it worked . . . If it worked, I would have what I had longed for in the months since discovering my feelings for Hathan but never imagined I would actually be granted: a glimpse into his thoughts. The idea was both heady and terrifying. What human suffering the pangs of unrequited love hadn't at some time or other longed for a portal into the mind of his or her beloved? And didn't most of us ultimately conclude that it was probably in our best interest that such knowledge was locked securely away? Some things were better left in darkness. I knew how cruelly revealing were the things people said about each other in unguarded moments. And those were just words. Thoughts were another matter entirely. I wasn't at all sure I had the courage to see myself as Hathan saw me.

And yet, I argued with myself, what did I really have to lose? There could be nothing in his mind darker than what I had already seen. The Flare had spent whatever poison was there. And if I refused his offer, I would deny myself the chance to see the world through his eyes. He was proposing to share his memories with me. What I had done with Saresh hadn't been nearly so intimate. I had sensed his presence, but he hadn't let me into his thoughts. That I should be invited to do such a thing by any Vardeshi was remarkable. That the invitation should come from Hathan himself was extraordinary. And I would never have another chance like this one. I knew him well enough to know that, if rejected once, he would never offer again.

He was watching me. I'd been silent for too long. I needed to say something. I racked my brain for a suitably preoccupying objection and seized on the first one that came to mind. "Just so we're clear, I'm not interested in reliving the Flare from your point of view. Once was more than enough. I can barely handle my own memories. I'm not about to throw yours into the mix."

"I wasn't thinking of the Flare. I had a different memory in mind." He looked at me questioningly. When I nodded, he went on. "The night before we launched on the *Ascendant,* I met with Suvi Ekhran to discuss the crew. She asked me what I thought about you, and I told her. I was honest. I had no reason not to be. It was a private conversation, and it was in my interest to tell her what she needed to know. Let me show you my memory of that night. I think it will give you the proof you need."

Skeptically I said, "And you're willing to do that? To share that with me?"

"I wouldn't be sitting here if I weren't."

"But why? The mission is over. I'm being sent home. Why does it matter what I think?"

He lifted one shoulder slightly. "Maybe it's ego, but I don't like the thought of you going back to Earth thinking the man you saw that day was the real me. I own my mistakes. I was wrong about you the first time, with Vekesh. But I've learned since then. I see humans differently now. I see you differently. And if there's the slightest chance that I can prove that to you through a Listening, why not try?"

Put in those terms, it seemed eminently reasonable. A Listening was the logical solution to a thorny emotional problem. It would be personal for Hathan, but not deeply so. He was Vardeshi. The sharing of memories was a social practice for his people. And while it meant something more for a Vardeshi to engage in a Listening with a human, he could have no idea how much it would mean to me. Saresh did though. And Saresh had been the one to suggest it. I wondered what he thought I would see.

A thought struck me, and I asked, "Isn't it against the rules though? I thought Listenings with humans were off limits now."

Hathan looked pensive. "As to that, the Council and the Echelon can advise us, but they don't control us. Ultimately we make our own choices. As the first human survivor of the Flare, you'll be given broad latitude to determine what you need to recover. If you think a Listening will help, we should act now and worry about getting permission later. That being said, if we do it, I think we'd be well advised to keep it quiet for as long as we can."

His flexscreen emitted a humming note, signaling an incoming high-priority message. He glanced at it. "The briefing just ended. We won't have the mess hall to ourselves much longer. Will you consider—"

"I'll do it," I said.

He looked taken aback. "You're sure?"

"I'm sure."

"If you need time to think—"

I cut him off again. "I said I'm sure. When can we do it?"

The part of me that had assumed he was bluffing all along expected him to put me off, but he said immediately, "Tonight, during the senek hour. In my quarters. I'll tell Saresh."

"I'll be there." I got up to clear my dishes away.

It was only later, when I was alone in my quarters again, that I recalled my long-ago promise to Zey never to participate in another Listening. I had been so certain then that I could keep my word. I had only agreed to the first Listening because of imminent danger to my life and the lives of my crewmates. I would never have risked my sanity for any circumstances less compelling. It had seemed impossible then that I might find myself in such a position twice. But I had reckoned without the Flare. And I hadn't known that whatever inexplicable hold Hathan had over me would only grow stronger, even after my trust in him was shattered, until the need to validate his innocence loomed as large in my thoughts as life and death. He had invited me into his mind. I couldn't refuse.

But it made me uneasy to think of Zey. It had wounded him deeply to learn that I had shared a connection with

Saresh that was forever denied to him as a Blank. How would he feel when he discovered that I had shared that same connection with Hathan? It was a secret for now, but I knew better than to believe such things stayed hidden, particularly when the two others concerned were Zey's brothers. Sooner or later, he would find out. The thought of hurting him again was almost enough to make me change my mind. I reached for my flexscreen more than once, a few keystrokes away from calling the whole thing off. But when the senek hour arrived, I found myself standing, just as I'd known I would, outside the door to Hathan's quarters.

I pressed the control to request entry, and the door slid open. I stepped inside and looked around curiously. Hathan's rooms weren't as expansive as Kylie's suite on Arkhati, but they were generous, with multiple tiers giving the illusion of larger space. The lowest level, where I stood, held a recessed seating area. The second level contained a workspace with stools and a table. The highest level was the smallest, with room only for a bunk the size of my own, set beneath a bank of viewports. The view was impressive, if one wasn't troubled by the thought of the cold depths of space only a hand's breadth away from one's pillow. Somehow I didn't think the idea would bother Hathan.

I saw immediately that Saresh hadn't arrived yet. We were alone. Hathan was on the second level, preparing senek at a small alcove with a washbasin and water taps. The privileges of command, I thought. He hadn't been eating cold cereal during the Flare. Then I remembered something I had overheard in the mess hall that morning. After Reyna had restrained the infected members of the crew, she had been driven to extreme measures to secure them. Unable to lock them in storerooms due to the override on the door controls, she had settled for putting them inside large empty containers in the cargo hold. Hathan had spent the second half of the outbreak locked in a metal carton roughly the size of a refrigerator box, bound at the wrists and feet. He probably hadn't been eating anything.

I felt the need to say something, if only to wrench my mind away from the image of him sitting there in his tiny dark cell as the rage ebbed slowly away. "Wow. Khavi quarters are nice."

"Feel free to look around. Saresh is on his way."

I did look around, eagerly, my senses heightened by the illicit thrill of trespassing on forbidden ground. The space was as immaculate as Zey's, but there were a few more personal touches scattered around. A shelf held a shallow bowl carved from the same smoky gray quartz as the whiskey glasses I had bought for Dr. Sawyer. The bowl contained perhaps a dozen memory crystals. What memories did Hathan deem important enough to keep in view? I wished I could plunge my hand into the bowl and pull out a crystal at random, but I knew it would be unpardonably rude to do so.

One wall held three ceremonial sashes, blue and orange and gold. "What are these from?" I asked.

Hathan looked up from the senek things he was placing on a tray. His private senek set, I noticed, was matte green ceramic, nearly a perfect match for the Japanese teapot I'd bought in college. "From left to right, coming of age, Institute graduation, betrothal."

Betrothal. Right. With an odd sense of unreality, I realized that Hathan's fiancée, whoever she was, had never been in this room. She had never seen the narrow bunk with its crimson and gray woven spread where he slept beneath the stars. There wouldn't have been room for her in it anyway. I remembered Zey telling me that couples serving on the same ship were given individual quarters. But what if they wanted to sleep in the same bed? Or was that a thing only humans did? I couldn't very well ask him.

I wandered up the steps to the second level. Above the work table hung a placard bearing a few lines of text in a script so stylized I had to squint to make it out. "Citizens of the Vardeshi worlds," it began, "the people of Earth send you their greetings across the void that divides us." I recognized these as the opening words of Earth's reply to the first transmission we ever received from the Vardeshi, more than twenty-five years ago now. Hathan had placed these words over his private workspace as, what, a reminder of his purpose? I felt a twinge of doubt. Maybe he really didn't hate humans. How he felt about me in particular, of course, was the more pressing question.

Hathan had gone down the steps to the first level. I followed him. The wall behind the seating area was dominated by a large piece of abstract art, intersecting circles and tangential lines, white upon black. I stood looking at it for a moment. He set the tray down on the table and came over to look as well. "What do you see in it?"

I studied the curves and angles, trying to make sense of them, but I couldn't make them resolve into any coherent picture. In the end, I fell back on my knowledge of who he was. "It looks like a star chart."

"It is." He sounded surprised. "It shows a flight path. Vardesh Prime to the third moon to Arideth. My first trip offworld."

The hiss of the door signaled Saresh's arrival. I wondered for a moment at the absence of a chime—I'd had to request entry, after all—then realized that Saresh, as Hathan's brother, probably knew his private door code. The three of us settled ourselves on cushions around the low table. Hathan poured the senek and passed a cup to each of us. Saresh looked at me over his. "Do you have any questions for me?"

"It's a one-way transfer, right?" Hathan had told me as much, but I felt compelled to clarify.

He nodded. "If it works, the connection will be one-way. Hathan will choose the memory, I'll transmit it, and you'll see it. It's a procedure we use frequently to settle legal disputes. A sharing between two latent telepaths can be unpredictable; cognitive slips can occur on either side. Having a Vox serve as intermediary helps to control the flow of information. Generally speaking," he added, and I had to suppress a smile. He went on, "I don't know for sure that it will work, but I'm more confident than before that your mind won't be damaged. The exchange went smoothly last time. That's an encouraging sign. Any other questions?"

I shook my head.

Hathan said, "I have one for you, Avery. Are you sure you want to do this?"

I took a gulp of my senek and immediately felt its calming effect. My voice steadied by the drink, I said, "I'm sure."

Saresh set his cup down and held out his hand for me to take it. "Then let's begin."

11

The instant Saresh's hand closed on mine, I found myself immersed in the weightless sapphire calm I remembered from our previous Listening. I was still adjusting to the sensation when he said, *I'm going to bring Hathan in now,* the words as clear as if he had spoken them in my ear. I heard them in English; I had a moment to wonder if he'd thought them in Vardeshi before he was gone and I found myself abruptly and unequivocally in Hathan's mind.

It wasn't at all what I had expected. With Saresh, I had been enveloped by his presence, but I hadn't been able to hear his thoughts. Now Hathan's thoughts were mine. My own were still there, but faint and tinny and somehow intrusive, like someone's cell phone ringing in the middle of a symphony. I saw the world through his eyes. More than that, I felt it. I knew the exact spot on his left heel where the standard-issue boot rubbed against it. He'd been planning to replace it before launch, but the debriefing sessions had consumed every waking hour, and now he'd have to pray that Khiva had a pair in his size down in Requisitions. I knew he was regretting that he'd just eaten his last starhaven meal and hoping Ahnir wouldn't find a way to incorporate mizik root into quite so many dinners on the next arc of the journey. A regional preference, of course, but they didn't spice their food quite so strongly on the Southern Continent, and it had been difficult to force the stuff down by the end. I knew he hadn't had a full night's sleep in weeks, and that while he longed for the cool silence of his bunk, he was all too aware that in a few short hours he would be expected on the docking level for the prelaunch walkthrough of the *Ascendant*. I knew that in the back of his mind there simmered a constant low-grade worry about Zey, who was showing signs of favoring piloting as his specialization. It had been one of his weakest subjects at the Institute, and Hathan was concerned about finding him a suitable mentor.

I watched him reach for the dice cup on the table and hold it up to the young woman in the Echelon uniform sitting across from him. "Game?"

"Khivrik sevens," said Reyna.

Hathan nodded and shook the dice out into his palm. Khivrik sevens was a formidably difficult variant of the standard Institute dice game, requiring near-perfect recall of one's opponent's preceding rolls. At this hour and after a full day of being grilled by Echelon examiners, he would have chosen something a little less taxing, and he thought she was probably testing him.

She was an interesting mix, he thought. Pretty in classical homeworld style—dark hair, dark eyes, sharp chin—but flaunting her Mirzand accent. Most offworlders dropped their accents as soon as they decently could; there was a strand of xenophobia running through both Echelon and Fleet, and the teasing could be intense. Somehow, though,

Reyna Ekhran didn't look as if she'd be discomfited by any amount of teasing. The gold sigil on her hand was that of Vadra House, but Hathan knew that was a recent acquisition. She had broken a long-standing engagement to a childhood friend when the match with Vadra offered itself. Her new fiancé, a fellow Echelon officer, was reportedly no prize in the personality department, but that wasn't why she'd accepted him. She was ambitious. She was also, to judge from her record, a skilled systems officer and a gifted ranshai fighter. The film of her last qualification trial had been appended to her file. She had won her designation of advanced seventh class with enviable ease, while he had fought like a cornered nivakh for his own intermediate fourth. She could take him apart at any time, probably one-handed and wearing one of the disorientation visors the Fleet used for antigrav training. And, of course, her English was impeccable. With all this she had evinced none of the typical Echelon arrogance during their two days of meetings. If she could be trusted, she would be an asset.

A server came by to see if their glasses needed refilling. Hathan waved him away. It was tacitly understood between him and Reyna that this was a professional rather than a social meeting. The preferred time for a commander to pass on essential yet sensitive personnel details to his newly assigned second was over a prelaunch drink. He had already summarized the most pressing items, beginning with Vethna's unfortunate rana habit, moving through the escalating tension between Ziral and Ahnir in the wake of the Echelon's efforts to recruit the former as a pilot, and concluding with Sohra's silent yet protracted battle with homesickness. He considered mentioning Khiva's extreme mood swings, but decided against it. An observant supervisor would spot them on her own in short order. He'd see how long it took for Reyna to mention them to him. Just as she would be assessing his competence in the days to come, he would be assessing hers. That, too, was tacitly understood.

Reyna cast her dice. The result was dismal, but she gave no sign of annoyance as she swept them into her hand and passed them to him. "And then there's the human," she prompted.

"Eyvri," Hathan said, with a flash of rueful inward humor. "What do you want to know?"

"What do I need to know to keep her safe?" Reyna countered.

It was the right question, he thought, though not easily answered. He stared down into his glass while he considered his answer.

This was the moment, I realized. This was why he had chosen this particular memory. At last I saw myself in his mind. It was a peculiar feeling, not unlike looking at a friend's photographs of an event we'd attended together. The subjects were familiar, but glimpsed from odd angles and through unexpected filters. I watched, horrified and enthralled, while he sorted through the swirl of contradictory images. There were a lot of them. At first he had seen me as incompetent but harmless, fumbling my kevet—the Vardeshi eating utensil that had given me particular trouble—and mangling my honorifics. I cringed. My accent in those early days had been worse than I'd known. Time passed, and his derision deepened into scorn. I watched myself whisper to Zey in the middle of a briefing, shout at Vethna outside the mess hall, stammer denials as Hathan himself presented me with the two surveillance devices he'd found in my quarters. Then, with a shock like plunging into cold water, came the report of Vekesh's gun. I cringed again, not for myself this time, as Hathan recalled cradling my limp body in his arms, guilt and horror and panic tangling together in his chest.

There followed a few images he dismissed before they could fully register. I saw myself laughing with Kylie in Downhelix, talking animatedly to Sohra, watching while Saresh demonstrated something on his flexscreen, my eyes intent on his face. Irrelevant, Hathan thought. Abruptly everything else fell away, revealing a handful of memories that glowed with significance. I saw myself in the interview room at the Villiger Center, in Vekesh's sham tribunal, in the corridor where I had run into Hathan after the explosion in the *Pinion*'s cargo bay. The most recent memory was from earlier in the day of his meeting with Reyna. I was standing with her and Tavri, wearing Kylie's black dress with the gold beads, looking both earnest and apprehensive. That was Eyvri, Hathan thought. Always outnumbered. Always underestimated.

"She's brave," he said aloud. "She's lonely. She cares too much what we think. And she deserves better than she's gotten from me. I should have worked harder to keep her safe."

"That's my job now," Reyna observed.

"It's yours because I failed at it."

She blinked. It was the strongest sign of emotion she had shown in the hour they had been sitting together. "You honor me with your candor."

He says that's enough, Saresh said.

I opened my eyes and looked across the table at Hathan. For a split second I knew with absolute certainty that I was in the wrong body, looking at my own face from outside. The feeling went beyond mere disorientation into deep, stomach-twisting horror. This must be what madness felt like. I tasted bile. I scrambled to my feet and sprinted for the half-hidden door at the far end of the room that I was sure concealed a sanitation room. I had better be right. If not, I was going to throw up in his closet.

It was a sanitation room. And I did throw up, humiliatingly, with the door open, because there wasn't time to close it. Then I sat on the floor with my head between my knees until the dizziness and trembling went away. The sense of wrongness took longer to subside. Even after my mind settled back into itself, accepting that I was Avery and not Hathan or some hideous amalgam of the two, the physical sense of displacement continued. My heartbeat was too fast. My senses were ever so slightly dulled, so that sounds were muffled and edges that should have been sharp looked blurred. I stared down at my hands. They were mine. This body was mine. I knew that it was. So why did I feel like I'd been put back into it slightly wrong? Had I lost some degree of nervous-system function during the Listening? I waited, and breathed, until I was sure that I hadn't. This was what being in a human body felt like. I'd just never had anything to compare it to before.

I looked up at the doorway, where Hathan and Saresh stood side by side, their faces drawn, and said, "Let's not do that again."

Their relief at hearing me speak coherent words was unmistakable. "Are you all right?" Saresh asked. Hathan didn't say anything, but he closed his eyes briefly and released his grip on the doorframe. I could see the tension leave his body. After what we'd just shared, I could practically feel it.

"I think I'm fine," I said. "I was . . . confused for a minute. I didn't know which body I was supposed to be in. It was awful. I don't think my mind is meant to do that."

Saresh took out his flexscreen. "Stay where you are, Eyvri.

I'm going to call Daskar."

"No!" Both of them looked startled by my vehemence. I
went on, "If we tell her, she'll have to report it, won't she? I
thought we were going to keep this quiet."

"Not after what just happened," Hathan said firmly. "We
took an idiotic risk. I'm not about to compound it by keeping
it a secret. You're clearly in need of medical attention." To
Saresh he said, "Call her."

Saresh went out into the larger space beyond the doorway.
After a moment I heard him speaking in a low voice, presumably to Daskar. Hathan said, "I'm sorry I suggested this."

"Don't be. It worked."

"You saw it?"

"Saw it? My body thinks I was there. I'm pretty sure that
if I took a polygraph test right now, I'd pass it."

"I don't know what that is," he admitted.

"It's a machine that tells you when someone's lying. You
guys don't need them."

He smiled a little. "I wish I'd known about those before I
talked you into another Listening."

"You didn't have to twist my arm very hard. I wanted to
do it. And, like I said, it worked."

"Then you know I don't hate you."

I met his eyes. "I do now."

He sighed. "Well, I guess that's something."

It was more than something, I thought. It was everything.

Daskar arrived after a few minutes, looking so much like
herself that I questioned whether I had imagined the gray ap-
parition I had seen in the clinic. When she had examined me
thoroughly, she said, "You seem unhurt. That was a very
foolish thing to do. I hope it was necessary."

"It was," I said.

"I'm glad it worked, then."

I looked up at her. "Are you going to report us?"

"I have no choice."

"Are they going to get in trouble?"

"Very possibly. But they knew that from the beginning."

She helped me up, made sure I was steady on my feet, then went into the outer room to speak to Hathan and Saresh. I washed my face and rinsed my mouth out in the sink. I wanted to laugh at myself for feeling so guilty about invading Hathan's privacy. I had been inside his head. Using his bathroom shouldn't feel like such a big deal.

I emerged, a little refreshed, to find that Daskar had gone. "Well," Saresh said ruefully, "so much for keeping it a secret."

"You're sure you're all right?" Hathan asked me.

"Believe me, I'd tell you if I wasn't. I'm not a martyr."

"I'm not at all sure that's true." He looked at Saresh, who said, "That must be my cue. I'll take my leave. Assuming that's all right with you, Eyvri." Both of them looked at me.

Bewildered, I said, "It's . . . fine."

When Saresh had gone, Hathan said, "I know you've been through a lot tonight. This won't take long, but there's still something I have to do."

"What's that?"

"Apologize."

My mouth went dry. "Oh. Okay."

"I would have done it before, but once I saw that you didn't trust me, I knew there was no point. Now, I think, you'll believe me."

I nodded.

"Eyvri," he said. "Look at me."

I did.

Hathan said slowly, "When I think about the things I did

that day, I feel more ashamed than I can say. No apology will ever be adequate, but to say nothing would be unthinkable. I hurt you, and I made you afraid of me. It was twisted and cruel. I will never forgive myself for that."

"It wasn't you," I said shakily.

"Yes. It was." Very slowly he reached out his right hand, palm flat. It was a moment before I understood what he wanted. Then, recalling the ritual apologies offered by Sohra and others after Vekesh led them all to ostracize me, I held out my own right hand. Light glinted along the silver tracery of the wrist brace, a reminder, if I had needed one, of what his touch could do. Hathan took my hand gently in both of his. He knelt on the floor and pressed my palm to his forehead. "I'm sorry," he whispered. I had a sudden vivid memory of Kylie teasing me about my fanciful visions of Vardeshi engagement ceremonies. *They probably don't go down on one knee either,* she had said. I looked down at the man kneeling before me in supplication and pressed the knuckles of my other hand hard against my mouth. It was the only way to keep myself from crying aloud in sheer frustration at what the Flare had made of us.

The next day I went to see Reyna. Her greeting to me was perfectly matter-of-fact, as if she hadn't scolded me for self-absorption the last time we talked. I knew she preferred the direct approach, so I got immediately to the point. "You were right. I changed my mind. I'll stay on the *Ascendant* if the Echelon will let me."

"The Listening," she guessed.

"Daskar told you?"

"She did. You know, when I told you to listen to the khavi, this wasn't exactly what I had in mind."

"I know."

"You took an appallingly dangerous risk."

Recalling Daskar's words, I said, "It was necessary."

Reyna seemed to accept that. "Have there been any side effects?"

"A headache. And I threw up. Nothing else. Yet."

"Good. I'll pass your decision on to the Echelon." This was what I liked about Reyna: her ability to take on unwanted information and move forward without unwarranted theatrics. "The next time you decide to do something reckless," she said, "tell me. I won't stop you, but I'd like to be there in case something goes wrong."

"Okay. I will try not to do anything else reckless."

"Your recent history suggests that you won't try very hard," she said dryly.

I went directly from Reyna's office to the galley, where Zey was tidying up after the midday meal. He started to speak, but I cut him off, a breach of Vardeshi decorum so egregious it made his eyes widen. I couldn't help myself; I was terrified that if I hesitated, I'd lose my nerve. "I changed my mind. I'm not leaving the ship."

He matched my bluntness. "Why?"

"You were right about the Flare. And about Hathan. I see that now. I had it wrong."

"Okay," he said slowly. "I mean, yes, you did, but how do you know? What's happened to change your mind?"

Throughout that morning, while my hands worked at one mindless task and then another, I had struggled to assemble the necessary words to explain what I'd done, as if there were some alchemical formula that would automatically yield his understanding. I couldn't remember any of them. It hardly seemed to matter; his expression suggested the possibility of forgiveness was remote. I said, "Hathan changed it for me."

"How?" In the next instant I saw comprehension flicker across his face. "You did another Listening, didn't you?"

"I—"

"That sucks, Avery. That was a shitty thing to do. You could have trusted me. I asked you to trust me. But you took the easy way out. You cheated. I guess my word as a Blank wasn't enough for you. Do you have any idea how many times that's happened to me? Do you have any idea how it makes me feel?"

"No," I whispered.

"And the worst part is that you didn't even have to! No one's life was on the line this time. This was just"—he gave a slow, contemptuous shake of his head—"lazy."

My eyes stinging, I said, "I know it must look that way to you. But I didn't have a choice."

"No?" he snapped. "Why not?"

I could almost taste the words. *Because I'm in love with him. I had to know.* I couldn't make myself say them. Saresh was bound by the Vox code of ethics not to speak of what he knew. Zey was governed by no such constraint. I couldn't take the risk that Hathan would find out, not now, when it seemed we had finally achieved a fragile understanding. I looked at Zey in helpless silence.

"Yeah, that's what I thought. You're going to have to do better than that, Eyvri. I can't hear what you're thinking, remember? I'm just a Blank." He turned away from the half-emptied cleansing machine and walked out of the galley without another word. I watched him go, sickened by the thought that I had reclaimed one Takheri at the cost of another.

I didn't say a word to anyone else about the fight, and I doubted Zey did either. But the Vardeshi were an observant people. I suspected the coolness between us hadn't gone unnoticed, and the sudden arctic chill certainly didn't. Saresh, catching me alone during the evening senek hour, said quietly, "I take it you told Zey about the Listening."

"I had to. It didn't seem right to keep lying to him."

"That couldn't have been an easy conversation."

I shook my head. "No, it was not."

"For what it's worth," he said, "I think you did the right thing."

"You mean doing the Listening, or telling him about it?"

"Both."

"Yeah." I sighed. "Me too. Amazing how much that doesn't help. If you can possibly find a way to drop into your next conversation with him that I'm incredibly sorry and would do anything to make it up to him, please do it."

"I'll try, but I'm not entirely sure when our next conversation will be." I looked up in surprise. He went on, "He seems to be avoiding me too."

"I thought you guys were . . . moving toward okay."

"We were," Saresh said. "Now we appear to be moving somewhere else. I'm not sure what he's"—he broke off, and an odd expression flashed across his face, half laughter, half anguish—"thinking."

Over the days that followed, I felt a gradual easing of strain, as if the broken edges grinding together inside me had been fractionally smoothed down. The Listening had done its work. I was as certain now of the essential goodness in Hathan as I had been certain before of his viciousness. I hadn't liked everything I saw in his mind. He had an incisive wit that turned easily to mockery. Quick to see patterns and implications, he was impatient with slowness in others. He had laughed at my mistakes in the beginning, and not always alone. That was hard to forgive. But if he was intolerant of error in others, he loathed it in himself. His shame and regret for the way he had treated me under Vekesh's tenure ran deeper than I could have imagined.

And I had felt the truth in every word he had spoken to Reyna. There was no longer any question in my mind that he was not the man he had been during the Flare. I didn't know how to explain what I had seen that day, except to conclude that it was something ineffably other. The real Hathan was the one who had knelt unprompted before me in the atonement ritual of his people. When I recalled that moment, most of my remaining anger sluiced away like rain.

Recalling Reyna's advice from before the Listening, I focused my energies on my work. I had been doing my novi tasks unthinkingly for a long time. Now I forced myself to think about them again. There was a kind of solace to be found in doing simple repetitive things mindfully and well, and a kind of grace in caring for my crewmates. One afternoon I went by the medical clinic to bring Daskar a cup of her favorite tea. Her smile warmed my entire day. I sought Sohra out in the lounge to ask her questions about Vardesh Prime, knowing now that her reticence concealed a fierce longing for home. Seeing Khiva sitting alone in the mess hall, her plate untouched, I carried my tray over to her table and made banal but insistent small talk until she couldn't ignore me any longer. I could see the effort it cost her to pull her attention back to the present. I understood. It was an act of will to keep my own mind from straying down the too-short stretch of corridor that led to the conference room on helix three.

My days were beginning to feel familiar again, but my estrangement from Zey was a fracture running through them, and it would take more than a cup of herbal tea or a little small talk to mend it. At briefings now he sat next to Ziral, ostensibly to ask her questions about piloting. He ate most of his meals at the lower-ranking table, but he avoided it if I was the only one there. It was the same in the lounge. He would join a dice game that I was a part of, but he wouldn't sit in one of the curtained alcoves with me and Sohra, and I knew it was because he didn't want to risk finding himself alone with me. He didn't come to my evening English lessons any more. There were no more private jokes, no sly digs at Vethna. He contrived to be entirely civil without showing the faintest trace of warmth. It was like the worst days on the *Pinion,* when Khavi Vekesh had ordered the rest of the crew to ostracize me, except that this time Zey was doing it all on his own.

One evening as the crew was assembling for the late briefing I heard him teasing Khiva about an error she'd made in the ranshai drills that morning. I listened eagerly, glad to hear laughter in his voice again. "Come on, Khiva," he was saying. "That's a second-rank move at best. You shouldn't even have to think about it. I bet you're the reason we're still having morning practices."

"Suvi Ekhran," Khiva called in half-feigned irritation. "Novi Takheri is being insubordinate. Can you—"

I didn't hear anything past the word "insubordinate." The flexscreen slid from my nerveless fingers and clattered on the floor. The axis chamber went dark. The conference-room lights clicked on. After an undefined interval, I came back to myself, blinking dazedly, wondering why my throat felt so raw. It came to me that I'd been screaming. Saresh had hold of my shoulders and was calling my name urgently. Daskar, beside him, was paging through messages on her flexscreen. The room had emptied out around the three of us. "I'm okay," I said. "I'm okay." Saresh let go of my shoulders and stepped back, but his eyes didn't leave my face.

"Has that happened before?" Daskar asked quietly.

"Never during the day."

"How often at night?"

"Maybe . . . three or four times since the Flare."

Daskar found the message she'd been looking for. "Flashbacks are a common manifestation of post-traumatic stress. Have any of Dr. Okoye's suggestions been helping?"

"I haven't, uh . . ." I looked at Saresh.

"You haven't viewed any of your messages from Earth." He spoke gently but with authority, and I saw that there was no point in denying his assertion. I should have realized that, as communications specialist, he would have access to the logs of my incoming messages. Since the Flare, I had received video transmissions from Ambassador Seidel, Dr. Sawyer, Dr. Okoye, my parents. I had deleted them all unwatched.

"They're bringing me home," I said. "I can't see that there's anything more to say. If I need therapy, I'll get it on Earth. I doubt they'll give me a choice."

"Earth is a distant proposition as yet," said Daskar. "Can you think of anything that might help you now?"

I sighed. "Vardesh Prime would have helped. I need to be outside. I need to feel sunlight on my skin. Any sunlight. All these little rooms . . . Sometimes I feel like I can't breathe."

They looked at each other. Daskar said, "It's unlikely that you'll be allowed soilside before Earth. The Council is calling for your immediate return. They're pushing hard to curtail your stay on Elteni."

"It's fine. That's what I figured."

"It will do no harm to ask," Saresh murmured.

Daskar nodded. "I'll send the message. In the meantime,

Eyvri, why don't you see if it helps to visit the hangar? It's the largest space on the ship. I'll see that you're given clearance to lock it from the inside."

"Thanks. I'll try that," I said, although I had no intention of doing so. A few days later, however, overwhelmed by the sense of being confined, I made my way down to helix one. I brought Kylie's portable speaker, which I had found tucked into the top of my duffel bag after we left Arkhati, along with the beaded dress and a handwritten note reading, "You need these more than I do. Be safe. Be strong." I recognized the last four words as the particular farewell the Strangers used among themselves. I locked the door and sat cross-legged in the center of the largest section of empty floor. For a time I just sat there, taking deep breaths, listening to the throbbing of the engine and the far-off hum of the air recyclers. Then I turned the speaker up to its loudest setting and played the album I'd been gravitating to since the Flare. Hathan wouldn't have liked it. It was abrasive. I held the speaker in my lap and wished I could crawl inside it. With all that noise in my head, there was no room for words.

Thinking about the Listening was another thing that kept the darkness at bay. At idle moments I found myself turning over the images I'd seen in Hathan's mind, studying them like gemstones, waiting for new facets to catch the light. I hadn't known whether the individual details would stay with me after the connection was severed. I was glad they had. Each new fact, however trivial, added to my store of knowledge about him. He didn't like mizik root. He had asked Reyna to meet him at the Afterburner rather than the Double Star because, although the drinks cost more, the viewports overlooked the docks. In the two minutes I'd been inside his mind, he hadn't thought about his fiancée once. He thought

Reyna was pretty. He thought I was brave.

My thoughts drifted again and again to the memories containing myself, particularly the ones he'd dismissed as irrelevant. What did they mean? The others had been easy to classify: Eyvri the inept, Eyvri the saboteur, Eyvri the beleaguered defender of humanity's good name. The fourth category eluded me. And why had he been so quick to suppress those particular scenes? That fact alone heightened their significance in my eyes.

"Do Vardeshi fall in love?" I asked Sohra in the lounge that night.

She picked up the thread as easily as if it had been hours rather than months since we last compared courtship traditions. "Most of our matches, arranged or self-selected, are about long-term compatibility. It's rare for us to feel infatuation as you think of it."

"Okay, maybe not love. But are you ever drawn to someone without knowing why?"

"Oh, we know why," she said wryly. "We experience attraction too. We just don't act on it. These are fairly pointed questions, Eyvri. Is there something you want to tell me?"

I gave what I hoped was a convincing laugh. "Me? No. I was just thinking about that human-Vardeshi couple, you know, the ones who slept together. Do you have any idea what happened to them?"

She looked surprised. "You didn't hear? His family had him recalled. He went home."

"He left? Just like that?"

"Of course. He was engaged. What did you expect, that he'd toss aside all his plans for the future? For something as fleeting as desire?" She sounded faintly alarmed by the idea.

"I guess not," I conceded. "That kind of thing probably

only happens in television." It was, in fact, the exact plot of the final season of *Divided by Stars*. I felt a sudden fierce longing for Zey. To cover it I said, "But there must be cases of Vardeshi couples who turn out not to be compatible. For whatever reason."

"Of course. We're not robots."

"So what happens then?"

"They reconcile. Or they separate."

"Has that happened to anyone you know?"

"Not anyone I know personally. You might ask the Takheris about it."

I looked at her in confusion. Then I remembered Saresh telling me on Arkhati that his mother worked on one of the outlying research stations and he didn't expect to see her again for several years. I had found the statement puzzling, since I knew Novak Takheri was a senator on Vardesh Prime, but there hadn't been time to pursue it. Now I said, "Their mother lives offworld. Their parents are divorced?"

"Separated, technically. Their mother still wears the Takheri sigil. But her birth house was lower-ranked, so that may have been a practical choice."

"Why? I mean, why did they split?"

Sohra shook her head. "I don't know the details. It happened a long time ago, just after the senator's trip to Earth. I know their mother belongs to one of the anti-alliance factions now. Perhaps she was against the idea of contacting your people."

"Huh. If that's how she feels, she must have been thrilled when all three of her kids signed on to go to Earth. Talk about taking sides."

"They're sending a message," Sohra agreed. "And not a subtle one."

God, I thought, if I hadn't just seen in Hathan's mind that he bore no ill will toward humanity, this would have been motive enough for the rage I'd seen during the Flare. His parents' marriage had broken up over the question of whether or not to contact Earth. I remembered Saresh telling me that Hathan had heard more than his share of anti-human sentiment. How much of it had come from their mother? I thought again of Zey. He must have been only a child when she left. I wished he would talk to me.

* * *

The days separating us from Elteni Starhaven passed swiftly by. On the last night there was an unofficial crew party in the lounge. I slipped on Kylie's dress and assessed my reflection in the mirror. I looked almost exactly as I had on my last night on Arkhati. The only missing touch was the eye makeup, which, lacking Kylie's sure hand with cosmetics, I had decided to forgo. The bruising around my eye had completely healed. Daskar had removed the wrist brace a week ago. I no longer carried any outward signs of the Flare. It had marked me, though, as surely as Vekesh's bullet had done. With one finger I traced the dark line across my right arm, thinking about the invisible tether that bound me to Saresh with its twin strands of terrible violence and the extraordinary intimacy of the Listening. Now I was bound to Hathan in the same way. Oddly reassured by the thought, I swiped on some lip gloss and went to the party.

As I stepped into the lounge, I was startled to hear familiar music playing. I spotted Saresh leaning against the bar, the device in his hand emitting an unmistakable blue glow. That wasn't his flexscreen. It was my phone. He'd asked to borrow it along with my speaker earlier that day. "Earth Night all over again, huh?" I said as I joined him.

He glanced up and flashed me a smile. "Hopefully without the elixirs. I've never had a worse hangover. I've been making a playlist. Care to put the final touches on it?"

"Let's see." I scrolled through the list and was touched to see that it was evenly divided between songs about homecoming and songs about the lure of the unknown.

"I tried to balance ivri avanshekh and ivri khedai," Saresh said. "I wasn't sure what you were feeling."

"I'm not sure what I'm feeling either. I think it's perfect the way it is." I passed the phone back to him and went to get a drink.

The evening passed swiftly and pleasantly. As I looked around the lounge, I had the sense that everyone was trying to keep things light without being obvious about it. I wondered who, if anyone, had requested new assignments. I knew, because Reyna had explained it to me, that there were two schools of thought on crew dispersal after relatively mild outbreaks of the Flare. Fleet policy was to keep the crew together, the theory being that the best way to prevent both victims and attackers from dwelling excessively on the trauma was to force them to interact. Echelon policy mandated reassignment of those who had become violent in order to take the decision out of the hands of the victims. In instances of the Flare involving fatalities, both institutions agreed, immediate dispersal was the only viable option. We were a mixed Fleet and Echelon crew with the additional confounding factor of my human presence. No one had any idea what to expect. It was Arkhati all over again.

Hathan and I had spoken a handful of times during the night, but never alone. I was trying to decide whether I wanted to approach him when he resolved my internal struggle by sitting down at my table just as Sohra was rising to get another drink. "Don't worry," he said immediately. "I'm not going to ask you to sing."

"Good, because it's not happening."

He had a dice cup in one hand, which he rattled inquiringly. "Game?"

"Khivrik sevens," I said in as offhand a tone as I could manage, and was absurdly gratified to hear him laugh.

We played—standard Institute rules—in silence for a few minutes. Then I said, "Can I ask you something?"

"Anything," he said, so simply I was sure it was true.

"Did you put in for reassignment?"

"No."

"Why not?"

"I told you on Arkhati that my mission wouldn't be over until you were safely back on Earth. That's still true."

I hazarded a joke. "Even after I threw up in your bathroom?"

He didn't smile, but his look was wry. "It's going to take a little more than that to balance the scales between us."

"Okay, another question. If we were landing on Vardesh Prime tomorrow instead of Elteni, what's the first thing you'd do?"

His expression turned distant. "In Khezendri, near the Fleet Institute, there's a street of food stalls, all selling—" He used a food term I'd never heard before. "It's a meat stew simmered in a clay pot. It was the only thing that made the North Continent winters bearable. I'd go there first. Then I'd go home to see my father. We'd make senek, and I'd tell him about the mission. There's something confessional about talking things through with him. He understands without judging."

"I wish I'd had the chance to meet him."

"Maybe on your next trip." He said it lightly, but he must have seen the dismay in my face, because he changed the subject at once. "What about you? What's the first thing you'll do when you get back to Earth?"

"Go for a swim," I said instantly.

Hathan shook his head. "That's one Earth custom I'll never understand."

"It's so elemental. Like being part of the water and the sky at the same time. My philosophy all through college was 'never pass up a chance to swim.' I was all ready to go swimming on Vardesh Prime, if I could find somewhere safe to do it. I brought a swimsuit and everything. Too bad there's not a pool on Elteni."

"No, but there may be another hydrotherapy tub."

Cheered by the thought, I reached for the dice.

"Giving me a chance to redeem myself?" Hathan asked.

"What?"

"The game's over. You won."

"Oh." I laughed. "I'm not like you and Reyna. I can't actually talk and play at the same time. I stopped keeping score a long time ago. I've just been throwing the dice."

He gave me an odd look, like I'd said more than I meant to, but all he said was, "In that case, maybe your run of bad luck is finally coming to an end."

Later, as I was walking back from the lounge to my quarters, someone called after me. I turned and was surprised to see Reyna. She caught up to me and we fell into step. She said, "Eyvri, I think it's only fair to give you some idea of what to expect on the starhaven. This isn't going to be like Arkhati. You've been exposed to a lethal pathogen. No one knows what that means, for your people or ours. The threat of contagion is real. Our scientists need to be sure you're not going to step out of quarantine and infect the entire star-haven—or trigger an outbreak on Earth. The tests are likely to be . . . rigorous."

I made a face. "I'm not sure I want to find out what qualifies as rigorous in your book."

"I'm not sure you have any choice," Reyna said soberly.

12

Elteni Starhaven had all the imposing darkness of Arkhati and none of its grandeur. It was the first large-scale starhaven the Vardeshi had built, and its architects had prioritized function at the expense of form. At my first glimpse of the narrow corridors with their murky green underlighting, I recoiled in visceral distaste. My impression of the place declined from there. I was separated from my crewmates almost instantly, ushered away with both minimal fuss and minimal explanation by anonymous figures in sinister black hazard suits that covered them from head to toe. Their features were obscured behind opaque face shields, which was unsettling enough on its own, yet somehow less troubling than their hands. I'd grown accustomed to the fact that Vardeshi fingers were longer than human, and it had never bothered me before. Now, though, I found myself staring at those slender black-gloved fingers, unpleasantly evocative of a score of low-budget horror movies. Well, shit, I thought, reaching for humor to fend off the fear. I think I've been abducted by aliens.

By the end of that day, I had both a fairly clear idea of

what Reyna had meant by "rigorous" and a newfound respect for her power of understatement. My duffel bag and flexscreen had been confiscated. I had been asked to strip off my uniform and undergarments, wash myself thoroughly with astringent-smelling blue soap in water that went beyond lukewarm into outright chilly, dry myself, wash a second time, and finally dress in a flimsy beige jumpsuit. I had then sat, shivering slightly, in a small gray room for an hour before I was cleared to advance to the next stage of processing. I had done all this in apparent solitude, following the commands of a disembodied voice issuing from somewhere in the ceiling. The man giving the instructions spoke quickly and with a regional accent I didn't recognize. The accent, added to my rising anxiety, had led repeatedly to confusion on my part, and I knew I must appear slow-witted to whoever was watching me. And there was no doubt in my mind that I was being watched.

Now I found myself sitting opposite two figures wearing the black hazard suits I'd seen earlier. The man on the left had spoken for both of them, introducing himself as Specialist Irnik, Elteni's resident expert on human anatomy, and the woman beside him as Specialist Anash, the starhaven's supervising doctor. His had been the voice giving me instructions before. My skin crawled at the thought that he'd been watching while I stripped and showered.

"You appear to be trembling," he observed after the introductions had been made. "Are you ill?"

"No, just cold. Could I possibly have my duffel bag back? I have warmer clothes in there." Also underwear, but I saw no need to draw attention to that particular omission.

"I'm afraid your belongings are still being processed."

I squinted at the opaque face shield. "Is there any way for

me to see your faces? This feels a little impersonal."

"Of course," said the woman, her tone as cool as her companion's. Each of them touched a control on the forearm of their hazard suits, and the face shields became transparent. Being able to see them made me feel a little better, but not much. Both doctors had dark hair and distinctly unwelcoming expressions. The man reminded me of Vekesh. Not a pleasant association.

"So what happens next?" I asked. "When do I get to move out of quarantine?"

Specialist Irnik said, "Not for some time. First there are the physical examinations, then the interviews. It may be several days."

"But I'll be able to see my crewmates, right?"

"For security reasons, you'll be kept in isolation until we're sure you don't pose a threat."

"Oh. Can I at least have my flexscreen back?"

"You are uniquely qualified to know that a flexscreen in the hands of one infected with the Flare can be an extraordinarily dangerous weapon. Your access to technology will be restricted until—"

"Right. I get it. Well," I said with false cheer, "let's get going on these tests then, shall we?"

What followed was like a dark counterpart to the hours of stamina and cognition tests I had undergone on my arrival at the Villiger Center. The difference was that I had had at least a vague idea of what information that earlier battery of tests was designed to elicit. The Vardeshi ones were longer and more difficult, and I had not the faintest idea what skills, if any, were being assessed. Something that felt like a vision exam, where I was asked to track the movement of a tiny dot of colored light swirling among other dots of colored light projected onto a distant wall, was followed by a claustro-phobia-inducing strength test in which I stood trapped between two door-sized metal plates, pushing feebly against them as they slid inexorably toward each other. For no reason I could determine, about half of the tests took place in complete darkness. I hated those. Every time the illumination clicked on again, I had to clench my fists and fight the memory of the conference room. What are they doing, I wondered irritably, trying to induce a flashback? Then I shuddered at the realization that that was exactly what they were doing. The epiphany didn't incline me any more favorably toward Specialist Irnik.

When the tests finally concluded, I was spent and shaking. I followed a pair of men in red and black starhaven security uniforms identical to Arkhati's to my temporary quarters on the quarantine level. As the door slid open, I was dismayed to see that the chamber within was roughly the size of the one where I had waited after my decontamination shower, and nearly as featureless. There was a bunk, a small table, and a single stool. I had entertained a faint hope that I might find my duffel bag waiting for me, but the only evidence that any of my belongings still existed was one of my emergency med-ical kits sitting on the table.

I stopped on the threshold and looked questioningly at my two escorts, one of whom explained that I was being housed in isolation for the obligatory three-day observation period, but that I was free to come and go as I pleased. In addition to my quarters, I had access to a shower room and a lounge area with one section partitioned off for a galley. The doors at either end of the corridor were sealed. An attendant would show me to my first debriefing session at eight o'clock the next morning. Was there anything else I required at the present time?

"I could still use some warmer clothes," I said. "And maybe something to read?"

The guard who had spoken murmured something non-committal, and both of them left.

I pulled up a computer interface and checked the time. It was a little after four in the afternoon. I turned away from my makeshift cell and set out to explore the other rooms accessible to me. They were small and bare but functional. Most of the doors on the hallway were locked, and I wondered what they concealed. Empty sleeping quarters, presumably. I whiled away a little time investigating the food that had been provided—Ahnir must have helped with the selection, as there were ingredients for several full meals—and a little more organizing the containers and equipment to my satisfaction. I cooked a pot of red beans and rice and ate it as slowly as I could. I took a long, hot shower, wishing I'd been allowed to keep my own toiletries. I walked up and down the hallway for a while. Finally I gave in and checked the time again. It was just past seven. I went back to my quarters, lay down on the bunk, and tried to think rationally.

Vekesh was gone. The Flare was over. My circumstances now might recall those earlier periods of imprisonment, but the likeness was superficial. The Vardeshi were a practical people who feared the Flare as humans had feared no disease since the bubonic plague. They were simply being careful. My treatment thus far on Elteni had been perhaps a little callous, but not inhumane. In two days, when it was clear that I was sane and well, I would be reunited with my friends. All I had to do was wait out the quarantine. So I told myself. All the same, it was a difficult night. My request for reading material had been either forgotten or ignored. I'd only been given the one beige jumpsuit, and I didn't want to soil it by working out, not that the idea of bodyweight exercises sans underwear held much appeal. I had access to the ship's computer, but I was no more eager than before to delve into the ever-deepening strata of unread messages in my inbox. I turned the lights off and eventually fell into a fitful, shallow sleep. When a young woman in an Echelon uniform arrived to collect me the following morning, I'd already been awake and pacing restlessly for hours.

I soon regretted the profligate waste of energy. My second day of quarantine was entirely given over to debriefing sessions like the ones Hathan and the others had endured on Arkhati. I was seated in front of a panel of four interviewers, two each from the Fleet and the Echelon. They wore uniforms rather than hazard suits, an encouraging sign that my contagion risk had been downgraded. They asked me an endless series of questions about the events leading up to the Flare. When had I realized what was happening? What behaviors had I observed in my crewmates immediately before the outbreak? What precisely had Saresh said to Zey in the axis chamber? And so on and so on. My questioners seemed preoccupied with the fact that I'd ignored Reyna's instructions. They asked me over and over again what her orders had been, whether I had understood them, whether I knew what an order was.

"Look," I said wearily after the fourth iteration. "I know I screwed up, okay? I was scared and lonely. And then I was worried about my friend. It's really that simple."

When we broke for lunch, the younger of the two Fleet officers walked me back to my rooms. She'd been the only other woman in the room, and by far the friendliest of my interrogators. The good cop, I thought without acrimony.

"I know the questions are repetitive," she said. "We're trying to ascertain whether your disobedience is a sign of
disordered thinking. If the disease presents with milder symptoms in humans, it will be harder to identify."

"You mean . . . You think I was infected and didn't know
it?"

"It's a possibility."

I thought about it. "I guess. But for what it's worth, I
think I probably just panicked and made stupid mistakes. Humans do that sometimes. No explanation necessary."

She gave me a conspiratorial look. "I think you'll find that,
with the Vardeshi, explanations are always necessary."

The morning had been draining. The afternoon was
much, much worse. The questions picked up again exactly
where they'd left off: the moment that I'd received the first
message from Zey's flexscreen. Forced to confront in exact-
ing detail the very thing I'd been more or less successfully
ignoring for weeks now, I made a titanic effort to appear
composed. I kept my sentences short and my tone neutral.
Pretend you're talking to Kylie, I told myself. You're telling
her about a movie you saw. A really terrible movie that you're
trying to talk her out of watching. Some poor stupid girl got
herself locked in a room with a violent psychopath. It didn't
happen to you. It didn't happen at all.

The deception worked, for a while, but the barrage of
questions was unrelenting. At some point I put my head in
my hands.

"Is something wrong?" the friendly Fleet officer asked.

"I can't . . . I don't think I can keep doing this. Reliving a
recent assault in this kind of detail is actually not the best
thing for my people."

One of the Echelon officers said coldly, "Your

compliance is appreciated. We're nearly finished."

But it was another grinding hour before I was dismissed to the lonely silence of my rooms. I stripped down in the corridor, careless of who might be watching, and stood in the shower for a long time. Then I collapsed into bed. And that night, for the first time in days, I dreamed of the Flare.

I wasn't sure whether it was my own cry that woke me or the hiss of the door opening, but as I sat up, my tiny room was abruptly flooded with light. Dark figures moved toward the bed, three of them, their gloved hands reaching for me. I fought wildly, but it was no use. Calmly they pinned my arms and legs against the mattress. I felt the hot sting of a needle in the side of my neck. It's over, I thought, an instant before the blackness rushed up to claim me.

* * *

I awoke to a crushing headache and a foul taste in my mouth. I started to sit up, felt sick, and lay down again until the nausea passed. My vision was blurry, and I had to blink to clear it. Sitting up groggily a second time, I looked around in confusion. Where was I? Not in my provisional quarters. This room looked like one of the medical bays I'd seen earlier in my stay. Cautiously I swung my feet out over the floor and slid down. My knees gave way, and I had to grab at the bed for support. I hadn't gone more than a step or two toward the door when it opened and three men in black hazard suits stepped in. In the center was Specialist Irnik.

"Avery," he said smoothly. "I'm glad to see you're—"

I cut him off. "Why do I feel like this? Was I drugged?"

"You don't remember?"

"I remember having a nightmare. I'm having a little

trouble figuring out where it ended."

He had the grace to look uncomfortable. "You were sedated, yes. We thought you might be manifesting symptoms of the Flare. We were concerned that you would injure yourself."

"I was not," I said with brittle patience, "manifesting symptoms of the Flare. I was having a nightmare. Which is extremely common among human trauma victims. As you would know, if you knew anything about us at all. Did it even occur to you to try talking to me before you held me down and stuck a needle in my neck?"

"You reacted violently—"

"To what? Three men breaking into my room in the middle of the night and attacking me? Jesus Christ, I hope I reacted violently!"

"It was a regrettable misunderstanding. I offer my apologies."

"Regrettable?" I repeated. "Yeah, I'd say it's regrettable. What time is it? How long was I out?"

"You were unconscious for approximately twelve hours. It is now late afternoon. If you're feeling sufficiently recovered, I'd like to run a few tests—"

"No," I said flatly.

"I'm sorry?"

"I said no. No more tests, no more interrogations. Cooperating with you has gotten me nowhere. I'm done. I want a nice room with my own shower, I want my stuff back, and I want to see my friends. You can give me those things, or you can take me to a holding cell and call me what I am, which is a prisoner of war." As I was speaking, I felt the color rise in my face, but the words came out clear and crisp.

Specialist Irnik frowned. "Our races aren't at war."

"How long do you think that's going to last once the Council finds out how badly you've been treating me?"

There was a pause. Then he said, "I believe I take your point. I'll have to consult with my superiors, of course. In the meantime, I'll have you escorted back to your temporary quarters. Will that suffice for now?"

"It'll have to," I said, and shoved my way past him to the door.

I was too keyed up to think of food, but as the sedative left my system, I began to feel queasy again, so I nibbled on a protein bar while I made coffee. I took my thermos out to the lounge, which I'd discovered had a projection wall like the one in Saresh's hospital room, and toggled through different views of the starhaven while I waited. I wasn't overly impressed with what I saw. As far as I was concerned, Elteni's main selling point was its proximity to Vardesh Prime, a feature which no longer had any relevance for me. A couple of hours passed before the door to the lounge opened to reveal Sohra and Reyna. The latter had my familiar paisley duffel bag slung over one shoulder. Without a word I walked straight into Sohra's arms and buried my face in her shoulder. Her arms folded around me. "I hate this place," I whispered.

I felt the comforting pressure of Reyna's hand on my back. "I knew it would be bad, but I didn't know how bad," she said quietly. "A sedative? What were they thinking?"

"Apparently it was all a—what did he call it?—a *regrettable* misunderstanding," I said, and broke into laughter that verged on the hysterical.

"Come on," Sohra said. "Let's get you out of here. Your diplomatic suite is only a few minutes' walk from here."

Reyna said, "Just a moment. You might want to change out of that"—she nodded at my beige ensemble—"before you leave quarantine."

"Right. Hang on." I took my duffel bag and began digging through the contents in search of presentable civilian wear. I would have preferred pajamas, but I didn't know exactly how far we had to go, and I was, after all, representing humanity. I pulled out underwear, jeans, a striped shirt, and ballet flats. Sohra and Reyna considerately turned their backs while I changed. Once dressed, I picked up the beige jumpsuit again, considered it, then crumpled it up and dropped it deliberately on the floor. I was tempted to make a rude gesture for the benefit of anyone who might be watching through the hidden cameras, but I didn't, mostly because I didn't know where they were.

Within two minutes we were standing in front of one of the doors that had marked the limits of my quarantine zone. Reyna keyed in a code and we stepped through into a section of the starhaven I hadn't seen before—and directly into a virtual phalanx of uniformed security officers, most of them male, all of them at the upper end of the range for Vardeshi height and breadth. One of them, a man with cropped silver hair and a direct blue gaze, stepped forward and lifted his hand in a Vardeshi salute. "Novi Alkhat, I'm Officer Rathis, head of your personal security detail on Elteni."

I returned the salute and saw him smile slightly. I thought I knew why; Zey had once told me only Vardeshi children presented an unadorned right hand in greeting. "Is this my personal security detail?" I asked. "All"—I made a quick head count—"eight of you?"

Officer Rathis said, "Does that surprise you?"

"Yes," I said emphatically.

Reyna said, "Novi Alkhat has a tendency to underestimate the scope of her role in the alliance." To me she added,

"Would you like me to enumerate again the ways in which you are now a figure of not only political but purely scientific interest?"

"Please don't," I muttered. She smiled. I went on, "I had two guards on Arkhati. That I could see, anyway."

Officer Rathis nodded. "Your circumstances have changed since then. Here you'll have an escort of four uniformed guards whenever you move about the starhaven. That's in addition to the undercover detail, of course." I tried to keep my expression neutral, but some of my dismay must have crept through, because he said, "I know you've been accustomed to moving freely around a small ship. We'll do what we can to keep our presence unobtrusive. A section of the starhaven has been cordoned off exclusively for human use. In addition to the basic amenities, there's exercise equipment and a private observation deck. It's your space, and we won't intrude into it any more than necessary. And we'll be ready at any time to escort you to virtually any area of the starhaven you might wish to visit. But you'll find your activities somewhat … curtailed, at least in comparison to your explorations on Arkhati."

"No Downhelix, huh?" I said. "Where am I supposed to get my kicks?"

"You'll think of something," Sohra murmured, and she and Reyna traded amused looks. I looked from one of them to the other in bewilderment, but no explanation was forthcoming.

Officer Rathis led the way to the section of the starhaven cordoned off for my private use. Sohra and Reyna walked with us as far as the door. I thanked them and said I'd see them later. When they'd gone, I made a game attempt to memorize the names of my security guards, then settled for taking pictures of them with my flexscreen and scribbling in the names by hand, a process which seemed to amuse them. Then Officer Rathis walked me through the diplomatic quarters. The rooms were small and simply furnished, but still a substantial improvement over my accommodations in the quarantine wing. The extent of the area set aside for human use surprised me: there was a lounge, a workspace, individual as well as dormitory-style sleeping quarters, and two sanitation rooms with adjoining showers. Plenty of room for one solitary human to rattle around in. One omission perplexed me. "Where's the galley? And my cooking gear?"

"On the next level up." Officer Rathis indicated a doorway at the far end of the lounge area, where a narrow ramp corkscrewed up out of sight. "The observation deck is above that. The fitness room and laundry facilities are below us."

"Great." I dropped my duffel bag on the floor. "I think I'll go up and check out the view."

Officer Rathis said, "I'll be outside if you need anything."

I went up the ramp and emerged into a corridor with a single door opening off of each side. I chose the right-hand door at random. As I stepped through it, I was assailed by the smell of frying garlic. I stopped, thunderstruck, and stared at a scene so confounding I was sure I must be imagining it. Twin camp stoves blazed blue-white at the center of a long table scattered with recognizably Earth-issue food packets and cooking utensils. Atop one of the stoves a pot of water bubbled merrily. Set over the other was a saucepan, the source of the delicious aroma I'd noticed upon entering, its contents currently being stirred by a spatula in the hand of a man I'd never seen before. A human man.

Human.

My mind, which had struggled gamely to keep up with the

permutations of the day thus far, faltered and seized.

"Hello, Stranger," the man said brightly. "Champagne?"

The words, spoken in what was unquestionably the American English of a native speaker, jolted me out of my stupor. I looked from the man to the green bottle chilling in yet another stainless-steel cooking pot—one of mine, I was almost positive—and said the only thing that came to mind: "Who the hell are you?"

His smile faded. "You're kidding, right?"

I said tightly, "Entertain, for a moment, the possibility that I'm not."

He looked from me to the variously sized knives laid out on the table and said carefully, "Okay. Let's start over. My name is Fletcher Simon. We overlapped at the Villiger Center, but we never had a chance to meet. I've been on Elteni for a month now. I sent you a message three weeks ago, when I heard you'd been diverted here. You didn't get it?"

"I . . ." I thought of my cluttered inbox, of the messages I'd batch-erased without bothering to look at the senders' names, and my bewildered rage began to drain away. "Oh. No. I guess I didn't."

He frowned. "That's weird. Maybe there was some kind of interference?"

"Yeah. Maybe." I blinked hard, trying to process the flood of new information. Something clicked into place. "Wait. Fletcher Simon? I've heard of you. You're some kind of prodigy, right?"

He winced. "I think that's putting it a little strongly."

"But you were second on the List."

"That's right."

I remembered Governor Tavri's show of false concern on the night before I left Arkhati. "I knew you were headed this way. I should have known you'd be here." So this was what Officer Rathis had meant by *A section of the starhaven has been cordoned off exclusively for human use.* Human use. Not my personal use. I'd just assumed that was what he meant.

"From what I understand, you've had a lot going on."

"You can say that again." Another thought struck me. "Wait a minute. Why are they even letting me talk to you? Isn't everyone on this starhaven terrified of infection? An hour ago I was locked in some kind of horror-show hospital ward. Why put the two of us in the same place? Isn't there a risk of contagion?"

"You spoke to Specialist Irnik, didn't you? Asking to be released from quarantine?"

"Yes." I considered that particular encounter and added, "Loudly."

"Well, either your arguments or your volume must have done the trick. I didn't think we'd be meeting face-to-face for another few days, but a little while ago I got a call from your ship's physician saying you'd been discharged from quarantine early and that you'd probably be pissed off and hungry." He added with cautious levity, "She was half right, at least."

"She was all right. She usually is."

"That's good, because I doubled my recipe." Another smile. Was this what humans did—scatter warmth like sunlight? Or was he trying to put me at ease? He waved to the bottle in its bath of ice. "I was serious about the champagne. Don't make me drink alone."

"I . . ." I hesitated. "Sure. I guess. I assume we're being watched, so if no one shows up to knock the glass out of my hand, it's probably safe with whatever they gave me last night."

His expression sobered. "Right. Jesus. What a

clusterfuck."

The word was so apt and so unexpected that I gave an unladylike snort of laughter. "Yeah, exactly. I wonder if the Vardeshi have a word for that."

"If they didn't have one before they discovered humanity, you can bet they've got one now." He opened the champagne bottle with a practiced hand and tipped its foaming contents into two senek cups, another startling juxtaposition. He passed one to me. "Care to make a toast?"

I clinked my cup against his. "To the Strangers." It was the same toast I'd used with Kylie.

"To the Strangers," he agreed. "And to not being the only human in the room."

For the next few minutes, while he put the finishing touches on his sauce, I studied Fletcher Simon. He must have known I was doing it, but he moved among the items arrayed on the table with a perfect lack of self-consciousness. He was a little taller than me and of medium build, which must make him one of the largest people on Elteni. The T-shirt he wore in apparent disregard for the starhaven's coolness revealed a physique that was trim but not overly muscled. It also revealed a skin tone several shades darker than my own. It hardly seemed possible that he'd been locked away from the sun, as I had, for six full months. After the monochrome grays of the Vardeshi, he was startlingly golden. His hair was golden too, and as he glanced up to meet my appraising look, I saw that his eyes were a lucent aquamarine. So much color. Its richness astonished me. Was this what I looked like to my crewmates? I reached deep into Hathan's memories, to his first glimpse of me across the interview table, but any response to my appearance had been swept cleanly away by his incredulity at being addressed in his own language. A dryly precise voice in my head that sounded more like his than it had three weeks ago reminded me that Kylie had blond hair and blue eyes too, and I hadn't been nearly so awestruck by the sight of her.

"Elteni to Avery," Fletcher said lightly, reclaiming my attention. "I lost you there for a minute. What were you thinking about?"

"Just . . . First impressions."

"And? How am I doing?"

I reached for deflecting humor and found it ready to hand. "Well, you're not a creepy medical examiner, and you haven't asked me any probing questions about the Flare, so it's safe to say you're doing better than anyone else on Elteni."

"I thought I'd save the interrogation for after dinner."

We ate sitting on stools pulled up to one end of the long table, the bottle of champagne between us. Between bites of a surprisingly good penne all'arrabbiata, Fletcher told me about his five months on the *Azimuth*. He was a sharp observer and a witty raconteur, and I thoroughly enjoyed his account of the journey. His experience had been similar to Kylie's, generally smooth sailing with the requisite handful of misunderstandings and cultural gaffes. He glossed over the language aspect, but I had the impression that communication, on the whole, had not been a problem. I wondered what his Vardeshi sounded like at this point. The little I knew of him suggested it was substantially better than my own. I was going to have to brace myself for the inevitable ego check. Over a dessert of authentic Swiss chocolate, which had unquestionably come from Fletcher's stash, as my own was long gone, he told me about his month on Elteni. I noticed a conspicuous lack of late-night room invasions and grueling quasi-medical trials in the narrative. I could hear in his voice that he was still enraptured with the strangeness of the place, and I had to fight the urge to tell him how much I hated it. "And then you showed up," he said. "The end. Your turn."

"Oh." I made a face. "You were serious about saving the interrogation for after dinner. I hoped that was a joke."

"You don't have to tell me anything if you don't want to."

"You've probably heard most of it already," I hedged.

"But not all of it. And not from you."

I looked down at the silver foil chocolate wrapper, which I'd been absently folding into precise squares while I listened to him talk. "I'm not against talking about it. But I don't think I'm up for it tonight."

"That's fine," he said easily. "What do you want to talk about instead?"

"How's it going overall? The exchange, I mean. I've been a little . . . out of touch."

Fletcher nodded. "There have been some growing pains. A couple more Strangers have tapped out. Pretty much what you'd expect, homesickness and problems with the language. Some idiot on an orbit crawler misread the label on a food canister and nearly died of anaphylaxis. And there's been some violence. On both sides. An anti-alliance faction jumped one of our guys at a bar on Evrathi Starhaven. Security got there fast, but he's got a concussion and a broken jaw. Right after that, there was an attempted rape of one of the Vardeshi reps on Earth." Here he stopped, as if uncertain whether to continue.

"That's awful," I said, wondering what response he was expecting.

"She's fine, obviously, and some sick asshole in Chicago knows a little more about ranshai than he did before. I think that about covers it."

I let out a cautious breath. "No dealbreakers, then."

"You tell me," he said, his gaze steady on mine.

"The Flare, you mean?" When he nodded, I said, "It was . . . horrific. But it's not the truth of who they are. It's not a dealbreaker."

"Then you better call it in, Alcott, because nobody on our side knows what to think. The Vardeshi are falling over themselves trying to convince the Council that they didn't put the brightest star of the exchange program in the hands of a human-hater. Again."

"They didn't," I said firmly, ignoring the accolade. I'd heard plenty of that kind of talk from Kylie, and I knew the surest way to prolong the teasing was to challenge it.

"You sound pretty sure about that."

"I have good reason to be."

"How good?"

"You know how we say actions speak louder than words? Well, so do thoughts."

Fletcher stared at me. "Don't tell me you did another Listening."

"I did."

"You know they're still forbidden, right?"

"I had to be sure I was safe." I was pleased at how smoothly the words came out. They were partly true, in any case.

"I think I'm starting to understand why you've been dragging your feet on calling home," he said with grim humor. "On that note, I'm under orders to put you in front of a camera within twenty-four hours of making contact, with or without your consent. So it would save me a lot of trouble if you'd message Earth tonight when you get back to your room." Seeing my resistance to the idea, he added gently,

"People are worried about you. And not just the Council. There's a lot of chatter among the Strangers. You're kind of an icon for us. Knowing you're safe is going to make a lot of people feel safer."

"I didn't think of that," I admitted.

"I find it's getting harder to think clearly after being alone for so long. And I haven't been put through the wringer like you have. I think they should send us out in pairs next time."

"Next time," I echoed.

"Consensus among the Strangers is that the alliance will go forward. The *Azimuth*'s crew thinks so too. What are they saying on the *Ascendant*?"

"The same."

"Well, there's another reason for you to phone home sooner rather than later."

"How so?" I asked.

"Remember, you don't just work for the Fleet. You work for Earth too. And if you ever want to be allowed offworld again, you need to show the Council you can meet their expectations even under stress. Regular check-ins are part of the job description."

"They're bringing me home," I said. "I figured they were grounding me for good."

Fletcher shook his head. "I wouldn't make that assumption. You're too valuable. If they can verify that you're not broken, they'll send you out again."

"I'm not broken," I said.

"They don't know that."

"All right, you've made your point. I'll send a message." I got up and began stacking dishes together. He waved me away. "Let me handle the cleanup. Before you go, though, there's one thing I have to say, and you're not going to like it.

I'm hoping I've won you over enough tonight that you won't hate me."

"How could I hate someone who gave me chocolate?"

"That was a calculated move, as you'll see." He spoke casually, but his eyes were serious.

Unnerved, I asked, "What is it?"

Fletcher said quietly, "I launch in a week for Vardesh Prime."

At first I couldn't make any sense of the words. I looked at him incredulously. "What?"

"They're sending me to Vardesh Prime."

"Oh," I said in a small voice.

"I'm sorry."

"It's . . ." I waved a hand. "It's fine. I knew . . . I should have known. I was warned. Well, congratulations. I guess you're number one on the List now."

"That's not how I see it."

"Whatever. Thanks for the food." I bolted for the door. He made no move to stop me.

I walked in a daze down the narrow ramp to the common area where I'd left my duffel bag. I retrieved it, went into one of the single bedrooms I'd noticed on my tour, and closed the door behind me. Why had I been so naïve as to assume that, if the Council wasn't sending me to Vardesh Prime, they weren't sending anyone? Fletcher was intact. He hadn't sustained unacceptable levels of physical and emotional trauma. He hadn't blown off a month of transmissions from Earth. He hadn't been ostracized, shot, or assaulted. He hadn't exposed his mind to the unknowable stresses of telepathy on not one but two separate occasions. He had spent five calm and predictable months aboard the *Azimuth* and a calm and predictable month on Elteni Starhaven. And now he was going to Vardesh Prime. Not after me. Not with me. Instead of me.

* * *

When I awakened nearly twelve hours later, my first thought was that I'd forgotten to record my video message for the Council. My second was that Fletcher Simon was going to Vardesh Prime in my place. I dragged myself through a shower, dressed, and settled on my bed to record my long-postponed transmission. I began my transmission with an apology for my delinquency in not reporting in before now. With quick, broad strokes I laid out the events of the Flare and the succeeding weeks. I left nothing out, not the flash-backs nor the second Listening, for which I offered the same justification I'd given Fletcher. I assured the Council that the Vardeshi had been accurate in their description of the Flare and that it was not, despite appearances, indicative of latent aggression and hostility. I finished with a caustic critique of what passed for hospitality on Elteni. I seeded the entire re-cording liberally with covert signals confirming the truth of my words.

After assuring myself that the message had been sent suc-cessfully, I went to find something to eat. I moved through the common areas with trepidation at first, relaxing when it became clear that Fletcher was either sleeping or absent. Per-haps he had recognized the better part of valor and gone exploring elsewhere in the starhaven. If so, I applauded his wisdom. In the galley I found a plate of freshly baked muf-fins—how had he managed to bake anything with the equipment on hand?—conspicuously placed beside a carafe of coffee on the long table. He's trying to win me over with food again, I thought in some irritation, and then, grudgingly, It's working.

By the time I'd finished eating, I had reached the conclusion that I didn't resent Fletcher nearly as much as I missed him. After all, it wasn't his fault that the Vardeshi had chosen him to replace me. And, barring any unforeseen stops on the way home, it would be five long months before I saw another human. What could I accomplish by avoiding him except to punish myself unnecessarily for a situation neither of us could control? Besides, I had had more than three weeks to come to terms with the fact that I wasn't going to Vardesh Prime. Now that the initial sting of Fletcher's revelation had passed, I found myself able to take a reasonably impartial view of the situation. He had come as far as I had. He had learned a new language. He deserved to go. But, I promised myself, if he gloated even once about his last-minute promotion, I'd measure out exactly ten months of our combined food supply and vent the rest into space, dooming us both to an express trip home. I knew how to identify an airlock now. I knew how to open one too.

He didn't gloat. When I messaged him, asking if he was free to give me a tour of the starhaven, his response was immediate and affirmative. Five minutes later, he joined me in our de facto mess hall. "I'm glad you texted me," he said at once, sitting down beside me and helping himself to the last of the coffee. "I would have done it, but I thought you might, how shall I put this, need some space?"

We both laughed a little harder than the joke warranted. "It's okay," I said. "I mean, I'll be honest, I'm not thrilled. But I'll get over it. That being said, it wouldn't hurt your case to send a little more of that chocolate my way."

"It's yours. And, Avery, for what it's worth . . ." He waited for me to look at him before continuing. "I'm not going to say I envy you, because that would be incredibly callous after what you've been through. But I've been out here almost as long as you have, and no one's asked me to wear a uniform, let alone mind-meld with them. Did you ever go to Disney World as a kid?"

Perplexed, I nodded.

"Good. Then you'll know what I mean when I say that you're riding Space Mountain, and the rest of us are still dicking around on It's a Small World."

"Yeah, well, I admit it's been a while, but I don't remember having to switch cars on Space Mountain because my first one exploded halfway through. Or being turned back right before the end."

"And with all that," Fletcher said firmly, "it's still a better ride."

Unwillingly I laughed.

We spent the next few hours wandering around Elteni, inasmuch as it was possible to wander while politely hemmed in by our combined force of eight security guards. It wasn't, I had to concede, as repellent a place as I'd initially thought, but its chief attraction in my eyes was Fletcher himself. He was sublime company. I knew the counterfeit intimacy of like-minded strangers thrown together in unusual circumstances, but this was something more. We shared a fascination with language and wordplay in both English and Vardeshi. He was intensely jealous of my stock of borrowed idioms. I was secretly relieved that there was one linguistic arena in which I was able to best him, even if accessing someone else's lexicon should rightly be considered cheating. I had watched the accelerated progression of my language skills in Hathan's memories. I knew my Vardeshi was good. Fletcher's was better. I would have resented him for it if he had betrayed the slightest hint of either smugness or false self-deprecation, but he was entirely matter-of-fact about his fluency. I accepted my defeat with good grace, sharing in the laughter when he called a senek vendor out on a provincial accent too subtle for me to hear, let alone place. It wasn't until I heard him trading what I assumed to be jovial insults with a pack of young men in Fleet uniforms that I let my irritation show. "Oh, come on! Standard Vardeshi wasn't enough for you? You had to learn the North Continent dialect too?"

"It's as good a way as any to set myself apart from the competition."

"What competition?"

He gave me a sidelong glance, then said with disarming frankness, "You, for one."

"Well, you're going to the planet, so it must have worked."

"I'm going as your understudy. For two weeks. Next time I want to go for months, if not years. And I want to be the one they ask for, not the consolation prize."

"That's the second time you've brought up your next mission. You're already planning for it." I shook my head. "I can barely think about tomorrow."

"Like I said," he said lightly, "you've been on a different ride."

For the most part we were treated with either kindness or neutral courtesy by vendors and passers-by alike. At one point, however, Fletcher took my elbow and guided me gently onward when I would have stopped at a jewelry vendor. "What's wrong?" I asked.

"You didn't see the sign?"

"I saw it. It's a nice name." The sign bore the name of the shop, Shards of Starlight, in stylized gold script on an indigo background. It had caught my attention because the phrase reminded me of the transmission with which the Vardeshi had reopened contact with Earth. *Bright shards of yourselves,* they had said, referring to the fragments of radio and video communication they had intercepted from Earth over the years, the glimpses of our identity that had first piqued their curiosity about us.

"Not the name," Fletcher said. "The symbol in the corner."

I looked back over my shoulder. In the lower right-hand corner of the sign was another symbol, a small glyph I didn't recognize, also printed in gold. "What is that?" I asked.

"It represents purity. It means they're anti-alliance. It's the third or fourth one I've seen today."

"Anti-alliance?" I echoed in disbelief. "Are you serious?"

"You didn't see them on Arkhati?" Fletcher sounded equally surprised.

Rathis murmured, "Fringe starhavens tend to be more liberal in their politics. And, given Arkhati's proximity to Earth, the symbols may not catch on there at all."

"I hope not," I said, shaken.

Fletcher nudged me onward. "Come on. It's not a big deal. The alliance isn't universally popular on either side. That's not new information. Unless the movement gains enough traction to impact policy, which it won't, all they're doing is advertising their bigotry. Right?" He looked to Rathis for support.

"Yes," Rathis said. "And you should expect to see more of it. The consensus is that the trial year is proceeding well. Anti-alliance groups on both sides are likely to escalate their tactics out of desperation as the experiment draws to a close."

Fletcher nudged me with his elbow. "Get it? Because

we're winning."

I had to smile. "Okay, okay, you've made your point."

As we walked on, I tried to let the conviction I'd heard in his and Rathis' voices carry me past my unease. But I couldn't resist checking the corners of each sign we passed. To my relief, I spotted only two more of the purity glyphs. I avoided the eyes of the vendors running those shops. It might be only politics, and not intended to be personal. But I was one of only two humans on Elteni, and it felt awfully personal to me.

As the day unfolded, I had the same sense I'd had with Kylie of being pulled gently but insistently back into myself. Was it even possible, I wondered, to preserve the integrity of one's identity when surrounded by members of another species? Was I, after six months among the Vardeshi, ever so slightly less human? Maybe Fletcher had been right about the wisdom of sending us out in pairs next time. Maybe we needed to see our own humanity mirrored back to us by others in order to maintain our grip on it. I remembered the fears I'd had on Arkhati about Stockholm syndrome and going native. I hadn't thought in those terms in months. Was the omission meaningful in itself? Exactly how far out of myself had I gone? Remembering the peculiar sensation of settling back into my own body after the Listening with Hathan, I knew it was a long way.

By the end of the afternoon, I knew I liked Fletcher. I also knew—and in my mind the two facts were distinct—that I was attracted to him. After months of wrestling with my half-guilty fixation on Hathan, it was almost a relief to feel the clean, straightforward pull of desire. I had collected a handful of ex-boyfriends over the years. None of them had ever drawn me so forcefully. Was it something about Fletcher himself, I wondered, or was it only that I was emerging from what was essentially a six-month-long signal shadow? I knew that male and female bodies communicated in ways we only dimly understood, that an intricate dance of pheromones and subtle kinetic cues took place beneath and around any verbal interaction. I had never known that silent communication to be so powerful. Every time Fletcher spoke to me, every time our eyes met, I felt a giddy rush of heat. With every seemingly incidental brush of his arm against mine, I breathed in the commingled scents of Earth soap and deodorant warmed by his skin. When he left his jacket on a stool, I wanted to grab it up and bury my face in the fabric. His presence made me edgy, restless, but I wasn't sure if I wanted to move toward him or away. Both at once, maybe.

Whichever one I chose, I was fairly certain that the decision fell to me. From what I understood of the male libido, a young heterosexual man, celibate now for six months at minimum, was unlikely to turn down a brief casual liaison if one offered itself. I didn't think I was overestimating my personal charms to conclude that Fletcher was mine if I wanted him. So, I asked myself as I watched him making effortless small talk with another vendor, did I want him? I wasn't sure. I felt an odd compulsion to see him interacting with Hathan. In my mind there was no contradiction between the simple desire I felt for one of them and the love, with its attendant longing, that I felt for the other. But I couldn't interpret either feeling in isolation. I needed to put them into context, and there was no way to do that except to see the two men together.

Later that night I did. After a last draining cross-examination by another joint panel of Fleet and Echelon investigators, I was finishing up a leisurely dinner with Fletcher when I received a message from Sohra. Some of the *Ascendant*'s crew were meeting for drinks later, she said, and named the time and the bar. Fletcher had already suggested a quiet night in the Green Zone, our name for the humans-only section of the starhaven, with a bottle of wine and a movie. When I relayed the content of the message, however, he said decisively, "Let's go out. I want to meet these crewmates of yours."

A little later we made our way down to Elteni's bar level. I could have wished our security escort were a bit less efficient; my memories of Downhelix were still fresh, and I would have enjoyed wandering around looking for the place we wanted. On our way we passed one establishment whose purple gloom I recognized from Arkhati. I pointed it out to Fletcher, who had never heard of a rana club. Officer Rathis pointed out the sign for the Supernova farther down on the same side. Inside, I found my crewmates without difficulty thanks to Reyna's distinctive uniform. Fletcher introduced himself, and I watched with a mixture of envy and proprietary pride as their eyes widened at the authenticity of his accent. Hathan arrived shortly after us.

"Ah," he said as he sat down. "This must be the second most qualified representative of humanity."

As opening lines went, it was a bit aggressive, at least to my ears. Fletcher retorted, "And you must be . . . Novi Takheri, is it?"

He had to know that was wrong, I thought, even as Hathan glanced pointedly at the insignia on his sleeve and said, "Guess again."

"Oh, right. My mistake. You're the guy charged with transporting the most qualified representative of humanity safely to your homeworld. How's that going?"

"From your point of view," Hathan said, "it appears to be going exceptionally well. Our misfortune works to your advantage."

"Your 'misfortune,'" Fletcher repeated. "That's an interesting way to describe nearly beating someone to death."

"Just think, if you'd been first on the List, it might have been you."

Each of them spoke so lightly it was hard to reconcile the coldness of the words with their tone. I glanced around at the others, wondering if someone ought to intervene, but Reyna was as inscrutable as ever, and Saresh and Sohra actually looked amused. Was this a peculiarly Vardeshi type of verbal sparring which Fletcher had mastered on the *Azimuth* along with, apparently, everything else? Or was it exactly what it seemed to be, which was primitive masculine posturing, regardless of species? Either way, I decided to let it go and enjoy the illusion of being fought over.

"When do you launch for Prime?" Hathan was asking.

"A week."

"What ship?"

"The *Sidereus*."

"That's an Echelon ship," Sohra said in surprise.

"It seemed the safest course," said Reyna.

"Are you going?" I asked her.

"I was offered the posting. I declined it."

"So you could keep me from doing more stupid things," I guessed.

"Or try, at any rate," she agreed.

And just like that, the tension dissipated. The conversation became lively and general. Some time later, returning from a drinks run with Sohra, I found Fletcher and Hathan engrossed in what appeared to be a perfectly amicable dice game. I seized the opportunity to study them covertly. Viewed in profile, they were like an unconscious portrait of their respective species: Fletcher lounging back with a kind of insouciant grace, one arm stretched across the cushioned back of the seat beside him, Hathan sitting forward with his elbows resting on the table, fingers woven together. In attitude, in coloring, they were as different as sunlight and shadow. Absorbed in contemplation of the ways in which they diverged, I was caught off guard when Fletcher made a comment in the North Continent dialect that won a soft laugh from Hathan. Hearing it, I felt the same wistful ache I always had, and I acknowledged to myself that my feelings for him were unchanged. But. There was zero chance that anything would ever come of them. And I was lonely, and Fletcher was here, and it required no great leap of the imagination to speculate that he was lonely too. Was I obsessed enough to turn away from a real if transitory connection in favor of a fantasy? I still didn't know. The moment of decision came only later, during a lull in the conversation, when Hathan checked his flexscreen and said it was time for him to be on his way.

"Early night?" Saresh asked.

"Late one, more likely. I'm meeting Rhevi Garian for a drink."

"Sidra's brother?" Reyna inquired. "Is he still on the *Meridian*?"

"He's transferring to the *Star of Erasik*." Hathan rose to leave.

I waited until he was gone before asking, "Who's Sidra?"

"His fiancée," Saresh said, his tone carefully neutral.

I nodded and sat back with my glass, manufacturing an expression of polite interest, as Fletcher began telling a story about his time on the *Azimuth*. My mind, however, was whirling. At last I had a name to attach to Hathan's mysterious betrothed. Sidra Garian. Who had a brother in the Fleet, a brother with whom Hathan was sufficiently friendly to meet for a drink. Why, I asked myself tartly, did that information make me want to slink back to my room, crawl under the covers, and cry? I had spent enough time over the last six months staring at the gold sigil on his hand. It wasn't like I hadn't known the woman existed. Finding out that she had a name shouldn't be such a big damned surprise.

Soon afterward there came a more general fracturing of our party, some people moving on to another bar while others returned to their rooms. I glanced at Fletcher and found him watching me. I took a last moment of internal quiet to weigh my decision, then said casually, "Want to get out of here?"

"Sure," he said, matching my tone.

We said our goodbyes to the others. I asked Officer Rathis to take us back to the Green Zone. Fletcher walked beside me in a charged silence that made my heart beat faster. When we reached the door, I keyed in the entry code and stepped inside. Fletcher followed and closed the door behind us. We stood there a moment, alone in the stillness, looking at each other. Then I took his hand and drew him after me toward my room. Inside, I dropped his hand and turned toward him. His arms closed around me. I felt the warmth of his body against the entire length of mine. I gasped, dizzied by his scent, intoxicating at such close range, and by the sudden ferocity of my need. He ran his thumb along the line of my jaw, lifting my chin. His lips brushed lightly against mine. The teasing contact was maddening, inadequate. I put my hand on the back of his neck and pulled him down to me again, my mouth seeking his. He met my urgency with his own. In that instant I knew I had been right: about his loneliness, about his desire. We felt the same things. We were the same. It was only when we were stumbling toward my bed across a floor already littered with most of our clothing that he pulled away long enough to ask, "Are you sure you want to do this?"

It was the same question Saresh had asked me before each of the Listenings. The unbidden echo was jarring, but the answer was the same. "I'm sure."

"Oh, thank God," he said fervently. I laughed and pulled him down with me onto the bed, all thoughts of other men and other intimacies forgotten once again.

13

One night with Fletcher turned into two and then three. There was no talk of love or promises or meeting up again on Earth. I didn't ask him if he had someone waiting back home, and he didn't ask me. We both understood that whatever there was between us existed only for this stolen handful of days on Elteni. I was glad he saw it that way too. I needed his companionship and his humor and his warmth in the night. I didn't need anything more from him than that.

We agreed that, to maintain our professionalism, it would be best to be discreet. The logistics of our assignations, of course, were easy to conceal. The Green Zone was our private territory; Vardeshi intrusions were rare and never unannounced. The connection between us was harder to hide. In every social gathering we watched each other, drawn by the transparent play of emotion on another human face. When speaking Vardeshi, we constantly interrupted ourselves and each other to confer on translations and analogies. Fletcher's grammar was better, but mine was the richer lexicon, a consequence of my being a crew member rather than a passenger. Speaking English, we made pointless cultural references for the sheer delight of having them understood. We tested each other's humanity with endless rapid-fire trivia questions. "Worst childhood fear?" "Quicksand." "Favorite ice-cream flavor?" "Peanut-butter cup." "How many days in a week?" "Eight. Oh, sigils, I mean seven. Seven!"

Saresh, overhearing one of these exchanges, said in some alarm, "Eyvri, have you spoken to Daskar about these lapses in memory? They could be related to the Listening."

"Oh, no! It's a game," I assured him hastily. "We're just pretending."

"Pretending . . . to forget things?"

I looked at Fletcher, who waited, his eyes dancing, for my explanation. "We're . . . It's kind of hard to explain. I guess you'd say we're pretending to be Vardeshi spies impersonating humans."

"Poorly," Reyna added.

"I'm sure your real spies are much more convincing," Fletcher said.

She replied coolly, "They've escaped detection thus far, haven't they?"

"I can't tell when your Echelon friend is joking," he confided to me in a perfectly audible voice.

"Reyna never jokes," I said, deadpan, and caught the gleam of approval in her dark eyes.

It was the fourth day after my release from quarantine. We were standing on Elteni's largest observation deck, whose several tiers afforded panoramic views of the snowflake-shaped starhaven and a nearby nebula through a wall of viewports perhaps three stories high. Even I had to concede that the effect was stunning. I wore a simple dress and a brightly embroidered scarf I'd bought in the marketplace after Khiva assured me that it had no potentially embarrassing cultural significance. Fletcher was distractingly handsome in jeans, a blazer, and a crisp white shirt. My colleagues, in darkly elegant Vardeshi formal wear, each had a glass of some unidentifiable crystalline spirit in hand. Fletcher and I were once again drinking champagne, a case of which, I now knew, had been sent out with him on the *Azimuth* in the hope that it would eventually be approved for Vardeshi consumption. It hadn't been, and we were conscientiously eliminating the need to transport it back. The occasion was my official welcome reception, which was to follow the familiar pattern of cocktail hour, dinner, and brief performance. The cocktail hour was drawing to a close. I had been introduced to the commanders of Elteni's Fleet and Echelon branches and had made dutiful small talk for the requisite half hour before taking refuge in the company of my friends.

"There are a lot of Vardeshi who could pass for human," Fletcher said thoughtfully. "Not so many humans who could pass for Vardeshi."

I said airily, "Speak for yourself. I'm told I blend in perfectly."

Hathan joined us in time to hear my assertion and the laughter that followed it. "Blend in with who?" he asked.

"Us," Saresh said.

Hathan nodded. "Ah, yes. Virtually indistinguishable."

"Suvi Ekhran could probably pass for human." I heard the error in my speech too late to correct it. Once again, I'd used the wrong honorific. Now that Hathan had joined the group, Reyna was no longer its highest-ranking member. Hathan murmured the correction. So did Fletcher. Reflexively I whacked him hard on the arm, forgetting that he was holding a champagne flute. He kept hold of the glass, but half of its contents splashed onto the floor. Laughing, he pulled out his flexscreen and pretended to speak into it. "Paging Specialist Irnik. Avery's becoming violent. We're going to need some more of that tranquilizer, stat."

"Very funny," I said acidly. "I didn't realize the assholes of Earth were sending a delegation."

Fletcher's grin was unrepentant. "Call me whatever you want, just get the honorific right." He went off to look for a refill while I was still searching for an adequately scathing reply.

Hathan said quietly, "I didn't know you minded being corrected."

"You get to correct me. He doesn't. He's supposed to be in my corner."

He watched Fletcher make his way back to us from the drinks table, stopping on the way to speak with Elteni's governor, a man named Edris who had welcomed me with a cool courtesy I infinitely preferred to Tavri's manufactured warmth. "Is he?"

"Yeah. I think he is."

"Good." He hesitated, then added, "I'm in your corner too, you know."

An exhilarated thrill ran through me, but my reply, I was pleased to hear, sounded perfectly steady. "I know."

It had all the makings of a wonderful evening. At dinner, Fletcher and I were seated side by side, surrounded by a mix of friends and dignitaries. The conversation was effervescent, the cuisine superb, at least to a palate starved for fresh ingredients. The list of Vardeshi foods approved for humans had more than doubled in length since our departure from Arkhati, and Specialist Irnik, whatever I might think of him personally, had at least thought to include allergen tests in his battery of examinations. It was with shocked delight that I now found myself permitted to eat something approximating a salad. Fletcher was less enthusiastic about the vegetables, but he attacked the main dish, a small roasted fowl, with gusto.

"Tastes like chicken," he said gleefully.

I laughed. "Of all the stupid clichés—"

I never finished the sentence. With an odd sense of dislocation, I found myself standing beside the door to the corridor, my hand on the panel. I had no memory of getting up or crossing the short distance from my chair. The blood was thundering in my ears, and my breath came in gasps. Bewildered, I looked back toward the table. No one else had moved. Everyone was staring blankly at me. Everyone, that is, except Hathan, whose eyes held grief and terrible knowledge. There was an agonizing silence. Then two servers came cautiously forward to sweep up the remains of Khiva's water glass, which had just shattered on the floor. The sound of breaking glass must have tripped a flight instinct so primal it had bypassed my mind and taken direct control of my body.

With unhurried movements, Fletcher put down his kevet and pushed his chair back from the table. He came over to me and said gently, "Let's get some air."

I nodded jerkily. "Yeah. Good idea."

We walked down one corridor and then another, preceded and followed at a discreet distance by our security staff, until my adrenaline began to ebb, leaving me feeling shaky and sick but once again in full control. I was glad Fletcher was there. He didn't pester me with questions or conjectures. He reserved his attention for the signs at each corridor junction, glancing my way only once or twice. When we'd been walking for about ten minutes, I stopped in a sanitation room to drink from the tap. The cold water on my wrists as I held my cupped hands under the stream pushed the nausea back a little further. When I came out, Fletcher was speaking to someone on his flexscreen. Seeing me, he pressed the screen against his shirt, not to conceal it but to keep it from picking up our voices. I wanted to laugh. I'd never been able to locate the mouthpiece on mine either. "It's Rhevi Daskar," he said. "Do you want to talk to her?"

I shook my head. "Just tell her I'm okay. It wasn't a flash-back, more like a . . . reflex, I guess."

He finished the call, put away his flexscreen, and studied me. "You're shivering. Do you want my jacket?"

"Actually, I'd rather be cold. But thanks."

"Where do you want to go now?"

I sighed. "Back to the dinner, I guess. If I don't go back, it becomes a thing, right? More of a thing, I mean. I'm sure they're all talking about me right now."

Fletcher put his hands on my shoulders and looked into my face. "Avery. Forget what anyone thinks. Where do *you* want to go?"

With a laugh that was half a sob, I leaned forward until I could rest my head on his shoulder. He folded his arms around me, careless of the security personnel looking on. I said into his jacket, "I want to go to Vardesh Prime. And I want to go home. But neither of those things is going to hap-pen tonight, so for now let's go back to the stupid dinner. Just promise me you won't leave me alone in there."

"I promise," Fletcher said steadily, "that I will not leave you alone."

We retraced our steps to the observation deck. As we set-tled into our seats again, I had cause once more to be grateful for the Vardeshi habit of discretion. No stifled laughter or sudden embarrassed hush heralded our arrival. The conversations taking place around our end of the table had clearly been going on for some time; they hadn't been hastily snatched up like dropped knitting when we walked in. In our absence, our fellow diners had moved on to the savory course. Our plates had been cleared away, and smaller ones with artfully arranged cheese and olives had taken their place. I wasn't hungry, but I picked at my cheese and watched Fletcher chase an olive around his plate with his kevet, cursing under his breath. I was fairly sure he was doing it for my benefit. It was still funny. I watched Saresh ask the Echelon officer next to him a dull question about ship resupply protocols and listen with every appearance of interest to her equally dull response. That, too, was for my benefit, I knew. At one point I looked up to see Zey watching me from across the table. It had been a very long time since he'd looked at me directly. His eyes, in the lantern-lit twilight, were twin pools of darkness. We stared at each other for a long time, two islands of quiet amid the low hum of conversation that surrounded us. I was the first to look away.

The cultural-exchange portion of the evening went off without incident. The Vardeshi gave a demonstration of something called wind painting, which had to do with manipulating charged particles that left fiery trails in the air, allowing a skilled artist to write lines of calligraphy that faded well before I could decipher them. Fletcher offered to translate for me. I stepped on his foot. When our turn came, improbably, he produced a guitar and sang a rendition of "Blackbird" so clear and light it was like the dream of a song. I sang along with him, softly, after making sure Hathan was nowhere nearby.

By the end of the night, I was reasonably confident that

I'd salvaged my reputation among the notables of Elteni. I was in the midst of saying goodbye to the governor when Khiva interrupted us, her mortification obvious, to apologize for catching her water glass with her elbow and knocking it off the table. I quickly reassured her that she hadn't done anything wrong.

"Come on, Khiva, I drop something every other day. Usually at officers' dinner. It wasn't your fault." I added, conscious that the governor was listening with frank interest, that the sound had probably triggered a memory of my flexscreen shattering during the Flare.

"A flight instinct?" Governor Edris asked in a tone of neutral interest, as if we were once again discussing ship resupply protocols. "That seems so—if you'll forgive the term—primal."

"Unfortunately we still live in a world where those instincts are advantageous to survival," said Fletcher, who had kept his promise faithfully and returned to my side after his performance was over.

"Evidently so do we," the governor said. The words might have been merely for form's sake, the career diplomat ensuring the discreet exit of a problematic guest, but I liked him for saying them.

* * *

Fletcher had always been tender with me, but his lovemaking that night was cautious in a way it hadn't been before. I wondered at the change but didn't ask about it. As I was beginning to drift toward sleep, however, he spoke into the quiet. "You've never talked to me about the Flare."

"I know."

"That's what your … non-flashback tonight was about, right?"

I nodded against his shoulder.

"Hathan attacked you."

It wasn't a question, but I said obligingly, "Right."

"You were alone with him." I nodded again, wondering where this was going. He said slowly, "The report that went out to the Strangers was pretty vague. It just said you had bruises on your face and a sprained wrist. How did that happen?"

All at once his odd hesitation when telling me about the attempted rape of one of the Vardeshi representatives on Earth clicked into place. "Are you asking if he tried to force himself on me?"

A pause. Then, "Yes."

"No, he didn't."

Fletcher pulled back a little and raised himself on his elbow to look into my face. I said steadily, "It wasn't like that."

"Do you want to tell me what it was like?"

"I think I'd rather not talk about it."

"Okay," he said. I liked him for his willingness to accept the refusal without arguing or accusing or otherwise trying to twist my private pain into somehow being about him. I liked him, I realized, much more than I'd ever expected to, even after I'd decided to invite him into my bed. I shifted in his arms, settling my head more comfortably on his chest. His fingers moved lightly in my hair. We lay awake for a long time, each thinking our own thoughts. Neither of us mentioned the Flare again, but it was there with us like a shadow in the room.

* * *

We were in the Green Zone's galley the next morning, assembling a late breakfast, when my flexscreen signaled an incoming message. I checked it and made a face. "Ugh. Looks like the Echelon's made its ruling on the *Ascendant.*"

Fletcher paused with a pancake balanced on his spatula and looked up, his expression oddly intent. "And?"

I shrugged. "And nothing. That's all it says. I have to go to some kind of formal announcement this afternoon with my crew and a bunch of high-ranking Fleet and Echelon people."

"Sounds fun," he said sardonically.

An instant later his flexscreen chimed too. I laughed. "I bet that's your invite."

He read the notification. "Apparently we're both in for an afternoon of long-winded speeches."

I spent the intervening hours catching up on my correspondence with Earth. Fletcher helped by triaging my unviewed messages and offering suggestions when I found myself stuck for a word. I was grateful for his help; the phrases he suggested had a brevity and directness that I knew would assuage the Council's lingering doubts about my professionalism. When we arrived at the designated room that afternoon, there were several dozen people, most of them in Fleet or Echelon uniforms, already waiting for the proceedings to start.

"Good luck," Fletcher said and went to take his place on the tiers of benches lining the far wall of the room.

Officer Rathis led me to my crewmates, who were gathered before the dais on which the members of the tribunal sat. "What's the deal?" I asked Sohra in an undertone. "We don't get to sit down?"

"It's traditional to stand when receiving judgment," she explained.

"Just like last time." I shivered. "I figured that was just one of Vekesh's little personal touches."

"Vekesh was cruel, but he wasn't very original," Saresh said dismissively. "And that trial was a farce. This is the conclusion of a thorough and impartial investigation by a legitimate tribunal."

"Why doesn't that make me feel better?" I muttered.

As the proceedings began, I admitted to myself that while knowing I had received the Vardeshi equivalent of due process wasn't especially consoling, at least I wasn't facing this tribunal alone. Sohra was standing to my left. I watched her out of the corner of my eye, trying to imitate her attentive stillness.

Governor Edris was the first to speak. He made a few brief introductory remarks, then ceded the floor to the First Rank officer of the Fleet, a woman named Riash whom I recognized from dinner the night before.

"Many in this room vividly recall the last confirmed outbreak of the Flare, more than forty years ago now," she said. "It claimed more than a hundred lives. I know the experience of the *Ascendant*'s crew was emotionally devastating. But there can be no question that, placed in the proper context, the toll of the disease in this case was extraordinarily light. What makes this instance unique is the presence of a human. The most troubling event of the outbreak was also the most potentially damaging to interstellar politics. I will address that incident directly before giving our decision."

Oh good, I thought. Let's talk about it some more.

"There was some dispute among the members of this

tribunal as to how to handle the involvement of Eyvri Alkhat. The purpose of debriefing is to understand the chain of cause and effect and, where necessary, to assign blame. It was recommended by some that we exempt Novi Alkhat entirely from the debriefing process. However, as her title indicates, she is a contracted employee of the Fleet. She has served us successfully for six months, and she has demonstrated her allegiance on many occasions. We chose to evaluate her actions as those of a competent and informed member of the *Ascendant*'s crew, rather than a civilian passenger. After extensive interviews with both her and Khavi Takheri, we conclude that they bear equal responsibility for their disastrous encounter."

I glanced toward Hathan. He raised his eyebrows slightly.

The speaker continued, "They have since reconciled, as have the other crew members involved in violent incidents. Given that this is the case, we have elected to follow Fleet protocol with regard to reassignment. The *Ascendant* will launch in three days' time for Earth with its current crew, with one exception. On behalf of the Fleet, I congratulate Novi Takheri for his year of exemplary service and wish him clear skies in his new posting on the *Star of Erasik*."

"What?" I said.

Sohra looked over in surprise. "You didn't know? Zey asked to be reassigned."

"He what?" The words came out louder than I'd meant them to, but they were lost in the rising commotion as people began discussing the verdict with their seatmates. I looked for Zey. He was already far away, his diminutive silver-haired form nearly lost in the throng of taller uniformed figures filing toward the door. "Zey!" I shouted. He didn't look back. I went after him, fighting to master my impatience as Officer

Rathis and his companions decorously cleared a path for me. Out in the corridor I looked one way and then another, finally locating him near a junction. "Zey!" I called again, and would have sprinted after him if not for Rathis' gentle restraining hand on my arm. "Wait," he said. "I know you want to go after him, but you can't run around the starhaven alone." He nodded to one of the other guards, who went in pursuit of Zey. I followed with my remaining seven attendants at an infuriatingly sedate pace.

Within a few minutes we were standing in the corridor that housed the *Ascendant*'s crew. I recognized it because I had visited Sohra's quarters a few days before. I hadn't visited Zey's. I didn't even know which door to go to. Officer Rathis had to point it out to me. I pressed the control to demand entry. Instead of a welcoming chime, I heard Zey's voice say distinctly in English, "Fuck off."

He had to know I wasn't alone. Torn between rage and humiliation, I punched the control again. "Zey, come on. Open the door."

After a moment he did. He stood blocking the doorway with his body. I saw both weariness and resolve in his face. "What do you want?"

"To talk to you without eight other people listening."

He gave my security detail a cursory glance. "I don't care who's listening. If you came here to say something, then say it."

"Fine. You can't leave."

He lifted one shoulder in a perfect copy of Hathan's one-sided shrug. "I can't stay."

"I can't do this without you."

"You haven't needed my help in months."

"I wasn't talking about the work," I said.

He sighed. "Look, Eyvri, I'm not exactly happy with the way things have turned out either. And maybe it's my fault. I thought we were friends. I thought that meant the same thing to both of us."

My eyes stung. "It does."

"Not from where I'm standing." He made a shift, an incremental movement, toward the panel that housed the door controls. In that moment I knew I was about to lose him, and I knew, as well, that there was only one thing that might possibly win him back. I said, "I need to tell you something. It's private. It involves your family. And I don't want to say it in front of all these people, but if I have to, I will."

With visible reluctance he moved aside. I stepped forward. Officer Rathis caught me again, as gently as before, and drew me back, murmuring an order to the nearest security guards. She slipped past Zey and into the room. Two long minutes passed. The guard emerged at last and said, "It's clear. Go ahead."

I went in. Zey followed me and closed the door behind him. I pointed at his bed. "Sit down."

He sat. I started to talk. I told him the entire story, beginning with the first chime of my flexscreen on the storage-room floor, ending with the moment when Sohra and Ahnir found me in the corridor cradling my sprained wrist. For once I felt grateful to my questioners in the quarantine wing. Forced to repeat the grim saga over and over again, I had pretended I was talking to a friend. Now I was, and the words came easily. Only once or twice did I pause, knowing myself to be precariously balanced on a threshold between Zey's tiny quarters and a cold, bright, silent room that only I could see.

Zey was quiet for a long time after I finished speaking. Then he said, "That's awful, and I'm sorry it happened to you, but it doesn't change anything."

I rubbed a hand across my face. "I know. It shouldn't. This is the part that changes things. Zey, I'm in love with him."

"With who?"

I gazed at him, waiting.

"Hathan?" he said incredulously.

"Yes."

He screwed his face up in mingled bewilderment and distaste. "In the name of all the ancient sigils, *why*?"

I wanted to laugh, despite the gravity of the moment, at the glimpse of the old carefree Zey. "It's hard to explain."

"It's not just hard, it's impossible. After what you just told me . . ." He went still. Then he said slowly, "Now I see why you wanted me to hear that."

"I was wrong the last time we talked, when I said I didn't have a choice. Of course I did. I could have trusted you. I've been a terrible friend, and I'm sorry. But I couldn't live with not being sure. It's not like you and Saresh. I don't have a lifetime's worth of memories of him to fall back on. I only have six months, and he spent three of those hating me. I had to know if he still did. I had to know if he meant the things he said during the Flare. It had nothing to do with your being a Blank, and everything to do with how I feel about Hathan. Words just weren't enough. Not even his."

"You should have told me you were going to do another Listening. You should have told me why."

I nodded. "I wish I had."

"I don't know what it's like to be in love. I've never felt that. But whatever it is you're feeling, Hathan doesn't feel it about you. I don't have to see into his thoughts to tell you that."

"Yeah." I sighed. "I know."

"Who else have you told?"

"No one. But Saresh has known since the first Listening."

"That was months ago," he said, disbelieving.

I nodded.

Zey frowned. "That's why you didn't want to do it?"

"No, I didn't even know it myself until afterward. I never would have let Saresh into my head if I had. And I wouldn't have told you now if I thought there was any other way to keep you on the *Ascendant*."

His face darkened at the reminder of our present situation. "I'm committed to another ship. I launch in the morning. If I cancel my contract now, I'll look unreliable."

"Tell them you want to stay with your family. Tell them you're doing a favor for your weird human crewmate. Tell them whatever you want. You just survived the Flare. No one is going to think less of you for changing your mind." Reading the indecision in his face, I pressed the point. "The *Star of Erasik* has a crew of what, two hundred? Three? They'll be fine without you. The *Ascendant* won't. I won't. And," I added, hoping I wasn't completely misconstruing his silence, "Fletcher has *Divided by Stars*. All five seasons. I was going to surprise you with it after we launched."

"I would like to see if Sirran and Zoe make a go of it," he admitted. Then his eyes narrowed. "All of a sudden I'm seeing that show in a whole new light. No wonder you like it so much."

"Oh, trust me, things will be a lot more interesting now that you know my secret. You can spend the next five months watching me fall all over myself in front of your totally indifferent brother. It'll be like your own private Vardrama. And then we'll be on Earth, and I know how much you wanted to see Earth."

"I did," he said. "I do."

Unable to contain my hope any longer, I said, "Does this mean you'll come back with us?"

Zey said slowly, "I think I will."

I could have wept. I wanted to throw my arms around him, but I was afraid he'd startle like some wary forest animal. Instead I said simply, "I'm glad."

"Yeah, me too." He stood up. "Am I allowed to leave now? Because I should go talk to the *Star*'s khavi. She's going to have to find another novi in a hurry."

"Will she be angry?"

"Probably not. I'm staying with my family. It's a respectable excuse. And, like you said, everyone treads a little more carefully around the Flare."

"I'll walk you there," I offered.

"You have no idea where I'm going."

"Then you can walk me there."

"Okay, but I'm walking you to a senek shop afterward, and you're buying."

"Deal," I said.

"Oh, and I should message Rhevi Garian, he helped arrange my transfer." Zey looked up to gauge my response. "You know, Sidra's—"

"I know who he is," I snapped, and heard once again the silvery, irresistible, longed-for sound of his laugh.

It was as if we had never been estranged. After Zey spoke to his khavi, who he said took the news better than he'd expected, we made our way to Elteni's market level. On the way I intercepted a few curious glances from my security escorts, but none of them commented on the fact that I had gone into Zey's quarters an enemy and emerged a friend. We lingered at a senek shop, where Zey listened in fascinated horror while I described my time as a test subject in Elteni's quarantine ward. Then we wandered into the maze of shops. He dragged me to a sigil vendor, where, over my increasingly strident protests, he began negotiating the cost of a gold Takheri sigil for me. The vendor, clearly discomfited by the presence of a human and a visibly deranged Vardeshi, was quick to offer a price.

"Too much," Zey said dismissively, and dragged me away again.

"Are you out of your mind?" I hissed when we were a suitable distance away from the stall. "What if someone heard you?"

"Who, these guys?" He gestured to my implacable security contingent. "They don't care."

"Maybe not, but I do!"

"All right, all right, I'm sorry." He raised his hands. "I won't do it again. Here, try on this sash, it's a good color for you."

"It's gold!" I said, outraged. "That's a betrothal sash!"

His face fell. "How did you know?"

"I've seen them before."

"You have? Where?"

I gestured vaguely. "Just . . . around."

"You've seen Hathan's!" he crowed. "In his quarters! You're right, this makes everything a lot funnier."

"I'm glad you're amused," I said sourly. "Do you have any intention of actually keeping my secret, or should I just ask for reassignment now? I hear the *Star of Erasik* is looking for a novi."

"Ask away. The *Star* won't take you. It's going the wrong way. And just in case you've forgotten, Rhevi Garian is still on it."

"Well, then I guess I have five months of humiliation ahead."

Zey grinned. "Aren't you glad you talked me out of leaving?"

It was late afternoon when we parted ways. He had arranged to meet up with his brothers for a farewell dinner. In typical Zey fashion, he planned to surprise them in person with the news of his cancelled transfer. He asked if I wanted to tag along and see their reactions. I declined, but agreed to meet up with them afterward for a drink. That way, I thought as I walked back to the Green Zone, I would have at least a couple of hours to ready myself mentally for being in the same room with all three Takheris, two of whom now knew my secret concerning the third. My predicament was becoming farcical. But I had my best friend back, and that was the important thing. I was in a cheerful mood as I changed out of my uniform and headed to the galley.

Fletcher, I saw from his scowl, was in a very different kind of mood. He was rifling through our cooking supplies, picking up containers and banging them down again with unnecessary force. "Hey," I said tentatively.

"Hey." He didn't look at me.

"Is something wrong?"

"How could you tell?" He slammed a glass jar onto the table.

I winced. "Are you pissed at me?"

Now he looked up in surprise. "God, no. Of course not. I'm pissed at the Echelon. And the Fleet. And whoever was in the room when they decided to put you back on that damned ship."

It took me a moment to process what he was saying. "You

don't think I should stay on the *Ascendant*."

"No, I don't."

I felt as if he'd flung a bucket of cold water in my face. The lingering glow of Zey's company evaporated. "Why haven't you said anything about this before?"

"I was hoping I wouldn't have to. I was sure you'd be reassigned. No one in their right mind would think that the *Ascendant* is a safe place for you anymore."

I said slowly, "Is this about last night?"

He spread his hands wide. "It's about everything. The flashbacks, the Flare, the shooting. I don't have any psychological training, but it's pretty damn clear to me that you're working through some serious trauma. And I don't think the Vardeshi have the first clue how to deal with that. Look at this afternoon. They actually said you were responsible for your own assault."

"Partially responsible," I corrected. "And they're right."

"The hell they are!" he snapped. "This is exactly what I'm talking about. How can you defend their bullshit?"

"I work for the Fleet. I wear a uniform. I was given an order and I ignored it. Like it or not, I am partially responsible for what happened."

He shook his head. "That's exactly what Kylie said you'd say."

I felt chilled. "You talked to Kylie?"

"She sent me a message. She's worried about you. And from what I can see, everything she said was pretty much spot on."

"What did she say?" I demanded.

"You'd know if you'd read it. She sent it to both of us. Let me guess, you deleted that one too." He waited for the words to sink in. "I talked to your hadazi. The *Ascendant* has a log of every incoming transmission. Including mine."

I stared at him, lost for words.

"Can't you see it? You're compromised. You're not making rational choices. And your crewmates aren't either. They thought it was a good idea for you to have telepathic contact with the man who assaulted you. And you agreed with them! Do you have any idea how fucked up that is?" He studied my face. "You don't, do you? Jesus."

I stared at the floor, searching for the words that would persuade him that he was mistaken. I couldn't find any. The silence stretched out. Finally I said, "So what?"

"What do you mean, so what?"

"Say you're right. Say I am compromised. I have to get back to Earth somehow. And I feel safe with my crew. How would it be any better for me to get on a ship full of strangers?"

He nodded, as if he had been waiting for precisely this question. "Those are two options. There's a third."

"Not that I can see."

Fletcher spoke slowly, feeling the words out, as if each one was a step onto uncertain ground. "You could come with me."

"To Vardesh Prime? Is that supposed to be funny?"

"I know Earth doesn't want you going soilside. But I'm sure they'd let you wait on the *Sidereus* while I'm on the planet. I know," he said quickly, seeing that I was about to interrupt, "it's lame. But it would only be for two weeks. Then we could go home together."

"Fletcher, we . . . I mean, we aren't a couple."

"I'm asking you to come with me as a friend. As a fellow human. So that neither of us has to be alone for five months. Or seven."

I made a sketchy gesture in the air between us. "And what if . . . whatever this is . . . doesn't last that long?"

He shrugged. "Things would be awkward for a while. And then I think they'd be fine. We're both adults. Each of us knows what it's worth to have an ally. Someone to look out for you, someone who understands how you think. Isn't that worth risking a little awkwardness?"

I shook my head. "I can't. I'm sorry. I appreciate the offer, I really do. But I can't do that."

"Just think about it. If you change your mind, you know where to find me." He came around the table toward me, put a hand on my arm, and said gently, "Please change your mind, Avery." Then he went through the door, leaving me alone with my uncertainty.

14

When Fletcher had gone, I sat down on a stool at one end of the long table, put my head in my hands, and tried to think. His suggestion was absurd. Wasn't it? He was asking me to leave my friends, the *Ascendant,* the Fleet itself for . . . what, exactly? The chance to sit in orbit above Vardesh Prime while he became the first human to set foot on its surface? The thought was infuriating. Or it should have been. I wanted to be angry. Anger was safe. But Fletcher had done nothing to provoke it. He was trying to be kind. I had no defenses against kindness. And there was something impossibly seductive about the idea of finishing my journey with a human companion. With him at my side, I wouldn't have to police every word I spoke for unintended insults or inaccuracies. I wouldn't have to worry that he was extrapolating an entire culture from our briefest interaction. I could just be, fully and unapologetically, myself.

I walked as if in a dream to the bar where I had agreed to meet the Takheris. They were in high spirits; Zey's announcement had clearly had its intended effect. On any other day, my mood would have risen instantly to meet theirs, no matter what I was feeling when I walked in the door. It had been weeks since I'd seen Zey and Saresh laughing together. And Hathan's indulgent smile as he watched his younger brother openly cheating at dice should have been reason enough for elation. The others would be joining us later, but for now, for this one golden hour, I had the three of them all to myself. It was a perfect beginning to what Hathan would have called the final arc of our journey together. I wanted it to be a beginning. But there was a very real chance that it was, in fact, an ending.

I had drifted too far. Zey nudged me with his elbow. "Eyvri, you haven't said three words all night. What's the matter, did you forget all your Vardeshi? That's what happens when you hang around with humans, you know."

"Is something troubling you?" Saresh asked. I looked at him, stricken, knowing there was no truthful answer I could give that didn't either threaten his happiness or reveal things Fletcher had said to me in confidence. He saw the alarm on my face and said swiftly, "Forgive me. I didn't mean to intrude on your privacy."

"No, you didn't. And it's nothing important. Just . . . human stuff."

"I'm afraid none of us will be much help there," said Hathan.

He was offering me a smooth exit from the subject. I seized on it gratefully. "Probably not. Although Zey is going to be an expert by the time we get to Earth, if he watches half as much TV as he says he will. Who's up for another round?"

When I returned with the drinks, I saw that Reyna had arrived. Zey repeated his news. In the ensuing flurry of questions and congratulations, I worked to recapture the appearance, at least, of a good mood. I stayed for a second drink and a couple of dice games, and when Reyna went to refill the carafe of water, I had a glimmer of inspiration. I slid out of my seat and followed her. At the water dispenser, out of earshot of the Takheris, I asked, "Can I meet you for senek tomorrow morning? I need to ask your advice about something."

"Of course." Reyna sounded utterly unfazed by the request. I wondered what it would take to surprise her. If I demanded that she switch clothes with me in the middle of the bar, she'd probably reply with a calm observation about the difference in our sizes. She went on, "Breath of the Forest, on helix nine, around seven o'clock?"

"Perfect. Thanks."

Entering my dark bedroom later that night, I realized afresh how much I missed Fletcher. After only a handful of nights with him, it seemed oddly lonely to go to bed on my own. I wanted to message him, or just go down the hall and knock on his door, but I knew there was no point. There could be no return to the purely physical connection we had shared. Things had been simple between us. He had made them complicated. Here, at last, was a reason to resent him. I drifted off to sleep on a rising tide of irritation.

* * *

The next morning my security team delivered me to the senek shop—or a senek shop, at any rate—promptly at seven. I looked at the sign in surprise. "First Light? I thought Reyna said Breath of the Forest."

"She did," agreed Officer Ekeyn. I'd had to double-check her name on my flexscreen, as she was one of the night-shift guards, whom I rarely saw. "Rathis changed the venue. There were quite a few people at the bar last night when your friend named Breath of the Forest as your rendezvous. One of them is in contact with an anti-alliance activist on our watch list. There's an anti-Earth demonstration planned to coincide with your arrival at the shop."

"A protest? Now?"

"The timing is logical. Most of Elteni's day-shift staff will be passing through the marketplace on their way to work."

"So what's going to happen?" I asked. "Will security shut it down?"

"We don't forbid peaceful demonstrations, assuming they don't impede the flow of traffic. But neither you nor Representative Simon will be going anywhere near helix nine until further notice. We're hoping the demonstrators will lose interest when they see that you're not coming."

I felt a surge of relief at the knowledge that Fletcher was safe, followed by the realization that this was exactly what he had meant when he suggested we travel home together. "What about Reyna? Does she know there's been a change in plan?"

"She knows. She should be joining us shortly. She and Rathis are in the marketplace, gauging the response to the demonstration."

It was twenty minutes or so before Reyna arrived. "What happened?" I asked anxiously. "Are you okay?"

"I'm fine. It was peaceful." Her expression of distaste was so fleeting it was scarcely more than a twitch. "Unpleasant, but peaceful."

"Were there a lot of people?"

"Twenty or so. More than I expected, but still not many."

"What does a Vardeshi protest even look like? Were they

chanting and waving signs?"

She didn't smile, but there was humor in her glance. "No chanting. They were silent. All of them wore black, the color of spiritual purity in several of the ancient religions on Vardesh Prime. They were kneeling in a line beneath a hovering banner like the ones you saw on Arkhati."

"What did it say?"

"'The light belongs to us,'" she said.

"As in, you all should go away and leave us in the dark ages where we belong?"

"Precisely."

"What was the response like?"

"At demonstrations of this type, there's a bowl of colored chalk placed at the end of the line. If you sympathize with the cause, you take a little of the chalk and write a single line of the tribute glyph on the floor or the wall nearby—somewhere visible. The next person adds another line, and so on until the glyph is complete. I saw two completed glyphs and half of another one. Not very impressive, given how crowded the marketplace is at this time of day."

"And that's it?" I tried to picture the scene. "I think I would have walked right by that without even knowing it was a protest."

"You wouldn't, because I wouldn't have let you."

"Still protecting me, huh?"

"It's why I'm here. Well" —she cast a pointed look at the senek counter— "that, and to drink senek. Which I believe you're buying."

"Of course." I went up to the counter and purchased senek for Reyna and tea for myself. We found a place to stand that was out of earshot of anyone waiting in line, and Reyna sipped her drink and sighed appreciatively. Then, with a decisive movement, she lowered her cup. "So. You need advice."

"I don't know," I said dubiously. "Suddenly my problem doesn't seem all that important."

"It was important last night."

"Yeah." I sighed. "It still is. Okay. If possible, I'd like to keep this between us."

"Naturally."

"Fletcher asked me to leave the *Ascendant* and come back to Earth with him."

"On the *Sidereus*?"

"Yes." I gave her a slightly edited description of yesterday's scene in the galley. "He thinks I'm compromised," I finished. "I don't. And I have absolutely no idea how to tell who's right."

Reyna considered the problem, her head a little on one side. I drank my tea. After a little while she said, "Do you think his concern is sincere?"

"Why else would he be asking me to go with him?"

"I can think of one obvious reason." At my blank look she said dryly, "While there are plenty of unattached Vardeshi who find humans attractive, the odds of his meeting one of them on the *Sidereus* are vanishingly low."

"Oh. Right." I laughed a little self-consciously. "I didn't know you knew."

"That you were sleeping with him? I suspected."

"And that doesn't shock you?"

"Not at all," she said calmly. "Most Vardeshi don't become engaged until a few years after they come of age. A certain amount of . . . experimentation is expected in the intervening years. Those connections are, by necessity, brief and primarily physical."

Scandalized and delighted, I said, "I didn't know that!"

"It's not something we broadcast."

"Do those relationships ever lead to marriage?"

"Rarely." I remembered what I'd learned in Hathan's mind about her broken engagement to a childhood friend. Had that been a euphemism for a different type of youthful attachment? "But," she prompted, "we were talking about you."

"Right. I don't think Fletcher's motives are personal."

"Then let's assume that he's genuinely trying to protect you. He thinks you'll be safer on the *Sidereus* than on the *Ascendant*. He doesn't trust Hathan. But you do. You made your peace with him in the Listening. Setting aside these . . . cognitive aftershocks of the Flare, like the one you experienced on the observation deck, you're on better terms with him than you've ever been. You feel safe under his command." I nodded my confirmation. "So Fletcher's concern is only valid if you accept that his judgment is superior to yours, that your ability to think coherently has been impaired. Do you believe that to be the case?"

"No." I swirled the last sip of tea around in my cup. "But I can't pretend it's not comforting to have him around. We do understand each other. Perfectly. Effortlessly. I'd almost forgotten what that felt like. I didn't know how much I missed it."

Reyna lifted a hand to signal for more senek. We stood silently until the server had refilled her cup and moved to another table. Then she said, "You could have asked Saresh for advice. Or Sohra. Do you know why you came to me?"

"Because you see things clearly."

"That's part of it." She held up her right hand, showing me the gold Vadra sigil. "But so is this. You know that I go after what I want. You're looking for permission to do the same. So here it is. Do what you want, Avery. Without reference to what Fletcher or Hathan or anyone else thinks you should do. Are you broken? I don't know. It doesn't matter. There's no one out here who can fix you. You're five months from home. You need safe transport to Earth, which either the *Ascendant* or the *Sidereus* can provide. There's no empirically correct choice. There's only what you want."

"And if I don't know what I want?"

"I can't help you there. But at least now you know you're asking the right question." She drained the rest of her senek. "You have two days to answer it. You'd better get started."

We went our separate ways after that, Reyna going off to meet Hathan for launch preparations while I went in search of a place to think. I had declined the offer of a formal tour of the starhaven in favor of roaming aimlessly with Fletcher, but now I reconsidered. Within moments, it seemed, of asking Officer Rathis if a tour might be arranged, I was joined by a silver-haired Echelon officer who introduced herself as Almai. I wanted to laugh when I saw her. She was Zey's virtual twin for youth and excitability, and it was obvious that she'd never been in the presence of a human before. She chattered endlessly away in impeccable English about Elteni's long history—the starhaven was over a thousand years old— and its strategic importance as the gateway to Vardesh Prime. I nodded and made interested noises but reserved my real attention for the places she showed me. The oldest section of the starhaven, where we went first, I rejected as too dark and cramped. Next was a botanical garden, perhaps the inspiration for Arkhati's Arboretum, but smaller and visibly bounded by stark metal walls. "What's next?" I asked the uniformed sprite at my side.

"Elteni's main observation deck is one of the starhaven's most popular—"

"I've been there," I said a little abruptly. "I don't need to go back."

She flapped her hands in almost comical distress. "You— please pardon the correction—you've already visited the Echelon's private observation deck. Your welcome reception was held there. The public one is on the opposite side, above the docking levels."

"Oh," I said grudgingly. "That sounds okay."

The public observation deck was a ring-shaped gallery whose outer wall was entirely comprised of viewports. Wide and spacious, it was one of the newer areas of the starhaven, and I could see the beginnings of the aesthetic that had informed the design of Arkhati. A scattering of tea and senek stands offered refreshment to visitors. Despite its size, the place was nearly empty. When I expressed surprise, my guide explained that it tended to be busy early in the morning, when the majority of ships launched, and late in the evening, when they docked. We strolled along the wall of viewports. Officer Almai helped me to identify the sleek bronze shape of the *Ascendant* and the distant gray gleam that was all we could make out of the *Sidereus*. I thanked her for her help and politely but firmly communicated my lack of interest in continuing the tour.

She departed. Glancing around, I saw that my security team had apparently cordoned off the entire observation deck. They had stationed themselves at the entrances and near the few open senek stalls, leaving me in near-perfect solitude. Ordinarily I would have objected to the celebrity treatment, but I had to admit that, after the claustrophobic handling I'd received on Elteni thus far, the idea of wandering without a uniformed shadow at my heel was appealing. I purchased another cup of tea and walked up and down some more, looking out through the viewports at the different ships.

For most of humankind, I knew, such sights were still the province of fantasy. In my anger at being denied Vardesh Prime, I had forgotten what an astonishing gift it was to be granted entry for any length of time into a world so entirely beyond my own. Now I rediscovered something of the incredulous thrill I had felt at my first glimpse of the *Pinion*'s shuttle descending over Zurich. Beneath me, arrayed in glittering ranks, were ships harnessing speed and power that exceeded the scope of human imagination. I had lived on two of them. I had seen cities in the sky. And I had no reason to believe that I would ever see them again. I didn't share Fletcher's easy confidence that this was only the first of many such journeys for me. It might very well be the last. The Council might declare me compromised, broken, permanently grounded. All at once my departure from Elteni loomed in my eyes as impossibly final. It didn't matter that Earth was still five months away. My first step onto the *Ascendant* or the *Sidereus*, two days from now, would be my first step home.

Before I left the observation deck, I had found the clarity I sought. I returned my empty cup to the tea stand and sat down on one of the stools. Then I took out my flexscreen and sent a message to Fletcher. It read, *I'm sorry. I can't go with you on the* Sidereus. *I'd still like to see you again. I understand if you don't want to see me. Be safe. Be strong.* I didn't wait for a reply. I wasn't sure there would be one. I put the device away and went in search of Zey.

Over the day and a half that remained to me on Elteni,

my sense that I had begun a slow turning away from the Vardeshi grew ever stronger. I spent as little time as possible in my quarters, preferring to roam the corridors of the starhaven with phone in hand, preserving what memories I could. I recognized the feeling from the last days of my college study-abroad program. Everything was imbued with significance by the simple fact that it might be the last of its kind I ever saw. I spent hours in the marketplace, watching the ceaseless flow of people intent on unfathomable errands, studying their features and postures and gaits, so like my own and yet so different. I spoke to some of them. On Arkhati I had begun photographing Vardeshi faces with the vague idea of creating a portrait series, an idea shared no doubt by every Stranger who had visited a starhaven. I continued that project now, having been assured by Sohra that I would offend no one by asking to photograph them. She and Zey helped me identify promising subjects and, on the rare occasions when English and standard Vardeshi proved insufficient, communicate with them. I found that nearly everyone I approached was happy to oblige my camera. I didn't ask for their names, only their ages and provinces of origin, which I scribbled down in my sketchbook.

I liked the project because it gave me a reason to overcome my shyness and speak to strangers with interesting faces. It had another unanticipated benefit, in that it provided me with a thoroughly unexceptional reason to take a beautiful high-resolution photograph of Hathan. It was Zey who facilitated this triumph, and he did it so casually I knew I could put to rest any remaining doubts about his discretion. Hathan looked over my shoulder as I wrote my notes. "Male. Nasthav Province. Do you want my age in Vardeshi or Earth years?"

"Earth, if you know the conversion."

"About . . . thirty-seven."

"Really?"

"Yes, really." He sounded amused. "Our average lifespan is a little longer than yours. Not much, twenty years or so. In your terms, Saresh is forty. Zey is thirty-four."

"Thirty-four?" I said wonderingly. "He looks about seventeen. And didn't he just graduate from the Institute?"

"Our children start school later than yours. And the standard education program takes longer to complete."

"Bigger curriculum," I said dryly, but I was thinking, Thirty-seven. With a lifespan of, say, a hundred years. It could have worked. I had to suppress a sigh.

I saw Fletcher twice during those last days, once at a panel discussion on interspecies communication, once at a farewell dinner held jointly in our honor. Both times he was subdued and achingly polite. He hadn't responded to my message. I understood. But I missed him desperately, and as I sat beside him at the dinner, I had to keep my right hand hidden in my lap, balled into a fist, to stop myself from reaching for him.

The sudden coldness between us didn't go unnoticed. Most of my crewmates were too tactful to comment on it, but Zey crashed through their forbearance with characteristic energy.

"Where's your human?" he demanded on our last day on the starhaven. It was evening, and we were finishing up a last stroll through the market level. "I haven't seen him in days. You used to be inseparable. I was getting ready to sneak him onto the *Ascendant* in a packing crate. I didn't know how else we'd get you off Elteni."

I knew I was blushing. "He's not my human. And he was at dinner last night."

"But you barely even talked to each other. And he didn't

come out with us afterward."

"Leave it, Zey," Saresh said quellingly.

"What? I'm just asking—"

"Look!" said Sohra. "There's someone from Irinesh. See her, Eyvri? In the Echelon uniform? You should try to get a picture."

Grateful for the distraction, I grabbed my phone and went to accost the young woman she had pointed out. The Irinesh skin tone was the rarest, and I didn't have any other examples of that delicate lilac hue in my photo series, but I knew Sohra was less concerned with the portraits than she was with my obvious embarrassment. I stood talking with the woman from Irinesh a little longer than was strictly necessary, and when I got back to my table, a visibly chastened Zey was listening mutely while Sohra and Saresh discussed the songs they planned to perform at the launch party that evening.

I ate an early dinner that night—dodging Fletcher in the galley had turned out to be the most problematic aspect of our estrangement—and spent a quiet hour sitting in Elteni's little botanical garden before I went to get ready for the launch party. I had resolved to have a good time through sheer force of will, if need be, but in the end it didn't take much work. The party was held in what I took to be some kind of meditation studio. It resembled a woodland grove, with several full-sized trees apparently growing out of the deck plates. Softly colored light globes hung from their branches. The walls displayed a panoramic image of a forest, and in the dim light, with real trees scattered around, the illusion worked surprisingly well. I wondered who was responsible for the decorations. Saresh, probably. The coppery gold leaves were those of the trees in Nasthav Province, I was almost sure.

Equal care had gone into the selection of refreshments, all of which had been approved for human consumption, including several varieties of fruit artfully suspended in baskets from the trees. As I helped myself to a handful of what looked like pale blue grapes and tasted vaguely like cantaloupe, I understood Hathan's reluctance to leave behind the bounty of a starhaven's hydroponics bays. The food plants grown on the *Ascendant* had been selected for quick maturation times and efficient use of a small space. On the trip home, I would be able to supplement my dried and frozen rations with the Vardeshi analogues of lentils and kale, but the next fresh fruit I tasted would have grown in the soil of Earth.

Having heard Sohra and Saresh discussing song choices that afternoon, and knowing the Vardeshi preference for performers who were known to them personally, I was surprised to find that the majority of the evening's music was furnished by strangers. One corner of the meditation studio was occupied by a troupe of five musicians. They played softly, sending their melodies drifting into the air like smoke, to complement conversation rather than compete with it. They were traveling artists, Zey explained, who earned passage with their music. They were typically hired by the largest vessels, those with passenger complements of five hundred or more, to provide entertainment on long-haul journeys across Vardeshi space.

"Five hundred?" I said. "I didn't know you had ships that big."

I didn't voice the dark thought that followed, but Zey seemed to anticipate it. "It has its risks," he acknowledged. "The last outbreak of the Flare, forty years ago, was on one of those ships. That's why there were so many casualties. But it's the only way to make cross-system travel affordable."

For families, I thought. With children. And then I snapped the thought off like a thread, unwilling to let it unspool any further, and refocused my attention on the music.

In a pause between songs I heard my flexscreen chime. Confused, because all my friends on Elteni were already in the room, I looked at it. The incoming message was from Fletcher. It read, *I'm outside. Can we talk for a minute?*

"Outside is a tricky concept on a starhaven," I said lightly when I joined him in the hallway a few moments later. "I was about to go look for a pressure suit."

Fletcher smiled, but his eyes were solemn. "I thought I'd save you the trouble. Look, I'm not here to try to change your mind. I know that's not going to happen. For either of us. I still think you're making a mistake. But I get that it's not my call. And you must have your reasons, although I honestly can't imagine what they are."

"I know," I said.

He nodded and looked briefly away, rubbing the back of his neck. "We're both going back out there tomorrow. And we're both going alone. This is our last chance to see each other. I don't want to fight about what ship you should be launching on. I just want to be with you while I still can. So I thought maybe you could invite me to your party and we could just shelve the whole question and try to have a good time."

"I'd like that," I said.

We were never more than an arm's length apart for the rest of the night. Fletcher's presence was an unlooked-for gift, and I drank it in greedily, as if I could somehow store it up against the loneliness to come. I knew he was trying to do the same thing. There came a moment toward the end of the party when the professional musicians stepped down, in a Vardeshi custom Zey had explained to me earlier, to allow for performances from the guests. Sohra and Saresh stepped forward. To my surprise, they began singing a bluegrass song. It was a sweet and poignant evocation of lost love, one of my favorites, as Saresh knew perfectly well. I had no idea when they could have rehearsed it. Fletcher and I stood a little apart from the other onlookers in the shelter of a flowering tree. Their clear harmonies came to us on a stirring of air scented with blossoms, an improbable breath of spring from another world. Impulsively I reached out and took Fletcher's hand. His warm fingers closed around mine. I felt a gladness so piercing it was almost a pain. I had been ready to let him go. I had been certain Zey was lost to me. Now I had both of them back. It might be only a temporary convergence. But I had seen enough of the night around us, in which ships and planets and stars sped endlessly away from each other, to know how rare that was.

There were a few more songs. Fletcher himself took the stage at Sohra's insistence and sang a folk song that was a favorite of my father's, accompanying himself on his guitar, which had been hastily retrieved by a member of his security detail. Then people began to drift toward the door. Lulled by wine and music and the promise of one more night in Fletcher's arms, I thought nothing of it when he stopped to speak to Hathan, who was standing with Reyna in the corridor. Their remarks in standard Vardeshi seemed innocent enough. Fletcher said, "Bright stars to guide your path, khavi." It was the farewell traditionally offered by the Vardeshi to departing spacefarers.

Hathan nodded. "And yours. If you get a chance, check out that museum in Khezendri."

"Yeah, I will." Fletcher made as if to turn away, then paused. "Oh, and one more thing." He added a few words so clipped it was all I could do to place them as the North Continent dialect. Hathan replied in the same language, glancing significantly at Reyna, who clenched her right fist and raised it slightly in a suggestion of the Echelon salute. Fletcher and Hathan studied each other for a tense moment. Then Fletcher nodded slightly. His next words, in English, were directed at me. "Let's go."

"What was that about?" I asked as we walked away.

Fletcher said, "Just a little friendly advice." I decided to leave it at that.

That night we paced ourselves more carefully than before, savoring the slow unfolding of intimacy. Toward morning we both slept a little. I resented the lost time, but falling asleep in Fletcher's arms was a luxury in its own right. When my alarm sounded, we went and stood in the shower together. We had spent all our desire. The need for closeness remained. I rested my head on his shoulder, tightening my arms around his neck, and felt his arms tighten around me in response. I closed my eyes. The hot water drumming incessantly down on both of us was an utterly prosaic comfort. We could have been standing in the shower in my apartment in California or his in Cleveland. When we emerged, I saw that it was much later than I'd thought. Fletcher laughed as he watched me towel my hair dry and hurry into my uniform. "Don't worry. They're not going to leave without you."

The *Ascendant* was scheduled to launch before the *Sidereus*. Fletcher walked with me down to the docking level, my duffel bag slung over his shoulder. We'd said our private farewells before leaving the Green Zone, but I found myself resisting the approaching separation with unexpected force. As we descended the ramp toward the *Ascendant*'s airlock, I looked up at him questioningly. He ruffled my hair and murmured in English, "Text me so I know you got home okay." The unexpected reference to our shared culture proved too much for me. I flung my arms around him, heedless of the curious and amused and speculative gazes of my crewmates. For the last time I breathed in his familiar scent and felt the warmth of another human body against mine. "Be safe," Fletcher whispered into my hair. "Be strong." Then he released me and stepped back. I turned away, dry-eyed, to join my waiting crewmates in front of the airlock.

Our orders were to meet in the axis chamber in thirty minutes for a prelaunch briefing. I dropped my duffel bag in my quarters, cast a fond look around the neat little room, and went to make senek. Hathan entered the axis chamber while I was still arranging the trays. I fussed unnecessarily with the alignment of the spoons while working up my nerve. Then I said, "Khavi? What did Fletcher say to you in the hallway last night?"

Hathan looked up from his flexscreen. "You didn't ask him?"

"I tried. He just said he gave you some friendly advice."

"I wouldn't call it friendly. He said"—Hathan cleared his throat, and when he spoke again, it was in a credible imitation of Fletcher's American drawl—"'touch her again and I'll rip your face off.'"

"No kidding," I said, shocked and a little pleased. "That's pretty gallant. And pretty ambitious. Aren't you guys about four times as strong as us?"

"That's essentially what I said."

"Essentially?"

He didn't smile, but I heard the humor in his voice, as I

had more and more frequently since the Listening. "I called him . . . There's a word in the Northern dialect for a menial worker who wipes down the ranshai mats after practice. It isn't a compliment. And I reminded him that you're already well protected."

"By Reyna," I guessed.

"Yes."

"Well . . ." I studied the tray in front of me, which was Saresh's, checking the colors of the sugar pellets a third time. "Don't hold it against him, okay?"

"I won't. He's worried about you. And he's disappointed. If he had his way, you'd be launching on the *Sidereus* right now."

I looked at him sharply. "You knew?"

"I guessed."

"Oh." I didn't know what to say. Should I apologize for not telling him about Fletcher's offer? What difference would it make now? I had chosen the *Ascendant*. I decided to let my decision speak for itself.

Hathan evidently thought it did, because he didn't pursue the matter. Instead he said, "Eyvri? What did you say to Zey? It must have been you. Saresh and I both tried to talk him out of transferring. We begged, frankly. To no effect. The last I saw, he was dead set on leaving."

I wondered what I could possibly say to answer the question without giving myself away. It took me a while to find an answer. Hathan didn't apologize or withdraw the question, as Saresh had done the other day. He simply waited, skimming through messages on his flexscreen in a manner that made it clear that I still had his attention. At length I said, "You might say I appealed to his humanity."

"That explains it, then. You're the only one who could

have done that. And I'm glad you did. He belongs on the *Ascendant.*" I had turned away and was halfway to my seat before he added, "You both do."

The next member of the crew to arrive was Zey. His gaze flicked interestedly from his brother's face to my own, which I knew still wore the slightly foolish smile engendered by Hathan's last words, but he didn't say anything as he settled onto the seat next to mine. The others filed in and found their places, and the briefing commenced. A wave of fierce gladness overtook me as I listened to the status reports from the different departments. I still missed Fletcher. But I belonged here. And not only because Hathan himself had said so.

"We're cleared to depart," said Ziral. "Except—sir? Elteni's asking us to confirm our destination."

"Novi Alkhat?" Hathan prompted.

Caught off guard, I stammered, "Uh. I mean. Earth. Right?"

Hathan said, "I expected better from you, Novi. Surely by now you've learned to read a star chart."

I heard the gentle mockery in his tone, but didn't understand it. "I'm sorry?"

"Look at your flexscreen," Saresh suggested.

Flustered by the attention, because everyone was watching me now, I studied my screen, which displayed the star chart Hathan had sent to all crew members just before the briefing began. Slowly I picked out the orange triangle marking Elteni Starhaven and the blue one indicating Earth. There should have been a single continuous line connecting the two icons. There wasn't. Instead there were two short lines forming an obtuse angle around a third icon, another blue triangle, this one labeled *Rikasa.*

I stared at it, uncomprehending, then looked around at

my crewmates and saw Hathan's affectionate humor reflected in their faces. Zey was openly grinning. "Rikasa?" I whispered.

"There's been a last-minute adjustment to our route," Reyna explained. "Your physician on Earth made a very strong case for the healing properties of fresh air and natural light. Apparently the Echelon saw the merits of her argument. We've all been approved for ten days of recreational leave. Soilside."

Hathan said, "You won't be the first human on Vardesh Prime, but it looks like you'll be the first one on Rikasa. If you want to be. We can also make directly for Earth, if you'd prefer. No one would fault you for being ready to go home."

"So which is it?" Saresh asked. "Ivri avanshekh? Or ivri khedai?"

I looked again at the little blue icon, blurred now by tears. "Ivri khedai. I want to see another sky. With two moons in it."

"Rhevi Ziral," said Hathan, "it looks like you're going home. Take us to Rikasa."

PART THREE:
IVRI KHEDAI

15

Three months later I stepped down from the ramp of the *Ascendant*'s shuttle and onto the surface of another world.

It was a beautiful afternoon on Rikasa. The sun, which was smaller and redder than Sol, burned brightly in a sky of deep violet blue. The air was dry, and the wind that brushed teasing fingers over my hair had blown across a forest before it reached me. It was scented with something like cinnamon and something like mint. I filled my lungs with it. Letting my hiking pack thud to the ground beside me, I dropped to my knees and placed both palms on the dusty red soil, feeling its warmth and solidity. Then I bent forward to press my forehead against the ground between my hands. "Thank you," I whispered. In my distinctly secular life it was the closest I had ever come to prayer.

Ziral, unsurprisingly, was next to descend. I heard a footfall beside me and turned to see her drop to one knee. Pressing her right hand to the ground, palm up, she bowed her head and murmured, "Sigils of my ancestors witness my safe return." She stayed there, unmoving, for a long moment before getting to her feet again. I followed suit. Only then did our crewmates join us on the ground. I wondered to which of our rituals they had shown deference by waiting.

I hefted my hiking pack again. After buckling the straps, I flexed my shoulders, testing its balance. I was carrying thirty pounds of gear. Rikasa's gravity was nine percent higher than Earth's. I was long acclimated to the additional two percent that was standard on all ships and starhavens in simulation of Vardesh Prime, but I could feel the drag of the extra weight, and I knew what it meant. Falls would be harder and faster here. I would have to choose my footing carefully.

The pack hadn't been part of the original plan. Our leave on Rikasa had been designated as strictly recreational. The planet's main revenue source was tourism, and there were resorts scattered across its surface. The idea—for me, at least—had been to spend ten restful days breathing in the crisp mountain air and doing as little as possible. All that had changed three weeks ago. Arriving a bit late to officers' dinner one night, I had overheard Hathan saying to Reyna, "The timing is remarkable. I don't see how you can refuse."

"Refuse what?" I asked.

"The Outmarch," said Reyna.

"The what?"

She explained. "It's an Echelon training exercise. Twenty-five eight-man teams competing in an overland race across difficult terrain. The race is held once a year in ten different locations throughout our space. Coincidentally, one of the sites for the next Outmarch is Rikasa."

"Let me guess," I said. "It's happening while we're there?"

She nodded. "I've been asked to join a team."

"What she's not telling you," Saresh added, "is that it's a tremendous honor to be invited. It's notoriously difficult to

gain entry to the Outmarch. With only two thousand participants a year, the lists are filled years in advance."

I shrugged at Reyna. "It sounds fun. Why not do it?"

"Because I haven't trained for it. Most competitors spend
months preparing for the specific conditions of the course.
Every location has its unique challenges. Sometimes the race
is held in the desert, sometimes on a glacier, or on a planet
with high gravity or low oxygen. Only a few days are allotted
for the race. It's a mark of distinction to even finish it."

"It's the making of a career to win it," Hathan said quietly.

Reyna glanced up at him and flashed her teeth in a brief
vulpine smile. "I know."

"So," I said, "the Outmarch is Echelon only? Not Fleet?"
Something in my tone caught Hathan's attention, because he
turned to look at me, his expression speculative.

"Occasionally, when numbers are low in a given location,
the Fleet is permitted to enter a few teams," Reyna said.

"Are the numbers low for Rikasa?"

"No. The planet is centrally located, and its climate is relatively temperate. It's expected to be a soft course. The lists
have been full for years."

"Too bad," I said. "I'd do it if I could. I've got a hiking
pack and everything."

There followed an odd little silence in which my companions carefully avoided each other's eyes. It dawned on me that
they were trying not to laugh at me.

"Eyvri," Saresh said gently, "while your ambition is . . .
laudable . . . I'm afraid you wouldn't be eligible for the competition. Whatever your level of physical fitness in human
terms, the challenge is designed for Vardeshi at the peak of
their strength. There are no roads or trails. The course runs
cross-country over difficult ground. Typically participants

will cover around a hundred straight-line miles in three days, but the real total will be much higher due to detours around cliffs, ravines, bodies of water, and so on."

"Well, I wasn't expecting to win," I said with unintended venom.

Hathan said, "I think you're forgetting the reason for our detour to Rikasa. The Outmarch stretches the definition of recreational leave to its breaking point."

"I don't see why. What could be more recreational than a nice hike through the mountains?" Seeing the look he traded with Saresh, both of them openly amused now, I protested, "No, I mean it. I'm in pretty good shape. For a human. And we'll be on Rikasa for ten days. I can probably do a hundred miles over rough ground in that time. I could set the pace for our team. It'll be like a gentle stroll for you guys. Relaxing."

"Our team," Zey muttered as he cleared away my salad plate.

Strictly speaking, it was a breach of protocol for him to participate in the conversation, but that rule had more or less fallen by the wayside since we left Elteni. I answered him directly. "Sure. Teams of eight, right? If you exclude Reyna, who's already on an Echelon team, and Ziral, who I assume wants to be with her family, and Daskar—" I faltered.

"Who would certainly be capable, but probably won't be interested," Saresh said diplomatically.

"That just leaves eight of us." I made a dramatic flourish with the hand that wasn't holding a wineglass. "Team *Ascendant.*"

"You actually sound like you're serious about this," Reyna said.

"I am! Look. I can sleep all the way from Rikasa to Earth. But we're only going to be soilside for ten days. Let's stretch our legs a little. Let's go camping." I looked imploringly at Hathan. "Khavi? You're going backpacking on Earth. Why not get in some practice now?"

He answered with another question, directed at Reyna. "How would the Echelon handle the problem of Eyvri's security?"

"Truthfully," Reyna said, "I don't think it poses a significant challenge. The diversion to Rikasa was last-minute, which works in her favor, as does the fact that the contest roster has been closed for years. There's no room for last-minute entrants with an anti-Earth agenda. And this near to the start date, Outmarch Control should already be fully staffed, which means they won't be bringing in any new hires. I imagine the Echelon would screen everyone involved for any history of anti-alliance sentiment and close the planet to new arrivals. Beyond that, as one member of an eight-person team, she'd arguably be as safe as she was on Elteni."

He nodded. "In that case, what are the odds that the Echelon would grant her another favor?"

Reyna looked pensive. "A twenty-sixth team?"

"Strictly non-competitive," Saresh pointed out. "And the optics are good. A human in the Outmarch would be a historic first. It's an easy way for the Echelon to gain points with the pro-alliance factions, at virtually no cost to itself, since we'll already be there."

"The optics would be better if she finished it," Reyna said.

"It's a soft course," Saresh said. "There's a chance that she could."

"A slight chance," Hathan murmured.

I knew a challenge when I heard it. I grinned at him. "Like I said. A nice hike through the mountains."

"I suppose it's worth asking," Reyna said, still sounding

skeptical.

To my surprise, as much as hers, the Echelon quickly sent back their approval of the scheme. Reyna reported a little grumbling on Echelon channels from those who had been denied slots in the competition, but only a little. "You won't actually be part of the contest, so it isn't like a Fleet team jumped the Echelon waitlist. And—with apologies, Khavi— we love to laugh at the Fleet, and you've made it pretty easy this time. The window for course completion is three days. Ten is unheard-of. It's just more proof that your conditioning regimen is a farce." She paused. "That's what they're saying, anyway."

It was a few days after our initial conversation about the Outmarch. On receiving the good news from the Echelon, Zey and I had decided to celebrate with an impromptu round of one of the more arcane drinking games from my college days. I was hazy on the rules, so we were making them up as we went along, which might, in fact, have been pretty much the way the game was intended to go. After the first boisterous hand, Hathan and Reyna, who had been playing dice in a nearby alcove, abandoned their own game to join ours. It was Reyna's turn to deal. She had taken advantage of a quiet moment to fill us in on the Echelon chatter.

"That's not fair," I objected, picking up my cards. "The extension was for me. It has nothing to do with the Fleet."

Hathan said dismissively, "Forget it, Eyvri. The laughter of cowards is a blade with no edge." The words flashed into my mind so quickly I was sure for a moment that he'd spoken them in English. I had to translate backward to find the original rhythm of the phrase in Vardeshi. I was no longer surprised that I'd found Hathan difficult to understand before the first Listening; of all my crewmates' speech, his was the most figurative. I was grateful once again for the quirk of telepathy that had given me access to what was looking more and more like Saresh's complete lexicon of idioms.

Reyna snapped a card down in front of him with excessive force. "Cowards, sir?"

"Yes, cowards." Hathan traded a conspiratorial look with Zey. "Say what you want about Fleet conditioning. We know the real reason you won't let us into your little footrace. You're afraid we'll win."

"A fear," Reyna observed, "which, if it existed, would hardly be borne out by the performance of past Fleet teams."

Zey gathered up his cards in a single flamboyant sweep. "Well, of course not. Those teams were handpicked. By the Echelon."

Reyna eyed him narrowly over her cards. "Handpicked to fail, you mean?"

"I think the implication was clear," Hathan said.

"Rigged," Zey said gleefully, immune to implication. "Totally rigged." He plucked two cards out of his hand and dropped them in front of Reyna.

She pushed them back at him. "You can't just discard the ones you don't like. It's not even your turn. No wonder you think the Outmarch is rigged. Stop laughing, Novi Alkhat, the rivalry is serious business. And the truth—as you'll soon find out—is that the Fleet just doesn't measure up. Your endurance is no match for ours. The Echelon trains longer. And harder. And, frankly, better." To Hathan, who was watching her coolly, dice poised to throw, she said, "Wait and see. Even with your seven-day head start, I'll still cross the finish line before you."

Hathan rolled the dice absently in his hand in such a way that they seemed to flicker between his fingers. I recognized the gesture. It was a coin trick that appeared, briefly, in a sitcom we had watched during one of my earliest colloquial English lessons. He'd done it without looking. I hadn't known he could do it at all. "Is that a challenge?"

"I think the implication was clear," Reyna shot back.

He cast the dice toward her side of the table with an understated flick of the wrist. "In that case, I accept. The first one to cross the finish line wins . . . what? A bottle of Rikasan brandy? I'll take your threes, by the way."

She extracted a card from her hand and passed it across, frowning slightly. "Too obvious. And too easy. It should be something . . . inconvenient."

"A week without night duty," Zey suggested.

Reyna nodded judiciously. "Good. But make it a month."

"Done." Hathan reached his right hand toward her. She touched the back of her hand to his. I watched in perplexity until I realized that they were pressing their sigils together. An oath-taking ritual? Distracted, I almost overlooked the significance of their pact. Then I put up a hand in protest. "Hang on. I thought I was setting the pace for our team. Did you just stake the reputation of the entire Fleet on my ability to outrun Reyna?"

Zey grinned at me. "Better hit the gym."

I did. So did everyone else. The lounge, typically the hub of evening activity on the ship, was virtually abandoned overnight. Now my crewmates spent their free hours in the fitness center or in Requisitions. There was a flurry of unearthing and testing and trading of equipment. Hathan, looking ahead to his backpacking plans on Earth, helped me check over my own gear and offered replacements here and there with an eye to reducing weight. I cheerfully set aside my solo tent in favor of a palm-sized device that projected a dome-shaped force field. The field was invisible, and my hand passed through it with no resistance. Still, Hathan assured me that it was actually there, and that in addition to repelling insects, water, and wind, it also maintained an internal air temperature of the user's choosing. Suspecting that I was being pranked, I followed his instructions to position the force field over my sleeping bag, then abruptly upended my water bottle over it. He and Zey both laughed at my cry of surprise when the stream of water suddenly changed direction in midair. "Unreal," I said, watching it trickle down an invisible incline and pool on the deck plates. "Does it work while moving? Can you carry it like an umbrella?"

"Of course."

"Great." I tossed my rain gear onto the reject pile. My water bottles and purification tablets quickly followed, replaced by a collapsible water flask with a built-in radiation filter.

It was a good thing I was able to eliminate so much weight, because I was bringing a number of items the Vardeshi weren't: special sunscreen and portable oxygen inhalers and sunglasses designed to filter out radiation my eyes weren't accustomed to. Daskar had picked carefully over the array of options Anton had sent along before choosing the best pair. They looked, to my relief, pretty much like normal sunglasses. I also had a fairly substantial medkit, although Reyna assured me that that was just a precaution. "The Outmarch is meant to be challenging, but it's not pointlessly risky. The location of each participant is tracked with a transponder, and their medical readings are continuously monitored. At the first sign of distress you'll be evacuated from the course. We'll all have our flexscreens too. There are certain unavoidable dangers, like falls, but on the whole, the program is as safe as we can make it."

Daskar concurred. "The most important thing for you will be to minimize interaction with unfamiliar organisms. Don't eat any new fruits. Don't smell the flowers. And keep track of insect bites or stings. It's good that you'll be traveling in a large group. The larger wildlife should avoid you entirely."

"What about aquatic life?" I asked. Daskar looked nonplussed. Her frown deepened when I confessed my desire to swim, but she promised to look into the question. Choosing to be optimistic, I tossed a bikini onto my gear pile.

I noticed a few of my crewmates making equally whimsical packing choices. Ahnir was bringing his mandolin. Reyna teased him about it. "Only the essentials, Ahnir?"

"My definition of essential may not align with yours," he said, unfazed.

"It aligns with mine though," I said. "It's going to be pretty quiet around those Echelon campfires at night." Rikasa's climate was temperate, but its mountains were high, and the predicted temperatures resembled those of a New England autumn: mild days, freezing nights.

"Campfires?" Reyna asked. I explained, and was immediately informed that the Vardeshi didn't build campfires. Not only were they environmentally destructive, the heat was superfluous. Vardeshi hiking clothes absorbed the warmth of the sun during daylight hours and radiated it back at night. Curious, I requisitioned an outfit for myself, but I packed my own cold-weather gear as well. I was all too aware by now that the concept of warmth was species-specific.

"And don't forget your formal wear," Khiva said as I turned to leave Requisitions with an armful of new clothes.

"Formal wear? For the woods?"

She laughed. "No, for the reception afterward."

I eyed her warily. "What reception?"

"Didn't you hear Suvi Ekhran at the briefing this morning? The Outmarch is more than just a training exercise. It's one of the ways the Echelon builds solidarity. They're a small force spread across a vast territory. It isn't often that they're able to get two hundred officers together in one place. They're not about to send them home without letting them at least talk to each other first."

"Fine," I said. "I can handle talking."

Khiva's eyes gleamed with sudden mischief. "How about dancing?"

I shook my head vehemently. "Oh, no. No way. I don't dance."

She looked surprised. "What, never?"

"Nope." It wasn't completely true, but I didn't think anything I had witnessed or attempted at a smattering of weddings and high-school formals would be recognizable to the Vardeshi as dancing. Seeing her expression, I relented. "Dancing is more of a thing in some Earth cultures than others. In mine, you can get all the way to adulthood without knowing how to do it. I did."

"Well," she said thoughtfully, "if you don't know any dances of your own, you'll just have to learn ours."

"Khiva, it took me a week and a half to learn how the door codes worked. There is literally nothing I can learn about your dances, except possibly their names, between here and Rikasa. I'm not like you guys." I had observed, envious and a little mystified, the ease with which my crewmates, and others on Arkhati, had picked up the routines—some of them quite complicated—in the music videos Kylie and I had shown them. If they danced the way they did everything else, I would save myself a lot of embarrassment by simply embracing my role as a wallflower.

"All the same, you'd better try," Khiva said.

"You think?"

"You're the guest of honor, so they'll be a little offended if you don't. Just ask someone on the ship to teach you a couple of dances. They're not hard. We all learn them as children."

Of course you do, I thought wearily. "Who would I even ask?" I regretted the question at once. What would I say if she suggested Hathan?

"Vethna?" She laughed at my expression. "All right, Zey, then."

"I guess I could do that," I said dubiously.

"You should. Soon. And Eyvri? Cheer up. At least there's one thing you don't have to worry about."

"What's that?"

Khiva gave me a knowing look. "Finding something to wear."

Back in my quarters, I dumped the Vardeshi hiking clothes onto my bunk and pulled the blue silk dress from the depths of my closet. I had no one to blame but myself. Participating in the Outmarch had been my idea, and mine alone. If I'd known there was a reception involved, I might have had second thoughts, but it was too late to back out now. Apparently a formal gala was the price I had to pay for a week in the Rikasan woods. And Khiva had emphatically vetoed all the other wardrobe options I put forward for consideration. Nothing else in my closet was dressy enough, and as the sole Fleet team in a roomful of Echelon officers, we would be effectively tossing down a gauntlet by wearing our uniforms. And I couldn't very well borrow anything. Even if any of the women on board were my size, which, as Khiva helpfully pointed out, they weren't, I was there to represent my own culture. This was it. It was why I had brought the gown along. It was why I had bought the stupid thing in the first place.

I slipped the straps free of the hanger, carried the dress into the sanitation room, and held it up to my shoulders in front of my mirror. Then, with a sigh, I threaded it back onto its hanger and put it on the hook by the door. I didn't try it on. What was the point? I had literally nothing else to wear.

The next day I dutifully asked Zey to teach me to dance. And he dutifully tried, until he fell down on the floor laughing, which took about three minutes. I folded my arms and tried not to look like I was about to cry. I was though. It was impossible, just as I'd known it would be. Vardeshi dancing, from the eight steps I'd seen of it, married the elegance of a waltz with the joyful exuberance of—what? The tango? A Bollywood dance number? I didn't know. Whatever it was, though, I couldn't do it.

"I can't do this," I said when I thought I could trust my voice.

"No," Zey gasped. "Sigils and emblems, no. You can't. Promise me you'll never try again. Especially not at the reception. No matter what anyone tells you. The alliance wouldn't survive it. Vekesh, yes. The Flare, yes. Not this."

"Thanks," I said tightly. "I think you've made your point."

He got to his feet, wiping his eyes and making a credible effort to school his expression. "It's okay, Eyvri. There had to be something you couldn't do."

"What are you talking about?" I counted my failures off one by one on my fingers. "I can't dance. I can't fight. I can't fly a shuttle. I can't do anything."

"That's okay. You can read a star chart. Kind of. And you can do the Listening. And"—he stepped adroitly back out of reach—"you clean toilets really, really well."

I didn't allow my dread of the reception, powerful though it was, to occlude my excitement for long. As the days ticked down, it became more and more real to me: this wasn't going to be like Vardesh Prime. I wasn't going to be turned away again. I was finally going to see another planet. The plan, as Reyna explained it, was simple. The traditional structure of the Outmarch was for the twenty-five teams to be dropped at exactly equivalent intervals along a circle drawn with mathematical indifference to geography around the endpoint of the race. The varied terrain meant each team had different obstacles in its way, an intentional randomness meant to heighten the challenge. Use of navigational aids to locate the finish was strictly forbidden; dead reckoning was part of the game.

The endpoint for our race, it was announced a few days prior to our arrival on Rikasa, was a resort called the Perch set high on a cliff in one of the planet's most beautiful and remote mountain ranges. The resort would be emptied in advance of the competition and the rooms set aside for the participants to use as dormitories in the interval between race completion and pickup by their home ships' shuttles. On a course as "soft" as Rikasa, Reyna said, toward the end of the race, the leading teams inevitably converged. If they sighted each other, so much the better; it was invigorating to have a visible opponent. The teams were monitored at all times, and sabotage of any kind resulted in automatic disqualification. Team *Ascendant* would be dropped with all our gear at one of the starting points offering a relatively facile approach to the Perch seven days to the minute before the race was scheduled to begin. Ziral, who would be piloting our shuttle, would transport our formal wear and overnight bags to the Perch for us. All we had to do was get there.

Scoring of the race was hearteningly straightforward. All eight members of a given team had to cross the finish line within the designated completion window in order for that team to be eligible for victory. When they did, their finish times were averaged and the resulting averages ranked. The fastest team won. Times were measured down to the microsecond. There had never been a tie.

The night before we went soilside, Zey and I sat in the lounge studying maps of the Perch and its surrounding mountains. We were looking more for fun than for any real hope of learning anything useful. Due to differences of gravity, air oxygenation content, topography, and various other factors, there was no standardized distance for the Outmarch. We could only guess at what the Echelon course engineers might have judged a feasible yet challenging distance for their officers to cover in three days. And even had we had an exact perimeter to draw around the Perch, it was anyone's guess at what point along it we might be dropped. After an hour of zooming in and out of stunningly detailed topographical maps, I said, "I know one thing for sure. We're not going to win this thing. I just hope I can finish it in ten days."

"It isn't that simple," Zey said. "There are the special challenges to consider."

I turned a dark look on him. "The what? We're at twenty-seven hours and counting, and no one's said anything about special challenges."

He waved a hand. "Relax, they're not mandatory. On a planet like Rikasa, where the conditions are favorable, the course engineers look for ways to spice things up. Sometimes they throw in extra challenges at random locations. They're marked off by black and white flags."

"Echelon colors," I said.

He nodded. "Not all the flags are accessible. Some are deliberately put in impossible places, like in the middle of a cliff face, or hanging in midair. If you see a flag that looks retrievable, you send a team member to get it. Attached to the flag will be a token of some kind. It's a bonus. Time deducted from your finish. But there's no way of knowing, when you're out on the course, how much time it buys you. It could be ten seconds, or two hours. You have to weigh the odds of earning back significant time against the potential waste if you spend three hours scaling a cliff face to gain back twenty minutes."

"So you send the slowest person on your team to get the flag? To improve their time?"

He put his head on one side like I'd made an elementary arithmetic error, which, of course, I had. "It all averages out, remember? You can send anyone. Or no one."

"It's a gamble," I said. "You guys just love games of chance, don't you?"

Zey passed his hand over the tabletop display, which obediently went dark. "I guess. They keep things interesting."

"And yet the arranged marriages."

He shrugged, unconcerned. "We don't gamble with the fuel mixture in our engines either. Some things aren't supposed to be interesting. Listen, don't worry too much about the extra challenges. If you see a black and white flag, tell Hathan. Ultimately it's his call whether to try for it or not."

Every team participating in the Outmarch was required to designate one member as the official leader. One of our earliest planning meetings had concerned the question of whom to select. Hathan's expertise in navigation, added to his interest in the outdoors, made him a natural choice. The vote had been nearly unanimous. I, along with six other members of Team *Ascendant*, had voted for him. He had voted for me.

"You're already the leader in everything but name," he had argued. "We wouldn't be going to Rikasa at all, let alone fielding a team in the Outmarch, if not for you. It's your show. You should run it."

Despite being outnumbered seven to one, he had shown no signs of yielding until I told him I'd have more fun if someone else was making the decisions. I was relieved when he conceded the point, but secretly thrilled, at the same time, that he thought me qualified to lead the team.

In late afternoon of the day following my map session with Zey, after several hours of decontamination and medical examinations on a tiny orbiting starhaven, we were finally cleared to go soilside. The Rikasan day was shorter than that of Vardesh Prime; our race window of ten standard days worked out to just over fourteen local ones. There were only a few hours of daylight remaining when Ziral set the landing craft down in the designated zone, a flat spot in a saddle between two mountaintops. While the others unloaded the gear, she and I stood together at the edge of the clearing, moved to silence for different reasons, taking in the view. All around us the mountains rose to towering heights, their exposed peaks slate gray and purple, their lower slopes carpeted in crimson forest. The silver thread of a river glinted far down in the shadow of the valley below us. I breathed in and out, sensing the incremental changes in gravity and light, and caught again the ghost of cinnamon in the air. It was at once strange and puzzlingly familiar, this new world. My second world. "Rikasa," I whispered. Ziral heard me and smiled.

Hathan and Saresh came over to stand beside us. They had clearly made their own, more effective study of the same topographic maps Zey and I had looked at, as they had already pinpointed the location of the Perch. From their talk, I gathered that it was high on a mountain hidden from view beyond the range directly opposite our current position. I listened as they discussed possible routes, my mind half on their words and half on the warmth of sunlight on my face, an animal pleasure too long deferred. It was odd, and somehow fitting, that the ten days allotted us by the Echelon should work out to fourteen Rikasan days. To my companions, accustomed to an eight-day week, fourteen was an odd, unsatisfying number. To me it was simply two weeks, exactly the length of my planned stay on Vardesh Prime. Nothing was lost. I remembered something Dr. Okoye had said to me long ago, in a different context: I had traded one world for another.

Ziral's flexscreen chimed. She spoke briefly into it, confirming with Outmarch headquarters that all eight of our transponders were functioning correctly. Then she wished us luck and departed. The shuttle's liftoff was swift and eerily silent, the only mark of its passing a brief stirring of warm air. Red dust swirled around us and settled.

"Okay," Zey said behind me, already impatient. "The clock is running. Let's go."

We went. The rocks around us were covered with a dense thorny undergrowth which would have been difficult to push through, but after a few minutes of scouting, Khiva identified an animal track running roughly downhill from our landing site. Ziral had assured me that the wildlife of Rikasa were notably shy, a fact I recalled with gratitude when I saw the width of the trail, which afforded us easy passage in single file. I quickly fell into the rhythm of hiking, which was no different here than in the mountains of home, apart from the need to pause every fifteen or twenty minutes to breathe from my portable oxygen inhaler. We were at high altitude, and Rikasa's air was thin. I concentrated on taking shallow, even breaths.

The air cooled rapidly as the sun's angle steepened, and I wasn't the only one to pull on a warm layer when we broke for water after an hour or so. We had been hiking for just over two hours, and the light had turned diffuse and golden, when we entered the trees. I looked around in fascination. The gray trunks bent and twisted at fantastical angles beneath umbrella-like canopies of dark red leaves. The trees were spaced widely apart, and the leaf litter was soft and springy underfoot. Sprays of scarlet fern made pools of brightness around most of the trunks. The landscape wasn't otherworldly so much as dreamlike. Forgetting Daskar's instructions, I knelt to brush my fingers across the delicate fronds of a fern. The woody fragrance it released, reminiscent of rosemary, clung to my fingers for hours afterward.

We hiked on, following the downward slope of the hill, until Zey and Khiva returned from scouting ahead to report a stream a few minutes farther on. It was a tiny trickle of crystalline water, so narrow I could step easily across it, chattering down over a series of shallow stone ledges. The water was ice cold, I found when I dipped my hand in. "Too small to swim in," I said in disappointment.

"It's only the first day," Sohra said consolingly. "Maybe tomorrow."

Daskar had reported—her expression as dubious as it had been when I first broached the subject—that Rikasa's lakes and rivers had been deemed safe for swimming. "Use your judgment," she had said sternly. "Tolerable water temperatures and an absence of large aquatic predators don't guarantee safety. Keep in mind that, should you encounter trouble, your crewmates will almost certainly attempt to save your life. And, since they don't know how to swim, they may do so by sacrificing their own."

Suitably humbled, I had said meekly, "I promise I'll be careful."

Immediately after that conversation, I had consulted Sohra and Khiva as to the appropriateness of wearing a bikini in front of our male crewmates. They had demanded that I put it on for them. After twenty minutes of giggling and speculation, they had decreed that my swimsuit, while revealing, wasn't so far removed from Vardeshi undergarments as to be culturally offensive. When I asked, half hopefully, if a man who saw a woman undressed was required to marry her, or something along those lines, Khiva laughed and said, "We're not that naïve." They were as baffled as Daskar by the appeal of swimming as a leisure activity, but Sohra, seeing that the matter was important to me, was determined to make it happen. So was Khiva, mainly, I thought, in anticipation of the expressions on the men's faces when I dropped my towel. I was determined not to be nervous about that part. I'd been working out diligently all year, and after all, a bikini was a legitimate expression of my culture. I would just have to avoid looking directly at Zey, who would undoubtedly find the whole thing hilarious, or Saresh, who wouldn't.

We followed the river downstream to where it slowed and broadened a little. The banks on either side were invitingly flat. Hathan dropped back to walk with me. "What do you think?" he asked.

"It's perfect," I said. And it was, once the twilight had settled over the trees, revealing a white moon, tiny and coin-bright, rising through a filigree of dark branches. The force fields of our tents, rendered slightly opaque by no mechanism I could fathom, made a cluster of glowing amber domes along both banks of the river. My tent dome, along with Sohra's and Khiva's, was on one bank; the men's were on the opposite side, a decorous distance away. Hathan had explained to me that it was standard practice during wilderness exercises to segregate male and female sleeping areas to afford both groups some privacy. There was, inevitably, some banter about river-hopping under cover of darkness. Not likely, I thought, laughing along with the others. I could daydream about what it would like to be out here alone with Hathan, but given his indifference, and the sensitivity of Vardeshi hearing, I couldn't do much more than that.

Setting up camp took only a few minutes, and preparing dinner scarcely longer; Vardeshi camping gear included a sheaf of round silver adhesive patches which, attached to the bottom of a cooking vessel, heated its contents instantly to boiling point. When we had eaten and cleaned our dishes, I rose to refill my water bottle, looked up, and gasped. "Oh my God, you guys. Look."

My companions turned, bemused, to follow my pointing finger. The sky above the river had darkened to a clear indigo. The stars were as brilliant as any I had ever seen, their constellations warped slightly from the shapes I'd known since childhood, but they weren't what had drawn my attention. The white moon still hanging above the trees had been joined by a second one: a hazy gibbous orb with an unmistakable gold tint. Two moons. The feeling of incredulous gratitude I had felt earlier, when I stepped down from the shuttle ramp, rose up in me again. "Oh my God," I repeated. "The ships were one thing. And the starhavens. But this . . ."

Sohra came over and put her arm around me. "It's an

incredible feeling, isn't it?"

"Ivri khedai," I said. "The longing for another sky. I knew what the words meant before, but I didn't really understand them."

"Now you do," said Hathan. "You've seen the sky over another world. You made it. You're here." As if echoing his words, something in the trees beyond us offered its haunting cry to the night: bird or animal, I had no way of knowing, but its voice was wild and lonely and like nothing I had ever heard before.

"I'm here," I whispered.

16

My time on Rikasa flickered past, one golden hour giving way to the next with disquieting speed. The dreamlike mood of that first night in the forest persisted, enhanced perhaps by the fact that my internal circadian rhythm was meaningless on a world whose days were only seventeen hours long. I woke when sunlight brightened my tent dome, which I left semitransparent for the sheer delight of sleeping under the stars, and stayed awake as long into the twilight as I could before drifting off to the murmur of my companions' nearby voices. I was always the first one asleep and the last awake, and I was always tired, but it hardly mattered. From the very first morning, when I sat cradling my thermos of instant coffee, breathing clouds of white smoke into the air and listening to Zey gripe halfheartedly about dust in his senek, I was utterly content. The Outmarch felt so right, so inevitable, that I wondered how I could have imagined the mission without it. I remembered the first time I had heard Rikasa mentioned, on the *Pinion,* a few days before we docked at Arkhati. I had been instantly captivated by Ziral's description—almost more so than by the description of Vardesh Prime offered by Saresh. It was as if some part of me had been headed here all along.

Hathan, to judge by his words, felt the same. "This is exactly what we need," he said over breakfast that first morning. "I should have thought of it myself. There's a reason why every year of Institute training includes a survival exercise. They're good for morale."

"I wish I could say I had that in mind when I suggested it," I said. "But, honestly, I just wanted to go camping."

He smiled briefly. "So did I. I've been trying to get into the Outmarch forever. Before I transferred to the *Pinion,* the Echelon turned me down three years running."

"You're not really in now though," I felt obligated to point out. "Not as a contestant, I mean. When you applied before, you probably weren't picturing crawling along at human speed."

"Who cares?" Hathan's offhand tone was a perfect imitation of Zey's. I smiled; sitting on his bedroll, senek cup in hand, he did look completely at home. He gestured to the trees around us, which had the look of a fairy-tale wood, misty and luminous in the early light. "Ten days of this is better than three. Reyna will remember the contest, but she won't remember Rikasa. I will. And I can always apply again. I have the form pretty well memorized by now."

"Oh, please," I muttered. "You've had it memorized since the first time you saw it."

He gave me a wry sidelong look. "Maybe I have."

This, for me, was the remarkable gift conferred by the Outmarch, more precious than double moonrise or tent domes glimmering in the darkness: Hathan and I were finally friends. Since the second Listening our interactions had been collegial but never warm. Fleet protocol aside, the simple fact was that, as the *Ascendant*'s highest- and lowest-ranking crew members, we didn't interact enough to smooth down the rough edges left behind by the Flare. Even on a vessel as tiny as ours, we led nearly separate lives. Now, on Rikasa, all the walls had come down. We weren't khavi and second novi any more. We were simply teammates. And Hathan was at last beginning to see what I, because I was so drawn to him, had recognized long ago: the likeness of mind between us. I had sensed it when we first discussed ivri khedai, and again when we sat in the *Ascendant*'s lounge exchanging backpacking stories. It was the same feeling I had had with Fletcher, amplified a hundredfold. We felt the same things. We were the same.

I knew all Vardeshi felt wanderlust to some degree. But our crewmates had seen other worlds before now. They had grown up in the reality of interplanetary travel. I hadn't, and now, finding myself confronted with fresh proof of it at every turn, I found my excitement impossible to contain. And Hathan, who had the chart of his first trip offworld displayed on his wall, who alone of all our companions was planning to spend his three weeks on Earth backpacking through the remote wilderness, found it hilarious and endearing and familiar. I had persevered through the trials of the past nine months, and in doing so had won his respect. But it was that quality—my transparent joy in wandering on foot through the forests of another world—that finally made him like me.

I sensed the difference, the new warmth in him, from the very first morning. Going down to fill my flask at the river after breakfast, I was astonished to see innumerable faceted blue crystals nestled among the pebbles on the streambed. Some of them were as large as my fist. I hadn't noticed them last night; in the swiftly falling dusk, they had simply looked like stones. I scooped up a dripping double handful and carried them back to the edge of the camp, where I deposited them proudly in front of Hathan. I didn't seek him out on purpose; he was simply the first person I saw. He was sitting on a rock, flexscreen on his knee, adding with light but sure strokes to the hand-drawn trail map he had begun drafting the day before. "Look what I found!" I said.

He leaned forward to examine them. "Pretty, aren't they? They're naturally occurring prisms, like your quartz crystals. They're as common as dust on Arideth—we've found them on at least a dozen different planets."

I picked out the most regular of the stones, about the size of a robin's egg, and polished it carefully on the hem of my shirt. "They look like memory crystals."

"They are. Or, rather, it's the same stone. But we don't source it on Rikasa. Too many impurities. May I?" Hathan took the one I had cleaned and held it up to the light. "Ah. There's an imperfection, but you have to look closely to see it. The encoding won't work unless the stone is nearly flawless." He handed it back to me.

I balanced it on my palm, admiring its color, a paler blue than sapphire in the sunlight filtering down through the leaves. If there was a flaw in the stone, I couldn't see it. "Maybe that's why humans don't have perfect memories. Too many impurities."

Hathan said lightly, "If that was how it worked, I'd be a lot worse at Khivrik sevens."

To me the words signaled an end to the conversation. I closed my hand around the crystal, thinking to keep it as a souvenir, and stood up. I was surprised when he said, "I hope you know how lucky you are."

I sat down again. "You think I'm lucky?"

"You and Saresh both. You've experienced something truly rare. Something unprecedented in both our histories." He turned his attention back to his map, began shading in the line of the river a little more deeply. I watched his face. He seemed tranquilly absorbed in the work, but the regret was clear in his voice when he spoke again. "I wish . . . If things had gone differently this year, I like to think I might have had the chance to see a human memory. Just one. Imperfections and all."

Setting aside the two occasions on which he had apologized to me, he had never voluntarily raised such an intimate subject before. I said slowly, "I had no idea that was even something you wanted."

"It's something I want very much."

He could have no idea what he was suggesting, what even the briefest contact with my mind would reveal. I spoke with a brightness that was as natural as I could make it. "Then you will. I'm sure of it. Cross-species Listenings won't be off-limits forever. Not if the only side effects are the ones we've discovered. For me, at least, the first Listening was the easy one. Going the other way, into your memories, that was where I had trouble."

He nodded. "Maybe you're right. But I've missed my chance this time around. And Saresh is no help. He won't tell me anything more about the first Listening than he did in the ten seconds after it happened."

I said neutrally, "You asked him? About my memories?"

"I did, and he was exceptionally vague."

Damn right he was, I thought. "The Vox code of ethics, huh?"

"Apparently it applies to humans too." His smile was so swift and brilliant I wondered again how I could have failed for so long to see his resemblance to his elder brother. "So don't worry," he went on. "Your thoughts are safe from me—for now. But I think you should know that, as far as I'm concerned, you owe me a memory."

His tone was teasing. If he'd been human, I might have called it flirtatious. A sudden recklessness took hold of me. I opened my hand and looked down at the blue gemstone. "Here. Take this. Call it a Rikasan bar coin, worth one memory of your choice. We'll probably never see each other again after the mission. But if we do, and if you still haven't seen a human memory, I'll make good on it. Whether or not the ban is still in place."

Hathan said, "I'll hold you to that. I think you know I'm not likely to forget it."

"I know." Abruptly overwhelmed, certain that I'd gone too far, I set the crystal down in the fallen leaves beside him and headed back to the campsite. I didn't look back to see if he picked it up.

I could feel Saresh watching me as I rejoined the others. I ignored him steadily until I'd finished snapping on my pack and adjusting the straps. By that point, the betraying flush had faded, and I was able to meet his eyes. "Ready to go?"

"Well, yeah," Zey said. "We've been waiting for you."

I moved to take the lead, nudging him with my elbow as I went past. "Get used to it, pal."

I remained a little on edge until our second oxygen break of the morning, when Hathan sought me out to ask about my rock-climbing experience. I knew at once from the nonchalance of his manner that I hadn't betrayed myself earlier. I remembered all the times I'd seen him working in the *Ascendant*'s lounge with Reyna. Their seriousness had been woven through with moments of levity. Of course he hadn't been flirting with me. He'd been being friendly, that was all. I'd misread the signals. I vowed silently that I wouldn't be caught quite so off guard the next time it happened. If there was a next time.

As it turned out, there were plenty of next times. By the end of that first day, we had drifted into the habit of walking together. It made sense, practically speaking. The team could only move as fast as its slowest member. There was no point in Hathan's planning out a tricky ascent of a mountain face only to learn that it was too steep for me to climb. From the second morning on, without an acknowledgment from either of us, we were a dyad. We hiked at the front of the pack, or at the back, or in the middle, and wherever we went, the others looked to us for guidance when there was a decision to be made. I nearly laughed out loud when it struck me that I, and not Saresh or any of our other eminently capable companions, had emerged as de facto second-in-command.

I was anxious at first, sure my pace must seem agonizingly slow to Hathan, but he never hurried me along or betrayed any sign of impatience. I knew he was alert to the passage of time; he sent pairs of scouts ahead of us in a near-constant rotation to find the most efficient way forward. Watching Zey and Khiva return, mud smeared and laughing, from one such excursion, I realized that the scouting missions weren't only a time-saving measure. They were also a welcome chance for my crewmates to move at their natural pace. After that, I wondered when Hathan himself would join one of the scouting parties. He never did. He stayed with me. And at length it dawned on me that there was more to our near-constant proximity than simple pragmatism. With Reyna gone, he had stepped quietly back into the role she had abdicated. He had no intention of leaving my side, even for a few hours. He was doing the job he had, to his own shame and self-recrimination, twice failed to do. He was keeping me safe.

As I watched our path take shape under his pencil, I wondered whether the starting point the Echelon had chosen for us really was as favorable as they'd claimed. Our route was torturously indirect. We were constantly dodging obstacles reported by our vanguard to lie ahead: cliffs, thickets of thorny brush, gorges too deep and wide to cross. Some of these we avoided for my sake, but most were simply impassable. If this was an easy approach to the Perch, I thought, what were the other ones like? What kind of pace would Reyna and the others be setting, to conquer more challenging terrain than this in just three days?

Team *Ascendant*'s pace was as fast as I could make it without actively courting injury. I had never been in better physical shape, nor carried a lighter pack on a multiple-day trek. In my own admittedly unscientific estimation, those gains balanced out the toll exacted by Rikasa's heavy gravity and unfamiliar diurnal rhythm. We saved time wherever we could. We kept our breaks short. We ate the first two meals of the day cold and prepared the next morning's senek and coffee along with dinner. I had been a runner long enough to know exactly how hard I could push myself, and I did it, over and over again. By the end of each day, I was drenched in sweat and trembling with fatigue. I had no idea how the Echelon had calculated their ten-day window, what data they had used, whether their concept of a traversable distance for a human aligned at all with mine. If it could be done, though, I was determined to do it. While there was daylight, we hiked.

In the evenings, though, I let myself relax a little. Ahnir had brought along a larger version of our individual tent domes, meant to shelter ten or twelve people sitting on the ground. We ate dinner under it, shielded from the bites of insects and the cold edge of the wind, our plates lit by the stars and whatever combination of moons was visible. I never made it very far past the meal. Once I was dressed in my warm fleece layers, with a stomach full of warm food, my body began to shut down almost immediately. But that half hour of quiet talk was my favorite part of the day. The others stayed awake late into the night, telling stories and playing dice and (some of them) drinking. Alcohol was out of the question for Echelon teams, not forbidden so much as understood to be counterproductive. We were playing by our own rules, however, and my companions were determined to enjoy their recreational leave to the fullest. Now and then a cry of mirth or outrage roused me briefly from sleep. I didn't mind. Those moments reminded me of falling asleep as a child: the strip of golden light under the door, the sound of adult laughter from another room. I had a flask of contraband whiskey tucked away in my own pack, waiting for the right moment. Daskar had strongly discouraged me from bringing liquor for myself, but she hadn't gone so far as to actually forbid it.

On our third full day soilside, we lost an hour for another reason, one I couldn't bring myself to regret. We had spent the day climbing up out of a valley, slowly but steadily gaining elevation. At midafternoon Zey and Sohra returned from a scouting trip wearing identical knowing grins. "We found something up ahead," Zey said. "Eyvri's going to like it."

We walked on. A few minutes later, Hathan paused, listened intently, and said, "He's right. You are going to like it."

We had gone another hundred yards before I heard it too: the muted thunder of a waterfall. Soon afterward we stepped out from under the trees into the sunlight, and I caught my breath in wonder at the beauty of the scene before me. We were standing on a ledge near the foot of the waterfall, a cascade two or three times my height. The pool into which it plunged was wide and still, with boulders at the downstream end forming a natural dam. The water was clear as a windowpane; blue crystals larger than any I had yet seen sparkled on the sand fifteen pellucid feet below. At the center of the pool was a tiny island, a broad flat rock with a single tree growing upon it. Its red leaves caught the light like stained glass. Without a word to the others, I dropped my pack, walked out to the end of the ledge, and knelt to dip my hand into the water. It was achingly cold. I looked at Sohra and Khiva. Both of them wore expectant smiles.

"Yes?" Sohra said.

"Yes," I said firmly, and turned to Hathan. "Can we—"

"Of course." He started unbuckling his own pack. The others, taking their cues from him, did the same. I fished my bikini out of my own bag and stepped back into the woods to change. I took a few extra moments to make sure all the pieces were in place—the suit was revealing enough when properly situated—before rejoining my crewmates. When I did, the various conversations that had begun in my absence faltered and died. Not since I laughed out loud in my initial interview with the *Pinion*'s senior officers had I been the focal point of such universally horrified silence. It dragged on for so long that I started to wonder if, my female crewmates' assurances aside, I had committed a serious cultural gaffe. Then Sohra and Khiva began to giggle helplessly. So did Zey. I looked at Saresh and Ahnir, both of whom had their eyes resolutely trained on the ground. Vethna wore the tormented look of a man fighting desperately to contain about eight different off-color jokes. As for Hathan, I had no idea what his reaction was, if any, because I simply couldn't look at him.

At last Vethna said cautiously, "Eyvri? Where are your clothes?"

I glanced down at my bikini, affecting unconcern. "I'm wearing them. This is a swimsuit. I'm going swimming."

"You're . . . going into the water? Intentionally?"

I had to smile. "It wouldn't be much of a swim if I didn't."

We were standing on the lowest in a series of steplike ledges that partially encircled the waterfall pool. I climbed up to the highest one, which was only a few feet above the water, and paused at its edge, willing a little more heat from the sun-warmed rock beneath my feet. Then I took a deep breath and dove in.

When I broke the surface, half-laughing, half-gasping at the cold, my crewmates were visibly relieved. I paddled around a little, allowing my breathing and heart rate to settle. I'd swum in water colder than this, but not by much, and I had taken Daskar's warning about my companions' misguided altruism very much to heart. Then I ducked under again and swam a few strokes just beneath the surface, testing my strength and lung power, reveling in the silken glide of the water along my skin. It was perplexing to feel sensations so utterly familiar in a setting so impossibly strange. Swimming on Rikasa felt identical to swimming on Earth. The buoyancy of the water was a reprieve after days of heightened gravity, and the chill of the water relieved the ache in my sore muscles at once. And I already felt cleaner. I surfaced and swam back to my crewmates.

Saresh was kneeling on the ledge, preparing to refill his water flask. He lowered a cautious hand into the water and instantly withdrew it. "Sigils and emblems. It's like ice. Exactly how much recreation are you planning to endure?"

"Are you kidding? I'm just getting started! You should come in." I flicked water at him.

He aimed a gentle splash at me in return. "Thank you, but I've had enough hydrotherapy for one year."

Hathan, beside him, said, "Eyvri gives hydrotherapy a whole new meaning."

"Khavi? How about you? Want to learn to swim?"

He smiled but shook his head. "Old prejudices are the hardest to shift. And I confess that I don't really see the appeal."

"Fair enough. But you should all keep in mind that the closest shower is still eleven days off."

"Two days," Zey said, almost too quietly for me to hear him. I sent another, more forceful splash his way and laughed when he recoiled with a startled curse.

The others were settling themselves down on sunny patches of rock. Sohra was taking her boots off. They were clearly amenable to staying a little longer. I pushed off from the ledge and swam a leisurely circuit of the island, then climbed up onto it. I walked in a slow circle around the tree. Each step left a wet footprint on the warm rock, an impermanent trace of my presence. I wished I'd brought a necklace or a bandana to hang on the tree, some emblem of humanity to leave behind where future visitors would be sure to see it. Inspiration struck. I returned to the far side of the island, to a place where some object, perhaps a stone falling from the mountain above, had impacted with sufficient force to crack the topmost layers of rock. I worked a few stones loose and stacked them into a vaguely humanoid figure. Finding nothing suitable for the head, I went back into the water, my breath hitching again at the cold, and dove down to retrieve a fist-sized blue crystal from the sand.

My fingers had just closed around the stone when I saw a glimmer of movement in the shadows under a rock outcropping. I jerked backward in surprise, expelling half my lungful of stored air before I realized what I was looking at: a school of fish, each as long as my forearm, their triangular bodies as slender and translucent as panes of stained glass in delicate tints of blue and violet. I hadn't noticed them at first because the light passed right through them. I watched their gentle drifting movements in fascination until dark spots danced before my eyes and I was forced to kick for the surface.

My ears were ringing when I emerged. I set the crystal on top of the little figure and swam back across to where Sohra and Saresh were sitting with their feet in the water. "There are fish down there!" I said as I lifted myself out onto the ledge next to Sohra. "I didn't even see them until they were right in front of me. They're transparent!"

Saresh leaned forward to look; Sohra immediately withdrew her feet from the water. "What did you build?" she asked.

"It's called an inukshuk. I used to make them all the time with my Canadian cousins. It's a sign of human passage." I began toweling myself dry.

"Is the crystal meant to be symbolic of memory?" asked Saresh.

I grinned. "It is now."

Once I'd dried off, I spread my towel out in the sun, then shouldered my pack and went to change. Pulling sweaty clothes onto clean skin was viscerally distasteful but necessary. I had packed as lightly as I could: one set of hiking clothes, one set of camp clothes. It was crucial—for my crewmates' sake as well as my own—to maintain that distinction. Maybe, if I was exceptionally lucky, we'd come to another swimming hole just at dusk on one of the days to come. With seven days left, it wasn't out of the question.

* * *

On the eighth day we came across something better: not a mere swimming hole but a real lake, and a good-sized one at that. It completely filled the narrow valley that lay between the mountain we were descending and the one we meant to climb next, leaving only a narrow margin of passable ground. We had no choice but to go around it. I cast glances out at the water when I could spare my attention from watching my footing on the stony shore. Even to my eyes, it didn't present a very enticing prospect for a swim. The day was overcast and cold; the water was dark and choppy, with here and there a wave curling over in a crest of white foam.

We had been following the shoreline for twenty minutes or so when Hathan called a water break. Before I could unbuckle my pack, he said, "Eyvri, come with me. There's something you should see."

I followed him down to the water's edge. The sun had broken through; its reflection on the waves was dazzlingly bright. I had no idea what had drawn his attention.

"Do you see it?" he asked.

"See what?"

He raised a hand to point. I squinted. Halfway across, I could just make out a square of metal reflecting the sunlight: a raft. High above it, a small black and white triangle snapped in the brisk wind. It took me a moment to place what I was seeing. Then recognition dawned. "Oh my God. It's a flag. A special challenge."

"It's for you," he said.

"How do you know?"

"There's no access from the far side. The rocks are too steep. And you're the only one who can swim."

"So what do we do?"

"Do you think you can reach it?"

I looked up at the sun, which was already dipping toward the horizon, and out at the water again. The wind was blowing in toward our shore, which I took for a sign in my favor. "I think so. But I'd have to leave right now. There's not a lot of daylight left. What do you think? Should I go for it? It might just be a colossal waste of time. I have no idea if the Echelon's still angry at me for turning down their ship."

"If I were you, I'd want to find out."

"You want me to go."

"I want more information. There's only one way to get it. But it's your challenge, not mine. And a lot of guesswork went into designing it. Too much, maybe. The Echelon doesn't know how far you can swim, or what qualifies as dangerously cold water for a human. You're the only one who can assess the risk."

I took a last look at the flag. Then I dropped my pack on the stones and started to dig through it. Hathan began giving orders to set up camp. When I protested, he said, "Whatever happens, we're not going any farther today."

After I found my swimsuit and my camp clothes, I started pulling out my cooking gear. Ahnir stopped me. "Go. I'll have hot food ready when you get back."

I stepped into the shelter of the trees and changed into my swimsuit, my mind already on the challenge ahead. Hathan walked with me down to the water. I stepped in and swore under my breath.

"Cold?" he said.

"Yeah."

"Too cold?"

"I don't think so." I gritted my teeth and waded farther in. When the water reached my hips, I turned to look back at the shore. He was still standing there, alone, watching me. I lifted a hand, turned toward the open water, and dove in.

It wasn't too cold, or too far. But it was awfully close. I was in good shape, and I'd grown up swimming in icy New England lakes, but I had been starside for nine months. I fought the chop all the way to the raft. When I reached it, I swam around it twice before accepting the fact that there was no ladder. I scrabbled for a handhold on the slick surface, then hung by one arm until a chance swell lifted me high enough to hook a knee over the edge. Once out in the chilly air, I immediately started to shiver. I stamped around on the surface, trying to warm up, cursing the Echelon in every language I could think of. The flag was lashed to a pole rising from the center of the raft. It took a few tries before my numb fingers could undo the knot holding the line in place. I hauled the flag down and found the token attached to it, a metal ring about an inch in diameter. It gleamed like chrome in the fading light. I untied my bikini top and knotted the ring securely onto one strap before tying it again. Then I walked to the edge of the raft. I didn't try to signal the shore. My crewmates' eyesight was keener than mine; they would have seen the descending flag and understood its meaning. Already the domes of their tents glowed against the dark trees. I looked up into the sky and was marginally heartened to see a flash of green and a gleam of silver high overhead. There was a rescue craft hovering directly above my position. The Echelon was watching. I took a deep breath and dove into the water again.

The way back was harder. The wind was rising, and it had swung around to push me away from the beach. Several times I was swamped by large waves and swallowed water. I bobbed on the surface, coughing, until I got my breath back. When I reached the calmer water near shore, I put my head down and swam blindly until the ground came up under me. Then I stood up. Rikasa's gravity slapped me down like a giant hand, shocking after the weightlessness of water, and I fell. Someone's arm locked around me: Hathan's. I looked down. We were knee-deep in the water. He had waded in, still in his hiking boots, to help me. I was too cold and tired to feel anything beyond simple relief at his touch. I stumbled and nearly fell again on the way into camp. Sohra and Khiva helped me out of my wet swimsuit and toweled me off. I felt no self-consciousness then either. The resistance of pulling dry clothing onto still-damp skin was almost too much for my strength. Ahnir had made spaghetti and hot cocoa. I silently ate and drank everything he put in front of me. Then I fell into my sleeping bag and into an oblivion that felt like dark water.

* * *

When I woke again, it was full daylight. I crawled out of my dome and was shocked to see how far up the sky the sun had already traveled. Mine was the only tent still set up. I retrieved my pack and began sorting through my gear. Zey brought me my thermos, which held still-scalding coffee that had probably been made hours ago. "Why didn't anyone wake me up?" I demanded. "We should be miles away from here by now!"

"Hathan said to let you sleep. I think he's worried about

you."

Hathan's first words to me when I found him in a shady spot on the beach confirmed Zey's assertion. "The challenge was a mistake," he said. "It was too risky. I should never have encouraged you to do it. I knew it the moment you were out of reach. I tried to call you back, but you didn't hear me."

I patted the top of my pack, where I had stowed my now-dry bikini top, the chrome ring still knotted into the strap. "I got it though."

"I hope it was worth the trouble," he said grimly.

"How much time do you think it'll buy us?"

"It could be five seconds—or five hours. We won't know until the finish."

I stood up and shrugged into my pack. "Then we'd better get there."

* * *

The next few days passed swiftly by. We spent the twelfth day climbing up alongside a brook, or more precisely a chain of tiny waterfalls, that threaded its way up a gradually narrowing seam between two mountains. The climb was grueling work, as much vertical as horizontal, and it had taken us most of the day. Mist-slick rock scrambles gave way to narrow ledges rendered nearly impassable by the vegetation already fighting for purchase there. I had passed one or two promising swimming holes without even pausing. Stopping midclimb would be pointless; the knowledge of more elevation to come would rob the swim of any enjoyment. I had scrapes on my knees and my palms, the muscles in my thighs were jumping with fatigue, and it was disheartening to haul myself over each rise only to see another beyond it. I was worried, too, about what Saresh and Khiva would find on their scouting run. Hathan had sent them ahead twenty minutes ago with orders to seek out a level place to camp for the night. What if they couldn't find one? I was all too conscious of Rikasa's tiny red-gold sun racing down the sky toward the horizon. A night spent up here on the mountain, the eight of us strung out in ones and twos across a series of tiny ledges, would be hellish.

I hauled myself and my thirty pounds of gear up onto the next rock and hesitated, still on my hands and knees, trying to summon the energy to stand. Hathan was already scaling the next tumble of boulders. "Are you all right?" he called back to me.

"Fine," I gasped. "Water break?"

He vaulted up onto the topmost slab and cast a cursory glance around before replying. "If you can make it this far, you'll have a better view."

Cursing Vardeshi strength and Rikasan gravity, I pushed myself to my feet and trudged to the next cluster of boulders. I stood paralyzed in front of them for a long time, unable to commit to an approach, a sure sign of exhaustion. When I was nearly to the top, Hathan leaned down and offered me his hand. I took it without hesitation. He locked his fingers around my wrist and pulled me up the rest of the way. "See?" he said as he let go. "I told you the view was better."

I looked around incredulously. "I don't believe it. We made it!"

It had been impossible to tell from just a few feet below, but we had at last reached level ground. We were standing on the edge of a plateau between two mountain peaks. Before us lay the source of the stream we had been following all day: an alpine lake, tiny and crystalline. A sheer rock face rose out of the water on one side, but a narrow crescent of pebbled beach ran along the other, flanked by scarlet trees. Beyond the lake, a wooded slope rose gently up to a narrow pass between the peaks.

Hathan took out his map. "If I've charted our position correctly, we should be able to see the Perch from the far side of that pass. I think it's located on the near side of this mountain range." He traced it with his finger. "By tomorrow morning, we'll know whether we still have a shot."

My entire body ached for rest, but I forced myself to ask the question: "Shouldn't we go look tonight?"

"To what end? You're not going any farther today, no matter what we see."

"No," I conceded. I was keeping myself upright mainly by force of will. There was no question of my descending the far side of the mountain we had just scaled—in the dark, no less.

There were murmurs of admiration and triumph behind us as our crewmates gained the plateau. It was gratifying to know the climb had taxed them too, at least enough to make them glad to leave it behind. We stopped for a few minutes to drink water and adjust our layers. When we moved on, it was in the distinctly laissez-faire attitude of weary hikers with camp firmly in their sights: pack straps unclipped, water flasks in hand.

We hadn't gone far when Saresh and Khiva came jogging down the beach to inform us that there were plenty of good-sized campsites scattered among the trees. We followed them to the nearest of these, where Hathan designated sleeping areas for men and women to either side of a clearing with ample space for Ahnir's communal tent dome.

A remarkably short time later, I was wading into the icy shallows of the lake, flanked by Khiva and Sohra. It was the first time I had bathed in company with my crewmates. I had swum alone at the first swimming hole; at the lake where I had retrieved the challenge token, I had still been fast asleep in my tent when everyone else bathed. As I had done before, I wore my bikini. The others wore the standard-issue technical undergarments furnished by Requisitions. These were predictably gray and conservative, and also, Khiva said, quick to dry. In spite of the underwear, which to my eyes provided more than adequate coverage, Hathan had directed the women to bathe separately from the men. The idea was so quaintly Victorian I actually laughed out loud when he said it. Not until I saw the looks my crewmates were giving me, half-amused, half-alarmed, did I realize he meant it. "Oh," I said. "You weren't kidding."

"It's standard policy during soilside training exercises," he explained, "to maintain discipline, just as with the tents."

"Sure." Privately I doubted that all the brandy on Rikasa, if it were magically to materialize at our campsite, would so much as dent my companions' self-control. Certainly it would take more than a few minutes of decorous splashing around in appallingly cold water. But I couldn't argue the point any longer, not without making it abundantly clear to everyone listening that my real agenda was to see what the male contingent of Team *Ascendant* had been issued for underwear. I let it go, but the laughter was still in me, and I couldn't resist a final comment. "It's a good thing you guys weren't on my last camping trip in college. Not much discipline there."

"Go on," Zey asked obligingly.

"We were backpacking in the White Mountains, just before graduation. It was supposed to be really cold, and for most of the trip, it was. But on the last day it turned warm all of a sudden. We stopped for lunch next to this beautiful river, and nobody had a swimsuit, but we all wanted to swim." I shrugged. "So . . . we swam."

"And then hiked out in wet clothes," Hathan said.

"Oh," I said blithely, "our clothes stayed dry."

I knew the exact moment he grasped the implication by his quick glance away and the indigo flush that darkened his cheekbones. I laughed again. It was getting easier, being friends with him. If that was what we were doing. To me it still felt like flirting.

I kept my swim brief. The lake was gorgeous, deep and jewel-clear, but the daylight was fading, and I knew there were others awaiting their turns in the water. Sohra and Khiva didn't venture farther in than the shallows, where they knelt to wash themselves efficiently with the biodegradable soap we had been issued at the starhaven. Their murmured comments told me exactly how little they enjoyed the process. I joined them in time to soap and rinse my hair, a less involved process for me than for them, since mine was so short. We waded out together.

A few minutes later I was seated under the group tent in my camp clothes, blissfully clean and warm, with dinner to look forward to and the knowledge of headier pleasures to follow. My silver flask was tucked into the pocket of my vest. The white moon was edging out over its trembling reflection in the dark water. In the dusk above the treeline, nocturnal birds swooped and dipped, trailing wings like tattered ribbons. It finally felt like the right moment—or one of them, at any rate.

"What's that?" Saresh asked when I brought the flask out of my pocket after dinner. I thought I heard disapproval in his voice.

I waved it at him. "This, my friend, is the good stuff.

Straight Kentucky bourbon."

"Are you allowed to drink that soilside?"

"What, you think I asked?"

His brows drew together. At once I regretted my flippant answer. "Don't worry, I won't overdo it. The last thing I want is to be hung over in this gravity." I offered him the flask. "Here, you should try it. It's good."

He considered, then said, "In the interest of lightening your pack for tomorrow, I will." He unscrewed the cap and tipped a little bourbon into his empty senek cup. I hid a smile. It hadn't occurred to me that he would do anything other than swig directly from the flask. He took a wary sip of the bourbon and nodded. "I can see how you might get into trouble with that. Thank you." He handed the flask back to me.

I uncapped it and drank, savoring the bourbon's warmth and its complex sweetness, then settled back against the bedroll I was using as a backrest with a sigh of utter contentment. "This night couldn't be any more perfect unless it had a campfire."

"I've got the next best thing," Ahnir said, and stood up. He returned a moment later with his mandolin.

I felt a stirring of something unexpected: eagerness mingled with fear. Zey rose to take the instrument from Ahnir. I tensed, suddenly afraid he would present it to me with some elaborate and undeniable public flourish. He didn't. He sat down cross-legged and began to tune it. I relaxed.

The song he chose was melancholy and restrained, a fitting accompaniment to the quiet night that surrounded us. I listened breathlessly, captivated by the sounds of archaic Vardeshi, the liquid rush and glide of unfamiliar syllables. They slid past me in a single continuous ribbon of sound, like a silk scarf slipping through my fingers. Strange to think modern

Vardeshi had sounded like that to me once. Now it was barbed with meaning, freighted with it. I couldn't hear it as simple noise any more. Comprehension was a gain and a loss, both.

When Zey finished his song, he passed the mandolin back to Ahnir. One song led into another, and then another, and my conviction grew. It was the right moment—and not only for bourbon. When Sohra finished her song, it felt perfectly natural to me to get up and take the mandolin out of her hand. I was glad the night was so dark; if anyone turned surprised or skeptical looks my way, I didn't see them. I sat down beside Zey, because although I could feel that the time had come, it made things easier to pretend this was just another practice session. He gave me an encouraging nod. I could feel Ahnir, the expectant tutor, watching us across the circle of listeners. I knew Hathan was there as well, sitting against a tree on the far side of the tent dome. With trembling fingers I picked out the first couple of notes. Hearing them gave me courage. It's not about me, I reminded myself. It's not about my voice. It's about the song.

I had never forgotten my promise to Hathan, that I would sing for our crewmates before our journey came to an end, and I had always known I would keep it; but it had taken me a long time to choose the right song. The one I eventually settled on was by a little-known Scottish folk singer. It was short and simple. It described a lover's difficult journey to his beloved, and while it sounded nothing at all like the lament Hathan had sung for me before we arrived at Arkhati, it seemed to me to capture a little of that same spirit. If it had been more overtly romantic, I would have rejected it as potentially too revealing, but all the imagery was of traveling, and as long as I didn't look at him—which I wouldn't—I didn't think there was anything to give me away. I had rewritten the second verse, which had never seemed to me to match the mood of the first, to extend the theme of wandering in unknown lands.

That had been the easy part. Language came to me naturally, musicianship less so. After we left Elteni, for weeks on end, Ahnir had spent an hour every night patiently instructing me in the rudiments of playing the Vardeshi mandolin. At first clumsy and halting, my fingers had acquired minimal skill through repetition and sheer resolve. When I achieved a modicum of polish, I added in the vocals. Here I was on firmer ground. My singing voice wasn't unpleasant, and it improved with practice and concentration.

The final step had been bringing Zey in to learn the harmony, which he had done, of course, after a single hearing. His talents as a singer far exceeded mine, which worked to my advantage. He caught the mood of the song perfectly. I liked it even better when I heard the light, dreamy complement his voice offered to mine. And he knew instinctively how to hold back, giving precedence to the melody, though he could easily have overpowered it.

About a month after we left Elteni, Ahnir had told us it was time to stop rehearsing. "You have it now," he had said. "Don't oversing it. You'll spend its freshness before you have an audience."

I had known he was right, and I knew now that the flutter I felt in my stomach was supposed to be there, but I still wished we'd practiced a couple more times. I tried to focus on what my fingers were doing, struck a false note, and grinned at Zey. It was easier after that. The tightness in my chest subsided. Singing helped too, because it forced me to take deep breaths. By the end of the first verse, I knew it would be all right. The song still felt like a good choice; it still spoke truth to me. I had traveled a long way too, and I was lonely, and carrying a love that felt like another kind of loneliness. On the second verse, I found a little more power and confidence, and Zey matched them effortlessly. I thought our voices had never blended so well before. When I reached the coda, with its line about homesickness, I sang it without restraint. The last few measures of wordless harmony were softer, just as we had practiced them. I played the final notes and strummed an emphatic closing chord. I'd done it. It was over.

I would have given a great deal for even a polite smattering of applause. I knew rationally that the thoughtful stillness following my last notes was meant to signify appreciation, but it was still disconcerting. After a pause that felt endless, Ahnir came to reclaim his instrument. As he bent to take it from me, he said, "That was better than the rehearsals."

"I made a mistake," I said.

"So what?"

"I don't know. I guess I just wanted it to be perfect."

He nodded. "And it was."

The lingering charge of the performance made me restless. I went down to the beach and stood at the water's edge. The wind was rising. I shivered and raised the collar of my fleece. Behind me I could hear Ahnir and Saresh beginning another song. I heard the rattle of stones that meant someone was crossing the beach and knew without turning to look that it was Hathan.

"I don't know why you waited so long to sing for us," he said. "You have a perfectly adequate voice."

Adequate. The echo of Khavi Vekesh's coldly dismissive assessment of my fledgling Vardeshi stung in a way he probably hadn't intended. I said, "Probably because, on a ship full of really incredible voices, mine is just adequate," in a waspish tone I instantly regretted.

Hathan said, "I didn't mean it as an insult."

I shook my head. "No, it's fine. You're right. But that's the answer. I said I'd sing for you, and I did, but I'm not about to make a habit of it, not with so many beautiful voices on the *Ascendant*."

He said slowly, "Your music is different from ours, but it's appealing in its own way, and you performed it well. I hope you'll sing for us again."

"Maybe sometime." I took a swig from my flask. My eyes were stinging, and I knew it wasn't just the wind. I had hoped for . . . I wasn't sure what. Not flattery, not from him, but perhaps slightly warmer praise. I knew there wasn't the faintest chance that I would ever sing in front of him again. After a pause, I heard the crunch of receding footsteps. There was plenty of bourbon left in my flask, but I knew it would be a mistake to continue drinking. The morning would come all too swiftly. I returned to the camp for a few more songs, accepted a handful of compliments substantially more generous than Hathan's, and went to lay out my sleeping bag, still feeling the ache of unshed tears in my throat. The song had been fine—better than fine. It was what had come afterward that fell short of my expectations.

17

The wind rose during the night; its mournful soughing in the trees stirred me from sleep more than once, finally waking me for good in the gloom before dawn. Most of my crewmates were already up. Zey, seeing me emerge from my tent in hiking clothes, went to rouse the others. Vethna muttered something about sleeping off the whiskey and catching up with us later but fell silent at a look from Hathan. As we packed, the wind flung droplets of a fine cold rain into our faces like handfuls of needles. The rain began falling steadily as we marched along the pebbled beach toward the far end of the lake. We stopped, and Hathan spoke briefly to Sohra and Saresh before sending them ahead. Ahnir helped me fasten my tent apparatus to the top of my pack and adjust the height and breadth of its projection. I watched in fascination while the water streamed down harmlessly all around me, as if I stood inside a transparent glass dome. Incredible though the technology was, it wasn't a perfect fix; stray gusts of unusually forceful wind were able to penetrate it, and the field extended downward only as far as my knees. My socks and

boots quickly turned sodden. I had hiked with wet feet before, although never in weather this cold. I tramped on,
determined not to complain.

We emerged from the mountain pass to find that visibility
had dwindled to nearly nothing. We might have been standing on a small rocky island in a mist-shrouded ocean for all
we could see of the mountain range opposite us, on one of
whose peaks Hathan thought the Perch might be located. If
it was, I couldn't see it. I couldn't see anything at all. Veils of
rain drifted past me like ghosts.

Saresh and Sohra rejoined us, stepping out of the rain so
unexpectedly I started. Hathan didn't seem surprised. "Make
the call," he said without prelude. "Stay or go?"

"Stay," Sohra said. "It's too steep. And too slippery. The
rain is freezing on the rocks. Eyvri—" She broke off with a
glance at me.

"It's okay," I said. "You can say it. I won't be insulted."

"It would be risky in any case," Saresh said. "With you,
it's too risky. It's that simple."

Hathan nodded. "Yes. It is. We stay put for now." He
turned to order the others back into the relative shelter of the
pass. I fell back a step to let them file past me, turning my
face away to hide my frustration. My throat felt tight, and
while I didn't think I would actually cry, I might if anyone
tried to comfort me. It was just too much: too many disap-
pointments strung too closely together. First the failure of my
song last night (because it did feel like a failure, no matter
what anyone said), and now this.

Hathan waited too. He didn't say anything. When everyone else had gone, and I thought I could trust myself to
speak, I said, "What do we do now?"

"We wait. The rain will pass." He paused. "Or it won't.

Either way, we'll get there."

"What if it just keeps raining? We only have one more day."

"The Echelon will give us as long as they can. If it looks like we won't reach the Perch in time for the reception, they'll send a shuttle for us."

I glared out into the gray abyss. "That's lame. We're so close. I would like . . ." I took a deep, calming breath. "I would like to finish this journey on my own terms. That doesn't seem like too much to ask." *Not after being turned away from Vardesh Prime.*

"I know," he said quietly.

We went back into the pass, where the others had gathered under an overhang. Ahnir was setting up his group tent. Most of the area it enclosed was wet, but there were ground cloths among the supplies, and my crewmates worked quickly to assemble a comfortable shelter. That done, they began changing back into their camp clothes, using a couple of personal tents set to maximum opacity as improvised screens. I was struck by how readily they adapted to the change in plans. That was how the Fleet operated, though, wasn't it? Last-minute changes were standard operating procedure. Headed to Arkhati? Guess again, you're actually going to Veynir. To those accustomed to reversals on the scale of planets and years, a surprise hiatus in the middle of a hike must be hardly worth noting. I set aside my own worries as best I could and copied their example, changing back into my camp clothes and draping my wet things over my pack to dry in the warm air.

Once I had accepted the delay as inevitable, I began to enjoy it. With the exception of an hour here and there, I had spent the entire Outmarch either hiking or sleeping. A little enforced idleness made for a welcome change of pace. While the rain tapped softly on the tent dome overhead, we sat on our bedrolls, drinking tea or senek and playing games. These began with simple dice games but soon entered more complex territory: lightning-fast idiom-association games I couldn't begin to follow, and others, question-and-answer games that felt older somehow, although I couldn't really follow them either. Watching the others break into appreciative laughter as Ahnir answered Sohra's idiom with one even more obscure, I felt a ghost of the bewilderment I had felt at my first-ever officers' dinner. I had come a long way toward understanding the Vardeshi since then, but in moments like this one, there was no denying that there were things they did, still, that I would never be able to do; chasms between us that I would never be able to bridge.

Zey, catching something of my mood, said abruptly, "We're leaving Eyvri out."

I said quickly, "It's fine."

Ahnir shook his head. "No, he's right. Eyvri? They must play games around those campfires of yours. Could you teach us one?"

"I could," I hedged, "but I don't know if you'd like it."

Hathan said, "Try us."

I ran through a couple of simple alphabet puzzles, typical summer-camp fodder. After the third one, I shifted without warning to a riddle game I had learned in college. The object was to guess which member of the group would be named next. The hint, ostensibly, lay in the placement of several objects relative to each other (in this case, three sachets of peppermint tea, a kevet with a bent handle, and a battered orange carabiner I'd found clipped to my pack). The secret was that the arrangement was meaningless. While setting up the display with my left hand, I casually pointed to the person in question with the forefinger of my right. My crewmates guessed again and again, their theories growing ever wilder. I could sense their frustration mounting. I was on the point of abandoning the whole thing when Zey, always the group's most ardent student of human facial expressions and body language, suddenly caught on. The look of wild glee that spread across his face was irresistible. At his insistence we played on. Sohra was the next one to spot the trick. In the end, despite or possibly because of his gift for strategy, only Hathan remained in the dark. When I finally explained that he couldn't find the pattern because there wasn't one, he leapt up from his seat, hurled his senek cup to the ground, and ran both hands through his hair in a transport of rage. Zey, over-joyed at this uncharacteristic loss of composure, shouted "It's the Flare! Eyvri, hide!" and tackled me, dragging me off my bedroll and into the partial shelter of a personal tent someone had forgotten to switch off. We lay there on our backs for the next few minutes, half in and half out of the opaque screen, giggling helplessly and repeating, "It's the Flare!" The joke ventured into questionable territory, but I knew it was safe to laugh at it. I had caught Hathan's eye before Zey succeeded in pulling me down, and he had been laughing too.

Toward afternoon, as the skies stubbornly refused to clear, the gaming enthusiasm began to pall. One by one my companions drifted off to private pursuits. A few—Vethna among them—napped in the privacy of their individual tents. Too restless for sleep, I settled down on my sleeping bag with my phone to scroll through my photos of the trip. I'd looked at a little over half of them when Hathan came over for a quiet conference. I reflected with a flash of interior humor that he had progressed as far as sitting on top of my zipped-up sleeping bag, which was, technically speaking, one step closer to actually crawling inside it. Vardeshi hearing being what it was, no conversation within the confines of the group tent could be truly private, but we kept our voices low, and the others pretended with varying degrees of success not to be listening.

"We've lost the day," he said. "Even if it clears off now, you're not going down that mountain in the dark."

"No," I agreed.

"It's unlikely at this point that we'll reach the Perch before the time limit runs out."

I rubbed a smudge from the back of my phone case. "Are you asking me if I want to quit?"

"Yes."

"Then no."

"Good." He glanced up through the transparent ceiling at the darkly overcast sky. "I'm not ready for walls yet."

I smiled a little. "Neither am I."

Dinner was a subdued affair. It was openly understood by now that any hope of my completing the course on time had been washed away by the rain. Toward the end of the meal I heard Zey mutter something about the dubious necessity of sleeping on the ground for another night. Hathan, hearing it too, briskly dispatched him to wash dishes outside. "To cultivate your appreciation of a warm, dry tent," he explained. I was secretly ecstatic that he had come to my defense. I had just finished putting away my cooking gear when Zey came in again, wide-eyed and dripping, his arms full of clean dishes. The rain had plastered his hair flat to his head, save for a few stubbornly upright tufts. He looked like a half-drowned cat. I took one look at him and started to laugh. I wasn't the only one. Zey himself joined in the laughter with his usual good humor. Hathan, clearly recognizing that his point had been made, presented his brother with a dry set of camp clothes.

"Are those clean?" Sohra said enviously. "You've been hoarding clean clothes all this time?"

"Holding them in reserve, yes."

"Are you holding anything else in reserve?" Saresh queried.

I said under my breath, "Just an extra pair of gloves."

I wasn't trying to be funny, or, for that matter, to be overheard. The evocation of our long-ago hour in the lounge, with its dream of shared adventure that had so improbably come true, was meant for myself alone. Hathan's laugh caught me entirely off guard. I looked up and found him smiling quizzically at me. "You remember that story?"

"Of course. It's only been a couple of months."

"Do you know which glove it was?"

"The right." I answered without hesitation. I had been staring at the hand in question while he told the story, tracing the dark sweeping lines inked onto the back of it, wishing I could trace them with my fingertip. And maybe, while I was at it, peel off that pesky gold overlay.

My eyes dropped to his hand again as he flexed his fingers thoughtfully. "That's right. You know, I think you've been underselling human memories. Yours are quite accurate."

"They're okay," I hedged. Our companions, excluded from both the joke and the conversation that followed it, were looking interestedly between the two of us. I didn't think I was imagining the sharpness in Saresh's gaze.

"What are we talking about?" Zey said brightly.

"When Hathan lost a glove," I said, and felt the blood rush into my face. In the months that we had known each other, I had called him by his given name precisely twice. The first time, just after an explosion ripped through the *Pinion*'s hull, I had been begging him to trust me. The second time, I had been trying to recall him to his senses during the Flare. I had done it now without even thinking. It had felt effortless. Natural. I wished with sudden fervency that the end of the Outmarch was still days off. Weeks, even. I liked the people we had become on Rikasa. I didn't want to leave them behind.

Hathan was saying unconcernedly, "My winter survival trial. I must have told you about it."

"Oh, yeah," Zey said, and snorted. "Sock-hand."

"I'll be needing those clothes back," Hathan said, just as Saresh murmured, "Missing your kitchen detail, Novi?" All three of them laughed.

On the other side of the communal shelter, Sohra was brewing tea, a floral blend we had sampled together on Arkhati. The air was filled with its fragrance. Ahnir had begun tuning his mandolin. The shadow of future loss fell over me, dark and chilling, just as it had in my last days on Elteni. I said good night in a voice that trembled only a little. Then I turned my personal tent to full opacity and crawled inside it. I lay there with my sleeping bag pulled up to my chin, tears running silently into my pillow, for a long time before the pensive notes of Ahnir's playing finally lulled me to sleep.

The next thing I knew, Sohra was shaking me gently awake. "Eyvri? The storm is passing. We should be able to see the Perch now."

I sat up, rubbing my eyes, and saw that it was morning. The rain had dwindled to an occasional spatter, and while the clouds were still heavy, they were pierced here and there by golden spears of sunlight. I shoved my feet into my hiking boots without troubling to lace them and followed Sohra out of the tent.

The veil of rain had lifted. Across the valley a line of mountains rose as dark and straight as if inked in by hand on a paper horizon. I scanned their higher slopes for the Perch and found it almost at once, a roughly rectangular shining like a chip of mica on the shoulder of a peak slightly below our current vantage point. A single glance down over the tumbled rocks to the valley floor below and back up to that tiny glittering point told me what I needed to know. With mechanical movements I took my flexscreen out of my pack and checked the time. Six hours. Impossible. I turned to Hathan, raised my hands a little, then dropped them to my sides. "Well, we tried."

"We did," he said, consulting his own device. "Outmarch Control is asking if we'd like to be picked up now."

"Not now, not ever."

"I didn't think so." He sent his response and put his flexscreen away. "Let's see how close we can get."

We broke camp and began our descent. Nothing we had seen in the past two weeks came close to equaling its level of technical challenge. In full daylight, and with mostly dry footing, it was difficult; in darkness and rain it would have been suicidal, at least for me. Three times we were stopped in our tracks by vertical slabs of smooth rock, each at least two stories in height. My crewmates, exhibiting still-untapped depths of resourcefulness, produced an assortment of climbing ropes, which Khiva swiftly anchored into place and Zey just as swiftly retrieved after the rest of the group had made use of them. Watching my friend nimbly spider-climb down what had registered to my eyes (and fingers and toes) as a nearly featureless wall was deeply unsettling. He and Khiva were the most accomplished climbers, but all of my companions were highly skilled. I had to look away when Saresh and Hathan rappelled side by side down the third and longest rock wall in a furious race to the bottom. I wasn't afraid of heights, but my prior rock-climbing experiences had all involved helmets and redundant safety systems. The cat's-cradle harnesses Khiva had thrown together from skeins of what looked like parachute cord were probably stronger, but they didn't look it.

I couldn't keep pace with my crewmates, but I thought I acquitted myself well enough. When my turn came, I stepped promptly off each ledge, only giving my harness a couple of surreptitious tugs beforehand. I dropped down a little more slowly than the others and expelled a sigh of relief as my feet hit solid ground for the last time. Hathan was close enough to hear it.

"Still think the Outmarch is a nice hike through the mountains?" he teased.

"It's not so bad," I said, trying to ignore the heat rising in my face, "for a soft course."

With that last rock face conquered, the worst of the descent was behind us. It was early afternoon. We took a short lunch break, which my crewmates filled with cheerful talk of the various amenities offered by the Perch. I didn't say much. I didn't begrudge them their anticipation. How could I? We had all been promised ten standard days soilside to spend however we wished, and they'd had plenty of time to plan theirs before I came along and signed us all up for a camping trip. Still, it seemed that their eagerness to complete the course was growing in tandem with my reluctance. When we'd eaten, we headed down into the trees that blanketed the lower slopes of the mountain. As the ground leveled out, and it became possible to move at a faster clip, I had to fight the instinct to dawdle.

There was a river somewhere below us, winding its way along the bottom of the valley. I knew because I'd glimpsed it from the last high ledge. I had noted a place where the water made a lazy curve around a half-moon of pebbled beach that ought to mark an easy crossing, not to mention a potential swimming hole. I had already promised myself that, time limit or no, if I saw an opportunity to fit in one last quick swim, I would take it. I had just begun to glimpse the bright flicker of sunlit water through the trees, and to wonder whether the river would be warmer or colder in the aftermath of rain, when I stepped off a low ledge and broke my ankle.

The stone that rolled under my foot had held steady for six people before me. It gave way the moment I touched it, and my leg gave way along with it. The pain was instant and sickening. I went down hard, the weight of my pack combining with Rikasa's heavier gravity to propel me toward the ground with disconcerting speed. I couldn't get my hands up in time to break my fall; my face and chest broke it instead. The impact stunned me briefly. After a few moments I began to gather myself onto my hands and knees. While I did so, I took stock of my injuries. In addition to the watery wrong feeling in my right ankle, I had cracked one lens of my sunglasses, torn my favorite hiking shirt, and gained a scratch on the bridge of my nose and another on my chest above my collarbone. As I levered myself upright, noting the rock that would have broken my nose rather than scratched it had I hit a couple of inches to the left, I felt a sudden easing of pressure on my back. Someone was lifting my hiking pack away from my body. I freed one arm, then the other, and looked up to see Hathan setting the pack gently aside.

He crouched down next to me. "Can you stand?"

I doubted it, but I said through my teeth, "I'll try."

He settled my arm across his shoulders and helped me to rise. When I was fully upright, I took a deep breath, set my right foot down—and gasped at the white-hot knife that pierced my ankle. It was no good. My Outmarch was over. I turned my face toward his shoulder and wept tears of pain and bitter disappointment. He drew me against his side in an infinitely cautious embrace. Bitterly I consigned the moment, along with that earlier one in which he had half carried me out of the lake, to the realm of romantic opportunities ruined by the insistence of pain.

After a subjective eternity Ahnir said hesitantly, "Eyvri? Can I look at it?"

I dried my eyes with my none-too-clean sleeve and transferred my arm from Hathan's shoulders to his. He lowered me carefully to the ground again and began to unlace my right boot. At the first touch of his fingers on my sock-clad ankle, I was vividly reminded of his careful probing for broken facial bones after the Flare. He issued gentle instructions which I obeyed with only half my mind. My real attention was with Hathan, who had paced a short distance away and was speaking softly into his flexscreen. I couldn't hear the words, but I knew what they signified. He wasn't waiting for a diagnosis. He was calling for a medical evacuation. He knew it was over too.

Ahnir sighed and drew my sock gently back into place. "I suspect it's broken, but it's almost beside the point, no? Broken or sprained, you can't walk on it."

"No," I agreed. There was no point in denying it. Standing had been agony. Walking was out of the question.

Hathan finished his call and rejoined us. He addressed me without raising his voice; the others drew in to listen. "Eyvri, the Perch is sending a flyer to pick you up. You'll be transported back to the resort clinic. Echelon medical personnel will determine whether your injuries are treatable on-site. If not, you'll be flown south to one of the larger cities."

"Oh," I said, a little taken aback. "Okay. What about the rest of you?"

"We'll finish the course on foot."

Zey said reassuringly, "We'll see you in a couple of hours. You won't even have time to miss us."

"I miss you already," I said, and meant it. "If they send me to the city, can I bring a friend?"

"I'm sure that can be arranged." Hathan shaded his eyes to look up at the sky. "This must be your ride now."

"Fast," I said. It came out as much breath as word.

"Of course," Saresh murmured. "This is their nightmare. You can be sure they're ready for it."

I smiled crookedly at him. "We've seen a couple of nightmare scenarios. I'm not sure this one qualifies."

Hathan said, "The Echelon doesn't know that yet."

"Want me to carry you to the shuttle?" Zey asked.

"If you do that, they'll definitely assume the worst. I can probably make it, if you give me a shoulder to lean on."

The shuttle that touched down a little distance from our group was white, with black markings and strikingly elegant lines. Zey helped me over to it. He had retrieved my backpack and was wearing it. My right boot hung from a strap, clipped to the same orange carabiner I'd used in the memory game. We went slowly. My breath hitched every time my right foot brushed the ground, but I didn't make a sound beyond that. As we approached the craft, a panel retracted in its side, and a young white-haired medic stepped out. She wore Echelon colors, but her uniform was simpler in design than Reyna's.

Her right cuff was banded with a triple stripe of red, indigo, and purple. The colors, instantly evocative of the Rikasan landscape, suggested an Outmarch uniform to my eyes.

"Translator?" she said curtly to Zey.

"Nah, she doesn't need one."

She absorbed that fact without blinking. "I'll take over from here."

"Good luck, Eyvri," Zey said. "Don't let them take the leg. It's probably still good for something." He passed my backpack to the medic.

She put it on, giving him a dark look as she did so, and draped my arm over her shoulders with conspicuous gentleness. We began our awkward tandem shuffle up the ramp. "Novi Alkhat," she said as we went, "Outmarch Control regrets that your Fleet escort permitted you to be injured, but you're in Echelon hands now, and we'll keep you safe."

"I appreciate that, but I think I'd be better off in Echelon feet," I said, and heard Zey laugh as he walked away.

The medic smiled too, just slightly. "I'm afraid the on-site facility at the Perch isn't equipped to clone Vardeshi feet on cue, let alone graft them onto human tissue." She helped me settle onto a stool in the flyer's tiny cabin, arranged my right leg as comfortably as possible, and set down my pack before signaling to the pilot to take off. "But," she went on, taking her own seat, "we should be able to re-knit a torn ligament or fractured bone for you without any trouble."

"Seriously?" I said, startled.

"Yes. The updated list of basic medical techniques approved for humans includes both of those procedures." She held up a syringe. "May I inject an anesthetic?"

"Please." I sighed as cool relief washed through my leg. "Re-knitting bones is a basic technique, huh? How long does it take?"

"Anywhere from twenty minutes to a few hours, depending on the severity of the break. Ligaments are a little faster."

"And when would I be able to walk on it?"

"That also depends on the extent of the damage."

"My hadazi had surgery on Arkhati," I said, recalling Saresh in his hospital bed, "to reconstruct his leg. He walked the next day."

"He's Vardeshi. The treatment was designed for our bodies, not yours. To my knowledge, only two humans have undergone bone-reconstruction procedures. Both of them responded well, but it's still only two cases." She rose from her stool, slung my pack on, and reached out a hand to help me up. I took it, belatedly registering that the flyer had landed. The pilot had been navigating by instruments throughout the short flight, and other than the swiftly changing readouts on the front display screen, which I still couldn't interpret, there was no visual or physical cue to accompany our touchdown. I leaned gratefully on her strong arm as I shuffled down the ramp.

Shuttles arriving at the Perch landed on an enormous hexagonal platform built slightly upslope from the structure itself. My first clear view of the building through the shuttle door brought a wave of intense disorientation. Seen from the other side, its shape was all wrong, and the many mirrored facets I had been scrutinizing in miniature now towered overhead, rising to a height of several stories. I shook off my confusion and went to greet the collection of Outmarch staffers—or so I inferred from their striped cuffs—who waited on the edge of the platform to receive me.

I saw at once that Saresh had been right. They had been bracing for the nightmare scenario. Their relief at finding me conscious, calm, and articulate was unmistakable. A volley of names and titles ensued, most of them flying harmlessly over my head. I managed to retain the two most important ones. Director Anziar, overseer of the Rikasan Outmarch, had cropped black hair and looked improbably young for her role. Specialist Reyansh, chief physician, was a gray-haired woman who looked to be in late middle age.

My memories of Specialist Irnik were sufficiently fresh to make me wary of her, but she greeted me cordially enough, and looked me in the eye while she did it. If her plans for me included syringes or cold showers, she was canny enough not to mention them. She did insist on ferrying me to the Perch clinic on a chair-shaped version of the hoversled I had used to transport heavy items up and down the corridors of the *Pinion* and the *Ascendant.*

I stopped protesting when the friendly medic, who was still at my side, quietly observed that the anesthetic she had administered was a Vardeshi formulation with a numbing effect, and I might inadvertently do further damage to my ankle by walking on it. Her name was one of the ones I'd missed, but I asked for it again on the way to the clinic. "Tenvi Lanakh," she said, and I worked on committing that one to memory too.

Tenvi and Specialist Reyansh floated me into the Perch and through a network of twisting corridors. I looked around eagerly, both to satiate my curiosity—this was the first Vardeshi building I had ever seen—and to distract myself from the fascinated glances of passersby. I saw a blend of textures. The floors were a matte blue-gray substance resembling concrete, while the walls were synthetic wood, interspersed with sections of bright metallic paneling. The corridors were high and surprisingly narrow, leading to a feeling of confined space

I didn't associate with the resorts of home. There wasn't room for Tenvi to walk beside me, so she followed behind, guiding my hoverchair with one hand. I saw no windows at all until we approached the rear of the building, and the ones there were viewport sized. The glass, or glasslike substance, set into them was amber. It dimmed the incoming light and warmed it, giving the place a dreamy, ethereal feel. That, at least, was spalike, I thought.

We went up a spiral ramp and around a few more turns before arriving at the clinic. I was shown into a room opening off the main space. It was small, clean, and flooded with that same sepia light from an angular window set high in one wall. The narrow bed was covered with a crisp gray sheet. I eased off the hoverchair, then stood balancing on one foot, looking dubiously down at my clothes. They bore obvious signs (not to mention smells) of having been hiked in for days on end.

"Go ahead," said Tenvi, seeing my hesitation. "We're used to the mess. All our patients are coming straight off the course."

"Have you had many?" I asked.

She shook her head. "A few broken bones, a couple of cases of dehydration, one concussion from a fall. Nothing unusual for the Outmarch."

"Still, they must have been disappointed to be pulled out of the contest."

"Oh," she said matter-of-factly, "we put them back in."

I sat on the bed. Tenvi ran through a now-familiar battery of standard physical assessments while Specialist Reyansh asked me questions about the fall. Next she examined my ankle, first with her fingertips and then with three delicate silver instruments. She confirmed that there was a break, "a simple fracture of the fibula," as she put it. She looked scandalized when I confessed to not knowing which bone was the fibula.

"I can tell you where the name comes from," I said a little defensively. "I'm strong on etymology, not so much on anatomy."

"The break is here." Reyansh showed me a magnified image on her flexscreen. "It's quite treatable. I see no need to send you to a larger facility. There's nothing in your medical records to contraindicate the application of our medical equipment. I can heal the fracture right here, using this." She held up a glass-tipped white instrument that looked like a touchscreen stylus. "With your permission?"

I nodded emphatically. "Yes. Please. Fix me up."

She pressed the little device against a spot on the back of my right ankle, glanced at her flexscreen, adjusted the angle, and touched a control on the screen. The stylus began to hum lightly. Tenvi watched the readout over her shoulder. "It's working," she told me.

"I can't feel anything."

"The anesthetic is still in your system," the doctor observed.

I watched the procedure curiously at first, but the sunlight was warm and the sheet beneath me cool and clean, and inevitably I began to drowse. I snapped awake again when Tenvi said worriedly, "She's losing consciousness."

"Look closer," Reyansh retorted in good humor. "She's at the end of a ten-standard-day survival trial. And she's adjusting to a new diurnal rhythm. That isn't unconsciousness, it's sleep."

It was. I slept for around an hour, or so I guessed by the slant of light across the little room when I woke. Tenvi was still there. She offered me water and asked if I'd like to stand up.

I twitched the sheet aside and gazed down at my right ankle, which had been wrapped in silver tape. "Do I need crutches?" I thought of Saresh again. "Or a cane?"

"Neither. It's fully healed."

My gaze snapped up to her face. "What?"

She said again, more clearly, "It's healed."

"I can walk on it? Already?"

"Yes."

The next question, to my mind, was self-evident. "Can I hike on it?"

"I . . ." Tenvi faltered. "I don't know."

"What's your best guess?"

She hesitated, studying my expression, then said, "I'll get the specialist."

Someone had helpfully put my backpack on the floor at the end of the bed. When the doctor returned, accompanied by Director Anziar, I was wearing it. I had laced my right boot on again. I saw Reyansh's gaze drop to my feet and spoke before she could. "I'm grateful for your help. My ankle feels as good as new. I wouldn't even know it had been broken. I'd like to return to the course now, please."

The two glanced at each other. Anziar said, "Miss Alcott, I appreciate your commitment to the challenge, but there's been no discussion of your returning to the course."

"That's fine," I said, trying to channel some of Zey's bright matter-of-factness. "We can discuss it now."

Reyansh said slowly, "You've been pushing yourself in unfamiliar environmental conditions for the last ten standard days—or ten months, depending on how one counts. You're fatigued. You've just been exposed to medical technology unfamiliar to your body. In my considered opinion, it would be prudent to rest."

"If you were to become injured again . . ." Anziar added.

"Then I would call for help again," I said steadily, "just like the first time." She drew breath to speak; I cut her off. "The spot where I fell was close to a river. If you drop me back there, I'll hike down to the water and make camp for the night. I'll rest"—I looked beseechingly at Reyansh—"like you said, and move on in the morning."

Reyansh said, "I'm afraid it's out of the question."

"But everyone else who was injured went back in."

"A fact which has no bearing on your particular case."

I took a deep breath. "I'd like to speak to my khavi."

Anziar consulted her flexscreen. "Your team should be coming in any moment now."

"Good luck," Tenzi whispered as I passed her.

"Sigil to the stars," I whispered back, and saw her smile.

I followed Anziar and Reyansh down through the Perch and out onto a broad terrace of the same blue-gray poured stone I'd seen indoors. The terrace overlooked the river valley. The dropoff beyond its edge was sheer. There were no railings; presumably Vardeshi could be trusted not to fall off. Doubting the same could be said of humans, I gave the precipice a wide berth as I followed the others across to the far side of the terrace, where a ramp curved down to the ground. The final approach to the Perch from below was a rock face nearly as sheer as the ones we had descended that morning. The rock was crisscrossed with natural seams offering minimal traction for determined climbers. The deepest such seam intersected the cliff edge a hundred yards or so from the terrace. My crewmates were spread out across it, looking like nothing so much as mountain goats clinging to tiny spurs of rock. I watched, trying not to think about how I was going to duplicate that ascent, while they scrambled up the last hundred feet or so.

Hathan was first to the top. I marched out to meet him, trailed by Anziar and Reyansh. I didn't even wait for him to finish pulling himself up onto the cliff before I started talking. "Please tell them to put me back in. They can drop me right in the clearing where they picked me up. It's an easy landing for a flyer, right? My ankle is as good as new, it's like the break never even happened, but they're saying I can't go back in, so will you please tell them that I'm fine?"

The words burst out in a torrent. Anziar and Reyansh, who in our brief acquaintance had heard neither such velocity nor such passion from me, looked startled. Hathan didn't. He didn't even glance my way until he had brushed his hands off, surveyed the result, grimaced, and examined an inky blue abrasion on one forearm. Then he looked up and said crisply, "What?"

He was holding back a laugh; I could hear it in his voice. Encouraged, I tried again, more slowly. "Please tell Outmarch Control to put me back onto the course where they picked me up."

"Why?"

The answer seemed so transparently obvious that my voice edged into shrillness. "Because I'm not done."

He addressed Reyansh. "Her ankle?"

"It was a clean break," Reyansh said, "and the bone appears to have integrated smoothly. But I'd advise against putting unnecessary strain on it."

Hathan looked at me.

"Please," I whispered.

He nodded, almost to himself, and said to Anziar, "I didn't know it until I saw her on Rikasa, but Eyvri feels ivri khedai as strongly as any of us. It's her first new world, and it might be her last. I don't know about you, but I'd rather work an ice mine on Zarakhat than be planetbound for life. I know it isn't what you planned. I know you'd rather have her here under your eye. So would I. But it costs you little, and it means everything to her, so why not give her one more day in the sun?"

My heart soared. Whether or not Anziar yielded to his argument, the fact that he cared enough to make it—and understood me enough to make it so well—filled me with radiant happiness. I thought distantly that it had been a sound instinct on his part to appeal to her sense of ivri khedai; if anyone could be expected to feel the lure of fresh air and exploration, it would be the Outmarch director.

Anziar said, sounding more sympathetic than she had before, "I'm afraid she doesn't have another day. Her window closed"—she checked her flexscreen again, ostentatiously, though I had no doubt she knew perfectly well what time it was—"over an hour ago."

"No," I said suddenly. "It didn't." I unshouldered my pack and dug through it while they all watched. Zey, who had reached the clifftop too, drifted over to see what was going on. After a tense moment I pulled a handful of damp nylon out of a side pocket: my bikini top, with the challenge token still knotted into its strap. I thrust it triumphantly at Director Anziar. "I have this. I earned it fair and square. It buys me extra time, right?"

She said reluctantly, "That's correct."

"How much?"

"Only the course engineers have access to that information."

"Then, for all you know, I'm still in the race. And I'd like to finish it."

She gestured at the other members of Team *Ascendant,* most of whom had now gained the summit. "Your team has already finished. Without you."

"That's fine," I said firmly. "I can do it on my own." I tried not to think about the sheer cliff a few paces to our right.

Hathan said, "Out of the question."

I looked at him in surprise; if he felt that way, why had he spoken so ardently in my defense? Before I could process the reversal, he said, "I'll go with you."

"You—" My voice caught. I cleared my throat and tried again. "You will?"

Anziar echoed, "You will?"

He answered her. "Why not? It's the easiest way to keep her safe. Look at it as an extra measure of security. If you put the word out that she's off the course due to injury, no one will be looking for her in the woods. At this point I assume most of the other teams have already finished anyway." She nodded slightly. He went on, "If it looks like we won't make it back in time for the reception, one of my crew can pick us up. They could stand to log some flight time in atmosphere." Seeing her skeptical look, he added dryly, "And, as it happens, I know the route."

I stared at Zey. He stared back at me. Our joint incredulity eclipsed speech. The suggestion was outrageous, and he and I both knew why. So did Saresh, who had finished his own climb and joined our little circle. He listened with a faint frown while Anziar said, "You're proposing to spend another day hiking the same ground you just covered in two hours?"

Hathan said, "Certainly. Why not? After tomorrow, we all have two months of darkness to look forward to between here and Earth. I'm not in any hurry to go inside."

"I . . .," said Anziar. "When you put it like that, I don't see how I can refuse."

"Neither do I." If there was a trace of ironic humor in Hathan's voice, it was gone when he spoke again. "Director, if you'll provide us access to a flyer, I'll have one of my crew drop us in the valley."

I couldn't look at Saresh. I looked at Zey instead. He opened his mouth, closed it, then opened it again and said, "I'll fly you out."

I thanked Anziar and Reyansh and promised to be careful and to signal at the first sign of trouble. The words reeled out almost too easily; I didn't think about them at all. I was filled with a queasy exhilaration, like I'd downed three glasses of champagne on an empty stomach. Somehow, in the last few minutes, events had veered from the merely unlikely into the outright fantastical. I was going back into the Rikasan wilderness. With Hathan. Alone.

Hathan offered his own terse thanks, and we walked away. As we rounded the side of the Perch, I saw the flyer on which I had been evacuated still sitting on the hexagonal platform. "I'll get the access codes," Zey said, and went toward the Perch.

When he'd gone, Hathan said, "Eyvri, this is all happening very fast. I'm trying to get you back on the course before they change their minds. But if our history makes the thought of being alone with me uncomfortable for you, I completely understand. Zey can come with us. He might complain about it, but he wouldn't really mind. One of the Perch staff can fly us out."

I didn't say anything for a moment. Misinterpreting my silence, he said, "If you'd rather I didn't go with you, I can arrange that too. If you don't mind, though, I'd like to go. I feel a certain responsibility to . . ." He paused, looked away, and it struck me that he was struggling to articulate his thoughts. It was rare to see him fumble for words. I listened, my heart pounding, as he went on. "I promised to protect you. I know I haven't done a very good job of it. But I can't do it at all from here. I hate the thought of sitting up here, waiting, knowing I can't help you if anything goes wrong."

"Actually," I said, "I think it should be you. It's our trip— yours and mine. It has been from the start. Everyone else was just along for the ride. And I'm not uncomfortable. I feel safe with you." I went on, surprised as before at how easily the words flowed out and how natural they sounded. "It might be different if we hadn't done the Listening. But we did. The Flare was awful, but it's over, and I'm sick to death of talking about it."

"So am I," he said quietly. "Then you don't want me to ask anyone else to come with us?"

I shrugged. "It's up to you. I'll be fine either way."

"It should be simple enough to arrange for a dropoff if you change your mind."

It wasn't long before Zey joined us in front of the flyer. He brushed his fingers across its metallic skin to bring up the login interface. Instead of keying in his newly acquired access code, however, he turned abruptly to face me. "Eyvri, I'll tell you straight, I don't love this idea. I know you're trying to play it cool, but I don't think you should be out there alone with him."

"Thank you," Hathan said mildly.

Zey gave him an irritated look. "You know what I mean. Or, more to the point, you don't. No one does, except Eyvri. And Ziral, but she's not here to agree with me."

"Are you telling me you'd be afraid to sleep out there alone with Saresh?" I challenged him.

"Probably not. But it's not the same."

"Because he's your brother?"

He gave me a look of pure exasperation. "No, you idiot, because I wasn't locked in a room with him."

Hathan said, "If you're so concerned, why not come with us?"

I stared at Zey, trying to drive the words *Back off* like a battering ram straight through whatever invisible wall kept the mind of a Blank insulated from the thoughts of others. I was fairly sure he could read it in my face, even if he couldn't hear it.

"I would," he said, "but I'm pretty committed to a dinner that wasn't flash-heated. And a bed that isn't the ground. I just didn't feel good about dropping you out there without saying anything." He continued, speaking just to me, "You know your doctor back home contacted me after the Flare, right? We messaged back and forth a couple of times. She told me about the metaphor she uses for the two sides of the human mind. The rational one and the animal one."

"And?" I said.

"And I think we both know the animal voice is louder at night."

I said grudgingly, "I get where you're coming from. But I really think it's going to be fine."

Zey nodded. "All right. Just keep your flexscreen close, okay? If anything happens, call me. I don't care what time it is. I'll come get you. Or switch places with"—he nodded at his brother—"him. Or whatever. Just call."

"I promise you I will."

"Good." He tapped in the access code, and the door slid open.

It seemed like no time at all before Zey was setting the

flyer down in the clearing where I'd broken my ankle. He came down the ramp with us. "You're sure?" he asked me again.

"I'm sure."

"Okay." He lifted his right hand, palm facing us: a human farewell. "Good luck." He turned and went back up into the cabin. The ramp retracted; the door slid shut.

And then he was gone, and we were alone.

18

The river was even closer than I'd imagined; it was only a few minutes later that we stepped out from under the trees. The stones underfoot were flat and bone pale. They clicked together like dice as we walked down to the water's edge. Here the river ran broad and shallow, just as I had pictured it. The upstream end of the beach was dominated by a sloping boulder the size of a house. The deep pool in its lee was half in sunlight, half in shadow.

"This is where we crossed," Hathan said. "We could camp right here, but I think the best sites will be up there." He nodded toward the downstream end of the beach, where a narrow spit of forested land reached out a stony finger into the water. We topped off our water flasks, then headed that way. Almost at once we found a level clearing with a view of the river. I started unpacking my gear. Hathan waved me away. "Go on. You'll be swimming in the dark if you don't hurry." I snatched my swimsuit and towel out of my pack and ducked off into the trees.

Despite my knowledge of his nearness, I felt surprisingly

unselfconscious as I picked my way across the stony shore. Afternoon had shaded into a beautifully clear evening. Rikasa's two moons hung in the sky as if placed there for my enjoyment alone. I spread my towel across the sun-warmed foot of the boulder and stepped in. The shallows were cool, the deeper pool shockingly cold. I floated for a while, then swam across to the rock ledge on the far side, finding the current strong but not frightening. Keeping close to the ledge, where the water was still, I worked my way upstream to let the current carry me back to the beach on my return trip. I looked over to gauge the angle and saw Hathan sitting on the boulder, his arms clasped loosely around his knees. I wondered how long he'd been there. Unhurriedly I crossed the current a second time. The sun had shifted, and the pool below the boulder was illuminated now by a shaft of tawny light that caused the scattering of crystals on the river bottom to sparkle. I took a deep breath and dived down to collect a handful of blue gems. Then I climbed to the top of the boulder and sat down, next to Hathan but far enough away that I was in no danger of dripping on him. The warmth of the day lingered, and I didn't yet need my towel. I tossed the crystals one by one back into the pool.

"One more day on Rikasa," Hathan said when we had been sitting quietly for a while.

"How many other planets have you visited?" I asked.

"Other than Vardesh Prime, you mean?" He considered. "Four. Five if you count Earth, but I don't—yet."

I looked again at the sky. The white moon was nearly full, the gold one, above it and slightly offset, a delicate crescent. Like so many things I had seen since leaving home, they were exquisite and impossible, too perfect to credit. "I never even thought I'd visit one."

"It isn't the one we promised you."

"I wouldn't have missed Rikasa for anything," I said firmly.

He nodded. "After this, I think, you'll start to feel ivri avanshekh."

"Maybe." I couldn't explain, even to myself, the mingled anticipation and dread that filled me at the thought of seeing Earth again.

The evening wind was beginning to stir, ruffling the surface of the pool. I shivered. Hathan stood up. "We should get back to camp." Then his expression changed. He tilted his head slightly.

"What is it?" I asked.

He listened a little longer, then nodded once, decisively. "We're not alone."

I followed his gaze toward the wooded point where we had made camp. At first I couldn't see anything out of the ordinary, but after a moment a running figure emerged from the trees, then another and another. I counted eight in all. They jogged down the beach in our direction, their steps light and perfectly synchronized. They had covered half the distance to the boulder when their leader threw up a hand. The group halted as one. They'd seen us.

An instant before, I had been perfectly at ease. Now I was acutely conscious of our isolation and my near-nakedness. Our situation was innocent, but to strange eyes, it wouldn't look that way. Shame washed over me, and I knew from the warmth in my face that it was flooding with telltale color. Why hadn't it ever occurred to me that we might encounter one of the other teams on the course? After all, there were twenty-five of them, and they were all converging on the same spot. As the group advanced again, now at a walking pace, my embarrassment gave way to fear. Was this a chance meeting, or had they tracked us here? And to what end? There were eight of them and only two of us. And, as the Flare had made abundantly clear, I didn't count for much when it came to self-defense.

Hathan stood up and began to climb down from the rock. When I rose to follow, he said, "Don't come down."

I settled obediently down again, leaning back on my hands, attempting to look nonchalant: just a girl in a bikini catching some rays at the local swimming hole. An image for which the strangers coming toward us could have absolutely no context. My pulse raced as I tracked their approach. Hathan stood a little in front of the boulder, his stance alert, hands relaxed at his sides. He was preparing to fight. To protect me. He must have been picturing this exact scenario when he insisted on coming with me.

As the strangers approached, I recognized a smaller figure toward the back. I said eagerly, "It's Reyna!"

Hathan said, "I see her."

"Seven against three," I said under my breath.

"Seven against two." I looked at him. Without turning his head he said, "If things take a bad turn, you go into the water. Head downstream. I'll signal for help and buy you as much time as I can."

It took all the self-possession I could summon to keep still as the Echelon squad drew up to us and stopped. They raked us with their gazes. After what seemed to me an interminable silence, one of the men in front said, "Well, isn't this cozy. If this is what hosting a human representative looks like, believe me, they've been advertising it all wrong."

"Sign me up for the next round," the man next to him muttered. They both laughed.

Resolving to steer the conversation in a safer direction, I called a cheerful "Hello!" in Vardeshi, using the neutral salutation exchanged among equals. "Anyone want to go for a swim?"

Hathan added, "Voluntarily or otherwise?"

The Echelon officer at the front opened his hands, indicating the absence of weapons. "Stand down, Fleet. We don't want any trouble."

"Good," I said, matching his battle-hardened tone. "Neither do we."

There was more laughter. I was fairly sure it was at my expense. I didn't care.

The man who had spoken first turned his head to the side. "Orders?"

Relief flooded me as Reyna said coolly from the rear of the pack, "Fifteen-minute rest. Packs off." She added, "You can come down now, Eyvri. There won't be any trouble, not with a human in the mix. No one's looking to earn the blue medallion today."

"The what?"

Hathan angled his hand across his throat, mimicking the slice of a blade.

"Oh," I said, enlightened. "Good. That's a relief."

As I scrambled down, Reyna came forward, unsnapping her own pack. She dropped it on the stones at the base of the boulder. "Where are the others?" she inquired, as if they might be huddling together just out of sight in the shallows behind the boulder.

Hathan glanced across the water and up, toward where the Perch blazed with reflected sunset fire. "Drinking senek on the terrace, I imagine. If they've managed to tear themselves away from the showers."

"They went on ahead?"

"Not exactly." He offered a precis of the afternoon's events.

At the mention of my token, Reyna said interestedly, "You earned a challenge token? How?"

I explained. When I'd finished, one of the women on the Echelon team who was filling her water flask nearby murmured audibly, "Too easy."

"If it'd been any harder, I'd be at the bottom of the lake right now," I snapped.

"In that case," she said, "it sounds about right."

Reyna checked her flexscreen. "Even with the token, it's two hours past the deadline. You're probably out of time. I've never heard of a challenge ring worth more than three hours, and that was an exceptionally rare case."

"Oh?" Hathan said aridly. "Rare, was it? Any humans on that team?"

I said, "It's never been about the time, anyway. I just want to finish the damn hike."

"So do I," Reyna said with a certain bitter humor.

"Speaking of which," Hathan said, "you're running late."

"Our route was mostly exposed. The weather has been … inconvenient." She glanced out at the water. "How's the climb on the other side?"

"Easy. For one thing, it's dry."

"Good." Reyna turned her attention to me. "Come on. Let's go for a walk."

The grammatical structure of the invitation excluded Hathan. Surprised, I said, "Okay."

Reyna turned and strode down the beach in the direction from which she and her companions had just come. They shifted aside to let her pass. I stepped into my sandals and followed. When we were out of earshot of the others, she said conversationally, "I'd say I could take Hathan's place, or stay behind with the two of you, but I can see that the offer wouldn't be welcome. And all this time I thought it was Saresh you wanted. My mistake."

My heart thudded in my chest. I said as casually as I could, "What are you talking about?"

Reyna shot me a sidelong look. "Please. From what I've seen, our cultures have similar notions of privacy. I wouldn't undress for someone I didn't want."

I abandoned my pretense of misunderstanding her. "I'm wearing a swimsuit. Which he's seen before. Him and everyone else on our team."

"That's different. You weren't alone then." The shadow of a frown crossed her brow. "Whose idea was that, by the way?"

"His. But"—I hesitated—"it might not mean anything."

"It might not. Or it might. Either way, nothing will happen unless you make it happen."

As always, Reyna's absolute matter-of-factness put me at ease. The conversation should have been surreal. Instead it felt necessary and surprisingly clinical. I said, "How do you know?"

"Put yourself in his place. He's made two very public mistakes with you already. Now you're alone with him, under his protection. A subordinate. A diplomat. He'll be careful. No matter what he wants."

Recklessly I asked, "Can you find out what he wants?"

Reyna glanced back down the beach to where Hathan stood talking with the other Echelon officers. "Not in such a short time. And not without being obvious about it."

"Damn."

"I could have," she said, something suspiciously like laughter in her voice, "at virtually any time in the last six months, if you'd asked."

I said irritably, "If I'd known you'd be so laid back about it, I would have. But I didn't think there was any point. Sohra told me your people don't sleep around."

"Sohra was being diplomatic."

My anger faded at once, replaced by curiosity. "What's the nondiplomatic answer?"

Reyna stopped, picked up a handful of stones, and began tossing them into the swift-moving current at the center of the river. "That affairs happen. Typically during the engagement period, not after, and typically in couples with birth houses of equivalent rank. Usually one or both lovers is Fleet or Echelon. Think about it: it's the perfect scenario. You're away from your fiancé for months or years. If you're discreet, no one knows. If you're not, no one cares. It doesn't affect the marriage."

"Because nobody falls in love," I said.

"That's right."

"Would you do it?"

"Me? No. I have too much to lose." Without waiting for my question, she went on, "Hathan doesn't. Takheri House is ranked higher than Garian. And his family is important in the pro-alliance movement. Sidra won't throw that connection away without good cause."

"You make it sound like a math problem," I said.

"Because that's what it is. Eyvri, do you remember what I told you before? On Elteni?"

I did. Her words had been in my mind more and more often since our arrival on Rikasa. "You said there's no empirical right or wrong. There's only what I want. You're wrong, you know. There is most definitely a right and wrong in this case. And what we're talking about is just plain wrong."

"Perhaps," Reyna allowed. "But it's only one night. And you'll never have another chance like this one."

"What makes you think I have any chance at all?"

Without shifting her eyes from the horizon, she said, "For one thing, he's looking at you right now."

The shiver that went through me was hot and cold at the same time. I went still, then reached up to brush a strand of hair away from my face, resisting the impulse to look back down the beach. Why was it that the conscious decision to act natural instantly excised all ability to do so?

Reyna said, "You lose nothing by asking."

"That is absolutely not true."

She looked her inquiry.

"We've worked hard to come back from the Flare. We're okay. We might even be friends. If I ask and he says no, it'll ruin what we have."

"Two months from now, there won't be anything to ruin."

She had thrown her last stone. By unspoken accord we turned and walked slowly back along the beach. Reyna's companions were stowing their water flasks and picking up their packs, making ready to depart. To leave me alone again with Hathan. I felt exhilarated all over again at the thought, and terrified too, in a way I hadn't before.

"What are you going to do?" she asked.

I sighed. "I have no idea. What would you do?"

"Me? I'd wait until he fell asleep, then strip down and crawl into his sleeping bag."

"Jesus Christ," I said with feeling. "Straight to the nuclear option, huh?"

"In my experience," she said with a trace of a self-satisfied smile, "it tends to produce results."

"Yeah, I'll bet it does. How about a less drastic approach? What would Sohra do?"

"Sing him a song, maybe?"

I made a face. "I tried that. It didn't go well."

"In that case," Reyna said, "You should consider that the nuclear option may be the only one you have left."

We rejoined the others near the boulder. Hathan was standing with two Echelon officers, a man and a woman. The latter was sketching out a possible approach to the Perch, her hands nearly as expressive as her words. Hathan was listening attentively, but as Reyna and I stepped into the little circle, he glanced from her face to mine with an expectant air I didn't understand.

Reyna, bending to adjust something on her pack, missed the look entirely. She straightened, lifted the pack, and slipped it on. As she did up the fastenings, she said to Hathan, "Are you short any supplies? We can leave you whatever you need. We'll be at the Perch in another two hours."

"One," said the man next to her.

Hathan looked at me. I shrugged. He said, "We're fine."

"Until tomorrow, then," Reyna said with a nod that included us both. "Khavi, you'd better rest up for those long duty nights ahead, because I appear to be poised to win our bet."

"You mean the bet I won earlier today when I crossed the finish line before you?"

"So you say," she murmured. "And yet here you are."

"Here I am," he agreed. "If you're content to win on a technicality, so be it."

"I'm content with anything that gets me a full night's

sleep. I'll see you at the top." Raising her voice, she called, "Team Ekhran, move out." She led the way down the beach to where a scattering of smaller boulders formed a haphazard line of stepping stones across the current. Without hesitation she stepped onto the first boulder. The seven members of her squad followed her across one by one. When they reached the far side of the river, they ran up into the trees, a line of darting shadows in the twilight. Within moments they were lost to view.

When we were unquestionably alone again, I said, "I'm sorry about the bet. I completely forgot about that."

Hathan said, "It doesn't matter. Another day in the woods is worth a month of starside night duty. I'm sorry they were so crude."

"They weren't that bad."

"Still, I feel a need to redeem us as a species. Maybe this will help." And with no more warning than that, he grasped the hem of his shirt, pulled it up over his head in a single fluid motion, and dropped it on the pebbles at our feet.

My stomach turned over. What was happening? "What are you doing?"

"Taking you up on your offer."

"My . . . offer." My voice trembled.

Hathan jerked his chin at the river. "Let's go for a swim."

"A swim? Seriously?"

"Seriously." He read my skepticism and added, "Consider it my personal contribution to the alliance. We've put you in enough strange situations over the last year. I think I can handle a little cold water."

"Great," I heard myself say. "Okay. Let's go for a swim."

He reached for the fastening at his waist. I looked quickly away, horrified and elated, wondering if perhaps this was all a delightful dream from which I would shortly be awakened by Zey shouting into my tent dome that it was time to get up. I closed my eyes. I didn't hear any shouting. Instead I heard a rustle of fabric as Hathan removed his pants and another as he dropped them on top of his shirt. When I looked back, he was standing with his hands at his sides, entirely still in that uncanny Vardeshi way, less like someone suppressing the impulse to move than like someone who has never felt it. My peripheral vision told me he still wore the Vardeshi equivalent of underwear, but I sensed that he would have been equally at ease wearing nothing at all. He didn't try to cover himself or fill the silence with laughter or meaningless talk. He simply waited, his eyes steady on my face. The dignity he brought to such an intimate moment transported me somehow past its awkwardness. I had the sense that he was permitting me to look at him. And so, after a hesitation, I did.

For the most part, he was as I had imagined him. Fleet uniforms were relatively form-fitting, after all, and I had had ample time to study him covertly. The lines of his body were those of a slim human man built to slightly smaller scale. But no amount of imagining could have prepared me for the androgynous beauty of his uncovered form. Studying the long slender limbs that tapered to narrow wrists and ankles, I felt renewed awe at the strength they contained. My eyes were drawn inevitably downward to the region of his body that was categorically masculine. The briefest of glances suggested that proportions there were comparable to those elsewhere. The fact was reassuring, absurdly so, given how unlikely it was to be a matter of personal relevance to me. And hadn't Daskar essentially told me months ago that, in her considered medical opinion, our peoples were most likely physically compatible? Still, I told myself, it was good to have proof.

For the future. In case I ever found myself dating an unattached Vardeshi man. In case I ever found one, period.

As the first heady excitement faded, I began to look closer, to identify the subtle differences between us, the things the uniform had hidden. Hathan's skin tone was impossibly even. What human my own age, with a complexion lighter than mine, would sport no freckles or blemishes, no scars at all? That wasn't quite true though; that patch on his left forearm, the one I had seen him examining earlier, was scored with dark blue lines. There were subtle differences in skeletal structure, as well. Unthinkingly I reached out to brush my fingertips along an unfamiliar ridge on his shoulder above the joint. "I don't think we have this one."

"Or this." He touched his fingers to his breastbone, where five distinct points pressed outward against the skin in a vertical line, like spines along the rim of a seashell. "Or these," and he showed me the bony spur on the back of each heel.

"No wonder you couldn't find boots that fit," I said.

He smiled, but his eyes were serious. "It's a little disconcerting, isn't it?"

"A little," I admitted. My head felt oddly light. I recalled a moment from much earlier in the mission, when I had cut myself in the *Pinion*'s galley, and the sight of red blood caused Vethna to vomit. We were so alike, most of the time, that the differences came as an unlooked-for shock. My mind offered another memory, this one from a few days ago, of the stunned silence with which my crewmates had greeted my first appearance in a swimsuit. I understood their response now better than I had then. Was this moment the same as that one? Were they two identical pieces of the work we were doing together, sharing vulnerabilities, acknowledging disparity in order to overcome it? Or was this deliberate uncovering something more? Reyna's words of mere minutes ago echoed in my mind. *I wouldn't undress for someone I didn't want.* Would Hathan? What did this moment mean to him?

Before I could delve any deeper into the question, he said, "Shall we?"

"Yes." I forced myself to move. The water had unquestionably gotten colder in the time since I'd left it. When I had walked in up to my waist, I turned to look back at the shore. Hathan stepped forward into the shallows. A look of alarm crossed his face. I laughed. "You're going to have to come in a little farther than that."

"It's certainly . . . invigorating." He waded farther in. "And this is something you actually enjoy?"

"I love it. But," I felt compelled to add, "most people would think this water was pretty cold."

"Not you though."

"I grew up swimming in water colder than this."

"*Why?*" He said it with such evident distaste that I laughed again.

As he joined me in the deeper water, I felt suddenly uncertain. I had never in my life taught anyone to swim. There was no Echelon ship hovering above us now, poised to rescue him from drowning. There was only me. And it was that fact, the certainty of being absolutely responsible for his life or death, that enabled me to maintain the necessary composure, to distance myself from the feel of his skin on mine as he took my outstretched hand. His presence here in the water was an act of trust, just as my first step onto the *Pinion*'s landing craft had been. We might be alone together, and practically naked, and all the things I felt about him might be humming distractingly just under my skin. But this, this moment, was unequivocally the work I had come here to do.

And wasn't water at night more like space than it was like anything else: the cold, the dark, the surrender to weightlessness? The thought was pleasing in its symmetry. "Okay," I said. "First things first. You need to learn how to float."

The swim lesson, in the end, took all of ten minutes. The real hurdle for Hathan was accepting that swimming in icy-cold mountain rivers at nightfall was a leisure activity in which people—any people—voluntarily partook. Once that was out of the way, he learned the actual mechanics of the sport almost at once. We raced across the river (of course he won handily) and stroked back at a leisurely pace. By tacit agreement we made for the shore. A sigh escaped me as my toes found the stones of the riverbed.

I didn't know he had heard it until he said softly, "All things end."

The words were more fitting than he knew. "Yes," I agreed. "They do. I promise you I'm not ungrateful. Everything about Rikasa has been perfect."

"Even the broken ankle?"

That more than anything, I thought, but I said only, "It was worth it."

19

We returned to camp and separated to dress in privacy. I'd let myself get colder than I realized. Even when I'd been fully dressed and moving around for a few minutes, I continued to shiver intermittently. I was also starving. Knowing the two problems shared a common remedy, I set up my camp kitchen in the shelter of a rock outcropping with a clear view of the river. Once my macaroni was simmering in its pot of flash-boiled water, I dug into my pack again, hunting for my flask. Bourbon wouldn't actually make me warmer, but it would make me feel that way until the food was ready.

By the time I located the flask, tucked into a spare wool sock under nearly everything else in my pack, Hathan had joined me and begun setting up his own cooking gear. He had donned a few extra layers too, I saw. I took a long swig from my flask and then offered it to him. To my surprise, he took it. To my greater surprise, he didn't bother to decant the bourbon into a cup before drinking it. He didn't even clean the opening with his sleeve. As I watched him lift the flask to his lips, I felt the better part of the heat I'd lost to the river rushing back in all at once, mostly to my face. It was another unlooked-for intimacy, so close on the heels of the first one—his casual disrobing on the beach—that I wondered, again, if I was wrong to read meaning into it. Things had changed between us since our arrival on Rikasa. Had they changed that much?

"Saresh was right," he said as he handed back the bourbon. "It would be easy to get into trouble with that."

I set the flask on the ground between us. "Help yourself. I've got another bottle back on the ship."

"Thank you. I had whiskey, but I haven't seen it for a couple of days. Not since Zey helped me reorganize my gear. I have a feeling he may have reorganized it into his pocket."

"Or into his mouth," I said.

"That was certainly the end objective."

When I judged that the pasta was ready, I drained off the starchy liquid directly into a cup of instant miso, a trick from my college backpacking days. I drank the soup as quickly as I could without scalding myself, then moved on to my macaroni and cheese. I was surprised at how rapidly the food cooled in the open air; I'd taken the temperature regulation of Ahnir's communal tent for granted. Hathan, clearly thinking the same thing, took out his own tent and adjusted the field to its maximum setting, which neatly enveloped the two of us sitting cross-legged on the ground. And just like that, I thought, we were officially sharing his tent.

We ate quickly, then lingered with mugs of warm liquid—tea for me, senek for him—in hand. There were dishes to be washed, and I knew I ought to at least take a pass at rearranging my pack for the morning's ascent, but I was in no hurry to leave our cozy pocket of warm air. The golden moon had set. I leaned back against the rock outcropping, drew my sleeping bag over my legs, and watched the track of white moonlight on the river. It bore an inescapable resemblance to another glittering path: one more ethereal still, one that existed only in my mind. That one had led me from Californian sunlight into outer darkness, through the path of a bullet and over the threshold of a conference room. I thought it had ended in the void beyond Arkhati, but it hadn't. It had merely gone dark for a while. Now it had led me here, to this moment, with this man. I didn't believe in destiny. I never had. There was nothing compelling for me in the image of some divine inscrutable intellect mapping lives across each other like the bright intersecting lines on a star chart. But I was beginning to believe in convergence, in the powerful significance of those intersections, driven though they were by blind chance. My life and Hathan's wove over and under and across each other in a complex braid of convergences. Most of them were behind us now. There were others ahead, but the moment was fast approaching when my line would run on in one direction, and his in another, and they would not cross again.

Even as I thought it, I reached for my flask and found him doing the same. Our fingers brushed. We both laughed a little self-consciously; he withdrew his hand. All at once I felt uncertain. For months I had been telling myself that the right thing to do, the only possible thing, was to keep my feelings for him a secret. But what if I was wrong? What if I was taking too many things for granted, projecting my assumptions about love—and men—onto someone whom they only appeared to fit because he was roughly the right size and shape? I had taken it all on myself. I had made the choice for both of us. Maybe he deserved to make it for himself. Maybe he deserved to know.

He spoke into my silence. "What are you thinking about?"

In my culture the question was flirtatious; in any culture, it was intimate. I said, "Stellar cartography."

"Really?"

I smiled to myself. "In a sense."

"What about it?"

"I was thinking how much I still have to learn." I waited, gauging the quality of his silence, then ventured, "Maybe you could teach me some more?"

"I could try," he said, "but it might be difficult from here."

"I guess it would be easier if we were back on the ship," I acknowledged, trying to keep the disappointment from my voice.

I heard a soft exhalation that might have been a laugh. "It would be easier if we were sitting closer together."

I gathered up my sleeping bag and hitched myself along the rock wall until my shoulder touched his. He didn't move away. A tingling warmth crept into my arm and spread slowly throughout my entire body. Hathan drew a breath, somewhat unsteadily, then let it out; I felt both through his arm.

Then he said, in a voice that sounded remarkably natural, "What questions do you have about stellar cartography?"

It was difficult to think. I racked my mind for a question. "Where's Vardesh Prime?"

"Underneath us."

"What?"

He laughed softly again. "It's on the other side of the planet. We can't see it from here."

I scarcely heard his answer. My entire awareness was focused on the pressure of his shoulder against mine. Why wasn't he pulling away? Distractedly I said, "Okay, where's Earth?"

He made an unhurried scan of the heavens. Then he pointed. I noticed that he used the arm that wasn't touching mine to do it. "Do you see that triangle of bright stars? There's a cluster of fainter ones just above and to the left of the topmost one. Sol is one of those."

I squinted. "I see them. I think. I might be looking at a cloud."

"In any case, you're looking in the right direction. What else?"

"Where's . . . Where's the *Ascendant?*"

"In orbit around the starhaven where we did our decontamination. The ship is too small to see, but . . ." He took out his flexscreen, snapped it out to its full size, and panned it across the horizon, all without withdrawing his arm from mine. Was it possible that he was actually leaning into the touch a little, just like I was? "We should be able to see the starhaven in a few minutes. It's below the mountains now. Look for a very bright satellite in that direction." He put away his flexscreen. We watched the horizon in silence for a time.

A breath of night air rustled the leaves of the nearby trees. The tent field, set as it was to maximum extension, couldn't quite keep out the chill. I shivered.

"Are you warm enough?" Hathan asked.

I shook my head; my hair whispered against the hood of my down jacket. "No."

"I could raise the air temperature in the tent."

There was a meaning in his statement unattached to the words. It wasn't like him to be indecisive. If he wanted to adjust the tent settings, he wouldn't ask my permission, he'd just do it. He was giving me an opening to suggest something else. I said, "Could you put your arm around me?"

There was a little silence. Then, "Would you like me to

put my arm around you?"

"Yes."

He lifted his arm. I eased closer, pressed myself against his side. His arm settled around me. I put my head on his shoulder; he rested his cheek on my hair. I offered him the edge of the sleeping bag, and he took it, tucked it around himself, enfolding us both in a second tiny cocoon of warmth. I cast a fleeting look at his profile. The moonlight reduced everything it touched to a simple two-color palette of black and white. He looked like a statue carved from alabaster and jet.

I said, "If you were human, I would kiss you right now."

He said, "If you were Vardeshi, you would ask my permission first."

I took a deep breath. "Do I have your permission to kiss you?"

"Yes," he whispered.

I turned toward him and laid my hand on his chest. I felt the smooth fabric of his shirt and, faintly, the heat of his body beneath it. If his heart was beating faster than usual, out of fear or excitement, I couldn't tell. My own was pounding wildly. Gladness and terror chased each other through my blood, along with the fiery remnants of the bourbon. Hathan raised his left hand and covered my fingers with his, adding a new sensation of cool pressure to the others. Then he lifted his right hand to cradle my chin. He ran his thumb lightly across my lips. That single touch brushed away my lingering doubts like so many cobwebs. I slid my hand into his hair and kissed him.

After what felt like a very long time, and also like no time at all, he disengaged himself very gently and said, "Eyvri, I can't do this. I'd like to, but I can't. I'm sorry. I've let it go too far already. I can't take advantage of you like this. It's wrong."

Disappointment and mortification were a hot, corrosive ache in my chest. I said shakily, "Because of the Flare, you mean?"

"That's one reason."

"You're think I'm"—the words were so bitter I choked on them—"emotionally compromised?"

"After what I've done to you, how could you not be?"

"What if I told you I wanted you before the Flare?"

He said disbelievingly, "Did you?"

I nodded.

"When did it start?"

"I'm not sure. A long time ago. Before Arkhati." My voice trembled, giving the words the lilt of a question.

"Before Arkhati," he repeated. "We left Arkhati six months ago."

"Like I said, it's been a long time."

Hathan said slowly, "Even if I believed you, there are other reasons. Many of them. You know I'm not"—he raised his right hand slightly, and the gold sigil winked in the shifting light—"free."

"I know. I'm not asking for . . . I knew it would only be for tonight." I fought to steady my voice. "I know it's wrong, by both of our lights, but I also know that she's not in love with you. And you're not in love with her. Are you?"

He didn't hesitate. "No."

"So who would it hurt?"

"The obvious answer to that question is you."

I said fiercely, "I'm telling you, I'm not broken, and I'm not confused. We both know exactly what we're talking about. One night, no strings. Tomorrow we walk away. Go back to our lives. Pretend it never happened."

"In nine months I've never seen you tell a convincing lie. What makes you think you can do it now?"

I had an answer for that, at least. "I just told you I've wanted you for six months. Still think I can't keep a secret?"

A hesitation. I could feel him thinking, turning the pieces over and fitting them together. The knowledge that he was willing to give the notion a moment's thought filled me with a tremulous hope. Finally he said, "If anyone ever found out, it would wreck both of our careers."

"Trust me, I know. Where I'm from, these things look worse for the woman. I have just as much at stake as you do, if not more."

He was silent for a while. Then he said, "I'm running out of reasons to say no. But I still don't feel right about this. I need some time to think. I think we both do."

I knew no amount of time would change how I felt, but I said, "Whatever you need."

"I'm going for a walk. You should go to bed. If in twenty minutes or so you still feel the way you do right now, switch the light on in your tent. If I can, I'll join you."

He reached out to brush his fingers lightly across my forehead in what was clearly a caress, although it wasn't one I'd seen before. Then he rose and walked away. I watched him until he was no more than a dark silhouette far down on the moonlit beach. I knew better than to go after him. I had been living with this particular quandary for six months, while he had had about six minutes with it. I couldn't make the decision for him. I wouldn't force his hand. I got up, shook out my sleeping bag, and found a level place out of the wind to lay it out flat. I fetched my tent from my backpack and set it up with the field at full expansion, plenty of room to shelter us both if it came to that. I went through the motions of getting ready for bed, observing with clinical calm that my hands were trembling. When I judged that ten minutes had passed, I switched on the illumination, limning the tent field in shimmering blue light where it touched the ground. I left the field itself transparent. Then I lay down on my sleeping bag to look up at the stars and wait.

It was close to twenty minutes later, not ten, when I heard soft footsteps coming up the slope from the beach. I sat up. Hathan reached the crest of the rise and turned unhesitatingly in my direction. When he reached the edge of the tent field, he knelt to turn off the illumination and take off his jacket. I watched, hypnotized by the unhurried grace of his movements. I should have felt awkwardness or apprehension. I felt neither. Desire seethed in me like an ocean, leaving no room for anything else. When his preparations were complete, he paused, and I knew an instant's irrational terror that he would tell me he'd changed his mind. Instead he said, "You're sure you want to do this?"

"Yes."

"So am I. Still, the power dynamic is a little troubling, so I'll let you take the lead."

I nodded, desperately relieved. "Okay."

He lay down on his back. I lay down next to him, on my side, our bodies not quite touching. I had lived this moment a thousand times in my imagination. Now, as I leaned over and pressed my lips softly against his, it felt less like a conscious movement toward him and more like an inevitable yielding to some hitherto undiscovered law of the physical universe. And why not? I thought a bit giddily. This was Rikasa. Anything was possible.

Three months ago, with Fletcher, I had savored the

pleasure, at once new and familiar, of discovering another body. This was like discovering lovemaking all over again. I was vividly reminded of the immensely cautious explorations of my first nights with my high-school boyfriend. I was glad Hathan had told me he planned to let me take control. If he hadn't, I might have mistaken his restraint for indifference. I counted each tiny proof of his desire as a unique triumph.

When we had been kissing for a little while, I slid my knee between his legs. An instant later I felt the warmth of his hand on the back of my knee. His fingers trailed upward along my thigh to my hip. The lightness of his touch was maddeningly erotic. I felt the chill of the night air as he lifted my shirt. Then his fingertips brushed the bare skin at the curve of my waist. His hand slid upward over my ribs, still with that same infuriating slowness. When he touched my breast, I gasped with pleasure and pressed myself closer to him. Then I froze.

He pulled back to look at me. "Did I hurt you?"

"No. I just—I've wanted this for a long time. I'm trying not to overwhelm you."

"Overwhelm me," he whispered.

It was all I needed to hear. I abandoned any attempt at self-control and climbed on top of him, pressing my body eagerly against his. I kissed his lips, the line of his jaw, his throat. He took my shirt off, then my pants, fumbling a little with the drawstring. Anticipating his next challenge, I pulled my bra over my head with practiced ease and heard his soft laugh of comprehension.

Shortly after that, when I summoned the courage to slide my hand down inside the waistband of his pants, I was shocked and disappointed to find no physical evidence of his arousal. Hathan, seeing my dismay, laughed again. "You'll have to be patient. Apparently we take things a little more slowly than you do."

Encouraged by his total lack of concern, I said, "How much more slowly? Because the nights here are about four hours long."

"We have time," he said, and pulled me down to him again.

He was right. Not more than a minute or two later, his energy changed completely. The dreamy languor was gone, replaced by an urgency as passionate as my own. I gasped when I felt his hands clamp down with sudden force on the backs of my thighs. "If you're going to stop," he said in my ear, "stop now." There was a new and thrilling roughness in his voice.

"I'm not going to stop," I whispered.

In an instant he had pinned me under him. With quick, deft movements he shed his own clothes. Feeling his bare skin against my own, I felt a delirious relief that there were no more barriers between us, no more distances to be closed. I reached down again, confidently now, and guided him into me. A sound came out of him that I had never heard before. I cried out too, then bit my lip, terrified that he would mistake the sound for pain. He didn't. Or he didn't care. Either one was fine with me. I was still terrified beyond all reason that he would stop. I kissed him hungrily, laced my fingers in his hair, locked my legs around his narrow hips, all the physical signals I knew for *yes*. I had no idea if they were the right ones. I was operating purely on instinct, in a realm beyond thought. Every point of contact between our bodies was a distinct and separate pleasure. Entirely too soon, they merged into one. Ecstasy rose in me like a tide. I surrendered to it. As if from far away, I heard Hathan, moving above me, murmur something indistinct on an indrawn breath. Then he shuddered and lay still.

I blinked, coming back to myself slowly. My face was buried in his shoulder. I licked my lips and tasted his sweat, which was salty, with an unfamiliar metallic tang. His hip bone was pressed into my thigh in a manner that was going to become excruciatingly painful very, very soon. If he had been Fletcher, I would have said so. I didn't say anything. I knew that any movement on my part, however slight, would trigger the inevitable separation, the disentangling of our limbs. I could bear any discomfort if it kept him in my arms a little longer.

Eventually he stirred, then shifted his weight, lifting his body away from mine. I let him go. I had no idea what would happen next. Would he withdraw completely, seek solitude elsewhere, leaving me alone in the tent? Some human men would have. I was thrilled beyond all reason when he rolled onto his back and drew me gently toward him again. I nestled into the crook of his arm, my head tucked neatly under his chin. There were a hundred things I wanted to say to him, or possibly just one, but I knew it would be a mistake to say it. I focused on the subtle rise and fall of his chest beneath my hand. His breathing was fractionally too slow for me to match it. I wondered if my own seemed unsettlingly fast to him, if my skin felt fever-hot to his fingers, tracing the line of my hip in a deliciously idle caress.

"What was it you said before?" I asked after a while.

"Did I say something?"

"It sounded like the Northern dialect."

He shrugged slightly. "I have no idea. Probably something about sigils."

"Huh. That's a first."

"One among many, I assume."

I started to giggle. After a moment I felt him trembling against me. It took me a moment to realize that he was laughing too.

Another stirring of wind rattled the leaves around us. Hathan reached down and drew the edge of my sleeping bag up over both of us. As he settled back into place, he said, "I had no idea you were so aptly named."

"Am I?"

"Don't you know what your Vardeshi name means?"

Baffled, I said, "Eyvri? Isn't it just Avery with a different accent?"

"Yes, but it's also a word."

I shifted to look up into his face. "It is?"

He said, "You really don't know what I'm talking about, do you? Do you know what an eyvrith is?"

"Never heard of it."

"It's a desert animal native to Arideth. A type of cat. They have golden fur and green eyes. Zey saw the resemblance immediately. Actually we all did, but he was the one who pointed it out."

Trying unsuccessfully to keep my voice steady, I said, "You mean my name is a joke? Like *the ahtziri?* All this time you guys have been calling me Eyvri, you've been making fun of me?"

"Not at all. It's a compliment. They're beautiful. And exceptionally rare."

I was too distracted by the music his voice made of the word *beautiful* to process his original point. Then it hit me. "Aptly named. Oh my God. You're saying I'm a wild animal." I pulled the edge of the sleeping bag up to hide my face.

Hathan tugged it down again. "That was a compliment too."

"If you say so," I said dubiously.

I had just begun to relax when a sound shattered the quiet: the unmistakable chime of a flexscreen. I gave a convulsive start. Hathan went perfectly still. Then he got up and went away, presumably in search of his pants. He returned presently and slipped under the sleeping bag again. I watched while he typed something into his flexscreen.

When he had tucked it out of sight again, I said, "Who was that?"

"Outmarch Control."

"What did they want?"

"They sent a status request. Our medical transponders flagged unexpected activity for this time of night."

"Oh my God." I slapped a panicked hand to the back of my neck as if stung by an insect. "The transponders! I completely forgot about them!"

He laughed. "I know. I didn't. It's all right; the telemetry is purposely vague about some things. To anything but a very close-grained examination, what we were just doing looks indistinguishable from, say, high-speed bodyweight exercises. The message was automatically generated. I sent back the all-clear. I doubt we'll hear anything more."

"What did you tell them we were doing?"

"Calisthenic exercises."

"In the middle of the night? Will they believe that?"

"They should. We're from offworld. Our internal clocks are out of step with the rhythms of the planet. I'm sure the transponders are picking up all kinds of odd activity at odd hours." He sounded, again, supremely unconcerned. As before, his certainty eased my doubt.

We were both quiet for a while. I lay feeling the rise and fall of his breath, tracing aimless patterns among the stars, connecting them in impossible trajectories.

"Tell me something," he said at length. "What proportion of the Outmarch have you spent trying out different schemes to get me alone?"

His tone was light. I said airily, "Oh, all of it."

"Did you break your ankle on purpose?"

"I would have, if I'd had any idea how well it would work out for me."

"For both of us." I heard the warmth in his voice and allowed the correction.

When he didn't speak again, I ventured a question of my own. "When did you figure out that I wasn't just being polite about being alone with you?"

"Somewhere between swimming and stellar cartography, I suppose."

I sighed. "I don't know what I would have done if that hadn't worked. Bourbon and moonlight are pretty much my whole playbook."

"It's a good one. The first thing I learned in my tactics seminar was never to reject a strategy just because it's simple." He raised himself on one elbow to reach for my water bottle. He drank from it as casually as if it were his own, then passed it to me. "Of course, as a fallback, there's always the old broken-tent trick."

"I thought about that. But I figured you'd just be noble and offer to sleep out in the open."

"I wouldn't have." He considered. "But I might have called in for a replacement."

Diffidently I said, "It's none of my business, but did anyone pull that broken-tent trick on you during your Institute survival trials?"

I felt another of his soundless laughs. "No one, I'm sorry

to say—although it would have been difficult, given that we didn't have tents. No, I spent the first trial starving in the desert, the second one starving on a glacier, and the third one starving in the jungle. Also hallucinating, because someone in my squad picked up an especially virulent local pathogen, and by the third day we were all running dangerously high fevers. My memories of that week aren't especially clear. But I'm reasonably sure alien seduction didn't figure into it."

"Oh my God," I said abruptly.

"What's wrong?"

"What you said. It just clicked. I'm the alien seductress." I groaned in dismay. "I'm a huge cliché."

"Galaxy-spanning, in fact."

"Don't tell me you guys have that one too?"

"We do. I always found it wildly improbable." He added quietly, "It's not the first time you've proven me wrong, and not the first time I've been glad you did."

Time, I thought, to ask the pointed question. "When you volunteered to come out here with me, was there any part of you that hoped this would happen?"

He put off answering for so long I began to wish I hadn't spoken. Then he said, "What did you see about yourself in the Listening?"

"I'm not sure. There were flashes of something . . . I thought maybe you were attracted to me. But it was confusing. I might have just imagined it."

"You didn't." He paused; I lay silent, stunned by the raw simplicity of the words, the way they crashed through months of accreted doubt like floodwaters through a makeshift barricade. Eventually he said, "I would never have spoken up if I thought my motivations were a shade less than honorable. I really did think I was just trying to protect you."

I settled more comfortably into the crook of his arm. "I feel very protected."

I was drifting off to sleep when I felt Hathans gently freeing his arm from beneath my head. I sat up. "What's wrong?"

"You were falling asleep."

"Is that a problem?"

"No. I'll go to the other tent."

Fully awake once again, I frowned up at him. "Why?"

"Vardeshi don't"—he gestured—"sleep together."

"Um. The evidence suggests otherwise."

"No, I mean really sleep. As infants, we share a bed with our mothers. After that, we never sleep in the same bed as another person again. It's too intimate. Intrusive, even."

Suddenly I understood the narrow single bed in his quarters. "Oh. Okay. I can go—"

"Sleep," he said firmly. And almost at once I did.

20

I awakened all too soon to the uncompromising brightness of day. I rolled onto my back and lay blinking in the light
that sifted down through the delicate fans of crimson leaves
overhead. Memory and slightly guilty consciousness flooded
over me. How many times in the past year had I fantasized
about spending the night in Hathan's arms? Now I had actually done it. I wasn't sure which was more startling: the fact
that I had dared to make a somewhat fumbling overture in
his direction, or the fact that he had accepted it. The events
of last night defied reason and all good sense. But they had
happened. Nothing would ever be same between us again.

I sat up, holding the sleeping bag against myself in a pointless attempt at modesty, and looked around. Hathan was
nowhere to be seen. The clothes I'd been wearing the night
before were neatly piled within arm's reach of my tent. I put
them on, made myself presentable, and went in search of the
makings for coffee.

I found Hathan sitting against the same rock outcropping
where we had drunk our whiskey the night before, senek cup

in hand, looking out at the sunlit river. When I dropped down beside him, a carefully judged distance away, he glanced over at me. His gray eyes were as direct as ever; I read inquiry in them, as well as humor. I smiled at him, an impulse which felt as natural as breathing, then turned my attention to my coffee.

He said lightly, "No regrets, I hope?"

"None." I hesitated. "You?"

He shook his head and mouthed the word *no*.

I felt a rush of affection that was both sweet and piercing. It was true; I didn't regret what we had done. What I had done. But it had been one thing to long for him from afar. Now I had had him, if only for a few hours, and it was going to make leaving him so much harder.

But that was a sorrow for another time. I cast around for a distraction, any distraction, and noted with surprise that his hair was wet. "Did you go swimming again?"

"Briefly. You may want to as well. We smell like the woods, which everyone will expect, but they won't be expecting us to smell quite so much like each other. Someone would notice. Probably Reyna."

Reyna was the least worrisome of the many possibilities, but I kept that knowledge to myself. I started to get up. His voice stopped me. "Eyvri? That wasn't an order."

"Oh." I laughed a little self-consciously. "Habit, I guess."

"Sit," he said. "Drink your coffee. There's no hurry. They won't start the party without us."

"That would be too much to hope for," I muttered.

"You're not looking forward to the reception?"

I settled back against the sun-warmed rock. "You know that cliff we rappelled down yesterday? I'd rather climb back up it. In the dark. In a snowstorm."

"I understand the force of your objection," he said, "but not the reason for it. What's so terrible about standing around sipping wine and making conversation?"

I wrinkled my nose. "Standing around isn't the problem."

"Ah," he said. "What happened to the dance lessons with Zey?"

"They ended," I said grimly. "He gave up. Your people have perfected artificial gravity, but apparently teaching one uncoordinated human to dance exceeds the scope of their powers."

"That may be a false equivalence. We've had artificial gravity for a few centuries now. Zey wasn't exactly a major contributor."

I laughed, partly at the joke, mostly out of relief that we still sounded—and felt, from my side of things, at least—exactly like ourselves. I'd been afraid he might shut me out completely, out of self-consciousness or fear that I would mistake friendliness for something more. Last night might have changed things between us, but it appeared to have left the essentials more or less intact.

When my thermos was empty, I went to retrieve my bikini from the tree branch where I'd hung it the night before. I slipped it on, grimacing as the damp fabric settled onto my skin. The sensation was unpleasant, but nonetheless preferable to having to explain to another platoon of Echelon officers, if one should happen along, why I was bathing naked in full view of my khavi. I found my sandals and towel and made my way down to the beach.

Last night, warmed by the brief Rikasan day, the water had been bracingly cool. Now it was frigid. I soaped up hastily and ducked under to rinse my hair. By the time I emerged onto the beach, my teeth were chattering. I dried myself aggressively with my towel, trying to scrub a little warmth back into my limbs, and pulled on my hiking clothes for the eleventh day running. Typically I would stay in my camp clothes for the last day of a long trek, but I had been wearing them for quite a lot of last night, and I was still wasn't sure exactly how sensitive Vardeshi noses were. It seemed wiser to play it safe.

I returned to camp to find that Hathan had already packed away our tents and most of the cooking gear. I stowed the last of my personal belongings, and we headed down to the beach. We crossed the river, as Reyna's team had done, by way of the stepping stones. Hathan led the way. Midway across, he slipped, submerging one leg up to the knee in the icy water. He regained his balance, swearing more creatively than I'd ever heard him do, and went on.

We climbed steadily as the day brightened around us. The slope was precipitously steep. Almost at once the tree cover gave way to exposed rock, and I found myself climbing with my hands as much as my feet. I kept up with Hathan, just. Despite being in front of me, he seemed to know exactly when my longing for a pause or a water break turned into desperation. Conversation was impossible, which was fine by me. I felt no compulsion to draw him into talk about last night; as far as I was concerned, the terms of our assignation were clear, and I had no intention of bringing it up ever again. But it might have been difficult to talk around the fact that we had made love only hours before, and I wasn't at all confident that I could do that particular verbal dance while scaling a mountain. Better not to try.

By midday we had reached the foot of the sheer cliff I had been dreading since I caught a good glimpse of it the day before. We stopped for water and a snack: handfuls of trail mix for me, unappetizing foil-wrapped cubes of some pressed vegetable protein for him. The air was chilly, but I had stripped off as many layers as I decently could, and I was still red and sweating. Hathan, naturally, showed not the slightest sign of being inconvenienced by the grade of the climb or the weight of his pack, which, as I discovered when I passed it to him, outweighed mine by a factor of three.

As we shouldered our packs for the last time, he hesitated, on the verge of saying something. Then he visibly dismissed the impulse. I wondered if he had been about to remind me of the importance of discretion. I could have told him there was no need. I was only too conscious of how high the stakes were for both of us. I took off my baseball cap, tucked away a strand of hair, put the cap on again, and nodded at him. "Ready when you are."

"I'm ready," he said. "Let's go lose the Outmarch."

I made it, in the end, because someone—I suspected Zey—had climbed back down the cliff at some point in the intervening hours and put guiding ropes in place at all the trickiest spots. Fastened at each end and knotted at intervals, they were as good as railings. I didn't know if using them qualified as cheating in the eyes of Outmarch Control, or whether the fact of our having been teammates excused the intervention. I didn't care. If they wanted to disqualify me, they could. But they could damned well do it after I'd finished my hike.

I climbed doggedly upward, eyes fixed on the next achievable ledge, testing each foothold and handhold before committing my weight to it. Each foot of altitude gained was a tiny triumph. Hathan was behind me for this last stretch, near enough to catch me if I fell. I trusted him, but I trusted myself more. It was by no means a quick or a graceful climb, but at midafternoon, a shade under a full Rikasan day after I'd intended to, I finished the Outmarch. I dragged myself over the last precipice, saw the number of people who had assembled to greet me, turned my back on them all, and sat kicking my heels over the abyss while I caught my breath. Now, at last, I could appreciate the view. And it was magnificent.

Zey came over and dropped down beside me. "How'd it go?"

I was drinking from my water flask, but I gave him a thumbs-up.

He grinned. "No nocturnal disturbances?"

"Not a single flashback," I said, which was the truth. "Was it you who put the ropes out there?"

"Yeah. Thought you might need a boost."

"Literally. Thanks. I wouldn't have made it without them."

"Now I have to climb back down and get them. But first let's go be political." He got up and put out a hand to help me to my feet.

I took it gratefully. My legs, it seemed, had done more of the work than I'd realized. I was laughing, half out of surprise at my unsteadiness, half out of relief at having conquered the cliff, when I came face-to-face with the Outmarch staff. I recognized most of them from the day before. I wasn't too tired to produce a friendly greeting and a crisp Vardeshi salute. Salutations were exchanged, first with the Echelon personnel, then with my crewmates, most of whom had come out to watch the finish. Reyna cut across the last of these with her habitual forthrightness. "Where's your challenge ring?"

"Oh." The events of last night had driven everything else from my mind. Flustered, I searched through my pack until I found my bikini top. "Right here." I tried to free the ring from the strap where it had lived for the past few days, but the knot proved too much for my stiff fingers. I shoved the entire thing at her and was mildly horrified when she handed it on to Director Anziar, who passed it in front of her flexscreen. A musical chord sounded. There was a murmur from those watching.

"My congratulations," said the director in tones of mild surprise. "Just under ten standard days."

"I think you mean eleven," I said apologetically. "I should have done it in ten. The next humans will be faster."

"No, I meant ten." She turned the screen around to show me a list of names. The bottom one was mine. Beside it was a square of pulsing orange light. I looked uncomprehendingly at Reyna.

"The challenge," she said patiently. "You earned back a full day."

"What?"

"The swimming task was unconventional. The course engineers assigned it a high value. The challenge ring deducted a full day from your time." Seeing my still-disbelieving expression, she said more emphatically, "You made it. Here." She held something out to me: a small square of gray fabric with something pinned to it. I took it, bewildered, and looked closer. It was a tiny circle of white enamel, about the size of a thumbtack. "You wear it next to your rank insignia. White is for completion, black is for victory. See?" Reyna held out her own arm, showing me an identical white pin beside the familiar brass studs on her sleeve cuff.

I was abruptly overwhelmed. Tears sprang to my eyes. I put a hand over my mouth in an attempt to hold in an undiplomatic squeak of surprise. My emotional response to her words was, I knew, all out of proportion to their meaning. The challenge system was arbitrary and ridiculous, as was the ten-day window. I had finished the course in eleven days. All those assembled knew it. The Echelon was choosing to declare that I had finished within the allotted time. It was a gesture of forgiveness, and a public one at that. They didn't hold a grudge against me for choosing to stay with the Fleet. The relief, added to the emotions already roiling within me, was simply too much. I had just enough presence of mind to spin my overreaction in a politically useful direction, blurting out, "This is so nice of you guys, I don't know what to say—" before I buried my head in Reyna's shoulder and sobbed.

When I calmed down, I found that the crowd had dwindled to a few onlookers, mostly medical staff. A couple of my crewmates were among them. Hathan wasn't. The stab of loss I felt at finding him gone was surprisingly acute. For one full day I had had him all to himself. I had known that time would end today, but I hadn't expected it to happen so quietly. I wiped my eyes and apologized for my excessive display in a voice still trembling with emotion. The Outmarch staffers brushed my excuses away with what I guessed to be the magnanimous courtesy of people secretly thrilled to find themselves on the front lines of a scandal.

Sohra, however, said anxiously, "Are you all right, Eyvri? I don't even remember seeing you cry like that after the Flare."

"It happens when she's tired," said Zey. I gave him a grateful look, which he met with one at once sympathetic and wary. He was worried too, beneath his willingness to dismiss the concern of others. I wondered what he knew—or guessed—about last night.

* * *

After two weeks of rallying physically to meet the challenges of the Outmarch, I found that the Perch presented a different kind of challenge. I quickly saw that the medical personnel I encountered yesterday must have been shielding me from unwanted attention. Now my presence here was openly declared, and as a human and a Fleet officer, I was doubly an interloper. I was also, unmistakably, a parcel. The Echelon had signed for me, and their first order of business was to make sure I'd been delivered intact. I was escorted to the clinic, where two Echelon doctors, both female, asked my permission to perform a physical examination. Tenvi was there too. Her presence calmed my nerves a little. I had scrubbed assiduously in the river that morning, but I was still terrified that they would somehow scent Hathan on me. If they did, I had a lie prepared. I would say I'd been cold the night before and had slept in one of his shirts. In the end, there was no need. They didn't ask any awkward questions.

They did ask, in a perfunctory way, about the unexpected activity flagged by our medical transponders the night before. I repeated what Hathan had said in his message, that I had been having trouble falling asleep and we had done some calisthenics. I was irrationally afraid the doctors would ask me to demonstrate. They didn't. They performed a thorough but gentle examination and said, with a relief evident even to me, that I appeared to be in excellent health, ankle and all, though my skin tone was a little darker than they'd been expecting. I chattered about radiation and the aesthetics of tanning until they cleared me to leave.

The evening's festivities commenced with a banquet, but by the time I had been shown to a tiny room on one of the upper levels of the Perch, it was clear that I wasn't going to be in time for dinner. I waved away both doctors' apologies. I'd been dreading the dinner almost as much as the reception itself. I devoured the hot meal someone had left in my room. Then I went down the hall to the shower. Tenvi had explained that there were no private showers at the Perch, but with everyone else at dinner, I was guaranteed a slot. I took my time about scrubbing the accumulated grime of Rikasa from my skin. Then I attempted to make myself presentable for the reception. I scowled at the scrapes on my nose and collarbone, now sporting white waterproof bandages, but there was nothing I could do about them. The Echelon doctors had told me to wear them proudly.

"They're badges of honor," one had said. "No one makes it through the Outmarch intact."

I was just slipping into my dress when my flexscreen lit up with a message from Zey. *Dinner's just ending. Are you coming down?*

Not alone! I wrote back. *Come get me. Five minutes?*

I ran nervous hands down over my hips, smoothing the line of the skirt, and studied the overall effect in the mirror. The dress had been elegant in the boutique in Zurich, but it looked better here, or maybe I wore it better. The fabric was as rich as I remembered, the style simple but flattering, and the blue set off my newly acquired tan. I slid my feet into ballet flats—possibly the best thing about Vardeshi height relative to human—and put in my diamond stud earrings. I was fussing with the clasp of the necklace I'd bought on Arkhati when the door chime sounded. "Come in," I called.

The door opened and Zey entered. He was wearing a long surcoat I hadn't seen before, a rococo confection in gold brocade which he sported with the same jaunty confidence he had brought to my graphic T-shirt and ripped jeans at Earth Night on Arkhati. There was a glitter of gold on his cheek-bones which I recognized as one of Kylie's eyeshadows. His silver hair, standing up in its typical crown of spikes, looked to have been dusted with it as well. He looked like a tiny and potentially deranged sovereign. "Wow," I said. "You look great."

"We both do. That's quite a color."

"Apparently." I sighed. "I didn't know that when I bought it. In my culture, blue is pretty neutral."

"Who wants to be neutral? I like it." He studied me critically. "Something's different. Did you darken your skin tone? Or lighten your hair?"

"Neither. Or both, but the sun did it for me." I held out an arm, admiring my tan.

"What's wrong with your necklace?"

"I think it's tangled."

"Turn around."

I did. He came up behind me and lifted the chain out of my hands, his cool fingers brushing the back of my neck. "So, now that it's just us, how was it really?"

I didn't ask what he meant. "Fine. Quiet."

He snorted. "I'll bet it was. I'll be honest, I was worried about you. Not about flashbacks, but about the other thing. The moonlight last night was pretty spectacular. I was afraid you'd give in to the urge to do something catastrophically stupid, like tell him how you felt."

There was laughter in his voice. I said irritably, "Of course not. Even I'm not that dumb."

"Okay, maybe not that. But something."

I was glad he couldn't see my face as I answered. "I did hang around in my bikini for an unnecessarily long time. And it was damned cold down by the water. A human guy would have gotten the message."

"He's not human. And the Flare casts a pretty long signal shadow."

And with that, I thought, it was time to close the subject. I said, aiming for the right note of wistful resignation, "In any case, it's probably for the best."

"Oh, it's definitely for the best. Just think how hellish the next two months would have been if you'd made a move and he'd turned you down. Which he would have, you know."

I said softly, "I know."

Zey stepped back. "There, that should do it. Are you ready to go downstairs?"

I checked the fall of my necklace in the mirror. My reflection gazed back at me, hazel eyes tranquil in her tanned face. There was no sign in her expression that she was in the midst of lying yet again to a cherished friend. This lie was different though. I wasn't only protecting myself this time. And some things demanded to be kept within. I could feel the memory waiting for me, resonant with a deep, secret calm, like clear water in a hidden well. I didn't need to draw from it now. It was enough to know that it was there. I fastened my Outmarch finisher's pin to the neckline of my dress, as Reyna had instructed, and nodded. "I'm ready."

I had only the haziest notion of where the reception was taking place, but as we made our way down to the main level, I could hear music and the hum of many voices. We entered a large room that was clearly the antechamber to an even larger one, and the noise seemed to double. Zey offered me his arm. I took it gratefully. "I didn't think you guys did this."

"We don't. I'm practicing for Earth."

"Oh, sure, you're all about Earth culture now that it's too

late to swim."

He laughed. We went under the archway and into the hall. My senses were assailed by music, lights, voices, and the people to whom those voices belonged: the two hundred participants of the Outmarch, gathered before us in their most dazzling finery. All of them were looking in our direction. An excited susurration ran around the room. I took a deep breath and tried to steady myself. Things had been simpler in the woods. And quieter.

The Outmarch reception was the first diplomatic event of its kind I had attended as the sole human present. I didn't have Kylie or Fletcher to cling to. I missed them desperately. My crewmates were there, of course, but I was wary of leaning too heavily on them. For one thing, they were doing delicate work of their own, representing the Fleet in enemy territory; for another, I needed to demonstrate independence to our hosts. It was a difficult evening. I couldn't dance. Everyone else could, and did. My avoidance of the dance floor was just one more thing setting me apart. The Echelon officers treated me with reserved courtesy, warming a little, some of them, when I spoke to them in their own language. But they watched me like photographers hunting for a coffee stain on a celebrity's shirt. Their gazes ricocheted from my face to my hair to my Outmarch pin to my unadorned right hand. I heard no less than three stifled exclamations about my earrings. Other than the doctors who examined me and implanted my medical transponder the day we went soilside, and the handful of medical staffers I had met yesterday while half-delirious on pain medication, I hadn't interacted with anyone other than my crewmates since we left Elteni. I had been living with most of them now for nine cramped months. Nothing I did or said or wore drew odd looks from them anymore. I had forgotten what it felt like to be an alien.

I spotted Hathan immediately, of course. When I arrived, he was standing in a group of people near the door. He gave the lie to the doctor's assertion that no one emerged unscathed from the Outmarch. He looked as fit and rested as if he'd just stepped down from the ramp of the *Ascendant*'s shuttle. His surcoat was deep red with copper-colored embroidery, similar in cut to Zey's, but with fewer embellishments. The fabric had the textured gleam of velvet. He ought to wear red more often; it suited him. As I watched, he said something that made the others in his group laugh. I looked away quickly. I knew what I had to do, and I knew that I could do it. But it would make things easier if I didn't look at him.

I wished again that Kylie were there beside me. She would have known what to say: something sharp and caustic, a calculated sting to draw my attention away from the steady ache inside. Fletcher would have commented on the names of the dances. Or he would have joined in. He'd probably learned to dance, too, during those five dull months on the *Azimuth*. I stood on the sidelines, senek in hand, mostly for appearances since I was so tired that actually drinking the stuff would knock me right off my feet, and watched.

The scene was undeniably enthralling. It reminded me of the long, intricate choreography of European dances of the eighteenth and nineteenth centuries—or, more accurately, the depictions of them I'd seen in movies. I quickly realized that, while they had seemed bewilderingly complicated at the time, the dances Zey had selected for me really were the simplest ones possible. They had all been straightforward partner dances. These changed fluidly from partner to foursome to circle and back again. Each individual dancer on the floor—

twenty or thirty of them at any given time—seemed to have an innate awareness of the position of everyone else. Like a flock of birds, they moved in concert, constantly making minute adjustments and realignments. Furthermore, they seemed to be able to do it all while carrying on effortless conversations with their partners. After a few minutes I gave up trying to follow the sequences and simply enjoyed the spectacle, which was not unlike the shifting patterns of a kaleidoscope. The Vardeshi favored black and white in their formal attire, but there were flashes of silver and gold and red and purple as well. There was little blue, and none lighter in shade than indigo. I didn't consciously look for Hathan, but he crossed my field of vision a few times, first with a woman in silver and then with another in white.

I was grateful when Saresh joined me. "How's the first human ever to finish the Outmarch?" he inquired.

"Good. Pretty tired."

"I'm not surprised." He gestured to the dancing. "What do you make of all this?"

I followed his gesture. My eyes went unerringly to the red surcoat. "As a cultural showpiece, it's stunning. So much history. The journal article practically writes itself. As a party . . ." I shrugged. "It's a little much, you know? It reminds me of the first night on Arkhati. That dance with the twirling fireballs."

"The harvest dance from Arideth," he said. "A strange kind of welcome."

"Exactly."

We watched the dancing for another minute. Then I said, "Is this what Earth Night felt like to you guys?"

"No."

"Good."

"I'm sorry you can't join in the dancing. So is Zey. He wanted to hijack the music. Play a couple of club hits from Earth. I talked him out of it. I hope that was the right thing to do."

"It definitely was! Jesus, what a horrible idea." I shuddered.

"He meant well," Saresh said, "but I persuaded him that the best part of the scheme was the intention behind it." After a little silence he said carefully, "Eyvri, did something happen out there? With Hathan?"

I didn't look at him. "No. Why?"

"You weren't at dinner. It crossed my mind that you might be avoiding him. And you haven't spoken to him since you arrived."

"You've been watching me?"

"Yes," he said simply. "As your hadazi, as well as your friend."

I nodded, acknowledging that. "I missed dinner because the doctors took forever making sure I checked out. And then I took a really long shower. As for tonight, I think we're both just making the rounds." When he didn't say anything, I added, "It was nice, having that time alone with him. It could have been weird, but it wasn't."

"I'm glad to hear it. For both of your sakes."

His ready acceptance of my denial should have been a relief, but I didn't feel relieved. I felt ashamed. Lying to him was harder than lying to Zey. I wasn't sure why that should be the case, but it was. I watched the distinctive crimson surcoat pass by again. "How long do I have to keep making the rounds?"

He scanned the room. "I'd give it another hour."

I sighed. "Fine. I can do an hour."

"I know you can," he said, and touched my arm, and left.

A few minutes later, Hathan came to stand with me on the edge of the floor. I'd just begun to think I ought to go find him and initiate an utterly banal conversation. Saresh wouldn't be the only one to notice if, after a full day alone together, we didn't speak to each other at all. We embarked on an utterly banal conversation. He asked about my ankle; I asked about his dinner. We compared shower lengths.

Feeling like we ought to make a show of talking a little longer, I said, "Do you ever find it hard to step back into your real life after a long hike?"

He answered without hesitation. "Always."

"Me too. Especially this time. I miss the quiet. Not just the quiet in the woods, although I miss that too, but . . . the quiet in my mind."

Hathan said, "Three things elude me tonight."

I looked for a connection between his words and mine and found none. Reluctantly, because we had been in perfect accord only moments before, I said, "I don't understand."

"You didn't get this from Saresh?" He followed the question with a sentence in archaic Vardeshi.

I recognized the words as poetry from their cadence. "He gave me a lot of proverbs. Not many poems."

"This one was written by a poet from Vardesh Prime on a tour of the outlying planets. It's one of my favorites." Beneath the music, in a voice pitched for me alone, he said in English, "'Three things elude me tonight: the stars of home; my lover's touch; a quiet mind.'"

My mind went blank. It was a love poem. He was quoting me a love poem. What could have possessed him to do it now? Here? Was it a test? I was profoundly tempted to say something like *I know the feeling*. In the end I settled for saying blandly, "It's beautiful. Where was it written?"

"Obviously not on Rikasa."

I blinked. Then I looked at him. He wasn't looking at me. He was still watching the dancers. There was the shadow of a smile at the corner of his mouth. He was teasing me, openly, about last night, after all our solemn promises to pretend it had never happened. I felt the heat rising in my face.

Before I could think of a response, I saw a young dark-haired woman in a purple-gray dress approaching us. She smiled engagingly and asked me loudly in standard Vardeshi, "Are . . . you . . . having . . . a . . . nice . . . time?"

I had been on the verge of laughter before she joined us. Her words gave me the excuse I needed to yield to it. "Wonderful. Thank you."

She laughed too, once she heard my Vardeshi, and said at a more natural pace, "May I steal your khavi for a dance?"

"Of course. Enjoy."

She held out her hand to Hathan. He accepted it. I looked resolutely away from the sight of his hand in hers as they walked out onto the floor.

I stayed another hour, had another drink, drifted in and out of a dozen more conversations of which I remembered nothing afterward. Then I thanked my hosts, my manufactured smile as bright as it had been all evening, and went back to my room.

21

The two drinks I'd had during the reception had long
since burned away, leaving me clear-headed and alert. Our
launch was scheduled for midday, a mere eight hours from
now. I wasn't about to waste a single moment of my final
night on Rikasa sleeping. I rinsed off in the shower and put
on matching underwear, a rare occurrence in my life, then
jeans and a T-shirt, white to set off my tan. I laughed a bit
uncomfortably at myself as I did so. It was an after-party outfit, and I hadn't been invited to any after-parties. By rights, if
I wasn't going to bed, I might as well put on my uniform.
Still, as indulgences went, it was a small one. I could pretend,
for these few hours, and only to myself, that anyone cared
what I looked like tonight. And there was a symbolic meaning
in selecting civilian rather than Fleet attire for the thoughts I
needed to think.

I straightened up my room—that too was part of the illusion—then turned off most of the lights and went out onto
the balcony. It was another exquisite night. The white moon
was setting; the golden one still rode high in a clear sky,

gilding the peaks of the surrounding mountains. My room was on the outward-facing side of the Perch. From my vantage point I could look down over the flank of the mountain to where the river wound its way along the valley floor. I could almost see the place on the far shore where we had made our camp the night before. The place where I had found my way, against all expectation, into the embrace of a man I loved. Who didn't love me. Who shouldn't have wanted me, but did.

At a few hours' remove, it all seemed more incredible than ever: incredible in its original sense, not to be believed. That circumstances had arisen that argued compellingly for my being left alone with a single companion. That Hathan had volunteered to be that companion. That I had found the courage—if an unethical act could be called courageous—to confess my desire for him. That he had rejected me, reconsidered, looked past a litany of perfectly sensible objections, and said yes. That I hadn't lost my nerve. That he hadn't. In how many alternate universes, I wondered, had that delicate chain of causality snapped? How many other Averys had slept alone last night, to give me one night in his arms? God, they must hate me right now.

I had had him for a night. I would never have him again. But the memory was there, every word and look and touch, locked away in my heart as securely as if it had been encoded in crystal. Nothing could ever take it from me. I felt an incredulous gratitude at the thought. Other emotions would doubtless follow in time. Shame, probably, for propositioning a man who wore the pledge of his commitment on his hand for all the universe to see. And fear, that he had consented to be seduced out of pity, to keep from humiliating me again, or because he felt he owed me something. But just now I felt neither shame nor fear. I stood there on the balcony, impossibly far from the stars of home, nearer to my lover's touch yet infinitely apart from it, with that most elusive of things: a quiet mind.

I had been standing there for twenty minutes or so when someone knocked on my door. I was so far from expecting an interruption that I felt only vague irritation at the noise. So there was an after-party, then. This would be Zey, or Sohra, come to cajole me into attending it. They wouldn't succeed. I sighed and went to the door. I was already readying my excuse as I slid it open.

Neither Zey nor Sohra was waiting outside my door. Hathan was. He wore his Fleet uniform, which to my eyes signified two things: he'd already been back to his room, and he wasn't planning on going there again tonight. I stepped back to let him in. He closed the door behind him. I reached past his shoulder and snapped the lock into place.

There had been, last night, a surfeit of words between us. We had needed every single one of them. Now we needed none. For him to seek me out, dressed for the morning, told me everything I needed to know. And that single act of mine, after what had happened the last time a locked door sealed us off together from the world, did the same for him. We took a simultaneous step toward each other. He cupped my face in his hands and kissed me with the assurance of a lover who knows he will not be refused. After that there was no more space for thought.

Sometime later, as we lay tangled together on my tiny bed, on top of the blanket because our bodies hadn't yet cooled down enough to need it, he said, "How long," and stopped. "I was going to ask how long it's been for you, but I think I already know."

"Three months."

"Fletcher."

I nodded. "Fletcher."

"Before that?"

"I guess . . . Two years?" In my first year of graduate school I'd briefly dated a student at the military language academy in the neighboring town. His face was a vague blur in my memory. "What about you?"

"Three years."

I felt an utterly unjustified wrench of disappointment. So he had been unfaithful to Sidra before. Why had I assumed I was the only one? And what did it matter? What bizarre ethical tightrope did I imagine him to be walking? The reality, at least among humans, was that if someone was willing to break his vows once, he was willing to do it more than once. And that was fine. He was here in my bed for one reason: I had been unprincipled enough to invite him, and he had been unprincipled enough to accept.

As if he heard my thoughts, he said, "It was just before my engagement."

"That was three years ago?" Something about the number struck me as odd. I dredged up the memory of my very first meeting with Zey. "Zey's been engaged longer than that. A lot longer. And you're older than him."

"Yes." When he didn't elaborate, I told myself again, more firmly than before, to let it go. I had no right to push for more detail. He had already told me more than he needed to. I closed my eyes, far from sleep, and breathed in the scent of his skin.

Again he surprised me by offering more information. "I waited a long time. Longer than most. I was . . . Some part of me was hoping for a more authentic connection."

"You mean love," I said, astonished. "You wanted to fall in love."

"Yes."

"You were the one. In a thousand."

"Evidently not."

"What happened?"

I felt him shrug. "Nothing happened. That was the problem. I had a few girlfriends, but I never felt more than a passing fondness for any of them. My parents started to worry. I started to think I was being unrealistic. And I got older. And lonelier. One day I just stopped looking. I sent a message home. Sidra is the daughter of one of my mother's childhood friends. She was finishing a five-year term on a ship doing deep-space exploration. She'd been waiting until the mission was over to start looking for a match. My mother wrote to her mother. The whole thing was settled in about a week."

"What's she like?" I asked.

"Honestly, I don't really know. We've only met a few times, and our conversations were . . . concise. You'd be better off asking Saresh—they were in the same class at the Institute. She graduated with distinction, which isn't easily done. She's currently serving a hadazi year aboard the *Vigilant*. Her field is engineering. I know that our mothers thought we were well matched in temperament. I know that she's beautiful. She looks a little like Sohra. She's smaller than Zey, but her ranshai designation is novice fourth class, which is impressive for her size. And I know that in a few years, when we feel the time is right, we'll meet on Vardesh Prime for our wedding. That's really all there is to tell."

I let out a breath that was almost but not quite a sigh.

He said, "You're going to tell me I should have held out

for love."

"No way. I'm not that arrogant. Also, in case you hadn't noticed, I'm still single, so my advice is worth crap."

He lifted my left hand in both of his. "Which finger?"

"This one." I waggled it helpfully.

He stroked my ring finger with his thumb, a slow, deliberate caress that sent shivers of heat through my body. "Strange to think of a sigil that can be taken off."

"Strange to think of a ring that can't." I added more tentatively, "Can I look at it?"

He turned his right hand over. With my left forefinger I traced the slightly raised golden lines I had tracked so many times with my eyes. "It's your life. I think you get to make the choices you think will give you the best shot at being happy. Without me, or anyone else, telling you you're doing it wrong."

Hathan said, "I don't know if I'll be happy with Sidra. I just know I won't be alone." He raised himself slightly, looking toward the balcony, and made a sound in his throat: recognition and, I thought, disapproval.

"What is it?" I said.

"Dawn."

"Already?" I pushed myself up to look as well. Through the open balcony door I could just make out the line of the mountains, now faintly visible, gray on darker gray, where before there had been only formless dark. Tears prickled behind my eyes. I turned my face into his shoulder to hide them. When I thought I could speak steadily, I said, "There must be a planet out there with thirty-hour days. Why couldn't we have gone to that one?"

"If you'd told me how you planned to spend them, trust me, we would have."

"See, that's kind of an awkward topic to bring up at morning briefing."

"'Any other matters of note?'" he said in a perfect imitation of the uninflected query with which Reyna closed each briefing. We both laughed.

The chime of a flexscreen sounded from the shelf beside the bed. I looked over at it. "Yours or mine?"

"Mine." He scanned the message. "Ziral wants to meet me before the crew breakfast." He sent back a one-handed acknowledgment.

Dreading the response, I said, "How long do you have?"

Hathan replaced the device on its shelf. "Long enough." He turned back to face me again. His eyes traveled from my face to the line of my body beneath the sheet in a frank appraisal. I had been waiting for months for him to look at me that way. I watched his face, knew he would reach for me a moment before he did it. That instant of anticipation was as exquisite as any physical caress I had ever felt. I moved into his arms, found his mouth with mine, tried again to say with my body the things I couldn't say with words. The irony was sublime. I had been hired as a linguist.

We both knew it was the last time. Perhaps that was the reason for the urgency I sensed in him. Certainly it was the reason for my own. At the end, impelled by love even if I was forbidden to speak the word, I did what I had promised myself from the start that I wouldn't: I said his name. I felt his whole body respond to the sound. I waited, breathless, to see what he would do. Had I gone too far? Implied an emotional bond that didn't exist between us, even when our bodies were tangled together under a sheet?

"Again," he breathed in my ear. And it was that whisper of command, of distance preserved in the midst of absolute intimacy, that drove me over the edge into pleasure. I didn't know what it meant, or if it meant anything at all, that it should happen that way. But I knew, with a dreamlike certainty, that hearing me say his name again did the same thing for him. And I knew I would be hearing his whisper in my nights for a long time to come.

Afterward I said, "Is it just me, or were you a little different that time?"

"In what way?"

"More . . . aggressive."

"Aggressive? Did I hurt you?"

"No. Not at all."

He frowned. Then a look of sudden comprehension crossed his features. "Oh. You're not used to the daybreak hormone shift. I haven't had my morning senek." He held a trembling hand in the air.

Enlightened, I said, "You were in predator mode."

He laughed. "It sounds dramatic when you put it that way. Really it's just irritating. Like being overcaffeinated for you." He checked his flexscreen again. "I should make senek now, but I have just enough time to shower."

"I'll make it," I said.

"You don't mind?"

"Of course not."

"Thank you." He unlaced his fingers from mine and sat up. I watched him walk to the shower room, that ineffable Vardeshi grace even more visible without clothing to hide it. He made no attempt to conceal his nakedness. I tried to etch the lines of his body in my memory. I had never understood before why people took illicit pictures of their lovers. Now I did. It was a hollow kind of possession, but possession nonetheless. All I had was my imperfect human memory: riddled with impurities, like the crystals of Rikasa. It was enough. It would have to be enough.

I rolled over into the warmth he had left behind and lay there until I heard the sound of the shower running. Then I got up and went to the alcove near the entryway, which housed a two-serving senek set of utilitarian brushed steel. I measured powdered senek leaves into the pot and filled it with steaming water from the tap provided. An inferior brew; by now I could tell from the fragrance. I sorted through the sugar pellets for the correct ones and laid them out in a saucer. That tiny domestic act, identical to making coffee in a hotel room back home, felt ludicrously poignant. I had brewed senek for Hathan a hundred times before. Never like this.

The shower was still running. I put on my clothes from the night before. I washed up in the sanitation room, which was separated by a door from the shower room. Then I wandered around the suite, taking in each small tangible proof of his presence. His boots by the door. His flexscreen on the shelf by the bed. I stood for a long time in front of the wardrobe, looking at his uniform hanging beside my own, distinguishable from it only by the khavi's insignia on the sleeve. I brushed my fingers across the unfamiliar pattern of brass studs. Then I went out onto the balcony to watch the mountains brighten in the sunlight. I didn't think he would leave without saying goodbye.

He didn't. He came out onto the balcony to join me. I turned at the muted click of his boots on the synthetic wood floor. From an arm's length apart we studied each other. He was a cautious-eyed stranger in his uniform. I was in my jeans and T-shirt, a little flushed still, my hair artfully mussed from our lovemaking. I knew what the mirror had told me. I had no idea what he saw.

"So," I said.

He echoed softly, "So."

"I guess this is it."

"I guess so." He glanced to the side, rubbed a hand along his jaw, then met my eyes again, his own as clear as ever. "This is difficult. I find myself wishing we had more time. I didn't expect to feel that way. I enjoyed these two nights . . . Really, more than I ever thought I would."

I had known he would be direct. I hadn't expected him to be kind. I wasn't ready for it. His words filled me with a delirious lightness that threatened to lift me entirely off my feet. I said unsteadily, "Yeah. Me too."

"I took a risk in coming here last night. I hope you understand why that can't happen again."

"I do. It would be like . . ." I remembered a long-ago comment of Kylie's and smiled. "Like sneaking around in a minivan."

"As khavi, I'm vaguely insulted by that analogy, although I can't say I fully understand it."

"Give it a couple of months," I said wryly. "You will."

"We should agree on a pretext. In case anyone sees me leaving your room. I stopped by to drop off . . . What would you have asked me to carry for you yesterday? It should be something heavy."

I thought about it. "My medical kit."

"Good." Hathan consulted his flexscreen. "I have to go." The words were simply stated, an observation, with no emotion of any kind to color them.

I held up a hand. "Just . . . One more minute."

He looked at me, mildly curious, as if I'd made an obscure cultural reference. The walls were in place again. Standing so close to him already felt like an intrusion. But I would never be able to touch him again. I stepped forward, put my arms around his neck, and hugged him tightly. Vardeshi senses be damned. If he smelled like me, so be it. He had an alibi already prepared. He must have had the same thought, because his arms closed around my waist. I breathed in his scent, which I recognized somewhat unromantically as being mostly the mild detergent we used in the *Ascendant*'s laundry room, and the neutral soap the Perch stocked in its showers. I noticed, for the last time, that his body against mine felt slightly too cool, like he'd just climbed out of a swimming pool. I pulled back a little, cradled his face in my hands, and kissed him gently on the lips. Then I laid my hands flat on his chest and pushed myself backward. "Okay. Go."

"Okay," he said, and went.

When the door had closed behind him, I went into the shower room and turned on the tap. I stripped off my clothes and stepped under the sheet of warm water. I didn't cry. I couldn't; there wasn't time. I was due to meet my crewmates downstairs in thirty minutes. I washed off every incriminating hint of his scent, toweled my hair dry, and dressed in my uniform. Then I threw my scattered belongings into my overnight bag and left.

My crewmates had colonized two tables near the edge of the terrace. They had arranged themselves by rank. Observing that fact, I understood that the Outmarch, with its days of haphazard seating on the ground, was now unequivocally behind us. Hathan was next to Reyna, looking at something on her flexscreen. His eyes lifted briefly to mine as I passed him. The moment stirred a decade-old memory of sprinting upstairs from adolescent fumblings in a friend's basement at the sound of my mother's car horn in the driveway. I had

feared, at the time, that I couldn't possibly be those two people at once: the girl who knelt in front of her boyfriend on a
dusty cement floor, the girl who talked inconsequentially on
the ride home about the movie she'd supposedly been watching. If I tried to span both identities, I had thought, the effort
would tear me in half. Now, abruptly, I was sixteen again. It
wasn't any easier the second time.

"You're late," Khiva said as I sat down.

I had my line ready. I delivered it with deadpan sincerity.
"Sorry. There was an Echelon officer in my bed, and he didn't
want to leave."

Zey said, "I've heard three versions of that joke in the last
day."

"And told one yourself," Sohra observed.

He gave me his overblown stagey wink. "What makes you
think I was joking?"

I laughed and reached past him for the carafe of kina juice,
a thoughtful touch by the Perch staff, as kina had been
cleared for human consumption last month.

And that was it. There were no more comments about my
tardiness. Nor were there any questions about my absence
from whatever post-reception festivities had taken place last
night. Vethna, arriving practically on my heels, was teased in
precisely the same way. It appeared that we had been careful
enough, or lucky enough, to escape suspicion.

I assembled a pleasingly intercultural breakfast—kina
juice and coffee, granola topped with powdered milk and a
Vardeshi seed and nut mixture—and dug into it with enthusiasm. Even factoring in the shortened day, dinner felt like a
very long time ago. I didn't look over at the higher-ranking
table until Reyna rose to announce that our shuttle would be
lifting off in twenty minutes. That was nothing new for me;

I'd spent a significant portion of the last year trying not to look at Hathan. I didn't think he'd been conscious of that fact before. He'd be conscious of it now.

We gathered on the landing platform behind the Perch to await the arrival of Ziral in the *Ascendant*'s landing craft. I turned my back on the others and stood at the edge of the platform with my eyes closed, my face tilted up to the sun. These last moments of warmth and natural light would have to sustain me for the two dark months that lay between Rikasa and Earth. I heard the sounds of the shuttle touching down and deploying its ramp, the soft scuffs of my crewmates' boots as they boarded. Someone came over to stand beside me. Even before he spoke, I knew it was Hathan.

"Come on," he said. "Let's go home."

Let's. It was remarkable how such a little word could say so much. He wasn't talking about Earth. He was talking about the ship. It was the only thing he could have said to soften the blow of leaving Rikasa. I pictured my inukshuk, my little stone statue, standing sentinel on its tiny island somewhere far below. Possibly no one would ever find it. But it would always be there, proof that I had crossed these mountains, had breathed this air, had slept under these stars. A sign of human passage. I smiled. "Yeah. Let's."

Hathan wasn't immediately behind me when I went up the ramp. It was a few moments before he joined me and the others in the shuttle's cabin. I wondered what he had been thinking as he stood there alone on the edge of the platform. Had he looked at the Perch, angular and glittering in the morning sun, or at the mountains rising in serried blue ranks beyond it? Had he thought of me? He had told me yesterday morning that he felt no regret. I hoped it was still true. Whatever his thoughts had been, his voice was steady as he gave

Ziral the order to launch. I watched on the main display screen as the shuttle vaulted upward, punching through Rikasa's atmosphere like a needle through cobweb, and burst out into the darkness beyond. A sleek bronze shape hung before us: the *Ascendant,* poised in orbit, awaiting our return. My heart lifted at the sight.

I was going home.

Glossary of Vardeshi and Translated Terms

ahtziri: a foxlike animal

azdreth: the Flare; a malady affecting deep-space travelers which causes temporary madness

Blank: one who lacks even latent telepathic abilities

Echelon: the governing body of Vardesh Prime

eyvrith: elusive desert predator resembling a leopard

hadazi: ship's mentor

ivri avanshekh: the longing for permanence; homesickness

ivri khedai: the longing for another sky; wanderlust

kevet: eating utensil

khadrath: alone

khanat: boarlike animal with long sharp bristles similar to porcupine quills

khavi: commander of a ship

Listening: a telepathic exchange

nivakh: a large, slow-witted bearlike animal

novi: the lowest rank in the Fleet hierarchy

rana: a drug that temporarily unlocks the abilities of latent telepaths

ranshai: a martial art

rhevi: lower rank analogous to lieutenant

senek: tea-like beverage with mild tranquilizing qualities

starhaven: space station

suvi: second-in-command

Vox: telepath whose abilities are under conscious command at all times

Acknowledgments

Since BRIGHT SHARDS began life as the second half of ASCENDING, I am still deeply indebted to the people I acknowledged in that volume. To those names I would like to add: Laura Flavin, who provided critical marketing expertise at a crucial moment; Beverly Bambury, who organized my blog tour; and all the readers who gave me encouraging feedback on ASCENDING. Lastly, I am grateful to Lord Huron, whose music captures the spirit of these books so beautifully I'm not sure why I'm still writing them.

ABOUT THE AUTHOR

Meg Pechenick is a lifelong lover of fantasy and science fiction. Her experiences studying anthropology in college and linguistics in graduate school informed the writing of this series. She enjoys running, swimming, and planning out imaginary backpacking trips. She lives with her family in New Hampshire.

Still want to keep reading? Awesome! I'm currently writing CELESTIAL NAVIGATION, the third Vardeshi Saga novel. To be notified when it becomes available, please visit my website, www.megpechenick.com, and send me a message on the "Contact" page. If you're already on my mailing list, I'll keep you updated. I will be uploading Chapter One to my website soon, so stay tuned!

The reader response to ASCENDING has been incredible. If you're enjoying the series, I'd love to hear from you. Please share your thoughts with me in a review on Amazon or Goodreads. Alternatively, you can email me directly at meg.pechenick@gmail.com.

Made in the USA
Columbia, SC
05 November 2019